"Why are you here, Sama[...]
edged with displeasure, can[...]

I clutched the railing tighter and squeezed my eyes shut, trying not to breathe at all, but that was kind of impossible. Even soulless, voracious monsters like me needed oxygen.

When I inhaled this time, his familiar scent—warm, spicy and totally devastating—slid over me.

Finally I forced myself to face him and my breath caught. I'd almost forgotten how effortlessly he affected me.

Bishop's dark brows were drawn tightly over intense cobalt-blue eyes. He towered over me—a full foot taller than my short five-two. Broad shoulders. Sinewy muscle rippled down his arms under his long-sleeved black T-shirt, which was drawn tight across his chest. His mahogany-colored hair was messy tonight. I had a sudden urge to slide my fingers through it to push it off his forehead. I fisted my hands at my sides to keep from automatically reaching toward him.

The angel had had that effect on me from the first moment I met him. Uncontrollable. Compulsive. Irresistible.

Praise for *Dark Kiss:*

"More, please! Gorgeous angels, suspense and romance...this book has everything I love. I was pulled in from the very first sentence."
—Richelle Mead, *New York Times* bestselling author
of the Vampire Academy series

"Awesome story line, awesome characters...
I highly recommend *Dark Kiss* as a must read."
—*I Heart YA Books*

"A must read for all you angel/demon lovers out there...
An outstanding start to this fab new series."
—*The Book Hookup*

"Fantastic writing style, a sweet romance and...original and intriguing angel/demon lore."
—*diminutivemimi.blogspot.com*

Books by Michelle Rowen
available from Harlequin TEEN

The Nightwatchers series (in reading order)

DARK KISS
WICKED KISS

wicked kiss

Michelle Rowen

NIGHTWATCHERS

Book 2

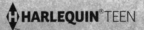

Recycling programs
for this product may
not exist in your area.

ISBN-13: 978-0-373-21064-0

WICKED KISS

Printed in U.S.A.

chapter 1

Crave used to be a prime hangout for dangerous monsters, but tonight I seemed to be the only one here.

A week ago, I lost my best friend in the whole world in this very club. Literally lost her, in a swirling black vortex that opened up and swallowed her whole, and took her…somewhere else. Somewhere horrible.

I didn't know how yet, or when, but I clung to that small yet resilient hope that had taken firm root inside of me: I *would* find her.

Carly had loved this all-ages nightclub and came here every weekend like clockwork, dancing till the place closed down. If I shut my eyes I could still see her on the dance floor, the one place she could forget her problems and let the music become her entire world.

Damn, I missed her.

But I had to come back tonight. I couldn't wait any longer.

There was somebody I had to find who used to hang out here a lot. Somebody I'd been searching the city for. Somebody who'd stolen something from me that I needed back before it was too late.

I had no real idea when "too late" was going to be. But I

had a sick, gnawing feeling in the pit of my stomach that we were getting really close.

"You look *way* too serious, Sam," Kelly said lightly from across the booth. "And you're not even listening to anything we're saying."

"Sorry," I began, my head still in a fog. I forced a smile to my lips and looked at Kelly and Sabrina—both blond and perky cheerleader types. I wasn't blond, nor was I particularly perky or cheerful. But they were both good friends of mine, anyway.

Well, maybe *good friends* was pushing it. We usually ate lunch at the same table and we had gym class together. I think they liked me. That totally counted.

After their invite earlier today, I'd decided to join them here for a "girls' night out." At least, that's what they thought it was. For me, it was an excuse to be here on the off chance I might find the boy who'd literally stolen my soul.

"Yeah," Sabrina agreed. "Like, earth to Samantha. What's up with you?"

"Nothing. I'm just a bit distracted tonight."

Understatement, table for one.

Kelly took a sip of her Diet Coke and eyed the remains of the nachos that sat on the table between us. There wasn't much left, thanks to me—just a bit of cheesy sludge and a couple soggy tortilla chips. A single jalapeño pepper remained, lying there mournfully after the battle its friends had lost.

I couldn't help it. I was really hungry tonight. And when I was hungry I needed to eat so my *other* cravings didn't kick into overdrive.

Unfortunately, the plate of nachos hadn't helped a bit.

"FYI, we were talking about Halloween," Sabrina reminded me. "Do you know what you're wearing to Noah Tyler's party?"

"Noah's having a party?" I asked absently, keeping my eyes on the club over her shoulder while still trying my best to appear attentive.

"Yeah. And he did tell me that he *really* wants you to be there." She grinned. "I think *somebody's* got a crush on you."

It took me a moment to clue in to what she meant. I cringed at the thought, and also the vague realization that Noah had been checking me out lately. I'd tried to ignore it. "He doesn't."

She shrugged and the girls shared a knowing look. "Whatever you say. But you're coming, right?"

"Wednesday night?" I forced a look of interest as well as a cheery smile though I felt anything but. "Wouldn't miss it for the world."

I was definitely going to miss it. No question.

They discussed their costumes. I half listened. The jalapeño pepper died a quick and painless death.

Then I stayed behind as a song came on that they got incredibly excited about and they made their way to the nearby dance floor. A sprinkle of colorful lights fell across their faces as they joined the swell of other kids dancing to the throbbing beat of the techno song—from a close bump and grind to a frenetic waving of arms and legs. I used to do a kind of uncomfortable shuffle thing when it came to dancing. I had always been hyperaware that somebody might be watching, judging, laughing. All of the above.

"Dance like nobody's watching," Carly always insisted.

"Did you see that embroidered on a cushion somewhere?"

She'd give me a grin. *"Probably. But it's still true. Gotta enjoy every moment because you never know when it's going to be your last."*

The memory of the eternal optimism of Carly Kessler made my throat too thick to swallow down another gulp of my ginger ale. I returned my full focus to scanning the club, the entrance, the dance floor.

We'd been here for an hour. An hour to consume a plate of nachos, chat with a couple girls who generously tolerated my company, watch a couple hundred kids having a good time on a Saturday night, remembering that I used to be one of them, and to realize that this wasn't getting me anywhere.

The scent in the air was intense and it made it increasingly hard to think. Not sweat or perfume—something else. Something deeper that slithered around me like a boa constrictor, squeezing painfully tight.

While I might look like a normal seventeen-year-old girl to anyone who didn't know otherwise, without my soul I was now a "gray," someone that had the ability to steal someone else's soul through a kiss.

It was a mistake to come here. It's only getting worse.

"Relax," I commanded myself.

But it was hard to relax when you couldn't let yourself breathe deeply. Shallow breathing was the best way to maintain control in a busy place like this. I'd come here to find a missing person, not to pick out a potential victim.

Finally, desperately needing to keep my mind off my unnatural but growing hunger, I pushed away from the booth and moved toward the brass railing that surrounded the dance floor and separated it from the seating area. I gripped the smooth, cold metal hard enough to make my knuckles turn white. After a few moments, my aching hunger finally eased off.

And then it spiked back up to maximum.

"Why are you here, Samantha?" His deep voice, edged with displeasure, came from right behind me.

I clutched the railing tighter and squeezed my eyes shut, trying not to breathe at all, but that was kind of impossible. Even soulless, voracious monsters like me needed oxygen.

wicked kiss

When I inhaled this time, his familiar scent—warm, spicy and totally devastating—slid over me.

Finally, I forced myself to face him.

Bishop's dark brows were drawn tightly over intense cobalt-blue eyes. He towered over me—a full foot taller than my short five-two. Broad shoulders. Sinewy muscle rippled down his arms under his long-sleeve black T-shirt, which was drawn tight across his chest. His mahogany-colored hair was messy tonight. I had a sudden urge to slide my fingers through it and push it off his forehead. I clenched my hands into fists at my sides to keep from automatically reaching toward him.

"Why am I here?" I forced myself to say it casually. "Why wouldn't I be? Crave's a great place to hang out with friends."

"You're looking for Stephen."

I shrugged a shoulder, tore my gaze away from his and studied the dance floor.

"Samantha."

The way he said my name always made me shiver. Still, this time my gaze shot back to his with more annoyance than nonchalance. "I know you want me to stay home every night with the door locked, but I can't do that. Besides, I haven't heard from you in a few days. I figured I was on my own again."

Bishop's expression remained frustratingly neutral. "I've been looking for him."

"Found him yet?"

His jaw tensed. "Believe me, you'd be the first to know if I had."

"Well, if you haven't found him, then it sounds like you need help. That's why I'm here."

He hissed out a sigh. "Seriously, Samantha. You need to go home and let me handle this."

Hot anger ignited inside of me, helping me resist my automatic pull toward him. "I'm not going anywhere."

Bishop's brows were drawn together, but a smile now tugged at the corner of his lips. "Feisty tonight, aren't we?"

"Define feisty."

"Samantha Day. Seventeen years old. Normally a realist who knows right from wrong, but is currently glaring at me like she wants to punch me in the stomach."

"Good definition." Something suddenly clicked for me. "You seem strangely okay tonight. What happened?"

The smile fell from his lips completely. "I'm not okay. But I've found another way to deal with my problem when I have to."

"How? I didn't think your particular problem came with a multiple choice solution."

"Neither did I."

He might look like a gorgeous eighteen-year-old boy, but Bishop was actually an angel who'd been sent here to Trinity to take care of the gray problem. But something went horribly wrong when he left Heaven. Another angel who wanted to sabotage his mission had made him a "fallen" angel—one with a soul. The soul was a punishment to those truly fallen. It wreaked havoc with their mental stability, causing them to go slowly insane. But it was also necessary for their ongoing survival. A soul to a fallen angel was a true double-edged sword. It messed up their minds, but without it they would perish.

I'd kissed Bishop once and taken part of his soul—it had been the most amazing and horrible kiss of my entire life. Now I instinctively wanted more. And part of him—like any gray's victim—wanted to be kissed again.

Yeah. You could say it was a complicated relationship.

"Well, I'm glad," I said. "I guess now I know why I haven't seen you lately. If you don't need me to help you find your sanity, then you can focus on the mission instead. Sooner it's completed, the sooner you can find a permanent solution to your problem. Right?"

"You think that's why I've stayed away? You don't think it's hard for me to be this close to you right now?" He leaned dangerously closer. "Remember, it's not just you suffering here."

My hunger level shot through the roof.

Oh, yes. I remembered.

When his hand closed on my wrist, a shiver of electricity zipped across my skin. My eyes snapped to his. "You really shouldn't touch me if you don't need to."

"I know."

The rest of the club seemed to fall away so there was only he and I left behind.

Right now, Bishop was too close and smelled way too good.

"I haven't had any slipups since I last saw you," I said, my voice strained. "I can control this until we find Stephen."

"I know you've been on your best behavior."

I looked up at him, confused. Then clarity dawned. "Wait. Are you saying you've been watching me the past few days?"

"It's not always me. And it's not all the time."

I gaped at him, the thought that he'd been monitoring me made me feel like a potential shoplifter. "You don't trust me."

His brows drew together. "This isn't about trust."

"Sure it is."

"If Stephen tries to contact you when you're alone, then I need to know."

I swallowed hard. "I'm worried you—or one of the others— is going to find him first and stick your dagger through his chest with no questions asked. One less gray to clean up later. But that can't happen. I need him alive, so you need to back off."

That painfully sexy smile touched his lips again as he studied me. "Yes, *definitely* feisty tonight."

I snorted softly, but refused to let down my guard completely. "I need my soul back. I can't live like this."

"I know."

The music shifted to a new song, even louder than the one before, if that was possible. The ground shook with the nearby dancers stomping on it. A waitress holding a tray of fried appetizers moved past us.

"Are you here alone?" I asked.

He glanced toward the far corner of the dark and noisy nightclub. "No. Brought some backup to help with the search while the others are out on regular patrol."

I looked to see who it was and cringed at the sight. Someone tall and blond and familiar.

Kraven worked with Bishop to save the city from things like me. At first glance I would have guessed that Kraven was another angel.

Nope.

Heaven and Hell worked together very occasionally on problems that threatened the integral balance of light and dark, good and evil.

Soul-eating monsters were just such a threat.

Kraven represented the dark side of the scale.

He was with a girl off in the corner and it was obvious that he was hitting on her. Heavily. He braced his hand over her shoulder, creating a partial cage she looked in no hurry to escape from. She grinned up at him as if in love. For all I knew, maybe she was.

As I watched him warily, wondering what his plans for that innocent—or not so innocent—girl were, he glanced over his shoulder at me. A cool smile curled the corner of his mouth.

"Yeah, he looks like he's really helping the search," I said with disdain. "If you're searching for slutty girls."

"Distractions happen."

I chewed my bottom lip and looked up at him. "I'm surprised that out of the whole team you'd pick your demonic brother to spend the evening with."

Bishop's expression tightened.

When he finally released his hold on my wrist, I grabbed the front of his shirt before he could move away from me.

"Are you ever going to tell me more about the two of you?" I'd come up with no reasonable explanation of how one brother became an angel and the other a demon, despite the tiny breadcrumbs of info I'd collected along the way.

"There's nothing to tell."

"Yeah, right. How about you at least tell me the name you had when you were human? I know one thing for sure—it wasn't Bishop."

"Okay." He eyed me. "It was Barbara."

"You're hilarious."

"And you still look like you want to punch me."

"I'm barely restraining myself, actually."

That smile returned to play at his lips. His gaze moved to the other side of the club and his expression grew grim again. "I need to talk to Roth. Wait here."

Another team member. Another *demon*. Roth, however, made Kraven look like a friendly teddy bear. And Kraven was not a friendly teddy bear by anyone's definition.

"I thought you wanted me to leave?" I said.

"I'll take you home when we're done here. Give me five minutes. Stephen's dangerous and I don't want you finding him by yourself."

"I can handle him."

Bishop returned my challenging look with one of his own. "Five minutes."

"Fine."

I watched as he walked across the club to where tall, handsome and hateful Roth stood by the long bar that only sold nonalcoholic beverages and appetizers. The crowd of kids swelled to cut off my view of the two.

Even with Bishop gone, my hunger hadn't faded one bit. Strange. I thought I'd get a chance to compose myself better.

"Hey, Samantha."

Damn. I glanced over to see Colin Richards standing right next to me. He was poised directly in what I'd termed my "orbit of hunger." Two feet or less. The danger zone.

"Colin," I squeaked out. "Hey."

I wasn't romantically interested in Colin at all, but unfortunately, the feeling wasn't mutual. He'd taken my rejection hard, especially when I showed very nonrejection behavior whenever he entered the orbit and I couldn't control my hunger quite so well. Most people respected your personal space. Colin wasn't one of them.

He swept his gaze over the short, black skirt and silver tank top I'd chosen to wear so I'd fit in with Kelly and Sabrina and the rest of the Saturday night crowd.

"You've kept a low profile this week," he said. "Are you specifically avoiding me, or just generally being a bitch to everyone?"

I winced at his sharp words, but then I smelled the alcohol on his breath. So much for this being a booze-free club. Some kids tried to sneak it in, anyway. Colin was becoming well-known for drinking too much and getting into trouble. When he dated Carly over the summer, he'd made a bunch of vodka-fueled bad choices, including cheating on her at a pool party.

"Nice," I said drily. "And maybe when you sober up, you won't be such an ass."

This earned me a humorless snort as he drained whatever was in his plastic cup. His gaze slid down the front of me again as if he was having trouble keeping his attention on my face. My cheeks grew warm at his blatant gaze.

"Who was that guy you were talking to?"

I blinked. "None of your business."

"Your boyfriend?"

"Again, none of your business."

He was being very confrontational tonight, which made me sad. Colin was actually a really nice guy, despite some of the more epic mistakes he'd made in the past. And I knew I'd hurt him last week, so I wouldn't hold this particular discussion against him in the future. This time, anyway.

Walk away, I told myself. But my feet refused to move. I fought my rising hunger with every ounce of strength I had. The more I fought, the colder I got until goose bumps broke out over my bare arms and I shivered, despite the club being at least eighty degrees. The cold was a side effect of not having a soul.

Colin leaned closer, which only made things worse. I didn't smell the vodka on his breath anymore; what I smelled was warm, tempting and entirely edible. Less so than Bishop, but still more than anyone else in this club right now.

"Heard from Carly?" he asked.

That woke me up like a glass of cold water thrown in my face.

Colin, like almost everyone else, believed Carly had run away with a secret boyfriend and was off having a misguided, but romantic adventure.

"No," I said softly. My eyes began to burn.

He snorted again. It was an unpleasant, mocking sound. "Look at you, all misty over Carly taking off with some guy. Feeling abandoned by your BFF? Poor Sam. Boo hoo."

I gave him a careful look. "I know I hurt you—"

"Hurt me?" he scoffed. "Please. I'm over it."

"Yeah, sure you are." I studied him, uncertain how to deal with this problem. "Look, Colin, I'm sorry. Really. But it's for the best. You don't need to be near me right now. In fact, I'd appreciate it if you backed off before my friend gets back."

"Jealous, is he?"

I'd had more than enough of this conversation and I needed him to step away from me now. "Leave me alone, Colin. I don't like you. At all. Get it through your head, okay?"

I forced myself to look at the dance floor again.

"You're such a liar." His words slurred together, heavy with enough underlying pain to make me flinch. "Everything that comes out of your mouth is a damn lie. You liked me. I know you did. I saw it in your eyes. You think you can just walk away from something like that? That I'd let you?"

Let me? "I think you need to go—"

But before I could say another word, Colin grabbed hold of me and crushed his mouth against mine.

chapter 2

No!

I tried to pull away from him, to shove against his chest as hard as I could.

But it was too late. The hunger that had swirled around me the entire time I'd been at Crave, which had intensified to an impossible to ignore level when Bishop was close to me, that waited patiently while Colin blurted out what was on his mind—

It spilled over.

The pounding dance music muted. The sparkling lights faded. The club disappeared. My rational thinking ceased. And my hunger took over.

This wasn't a kiss with a drunk boy who liked me and was mad I didn't like him in return. This was about feeding—that part of me that was missing a soul and was constantly trying to devour everyone else's.

It was what I feared the most. I didn't want to hurt anyone. But that was exactly what I was doing.

Feeding on Colin was so natural for me. In this mindless state, it was the most natural thing in the world—neither good nor bad. And with every bit of his soul I devoured, delicious warmth spread through me, chasing the horrible, endless cold away. My thoughts about hurting him vanished. I would feed until I was satisfied, and since I'd barely ever fed before, that would take a long time.

Someone grabbed my upper arm and painfully wrenched me away from Colin. Colin staggered back and dropped down into a nearby booth. Thin, black lines branched around his mouth and his skin was sickly pale. His eyes were glazed. His chest moved rapidly as he gasped for breath.

Haven't taken it all. Just a piece…

The grip on my arm tightened and I turned to see that it was Kraven now in front of me, shaking his head.

"Honestly," he said. "Can't let you out of our sight for a minute, can we?"

"Let go of me!" I was working on instinct only, still possessed by the hunger. I stared at Colin. "I need more."

"You need more?" Kraven grabbed my chin and forced me to look at him instead of Colin. "Try this."

He kissed me hard, releasing my arm to slide his hands into my long hair. I automatically tried to feed, but there was nothing there. Regular demons like Kraven didn't have souls. This was the proof. With no soul to feed from, this was just a kiss.

And yet, strangely enough, it still seemed to satisfy me. I wasn't feeding, but my hunger began to ease a fraction at a time.

But then the kiss stopped. Abruptly.

"What the hell are you doing to her?" Bishop snarled.

He grabbed hold of Kraven and wrenched him away from me, slamming the demon hard against the wall.

Bishop's eyes blazed bright blue. They did that sometimes. He'd told me it was a bit of celestial energy that rose up when he got emotional. Based on the current neon brightness, he was *very* emotional.

My head continued to clear, although not as rapidly as I'd have liked it to. I staggered back from them and landed in the booth across from the slowly recovering Colin. A quick sweep of the club showed that nobody was paying us any attention.

Neat trick that demons and angels had—they could cloak an area to gain a little privacy when problems arose.

Kraven shoved Bishop back from him. "Sorry, but your little girlfriend was in need of some help."

"That was you helping?"

"Worked, didn't it?"

I sent a look at Colin. My mind had now cleared completely and my control was back. Guilt and horror slammed through me at what I'd done. The black lines around Colin's mouth had faded completely, but his eyes were still glazed. A gray's victim seemed to go into a short-term trance while they were being fed upon. Since I'd experienced it from the victim's side, I knew that it felt way better than it looked. Exciting, exhilarating, amazing—just like a good kiss should be.

But there was nothing good about *this* kiss. If I'd successfully taken all of Colin's soul, I could have killed him. Or, if he was strong enough to survive it, he would become another gray, capable of hurting others.

Either thought scared the hell out of me.

My gaze shot to Bishop. "Colin kissed me. I—I'm sorry. I couldn't help myself after that."

Colin shook his head as if to clear it. He glanced at me, and then at the two tall boys staring at him.

"What—?" he began.

"How do you feel?" Bishop asked him.

He scrubbed his hand over his forehead. "Um, okay, I think. What happened?"

Bishop grabbed the front of his shirt and yanked him out of the booth. "Don't kiss her again. Ever. You hear me?"

Colin gaped at him. "Who are you?"

"You don't want to know. Leave now."

Bishop let him go and Colin staggered back, then glanced at me as if waiting for me to defend him. Instead, I forced myself to look down at my hands, which I'd clasped in my lap.

"Sorry," he began. "I, uh, don't know what I was thinking."

Without any further argument, he slunk away from us and was swallowed by the rest of the crowded club.

"Your girlfriend's a great kisser," Kraven said drily. "Her tongue is like…wow. She doesn't hold back. You're really missing out with that pesky soul of yours."

Bishop turned on the demon, his eyes flashing. "Stay away from Samantha or I'll kill you."

"This is the thanks I get for saving the day? She was going to suck that kid dry right here in the middle of the club. Besides, why are you mad at me? I think some of that angel attitude should be pointed in her direction. Or can gray-girl do no wrong in your eyes, even when she slips up? Or slips someone else the tongue?"

Bishop's expression didn't lose a fraction of its fury. "I think you *do* want me to kill you. Is that your goal?"

Kraven gave him a humorless smile. "Don't know. How many times can one brother kill the other? Are you looking for some kind of Guinness World Record here?"

"Try me."

Kraven liked to mess with the minds of others, but I wasn't in the mood for it now. He wasn't helping anything by baiting Bishop like this.

"Why do you have to be like this?" I asked.

He finally spared a look in my direction. "Please. You should be thanking me for saving your pretty little ass a minute ago. Instead, I get vilified. Whether either of you wants to admit it or not, the kiss worked. It snapped you out of your monster madness."

Bishop's brows drew together as if he was considering this possibility. His gaze then hardened. "We're leaving."

Kraven saluted. "Yes, sir."

I'd wanted to come here tonight so I could find some answers. I'd honestly thought I was in control of myself and my hunger.

But I'd hurt Colin, and if Kraven hadn't stopped me I could have killed him.

"I'm sorry," I whispered to Bishop as I pushed myself up from the booth.

Bishop didn't meet my eyes. "How much of that boy's soul did you take?"

I couldn't help but notice that he hadn't replied to my "I'm sorry" with a breezy "it's okay." Couldn't blame him for that.

I let out a shaky breath. "Not much."

"Be careful. He'll instinctively seek you out in the future so you can finish the job."

"How do you know?" Kraven asked.

"Believe me, I know."

I was definitely ready to leave. I'd done more than enough damage for one night. Stephen wasn't here so there was no reason to hang out a moment longer. I wanted to run home and hide my face from the world, but instead I tried to stay calm and not let anyone see how devastated I was. I said a quick goodbye to Sabrina and Kelly, who'd thankfully missed all of my drama while they'd been busy dancing.

Roth caught up with us at the front door past a poster advertising Wednesday's "Halloween Bash." We exited the club, and the cool, late-October air immediately chilled me. Stars sparkled in the clear, black sky and the moon, along with the parking lot floodlights, lit up the night around us. I ignored the cold, instead pulling my too-thin coat tighter around my shoulders.

Roth scanned the three of us silently trudging along the sidewalk. "Did I miss something?"

Bishop's jaw tightened. "No."

"Me and gray-girl just made out," Kraven said.

Roth made a face. "Disgusting. Why would you want to kiss something like her?"

"Research."

I expected no less from Roth. I was well aware that he despised me. Tonight only proved that I was in more trouble than I thought.

I scanned the night surrounding us, anything to take my attention off what had happened with Colin and Kraven.

"I'm taking you home," Bishop said.

I took a deep breath and let it out. "To keep me out of trouble."

"For starters."

At that moment I spotted something in the sky that grabbed my attention. I felt the color slowly drain from my face. "Can't go home. Not yet."

"Why not?"

I pointed at the sky behind him where a familiar searchlight had just appeared in the distance—although I knew none of them could see it like I could. "Looks like you're getting a new recruit."

chapter 3

"Don't know why a gray can do this," Roth grumbled as he trailed after us. "Why can she see the searchlights when we can't?"

He didn't know the truth and neither did Kraven. Only Bishop knew and he'd sworn me to secrecy about it.

I wasn't *just* a gray.

Bishop always talked about the universal balance and how important it was. Well, I was about as balanced as you could get. Equal parts dark and light thanks to my birth parents— whom I'd never met. Up until a week ago, I didn't even know I'd been adopted.

My father was a demon named Nathan, my mother was an angel named Anna.

Anna had been killed shortly after I was born and Nathan had joined her in the Hollow, her final resting place. The same place Carly had been sucked up into.

Theirs was a forbidden romance doomed from the start, but it had produced yours truly. Because of this, I was what was termed a "nexus"—the center, the connection—and the fact that I'd lost my soul meant I could allegedly channel the powers of both Heaven and Hell.

It helped me do things, see things. It made me special. It made me valuable. Clinging tightly to this thought after what I'd done to Colin was the only thing keeping me from completely freaking out.

"Why are they sending someone else?" Kraven asked, ignoring the other demon. He didn't sound happy.

"I don't know," Bishop replied. He walked so close to me that I could barely concentrate. My hunger still had me tightly in its grip and the scent of his soul, of him, did crazy things to my head. "You're sure it's one of *our* searchlights, Samantha? Not just a regular one?"

"Positive." The light that shone up into the sky was restoring my hope with each step I took. I moved toward it like I was following a rainbow to a guaranteed pot of gold.

A sixth member for the team would mean one more chance to find Stephen. At this very moment, I didn't care if he turned out to be a demon or an angel.

However, when we followed the searchlight to its origin, I found something I wasn't expecting.

"Well?" Bishop asked when I stopped walking. "Where is he?"

"Not a he." I pointed shakily in the direction of the girl up ahead. As soon as my gaze locked on her, the light disappeared. It only ever stayed on long enough for me to make visual contact.

She was young—like me. Seventeen, maybe. She had long, pale blond hair. She wore ripped jeans and a black sweater. She wandered along the sidewalk next to a busy street with her arms crossed over her chest as if trying to keep warm.

I'd always thought it was incredibly sexist that Heaven and Hell had only sent boys on this mission to save Trinity. Looked like they'd changed their minds.

"This is ridiculous," Roth said. "Girls are useless."

Just the sound of his voice rubbed me the wrong way. I didn't waste my breath in arguing with him, but he must have felt the heat of my glare.

"They are," he insisted.

"Whatever you say. Obviously, you know everything."

"Finally, you're starting to get me." He laughed darkly. "Let's hurry up. I'd rather be out killing things like you tonight than play follow the leader. At least, until we finally get a crack at you."

"Shut up, Roth," Bishop growled. He'd moved to stand between me and the demon while Kraven watched us, amused.

Fear slid through me at the way he'd said it. So bluntly. Like this was a guaranteed thing. "What are you talking about?"

He looked at me like I was stupid. "You're a gray. As long as things like you are still breathing, that barrier is up, trapping you—and us—in this city. When you're all dead, the barrier vanishes and we'll be pulled back where we belong. You think we're giving you a pass forever because of this magical mojo you can do?"

"Roth." There was a sharp edge of warning in Bishop's voice.

Roth snorted. "We're going to kill her, it's just a matter of time. You said so yourself."

My breath left me in a rush. "You said *what?*"

Bishop's gaze flashed to me. "I didn't say that."

"So he misunderstood you? Please tell me how that sort of message could get messed up."

Kraven laughed, an unpleasant sound that slithered under my skin. "Bishop didn't come right out and say we had permission to kill you. But he said if you slip up and start munching on souls then you'd become a problem we'd have to deal with. Better?"

"Is that true?" I shot a searching look at Bishop.

His expression was unreadable. "We'll talk about this later."

"No, we'll talk about it now."

"Later," he said again firmly. "Go home, Samantha. We can handle the girl."

I stared at him, trying to read his frustratingly hard-to-read face. I suddenly wanted to run—far away from here, far away from these three…even Bishop, who normally made me feel safe. At least, I thought he did.

But I stood my ground. I refused to be chased away that easily. I couldn't let myself give in to my fear. "I'm not leaving yet. I can still help you tonight."

Disapproval slid through his blue eyes. "Fine. Stay. Your choice."

I could prove to them that what happened at the club wasn't really me. It was a slipup, not an indication that I was losing it. And when I got my soul back, my hunger would be gone. The cold I always felt would fade away. I would be as normal as I could ever hope to be.

"Feeling a connection to the blonde chick?" Kraven asked with a smirk. "How sweet. Maybe you can be best friends. I know you're looking for a new one since the last got flushed away."

I didn't know why I was surprised that he could be so thoughtlessly cruel. My only defense was to put on a good game face. The best way to combat sarcasm was with more of the same.

"Or maybe you can bite me."

His grin stretched. "Is that an invitation?"

"Not tonight…*James*."

His smile fell.

I knew his human name. He'd shared it with me in a moment of weakness, and I knew it bothered him when I used it.

"Gray-girl's got a smart mouth," Kraven muttered. "It's going to get her in trouble someday."

"You're right," Bishop said. "It will."

He was mad that I hadn't tucked tail between my legs and scurried home like a good little monster. But I was staying for the ritual. I would be there for the new girl, no matter what.

I knew what was coming. She didn't. Right now, she'd have no memory of why she was here. The invisible barrier that stretched over Trinity, put in place by the combined powers of Heaven and Hell, was designed to keep supernaturals in the city. But it also kept supernaturals out. To get in, angels or demons had to be specially protected against it. It also stripped away memories. The only thing that helped pinpoint a demon or angel was the searchlight—the one only *I* could see.

The ritual was what restored them to their former demonic or angelic selves. If it wasn't performed, they'd wander the city forever with no idea who they were.

I would rather not have to witness the ritual again—to put it mildly—but I couldn't just walk away and let this girl deal with these three without a shred of moral support.

Her pace had quickened. She knew she was being followed. Before long, she found herself in a blind alley, in a less populated neighborhood. She turned to face us, holding her hands up in front of her.

"I don't want any trouble," she said uneasily.

"Do we look like trouble?" Kraven asked, looking down at himself. "Honestly. I'm a little insulted."

"Let's do this," Roth said.

Bishop shot him a look. "Patience."

The girl's gaze moved to me and a measure of relief went through her eyes. I knew I looked pretty harmless. Nothing more than a teenager dressed to go clubbing on a Saturday night, my long dark hair loose around my shoulders. Nothing to fear.

Not at first glance, anyway.

"Who are you?" she asked.

"A friend," I told her, forcing myself to sound calm. "My name's Samantha."

She swallowed hard. "Why are you following me?"

"Because we want to help you. We know you're having problems. We know you don't know who you are."

Her blue eyes widened. "How could you know that?"

"Magic," Roth said with a thin, unpleasant smile.

Bishop was the one who always performed the ritual, but he wasn't making any sudden moves.

"I think I hit my head." She scrubbed her hand through her blond hair. "I woke up earlier and I—I didn't know where I was. I'm sure I'll be fine in a little while, so…thanks, but I don't need any help."

Despite the chill in the air, sweat dripped down my back and my palms were damp. "You will be fine. I promise."

"Samantha's right. You'll be fine." Bishop finally pulled the curved golden dagger out of the sheath he wore under his shirt, along his spine.

Her eyes shot to it immediately and widened with fear. "What is that?"

"Check her back."

Kraven grabbed hold of both of her wrists in one hand. He pulled at her sweater and she let out a frightened shriek.

I stormed forward and punched him in his arm. "Do you have to be such a jerk? You're scaring her!"

"Sorry, sweetness. There isn't really a polite way to do this."

"Samantha, please don't let them hurt me," the girl begged. A tear slid down her cheek and she trembled, but didn't try very hard to break away from Kraven's grip.

My heart wrenched for her. "I need to check something real quick. Everything will be better soon. You need to trust me, okay?"

"O-okay." Her voice quaked.

I took a deep breath and pulled her sweater up her back a few inches so I could see her skin. The lines of the tattoo I'd been hoping to see were visible immediately, wrapping right around her sides and past the waistline of her jeans.

"Is it there?" Bishop asked.

A small but immediate measure of relief coursed through me. "She has an imprint. She's definitely the right one."

She stared at me with confusion. "An imprint? What's an imprint?"

I nodded and returned her sweater to its previous position. "Something that will make everything all right in just a minute." I looked into her blue eyes and the fear I felt for her must have been reflected there. The panic instantly returned to her gaze.

Her breath came quicker. "What do you mean? What are you going to do to me?"

"Do it, Bishop," I bit out, nausea coursing through my gut. "Quickly."

I thought he'd hesitate and show some sign of reluctance for what he had to do. Sometimes I mistook him for a gentle angel who struggled with sanity and needed help from time to time.

But he wasn't gentle. And he didn't need any help right now. He was a warrior who didn't flinch when it came to taking action.

He nudged me out of the way and looked in the girl's eyes. A coldness moved over his face that scared me.

"Be brave," he said, as if issuing a command. Then he thrust the dagger into her chest without another moment's hesitation.

My knees gave out at the same time hers did.

It's the ritual, I told myself over and over. *She's not human. This isn't really murder.*

The only way a demon or angel could get their memories back after passing through the invisible barrier and into Trinity was to temporarily die—provided that death came from Bishop's very special golden dagger. The dagger did something, some magic, which removed their protective shielding and restored their former sense of self.

If they were ever stabbed again with the same dagger, however, it would kill them.

I stared down at the blonde girl now lying on the ground of the alley with the dagger sticking out of her chest.

"That was so awesome," Roth breathed.

"You're sick," I snarled at him.

"Your point?" The demon leaned over and yanked the dagger out of her chest when Bishop didn't reach for it first.

My mind reeled over witnessing this horrible act yet again. "I need to talk to you, Bishop. Alone. Now."

"Uh-oh," Kraven said. "Somebody's in trouble."

"Fine." Bishop nodded to the left. "Let's go over there."

"Need a chaperone?" Kraven asked. "Wouldn't want her to get any ideas. Maybe fake murder turns gray-girl on."

Bishop sent a glare in his direction. "Stay here and watch over the girl."

"Eat me."

Apparently, Bishop took that as a "yes, I'll stay here and watch over the girl." He led me to a spot farther down the alley and just around the corner. I cast a last glance at the blonde now lying as if dead on the pavement of the alley while two demons lurked nearby waiting for her to wake up again.

"I told you to leave," Bishop said, his voice and expression equally tight. He wasn't meeting my gaze. "So if you're upset about what I had to do, you only have yourself to blame. I was doing my job. I didn't enjoy that."

I knew he was right. It was his job—one he was remarkably and chillingly good at. "Look, I—I'm sorry about what happened at Crave tonight. I know you're mad at me."

"You think I'm mad?"

"You should be mad."

"Should I?" He raised an eyebrow, his harsh expression finally thawing at the edges. "Okay, then I'm mad."

"I knew it."

"Still, you should have left. I know the ritual upsets you. Especially since it was a girl this time."

"Which is kind of ridiculous. I'd all but gotten used to it happening to boys. Why should a girl be any different? Maybe I'm the sexist one here."

"She'll be fine."

"You didn't hesitate. Not even a second."

"Does that bother you?"

"A little," I admitted, but held his gaze. "Are there a lot of female angels?"

"Is that what she is? I didn't see the imprint."

I nodded. Since angels and demons didn't have actual wings here in the human world—apparently such things were not physical as much as they were *metaphysical*—they did retain the mark of such wings. It looked like a large tattoo that stretched across their backs and down their sides. Angel wings were pale with delicate, feathery lines. Demon wings were bold and black and webbed. It was the only way to tell them apart at a glance.

"There are an equal number of male and female angels," he said.

"Equal. Everything's equal," I grumbled. "Got to keep the balance on the universal teeter-totter, don't you?"

He studied my face. "I know you're upset."

I didn't break our eye contact. "Did you really tell Roth he could kill me if I screw up?"

He didn't speak for a moment. "No."

The demon had said it with such certainty, there had to be more to this. I needed to know the truth. "Then what did you say that gave him that idea?"

His gaze grew fiercer. "You can't let what happened earlier with that boy ever happen again. It's too dangerous, Samantha."

It was so cold tonight—or maybe it wasn't. Maybe it was just me and my soulless side effects. My coat wasn't thick enough to keep me warm. The tights I wore under my skirt were too thin. I shivered. "That's the real reason you've stayed away from me this week. So I wouldn't be tempted to kiss you again. So I wouldn't hurt you again."

His vivid blue eyes burned into mine. "You didn't hurt me the first time."

"But I could next time."

"We don't know that for sure." He wrenched his gaze away from me, his expression shadowing. "I kept my distance because I needed to know if this pull I feel toward you was because of what you are. If this soul inside me has been a magnet drawing me closer to you since the first moment we met."

It was what I'd also feared. That this—this overpowering *thing* I felt for Bishop wasn't real. That it was just another side effect, like me being cold and hungry all the time. All because he had a soul and I longed for it. "And?"

His brows drew together. "Inconclusive. I'll know for sure when we get your soul back."

My heart pounded like a wild thing in my chest. "You think it'll be that simple? Find Stephen, find my soul, pop it back in like a battery pack? Snap, Samantha's back to normal and you won't feel so weird around me?"

"Nothing important is ever that simple." He searched my face. "Let me do my job. Let me find him. And then we'll figure everything else out."

I pushed a hand through my hair, tugging on a tangle, and realized I was literally trembling. "Quite honestly? Roth is right. Even if you purge the city of every single other gray, I'm still here. That means the barrier stays right where it is and you're stuck here."

"It's fine." Bishop rubbed his fingers over his temples, his frown deepening. "All is fine. All will be fine. I swear it will. Nothing to worry about. Nothing, nothing at all."

There was a worrisome edge of madness to his voice, something I remembered all too well from before. "Are you okay?"

"Why wouldn't I be? Everything's fantastic." When he laughed, it had a sharp, insane edge to it.

He wasn't okay. Far from it. "You said you'd found alternate ways of dealing with the crazy when it landed. How exactly is that? Deep breathing? Meditation?"

"Something like that."

"Care to expand?"

"Not really."

His insistence on always being evasive made *me* crazy. "Nothing's really changed, has it? You don't tell me anything."

"I tell you what you need to know. But some things…you don't want to know."

I flinched. "I thought we were in this together. Like a team. The others don't know the secret about me…."

"And you are never to tell them." He grabbed my shoulders tightly as if what I'd said had alarmed him. The craziness in his eyes intensified. "You hear me? None of them can ever know about your birth parents."

"I hear you. Relax." I reached down and grabbed his hand. Electricity sparked between us and the insanity began to ease from his expression.

Skin to skin. Touching him only spiked my hunger, but it was essential—at least right now—for him to calm down.

The others knew I could do this, just like I could see the searchlights. But they didn't know the whole truth like Bishop did.

"Better?" I asked.

"Much." He nodded, entwining our fingers together for a moment that was equal parts blissful and torturous before he reluctantly let go. "I know you're frustrated by some of the things I do, but you have to trust me."

"I want to…"

"But?"

My throat tightened as I locked gazes with him. "How can I trust somebody who won't even tell me his real name?"

"My name is Bishop."

"It wasn't always."

"No. Not always." He looked into my eyes and for the briefest moment I was certain he was going to tell me. Then something shuttered there, keeping me out when I only wanted in.

Don't get me wrong, I liked his name. I loved his name, really. It was right and it suited him. But it wasn't real. It was something made up, like an actor in Hollywood who wanted to leave his humble beginnings far behind.

If anything, I felt uneasier than I had before our private talk. I followed him wordlessly back to the dark alley to find Roth hovering over the angel while still holding the knife. The way he watched her was predatory.

"What the hell do you think you're doing?" I demanded.

"She's so hot. Too bad she's an angel." He gave me a cold grin. "I checked under her sweater."

A sudden flash of fury turned my vision red. "Touch her again and I'll kill you myself."

"Chill out, gray-girl." Kraven stood nearby with his arms crossed over his chest. "I was chaperoning from a disinterested distance. Don't worry, he didn't get frisky. It was just her back."

"She smells so good." Roth crouched down lower so he could put his face close to hers. "Like strawberries and whipped cream. It's making me hungry."

"Get away from her," Bishop warned.

"Make me."

All I wanted to do was protect this defenseless girl. I was about to move toward Roth and kick him as hard as I could, hoping to do a little damage with my high heels, when she let out a gasp and her eyes snapped open.

"Back from the dead." Roth gazed down at her lasciviously. "Welcome, beautiful."

She stared up at him hovering over her with the knife in his grip. Then her hand shot out and grabbed his throat.

"Get off me." She pushed him upward and then slammed him down to the ground. She easily disarmed him and held the knife to *his* throat.

He looked up at her straddling his chest, his eyes wide with surprise.

"That I didn't expect," Kraven said, from where he leaned against the wall. "But I kind of like it."

"Easy." Bishop approached the furious angel. "It's okay."

"How is this okay?" she demanded. "He was sniffing me like a horny dog. Very unprofessional. He must be one of the demons."

"I'm definitely enjoying this," Roth said with a lewd grin. "You can sit on me anytime, beautiful. Clothing optional."

"You're disgusting." She jabbed the knife into his throat

deep enough to cut him. He winced and blood trickled down his neck. The mocking edge to his expression disappeared. "I *despise* demons."

In a single effortless movement, she got to her feet and inspected the golden dagger. Her gaze flicked to Bishop. "Who's the leader here?"

"I am," Bishop said.

"Depends on the day, really," Kraven muttered.

The blonde's gaze shot to him. "You're another demon, aren't you?"

"Is it my cologne or my good looks that gave me away?"

I was becoming more impressed by the second. I'd expected her to be scared and uncertain, like she'd been before. But this angel could kick some serious ass.

"I'm Cassandra," she said when her attention fell on me. "You said your name's Samantha, right?"

"That's right. Samantha Day."

She cocked her head. "I thought you were human, but…" She looked at Bishop. "I sense that she's soulless—a gray. I don't understand."

"Samantha's different from the others. I'll explain everything later." Bishop's eyes flicked warily to the knife the blond angel clutched. "I'm Bishop. That's Kraven. And the demon on the ground in need of a Band-Aid is Roth. Welcome to Trinity, Cassandra."

"Glad to be here." She rubbed her previously injured chest and gave him a bright smile. "Stupid ritual."

"I couldn't agree more." He grinned back at her.

I'd been more than prepared to like Cassandra, but a dark ribbon of jealousy suddenly appeared out of nowhere to twist through me.

"Take me to your headquarters and we'll debrief," she said.

"Sure thing." Bishop glanced at me. "Samantha, go home."

The gorgeous, blond angel gets a killer smile and I get the brush-off. Awesome.

"No," Cassandra said. "She's coming with us."

"Is that necessary?" Bishop asked.

"I have a few questions for her."

He flicked a glance at me before returning his attention fully to Cassandra and he gave her another knee-weakening grin before offering her his arm. "Of course. Anything you like."

She took his arm and he began to lead her away, ignoring the rest of us.

I glanced at Kraven as that sharp-taloned jealousy I was trying to ignore began to leave claw marks on the inside of my chest.

He smirked at me. "Love hurts, sweetness."

chapter 4

I only had myself to blame. Bishop said I should go. Instead, I insisted on sticking around to help the helpless girl who wasn't helpless at all.

Now I felt like a specimen under the microscope as Cassandra had been watching every move I made since we got back to St. Andrew's, which was the abandoned church in an abandoned neighborhood the team had chosen as their makeshift "headquarters" and temporary hotel. Along with yours truly, the blonde angel swept her appraising gaze over the tall ceiling, stained-glass windows and rows of pews in the main sanctuary. Since there was no electricity, hundreds of candles were lit throughout, giving the area an eerie glow.

My feet hurt from these heels—which were meant for nightclubs, not brisk walks through the city streets. Still, the pain gave me a focal point. I concentrated on my aching feet rather than the threads of panic stitching unpleasant patterns through my gut. Even though I'd been given an uneasy pass when it came to the team, I still had a lot in common with a mouse in the middle of a group of feral cats. It didn't matter if they had halos or horns.

While Cassandra studied me, I studied Bishop. Hard not to.

My gaze was always drawn to him when he was in the same room as me. I couldn't ignore him if I tried.

I refused to believe it was just because I was attracted to his soul, even if that was his hypothesis for my unearthly infatuation with him.

I didn't feel like this toward Colin. Or anybody else with a soul.

Bishop was different for me. Different from anyone.

And when his gaze followed Cassandra through the sanctuary as if he couldn't look away from *her,* the gnawing ache inside me suddenly had nothing at all to do with hunger.

The other demons had taken seats in the pews on opposite sides of the church. Kraven sat three rows from the front.

"Why'd they send another angel?" he asked sullenly, cutting through the silence that had fallen since we'd arrived here. "I thought we were supposed to be all nice and balanced. Now it's four against two."

"An exception was made," Cassandra replied crisply. "Demons are rarely trustworthy enough to be part of a rare mission like this without causing trouble. Present company excluded, of course."

"Don't try to butter me up now, Blondie. You already said you despise demons." His lips curled to the side. "It's almost like you're trying to hurt my tender feelings."

She grimaced. "I apologize. That was rude of me. Truth is, I've never even met one before face-to-face."

Roth sat in the front row, eyeing her with caution while rubbing the shallow wound at his throat. Demons and angels usually healed much faster than humans, but after the ritual, when the wound was caused by the golden dagger, it was a different story.

It was more dangerous to a supernatural than any other weapon.

"Can you heal Roth?" I asked Cassandra. I needed to say something, to be part of the conversation, not just the helpless mouse who lurked in the corner trying not to squeak. "Not that you'd want to heal him, but I was just wondering if all angels had that ability."

"We can, in varying degrees of strength. I'm quite a strong healer." Her gaze shifted to the demon. "Do you want me to heal you?"

Roth shrugged. "Whatever."

Her expression soured as she moved closer to him. "A real charmer, aren't you?"

"I try my best." Roth stiffened as she reached toward him and brushed her fingers against his throat. There was a soft pulse of light and his tanned skin healed right before my eyes.

"You're very gifted," Bishop said. His angelic powers were limited due to his fallen status. He watched Cassandra with a wistful envy that made my heart hurt for him.

"Now that that's done we can deal with the problem at hand." Cassandra turned to the rest of us. "Your mission was to clear this city of its recent infestation of soul-devouring creatures. Yet one is here with us right now. Why?"

"Good question," Roth said.

I wouldn't underestimate this angel. She might look harmless, but she was anything but.

At the same time, I didn't blame her for her confusion. I'd ask the same thing if I was in her position.

"Samantha's different," Bishop said calmly. "She isn't ruled by her hunger."

Kraven snorted at that, and I shot a dark look at him.

"Something funny?" Cassandra asked.

"No, ma'am." He put his laced-up boot-clad feet over the back of a pew bench and crossed his ankles casually. I braced myself, expecting him to share what happened earlier at Crave, but he kept his mouth shut.

Shocker. But I'd reserve my gratitude for later.

Bishop raked his hand through his short, dark hair, his gaze flicking to me for a weighted moment before returning to Cassandra. In the shadowy light of the church, I wasn't sure if his eyes were glowing or if it was the candlelight.

"Samantha's important to us," he continued. "She has a special psychic ability—she can see the searchlights. I can't because I'm damaged from my fall."

"I did hear about what happened," Cassandra said, her brows drawing together. "I'm pleased you seem very capable despite the misfortune that's befallen you."

"Doing the best I can."

"You must be very angry."

"Someone sabotaged me, sabotaged this entire mission. Now I'm forced to deal with the consequences of having this soul. Can't say I'm happy about it."

"Nor should you be. What happened to you is unfair."

"That's putting it mildly." He snorted humorlessly, reminding me uneasily of his brother. "I hold out hope that it'll be corrected when the mission is complete and I'll be pulled back with the others."

"One should always have hope." Cassandra turned to eye me curiously. "So you have supernatural intuition. It's rare, but not unheard of. Perhaps you're mentally stronger than other humans."

"I do pretty well in school," I said as lightly as I could. "Mentally, that is."

Cassandra and the others could never find out what I really was. If demons and angels were forbidden to be together—to such an extent that this love had destroyed my mother and sent my father into the Hollow after her—I knew if anyone learned the truth I'd be in even worse trouble than I already was.

"Samantha isn't what I expected," Cassandra finally said. "When they briefed me about grays, I thought they would all be the same."

"I know." Bishop crossed his arms over his chest. "We were told we'd find mindless creatures driven by their hungers—created by an anomalous demon who devoured souls. That much was true. But it's not always like that for those who've been kissed—and I believe it's not only Samantha who's different. We've taken to eliminating only those who've completely lost their control and their reason. Anything else would be murder."

Something heavy inside me lightened at this confirmation, a part that was worried he and the others were indiscriminately slaying grays across the city.

"Is that why you're here?" I asked her. "Because all the grays haven't been wiped out of the city yet? Because the barrier's still up? Are you like…like some sort of quality control agent sent to assess how things are progressing?"

When I got nervous, I started talking and asking questions. I was surprised I'd been able to hold my tongue this long.

"Yeah, Blondie," Kraven spoke up. "Just what are you doing here?"

"I have a mission, of course. Part of it is to assess how the team is succeeding…" She paused. "Or failing."

"What is your main mission?" Bishop asked.

She swept her gaze over the four of us before she said anything. "We know the Hollow is not acting as it normally does."

Just the sound of its name spoken aloud made an unpleasant shiver race through me.

"Are interdimensional gateways to supernatural graveyards

ever that reliable?" Bishop's expression had relaxed and his tone felt almost too light.

Bishop had as snarky a sense of humor as Kraven did, only he usually kept it under wraps as leader. However, he seemed different with Cassandra around. More relaxed, more easygoing. I wondered if it was because he felt comfortable with her here...or if it was just the opposite.

"What have you learned about it?" Cassandra pressed, and she shifted her gaze to Roth.

He shrugged a shoulder. "It opens when it's supposed to—at the death of a supernatural. Sucks in the garbage. Then it closes up. Other than it spitting the Source of the grays back out to cause this current little citywide infestation, I don't think it's changed all that much."

She frowned. "So it's true. What has been cast into the Hollow now has a chance to return."

I didn't have to look to see that Bishop had drawn closer to me. I felt it.

"We think so," he said. "If a supernatural finds him or herself in the Hollow, there is the chance for escape. But the barrier is here to keep anything that gets loose in the city contained so we can deal with it."

"Keeping us trapped here like rats also," Roth grumbled. "All grays should die. Thinking any other way is just delaying the inevitable. And, for the record, I don't think that Bishop's pet gray should be given a break. We don't know that her soul can be restored."

"Excuse me?" Cassandra said, her gaze moving to me again. "Your soul is still in existence?"

"The one who took it managed to contain it," Bishop answered before I could. "We mean to find him and retrieve it."

She watched me again like a scientist studying a fascinating microbe. "This must be why you're different, Samantha." She looked at Bishop. "Right?"

"Perhaps," he conceded, but he believed I was different due to my secret origins.

Either way, I needed my soul back. It wasn't even a question.

"Very good." Cassandra nodded and slowly trailed her gaze over Bishop's body. It was leisurely enough that the sour taste returned to my mouth. "Despite your personal difficulties, you appear to have everything under control here."

"I do."

"Then why are you bleeding right now?"

My eyes shot to him.

"Excuse me?" he asked tightly.

She pointed at his abdomen. "How were you wounded?"

His jaw tensed. "It's nothing."

"Bishop!" I exclaimed. "What is she talking about? Are you hurt?"

He didn't look at me. "No."

"Pull up your shirt," Cassandra instructed. "Let me see."

After another hesitation, he reluctantly reached for the bottom of his long-sleeved T-shirt and raised it up to show his flat, muscled abdomen. My breath lodged in my throat. There were three deep cuts in his skin. The flow of blood had slowed, but it had soaked through his shirt. Since the material was black I hadn't noticed anything before.

I was horrified that he'd been walking around with these wounds all night and I'd had no idea. "Oh, my God! What happened to you?"

His gaze flicked to me. "Nothing. I was going to get Zach to heal me next time I saw him."

"Nothing? That's not nothing! Who did that to you?"

"He did it to himself," Kraven said with disinterest, exchanging a wry look with Roth. "It's his new thing."

All I could do was gape at Bishop. "Why would you cut yourself like that?"

"The pain helps me concentrate," he said through clenched teeth. "It takes my confusion away. I need to be able to keep my focus, no matter what."

I clasped my hand over my mouth, stunned. This is what he'd discovered during the days we'd been apart. This is why he hadn't needed me to touch him to help clear his mind.

Instead of sympathy for his struggle, hot anger surged through me. "That was an unforgivably stupid thing to do!"

His gaze hardened. "I found a solution. I used it."

A strangled sound escaped my throat. "Yeah, fantastic solution, Bishop. Self-mutilation. Really brilliant."

Kraven snorted.

It was as if someone had just drawn a blade over my skin as well and pressed down hard. He'd chosen to inflict injury on himself rather than seek me out. The realization stung like hell.

He lowered his shirt, frowning deeply. "I didn't want you to know about this."

"Such a martyr," Kraven drawled. "Spare me the drama."

"I assume you used the Hallowed Blade to do this. Otherwise, it would have healed by now." Cassandra was pushing Bishop's shirt back up. "Hold still."

She placed both hands over his wounds and a few moments later, with that soft pulse of light from before, the cuts disappeared.

She didn't let go of him right away, standing intimately close to him.

"Better?" She smiled up at him.

"Better. Thank you."

"I know how hard it must be for you to deal with the side effects of your soul. I wish I could do more to ease your pain."

I literally trembled with the effort it took not to close the distance between us and wrench her hands away from him. Even though I knew she'd helped him, I didn't like how she was touching him.

I'd known Cassandra the Perky Blonde Angel for an hour now and I was insanely and irrationally resentful of her immediate connection with Bishop. I hated feeling this way, all these gnawing doubts in my gut joining my ravenous hunger pains.

Cassandra was beautiful, capable, smart and strong—and she could heal injuries with a mere touch. She was an angel, too. They had everything in common with each other.

Irrational or not, I hated her stupid blond guts.

"Do you give everyone this kind of personal attention?" I asked. "Or just Bishop?"

She glanced at me and gave me a small smile. "I healed Roth, too."

I felt the heat of Bishop's gaze on me, but I didn't look directly at him. I knew every word that came from my mouth made me sound like a petty, jealous girlfriend. I'd always hated girls like that.

I fought hard to keep any discernible emotion out of my eyes. Despite our undeniable connection, Bishop wasn't my boyfriend. I had no real claim on him at all.

I mean, I didn't even know his real name.

That's what my brain knew—that Bishop wasn't mine.

My heart, however, had a totally different opinion on the subject.

Before anyone could say anything else, the side door clanged shut and a few seconds later, Zach and Connor entered the church sanctuary with us.

Great, I thought drily. *The gang's all here.*

Zach was tall and thin, with red hair, freckles on his nose and clear, green eyes. He was kind and thoughtful, and typically did the healing in the group. I knew this from personal experience. Connor was an inch or two shorter, with dark skin, and hair so short I considered it shaved. He always had a joke to help lighten the mood. The two had forged a close friendship since they arrived, and usually went out on patrol together.

"Patrol" was the term for their endless city walks in search of grays who'd lost their minds, their control, who were so driven by their hunger that they became a true and monstrous threat to anyone they crossed paths with. Those grays were targeted for death—their bodies swept away to the Hollow after the deed was done. The golden dagger wasn't required to kill a gray. They might be supernatural, but they were still mortal.

If I gave in to the kiss much more, I'd also become one of those zombie grays. Which was why what had happened with Colin had frightened me so much. Once a gray turned to that zombie state, there was no coming back from it. The horrible thought of losing myself completely kept me awake at night staring at my ceiling with my sheets pulled right up to my neck.

"We have a visitor," Connor said with surprise as he noticed Cassandra—and it was very hard not to notice the beautiful blonde. "Hi, there. I'm Connor."

"A pleasure." She nodded.

Zach's previous smile faded at the edges as his gaze widened with recognition. "Cassandra."

"Zachary. I'm glad to see you made it here all right."

"Stupid ritual."

"Totally agree." She smiled warmly at him. "So this is the entire team?"

"It is," Bishop confirmed.

"Why are you here?" Zach asked her.

"The same reason as the rest of you. To lend a hand with a difficult situation."

"Of course."

She chewed her bottom lip—which struck me as a nervous gesture. It surprised me that she and Zach already knew each other, although I wasn't sure why. Angels would be associated with each other on some level in Heaven, kind of like going to a big high school. Not everybody knew everyone else, but there were those you saw every day, some you made friends with, some you...didn't.

I got the strange feeling that these two weren't exactly best friends.

"Will you be staying with us here at the church?" Zach asked.

Cassandra swept her gaze around the sanctuary, ending with Roth. Her expression soured. "I don't think so."

"Oh, come on," Roth said, grinning darkly. "We can be bunkmates."

"Definitely not." She looked at me. "I'll stay with Samantha."

I stared at her. "I...uh, I'm not sure that's such a good idea."

"Of course it is."

I cast a look at Bishop, hoping for backup.

There was amusement in his gaze at her suggestion, which didn't bode well. "I think it's a good idea. Cassandra can watch over you at night when I'm not around. You'll be safe from any more...potential problems."

Kraven snorted again. Honestly, I'd think the demon had a head cold if I didn't know better. "Right. Wouldn't want you to have problems, sweetness. That story doesn't have a happily ever after."

Bishop shot him a look. "That's not what I meant."

The demon waved a dismissive hand. "I wouldn't know. I barely listen to anything you ever say."

Don't fight this, I told myself. *Go with the flow. Don't raise any alarms, not after what happened at Crave.*

"Fine," I said through clenched teeth. "Wouldn't want to be a problem."

"Way too late for that," Roth mumbled.

"Before you go, Cassandra…" Bishop beckoned for her to join him on the other side of the sanctuary. I watched them with a tight feeling in my chest, but I couldn't hear what they were saying anymore.

Zach moved to stand next to me and he scrubbed a hand through his short, red hair as he also watched the two beautiful angels in their tête-à-tête.

I glanced at him. "So you and Cassandra know each other, huh?"

"Yeah."

I twisted my index finger into my hair, pulling tight enough to squeeze off my circulation. "I bet when she was human she was, like, a cheerleader. One who stole other girls' boyfriends. I mean…not that this observation is relevant right now or anything. I'm just saying."

He grinned at my babblings before the expression faded. "She wasn't human. She's one of the hosts."

I blinked. "One of the what?"

"She was created as an angel."

I stared at him with shock. "Really?"

He nodded. "Really."

"Is…is that how it normally is? Or are angels usually human first?"

"They try to keep it balanced."

"Right. Balance. Can't forget that." I worked it over in my

head. "How does it happen? Like, do you do enough good deeds in real life and you're given the job when you die?"

"Pretty much. For me, I saved a kid from drowning. Saved him, but managed to drown myself in the process. I was only a week from graduating from Harvard top of my class. My father always wanted that more than anything—for me to be a lawyer just like him. He was so obsessed with my grades and my…my future. Sometimes I wonder if he'd approve of what I did become." He glanced at me guiltily. "Sorry, sometimes I still dwell on my past."

"Dwell away. Believe me, I totally get the parent angst. I've lived it all my life." It was crazy hearing someone talk about their own death, but he said it so matter-of-factly that I found I was able to take it in stride. "When was that? When did you, uh…die?"

"Fifty years ago, give or take. And, yes, I was given the chance when I died to choose between eternal rest or eternal…work." He shrugged. "I guess I like to keep busy. Never enjoyed taking vacations, anyway. Such a waste of time."

I couldn't help but laugh at that, but I quickly sobered. *Fifty years ago.* And he still looked so young. Wow. "So what happens to your body?"

"We get to keep our human bodies, which are resurrected and healed so they're even better and stronger than before." He frowned. "It's hard to explain if you haven't experienced it personally. Anyway, our mortal bodies then go through a very intense transition to become celestial and immortal. That part isn't fun."

That was when they'd give up their human souls and gain any special abilities as they were transformed into their angelic selves.

In two minutes I'd gotten more information about life as an angel from Zach than I'd gotten from Bishop in two weeks.

I was both stunned and grateful for anything I could learn. Now I knew Zach was the go-to guy for stuff like this.

"What about Bishop?" I whispered. "Do you know his story?"

Kraven shot a look at me as he rose from the pew. I wasn't sure if he was close enough to hear me and Zach talking. He gestured at Roth for them to leave, which they did. I figured they were sick of waiting and they wanted to go patrol. Connor swung into a pew halfway up the aisle.

Zach didn't speak for a moment. "I'm not sure I want to know his story."

I tensed. "Why?"

"Heard a few things about him before I left. He wasn't well liked. There were many who believed he didn't deserve his placement as an angel." He shrugged. "I don't know the truth. All I know is he was a workaholic...really driven. He took every assignment given to him without any argument as if he was trying to prove something. Frankly, I expected him to be a real dick. Maybe the fall knocked a lot of that attitude out of him. But knowing Bishop and Kraven were brothers once..." He sent a look toward the enigmatic angel in question. "I mean, it does make me wonder."

Me, too. I wondered way too much about the two of them and what it all meant. It had become a driving need inside of me to get to the bottom of the mystery of how and why one brother became a demon and the other an angel.

"Do me a favor, Samantha," Zach said.

"Sure," I replied, now distracted. "Of course. What?"

"Don't fall in love with him."

My gaze shot to his, and my cheeks immediately heated up. "Excuse me?"

He had the grace to look embarrassed. "Love...well, it

makes people do crazy things, even if they're not crazy to begin with. I don't want to see you get hurt."

I bit my bottom lip so hard I nearly drew blood. Out of the corner of my eye, I saw Cassandra give Bishop a hug.

A freaking *hug*.

I swallowed hard. "Any other sage advice tonight, Zach?"

"Yeah." He leaned closer so he could lower his voice to a whisper. "Be careful with Cassandra, too. Hosts are driven by their missions—they take them more seriously than anything else and never question their orders. It's why they were created—to serve Heaven in any way required. I don't know why they sent her, but no matter what she might claim, I know it's for something more than just tagging along on patrol with us."

It was all he said before Cassandra was there in front of me, ready to leave. I craned my neck to see Bishop again, but she whisked me out of the church before I even had the chance to say goodbye.

chapter 5

Cassandra had decided to stay with me. At my house. And I seemed to have no choice in the matter.

It made me mad. This wasn't a friend I wanted to help out. This was an uninvited problem that had barged into my life. If she was just a girl from school I would do my best to avoid her, but she wasn't.

She might look every bit as harmless as I did, but she was far from it.

I eyed her warily as we walked away from St. Andrew's and back toward downtown, the outline of the tall office buildings and St. Edward's Trinity Hospital a glowing beacon in the distance. I drew my coat closer to try to block out the constant chill that made me shiver violently. This was the abandoned part of town, what was once rather industrial, but after the economy tanked a while back, a lot of stores and businesses went bankrupt and shut down. I would definitely think twice about walking around here alone at night—or even with a friend. But Cassandra wasn't defenseless. She might be blonde and pretty, but she was every bit a warrior as the other guys. Maybe more so.

To tell the truth, she freaked me out.

"You know," she said after we'd walked in silence for nearly fifteen minutes. "I am getting the distinct impression that you don't like me very much."

Unfortunately, I wore my emotions on my face thicker than any makeup.

"You don't have to be afraid of me," she added.

I swallowed hard. "I'm not afraid."

Freaked out wasn't afraid. It was *freaked out.*

"If Bishop says you can resist your hungers, then I'm perfectly fine accepting his assessment. To me, you're the same as any other human. Just a little more interesting."

"I'm *not* afraid," I said again, firmer.

She smiled at that. "If you say so."

I needed to gain some sort of control here—even if I was only fooling myself. This was going to be a long walk and I'd spent all my bus money on the plate of nachos at the club as well as the cover charge to get in. I'd had no idea I'd be needing to find another way home other than with Sabrina and Kelly.

But here we were. Me hoofing it home on uncomfortable high heels with my new housemate, Cassandra the Perfect Blonde Angel.

"Zach tells me you're a host," I said. I was making the assumption it wasn't a secret. He hadn't said it was.

She raised an eyebrow. "And do you know what that means?"

Yeah, that I should watch you carefully for your hidden agenda. "You weren't human first. You were created as an angel."

"That's right."

"That's hard for me to wrap my head around. No parents. No siblings...not that I have siblings. But, I mean, most people do." Like Bishop and Kraven, who came immediately and vividly to mind.

She crossed her arms, keeping her gaze on the sidewalk stretching before us. "It's not as sterile an existence as you might think. I have a sibling—or someone I consider my sibling. She was created at the same time as me. We're like sisters."

"Oh." Yes, that was my fabulously snappy comeback.

There were some people you felt totally comfortable around. Like Carly, for instance. We knew each other so well we could basically finish each other's sentences. Also, we didn't have to be constantly talking. It was a comfortable silence.

I didn't have that with Cassandra. With her it was *uncomfortable* silence. One that pressed in on all sides like those collapsing rooms in sci-fi movies, threatening to squish the heroine into something the width of a piece of paper.

"Your supernatural intuition has helped the team," she said. "I'm grateful that Bishop found you."

"More like the other way around."

She looked at me with surprise. "You found him?"

I nodded, thinking back to that night—which was wonderful since I'd met Bishop, but also horrible because, well... I'd met Bishop. He represented the best and worst moments of my life, all in such a short time.

"He was having difficulties keeping his thoughts under control." That was putting it extremely mildly. "Our paths crossed. We realized that when I touched him his mind cleared."

"Incredible. You must be an asset to the team."

I shrugged. Kraven's earlier words echoed in my head: *don't try buttering me up now, Blondie.* "I want to help if I can."

"Now he's taken to inflicting pain on himself to get the same result."

I grimaced. "He has to stop that."

"I agree. It's barbaric. But I do have to wonder how he realized such a thing would work for him."

I'd wondered it, too, at first. But I think I'd figured it out.

Bishop must have realized that pain from the dagger helped clear his head when he'd been tortured by the Source of the grays—who just happened to have been my demon aunt, Natalie, my birth father Nathan's sister. This was another fact that nobody on the team knew but Bishop.

My aunt was anomalous—a demon with a scary glitch created in the conversion from human to infernal being. She had a disturbing taste for human souls and had been branded a problem that needed to be dealt with, especially since souls, both light and dark, were essential to helping keep the universal balance. She was tossed into the Hollow still alive as her punishment. Nathan, too, had an anomaly—according to what Natalie had told me, he could kill with a touch by absorbing life energy.

Seventeen years later, Natalie escaped and arrived here in Trinity. Her strange ability had evolved. Now she was able to create more creatures with her hunger through the "kiss." And they could do the same. Like a contagious disease. That was why there was a barrier up, so none of us "infected" could spread this disease to the rest of the world. It was an invisible citywide quarantine that would be here till we were all gone.

Natalie had known who I was. And being that I was the daughter of a demon and an angel, she thought that my nexus abilities could help her on her path of destruction and revenge. To do so, she got Stephen to remove my soul in a single kiss. She'd used the metaphor of removing a lid from a box. The soul was the lid keeping my supernatural abilities closed off to me. As soon as it was removed, the contents of this strange and scary box were finally revealed. She'd also promised that she was the only one who could lead me to my birth father, who still existed…somewhere. I figured he was still trapped in the Hollow.

And yet, even though she presented this "upgrade" to me as something good and beneficial, I still had to deal with the hunger of a gray. She'd told me she believed these hungers would fade for me since I wasn't totally human to begin with.

The evil woman was a liar about many things.

A week had passed since she'd been killed, and, if anything, my hunger was even worse than before.

So Natalie failed. She died before I could learn more information about my birth father's whereabouts. But before she was killed she'd used Bishop's dagger to carve him up as duress to get me to do what she wanted. It nearly worked. I'd been very close to doing anything to make her stop torturing Bishop. That must have been when he'd realized that injuries from the dagger would chase away his growing confusion.

"Are you all right?" Cassandra touched my arm, snapping me out of the horrible memory.

"Yeah, fine." I inhaled shakily and looked up at the sky. It was clear and black and studded with stars. My eyes burned, but I swallowed back my tears.

I tried to put on a brave face, but this was all still very new to me. I'd gone from being a normal high school student trying to keep a high average in order to ensure a bright future— to not knowing if I'd have a future at all.

Fear was not a friend. All it did was weaken me. I couldn't let myself be weak.

And I flatly refused to be afraid of this angel. I refused to be afraid of my future. *I* was in control here. I'd find Stephen and everything would be better again. My life would never revert completely to what I'd thought of as normal, but it would give me time to figure everything out. And it would give me a chance to find Carly again. If my aunt had managed to escape from the Hollow, then she damn well could, too.

I needed to change the subject to something more productive. Immediately.

"Can Bishop be helped?" I asked. "He's not supposed to have fallen. Somebody messed with him. But he gives me the impression this is permanent."

"There are only a few angels gifted with the ability to burn a new soul into a fallen one. It's not a process that is typically reversed."

"But it was a mistake! They have to make an exception for him."

"I completely agree and I hope that's what they'll choose to do." Her brows drew together. "He's dealing with these difficulties with admirable grace and strength. He's rather amazing, isn't he?"

"Yeah. He is." I agreed with everything she said, but it still rubbed me the wrong way that she was so impressed by him. I kicked my jealous thoughts into the corner like a pair of dirty socks and tried to ignore them. They weren't helping. Also, they smelled bad.

We'd finally emerged from the dark and abandoned neighborhood containing the church. This was more populated, more active, with a main road up ahead and lines of restaurants. It wasn't far from the shopping district known as the Promenade.

Still at least another twenty minutes before we got to my house, though.

I had to keep extra money in my purse for bus fare from now on. Like, seriously. I enjoyed a good walk, the chance to clear my head and get some fresh air, but this was ridiculous.

We passed a couple homeless people sitting with their backs against the fronts of closed-up shops. I scanned their faces quickly, but neither one was the homeless person I'd been searching for.

There was a man named Seth somewhere in this city. Just like Bishop, he was a fallen angel, one who'd fallen a long time ago. I knew he could give insight and help if I introduced him to the team, but I hadn't seen any sign of him in a week. I'd started to think that maybe he'd just been my imagination.

No, he wasn't. He was real. Carly had met him, too.

I'll find you, Seth. I swear I will. I need to talk to you again.

Cassandra slowed to a halt, studying an amorous couple on the side street we'd turned down. The streetlamps cast spooky shadows on the sidewalks and brick walls.

"It's not polite to stare at people making out," I told her.

"Is that what they're doing?"

"Yeah, I mean…" But I stopped talking. At first glance, I'd assumed they were doing just that—two people kissing passionately, so into each other that they ignored the world around them.

But at second glance…

Before I could say anything or do anything, Cassandra walked directly toward the couple and grabbed hold of the man's arm.

He broke off the kiss and turned to face her. His eyes were black, his skin so pale in the darkness that it seemed luminescent.

He was a gray.

I turned my horrified gaze to his girlfriend—or, victim, rather—who looked just as Colin had earlier. Glazed, dazed, with the telltale black lines branching around her mouth. She collapsed to the ground.

No one but us had witnessed this. We were fifty feet from the main road.

The gray looked to be in his early twenties, and was handsome when his pallor returned to normal and his eyes shifted back to human.

"Can I help you?" he asked calmly, wiping his hand over his mouth to remove traces of his victim's lipstick.

Cassandra's hands clenched into tight fists at her sides. "I know what you are."

"Do you?" He raised an eyebrow at the blonde angel who'd stopped him from continuing his dark kiss.

The girl who'd fallen to the ground wasn't moving. Her eyes remained glazed, and she wasn't snapping out of it as Colin thankfully had. The black lines remained around her mouth.

"Oh, God. No," I whispered.

This gray had taken her entire soul in that kiss, and she hadn't been strong enough to survive it.

"She's dead," I said, louder. My stomach convulsed. "You killed her!"

"Too bad," he said without emotion. "She was very tasty."

Cassandra's eyes flashed with rage. "You're evil. A plague upon this city. Upon this entire world. You must be destroyed."

He laughed. "Yeah, good luck with that."

She didn't pull out a weapon, but she stalked closer to him. I held my breath, watching, trying not to look at the dead girl again. I hadn't seen anything like this before. I'd seen the kiss before, I'd been guilty of the kiss myself, but I'd never seen it kill anyone.

This was proof that it could. That what I was, and what I could do—that this ravenous hunger I felt every hour of every day—was one hundred percent evil.

I felt no pity for this gray. Instead, all I felt was rage. I wanted Cassandra to kill him right here and right now. She was a warrior like the others; there was no doubt in my mind about that.

But as she drew closer to him, the gray watched her with open amusement. "You're one of the people I've been hearing about. The ones trying to stop us from having any fun in this town."

She launched herself at him, her hands out as if prepared to grab his throat and strangle him. But with a flick of his wrist, he backhanded her. It was so hard that she went flying through the air and hit the wall on the opposite side of the street with a violent smacking sound.

Cassandra crumpled to the ground unconscious.

I spun to face the gray, stunned. "What did you—?"

He grinned at me. "Impressed?"

I rushed toward Cassandra and snatched a jagged piece of wood from the side of the road, holding it in front of me.

The gray watched me carefully. "What exactly do you think you're doing?"

"Defending myself from a killer." My voice shook.

He laughed. "Seriously? You're one of us, in case you weren't aware. I saw you last week with Stephen at Crave."

Suddenly, I recognized him. He was one of my Aunt Natalie's minions who'd hung out at the nightclub. This was one of the grays who'd held Bishop in place while Natalie tortured him.

Fear and hatred stormed inside me.

"You're not supposed to feed!" I held the sharp piece of wood out in front of me like I was a vampire slayer. I wanted to check Cassandra and make sure she was all right, but I knew I couldn't turn my back on this monster for a second.

"I didn't. Not for a long time. I tried to follow the rules."

"Why are you so strong? Grays aren't any stronger than humans. What are you?"

He studied me without looking the least bit concerned about my impromptu weapon. "You know butterflies start as ugly caterpillars, right?"

My heart pounded so hard I could barely hear over the sound of it. "Is this science class?"

He shrugged. "You need to come with me. We can be friends."

"I don't want any more friends. Not like you." Something occurred to me. My gaze snapped to his. "Where's Stephen? I need to find him!"

His lips stretched over straight, white teeth. "Come with me and we'll all have a nice chat."

Crap. Even the possibility that he knew where to find Stephen was like throwing out tantalizing bread crumbs and then asking me to follow him to the loaf. But I couldn't trust him.

"No way. Tell me where Stephen is."

"Nah. Not if you're hanging around friends like these." He flicked a glance at Cassandra.

I swallowed hard, not sparing more than a worried glance at the unconscious angel. "Why are you different than other grays?"

"Am I?" He gave me a grin—one of those frustrating ones that showed that he believed he knew something I didn't know...and he wasn't talking.

Even from a distance, I felt his evil like thick slime spreading over my skin. He had no remorse about the dead girl lying four feet away from him. Not even a glimmer.

It was as if he had become one of the zombie grays—but he wasn't mindless. It shouldn't have been possible.

Whatever he was, it was wrong. Dark. Malicious. He knew right from wrong, yet he'd chosen to destroy someone's life anyway. He might have control, but he didn't bother to use it.

When he stepped closer to me I took a shaky step back. Cassandra was in my sightline, but she still wasn't moving.

"You need to join with the people who understand you," he said. "Don't get caught on the wrong side of this tug-of-war."

"How many are left?" I asked, my voice choked. "How many grays?"

"Have you seen the papers? They're calling us a kissing mob. A gang of people who randomly kiss strangers. They have no idea what we can really do. What we really are."

I'd seen it. It was buried in the *Trinity Chronicle* as an amusing fluff piece on page fifteen. Nobody realized what a threat it was. Nobody realized that the dozens of people who'd gone missing or turned up mysteriously dead in recent weeks—articles that ran much closer to the front of the newspaper—were related. It was a mystery. There were no signs of trauma found on the bodies, apart from the mysterious black lines left around their mouths. Those lines didn't fade on a dead victim.

"Give that to me before you hurt somebody." He looked so calm it was maddening.

When he reached for the piece of wood, I slashed it at him, cutting his arm.

He snarled at me. "Bitch!"

This time when he grabbed for my weapon I slashed the palm of his hand. Blood dripped to the ground as pain flashed across his expression.

He whacked me across the face so hard that the makeshift stake flew out of my hand, and hit the wall. White-hot pain momentarily blinded me.

I opened my mouth to scream, but he clamped his hand so tight over my mouth I thought he might break my teeth.

He began to drag me down the street. "I think you need to feed. I can set you up. Your head will get a lot clearer soon. Promise."

Michelle Rowen

"Let go of me!" My screams were muffled by his hand. I tried to bite him. I fought against him, scratching and clawing, but his bleeding arm may as well have been made of steel. This guy wasn't human. Not in any way. And he was more than just a gray.

If he shoved me in a small room with a human, based on how I'd dealt with Colin earlier, I wasn't sure if I was strong enough to resist. Maybe for a little while, but not forever. It would be my worst fear come to life.

Suddenly, Bishop stepped out from behind the corner up ahead. For a moment I thought it was all my imagination, that my brains had been rattled when the gray hit me. But it was true.

He was here.

And he looked mad enough to kill.

chapter 6

My heart leaped at the sight of him.

Bishop's gaze was narrowed and dangerously fixed on the gray. "Take your hands off her right now."

The gray removed his hand from my mouth, instead twisting it painfully into my hair to hold me still. I shrieked. "Is this the rescue party? Go check on the blonde. She's one of yours. This one…she's one of mine."

"Wrong," I snarled.

Bishop's eyes flashed bright blue. The dagger was already clenched in his grip. "Roth, check on Cassandra. I'll handle this."

Roth, who'd been standing just behind Bishop, moved toward Cassandra just as the gray shoved me away from him. I slammed hard into the wall, knocking my breath away and rattling my bones. I wheezed for a second and struggled to stay on my feet. This time, I tasted blood.

I whirled around to see Bishop charge the gray, dagger in hand. Much better than a piece of sharp wood.

"Be careful!" I yelled.

He wasn't being very careful. He didn't hesitate—just as he hadn't hesitated with Cassandra.

At the last second, the gray brought his foot up to smash Bishop right in the face, knocking him backward. He landed hard on his back, but leaped back up a moment later, shaking himself off.

"Interesting," Bishop said with a frown. He was now bleeding from a vicious cut on his forehead.

"Good word. *Interesting.* I'll take it." The gray grinned. "And I'll take the girl when I'm finished with you and your friends. She'll be happier with her own kind."

"You can try to take her. You'll fail."

"We'll see."

Bishop studied him with narrowed eyes. His gaze flicked to the victim lying nearby before grimly returning to the gray. "What are you? I thought you were a gray, but you're something else."

"Nope. Just a run of the mill 'gray.'" He even made sarcastic air quotes as his smile stretched. It was a term made up by Heaven and Hell, not by grays themselves. "Time changes things. By not slaughtering all of us last week, you gave us the time we needed to adapt, to evolve. We're glad you sent Natalie's ass back to the Hollow. She was a serious buzzkill."

"Bishop," Roth growled. "We need Zach. Her back's broken."

I stared at him with horror. I didn't think a broken back could kill an angel—only being stabbed by the golden dagger could do that—but if she didn't get healed quickly it could cause serious problems. She could be paralyzed.

Bishop swore under his breath. "Let's get this over with."

He stormed toward the gray again, but was deflected. He landed hard on his shoulder this time and I heard a sickening crunch. His dagger skittered across the pavement away from him.

"Bishop!" I yelled, terrified he'd been hurt as badly as Cassandra.

Roth got to his feet and rushed the gray but the gray easily slammed his fist into the demon's face.

I watched this with sheer disbelief. Grays weren't supposed to be any stronger or any more dangerous than humans. Except for the kiss.

But this guy...

He'd just taken down two angels and a demon without even breaking a sweat. What was going on here?

Bishop struggled to get to his feet, but the guy slammed his foot down on Bishop's broken shoulder. Bishop let out a roar of pain and rage.

Without thinking, I started for him, fists clenched.

"Stay back, Samantha," Bishop snarled. "Don't get closer."

My steps faltered. I trembled as I searched the side street, looking for something that might help.

The gray laughed loudly, and then glanced at me. "Ready to go?"

No. But I was ready to kill him. Seeing Bishop hurt had brought something out from deep inside of me—something that saw red and wanted to inflict injury.

But before I could take even another step closer—against Bishop's wishes—the golden dagger sliced through the air, hitting the gray directly in the chest. He snarled with pain, then yanked it out and threw the now-bloody weapon away from him.

I spun to see who'd thrown it. Zach had arrived and was crouched beside Cassandra. His eyes blazed bright blue in the darkness. Bishop's weren't the only eyes that did that; it was an angel thing.

Zach had thrown the knife with perfect aim. And here I

thought he was a peaceful angel who saved kids from drowning and could heal injuries.

He was also a deadly warrior when necessary.

For a horrible second I thought the dagger'd had no affect at all on this gray, that along with his super strength, he'd somehow become immortal and omnipotent.

Not the case.

He dropped to his knees. Blood soaked the front of his white shirt. He sent a hate-filled glare in my direction.

"Take a good look," he growled. "This is your future whether you like it or not. Soon enough, they'll kill you, too."

He shuddered, then he fell forward onto the pavement.

There wasn't even a moment to catch my breath before the Hollow appeared out of nowhere and opened wide.

I'd seen it twice before. Both times it had scared me so much I could barely function.

Seeing a black, swirling vortex appear out of absolutely nowhere wasn't the most natural sight in the world. It opened like a mouth with a bottomless hunger, ready to take whatever supernatural was in its path. It was triggered by a death, by blood, but it didn't seem to differentiate between the living and the dead. If you were in its path, then you were in serious trouble.

It was torture to think that Carly was in there somewhere—still alive. And I had no idea how to get her back out again.

The gray was closest. With fingerlike tendrils of living, breathing darkness, the Hollow reached out like a horrible hand and pulled him into the vortex. I swear, it was bigger this time, and stronger, as if all of the supernaturals it had taken had made it gain a few pounds. It shifted as if scanning the area, stopping on me for a brief moment. I swear, the Hollow looked at me. Right at me.

"Carly!" I screamed. "Carly! Where are you?"

Maybe if she could hear me. Maybe…

The horrific swirling gateway began to inch closer to me… nearer and nearer…

But then Bishop grabbed hold of me and tried to drag me back, his teeth clenched with pain from his massive shoulder injury. It was enough to snap me out of my daze. I held on to him tightly. The Hollow wouldn't hesitate to grab me. It had tried before, and I had the strangest feeling that it was annoyed that it hadn't succeeded.

"We'll find Carly," he shouted, barely loud enough for me to hear him over the roar of the Hollow. "But it won't be tonight. I'm not losing you like this."

To my right, I saw a horrific sight. Cassandra's unconscious body was sliding across the pavement toward the vortex that had moved away from me. It reached for her, black smoky fingers curling around her ankles.

But then seemingly out of nowhere, Roth launched himself through the air, tackling Cassandra, and rolling them both out of range.

With no one left in its sights, the Hollow began to swirl smaller and smaller until it finally, thankfully, disappeared completely. The thunderous sound—like being in the middle of a tornado—vanished like somebody had pressed the off button on a gigantic stereo.

I still clung to Bishop. He pulled back from me, checking my face, my arms, making sure that I wasn't hurt. His brows were drawn tightly together and his left arm hung slackly at his side.

"Are you okay?" he demanded.

I fought to breathe normally, but I nodded. "Bishop, your shoulder…"

"It's nothing."

"It's shattered."

"I'll live. But you…" His gaze moved over my face, his brows tight together. "You're not seriously hurt."

"No. But Cassandra is."

He swore under his breath. Then, with a last searching look, he pushed up off the ground and went to Cassandra's side.

It was so quick I'd barely had a chance to let the tantalizing scent of his soul affect me. I wished I could say that after what had happened with the gray it didn't bother me, but it had. My hunger surged forward. I squeezed my eyes shut and tried to push it back.

"Can you fix her?" Bishop's words to Zach were tight. Roth, Zach and Bishop gathered in a circle around Cassandra.

I stayed where I was, a safe distance away, watching tensely.

"I think so." Zach gently rolled Cassandra over onto her stomach.

I'd experienced something extremely similar nearly two weeks ago when a searchlight had led me to Roth. When he'd been "reborn" after the ritual, he'd immediately sensed I was a gray. And he'd been sent here to *kill* grays. He quickly and efficiently broke my neck. I'd been only moments away from death when Zach managed to heal me. And I swear, when an angel heals you, it's as if nothing ever happened. Better than that, really. My neck had honestly never felt so good. Still did. He was like a Heaven-sent chiropractor.

"Cassandra, can you hear us?" Bishop asked, touching her shoulder gently.

"Yes," she whispered.

"Hold still and let Zach help you."

"All right. Go ahead." Her pain-filled eyes narrowed. "And hurry up."

I couldn't help but smile shakily at that. The angel was very bossy and it didn't matter what the situation was. I wondered if all host angels were the same.

Zach pushed her sweater up farther to reveal more of her winged-tattoo-like imprint, identical to Bishop's and the other angels'. Then he placed his hands on Cassandra's spine and closed his eyes. His hands began to glow white. Cassandra cried out, and every muscle in my body tensed in sympathy.

I remembered that this felt worse before it felt better—like fire burning straight through your flesh and into your bones.

Finally, Zach returned her sweater to its regular position and helped her to her feet. She wavered unsteadily for a moment, but then got her balance.

"You're next," Zach said, before he quickly worked to heal Bishop's broken shoulder and facial cuts and scrapes.

This was close. Too close. That gray had wanted to crush him into dust right in front of me.

Cassandra looked at Zach. "Thank you." Then at Bishop. "Both of you."

Roth cleared his throat. She flicked a glance at him.

"I saved you, sweetheart," he told her flatly. "You almost got sucked into the Hollow."

Her expression tightened, but she finally nodded. "Thank you, Roth."

"Yeah, whatever." He laughed. "I saved an angel's ass. Can't believe it. Good thing you've got a nice ass."

Her cheeks turned red before she looked at me. "I apologize for failing you."

I stared at her, stunned. "Failing me? He knocked you out cold."

"It's unacceptable." She shook her head, looking angry at herself. "I should have expected—"

"Expected something like that?" Bishop said, crossing his arms over his chest. "You're not omniscient. You didn't know. That was different than anything we've ever been faced with before."

"It was horrible." She let out a shaky sigh and let Bishop put his arm around her shoulders. She leaned into him.

Despite everything we'd just experienced, the sight made my face start to burn. I fought hard not to let my inner flare of jealousy show on the surface. "He knew where Stephen was."

Bishop's gaze flicked to mine. "Did you want us to let him live?"

My attention brushed against the dead girl nearby and my throat closed. "No. He was a monster. But I—I don't understand why he was that strong."

He let go of Cassandra to come stand right in front of me. I studied the ground, feeling his gaze on me, before I finally looked up to meet it. He raised his hand as if to touch me, but then his hand dropped to his side, clenching into a fist. "I haven't seen anything like that before. Feeding too much… it must make them very strong just before it destroys their minds."

"Maybe he was about to change," Roth said. "Maybe this was the last gasp of strength before he lost himself completely."

"I'm glad Cassandra will be staying with you," Bishop said. "She can keep you safe."

"I'll do my very best," Cassandra said softly.

She hadn't exactly kept me safe a minute ago—or herself, for that matter. That gray would have easily dragged me out of here if Bishop hadn't shown up. But I couldn't hold it against her. That gray's strength had been a surprise to all of us.

"Go home. Get some rest," Bishop said to me, then turned to Cassandra. "We'll talk more tomorrow."

She nodded. "Again, thank you for your assistance. I thought we were on our own."

"Bishop tends to stalk from a discreet distance," I said. "You'll hardly notice him, really."

His gaze snapped to mine and a smile tugged at his lips. "I'm not stalking you. Never have."

The smile helped warm me. "Watching from a distance. Secretly observing my every move. I think you might need a dictionary, angel."

"You're welcome, by the way."

My cheeks heated again, for a completely different reason this time. "Thank you."

Finally, with effort, I tore my gaze from his and began walking away. Cassandra caught up to me a block later. We exchanged a look, and I couldn't help but notice her expression and mood were much graver than they had been when we'd left the church.

"You okay?" I asked.

She just nodded, keeping her eyes on the path ahead of us.

Even for an angel, being broken and then healed again had to be a traumatic experience. I'd planned to dislike her forever, especially due to her immediate connection with Bishop, but I found I couldn't after what had happened.

I wasn't saying I liked her, but despising her for being perfect, blonde and beautiful wasn't a good enough reason for absolute and immediate dismissal.

I wasn't positive, but I was pretty sure Bishop followed us back to my house at a discreet distance.

I'd only been kidding before about him being my stalker.

He was definitely my guardian angel.

chapter 7

So much had happened tonight, it was hard to believe it was only a little after nine o'clock when we finally arrived at the small bungalow I shared with my mother.

Home sweet home. I had to say, just the sight of the familiar house helped calm my nerves. Even considering who was with me.

I'd lived here all my life. Until a couple years ago, it was me, my mother and my father. Since the separation, it was just me and Mom. My father lived in England now. I only saw him rarely. Even the emails had started to come with less frequency than they used to.

It would make me sad if I let myself think about it too much.

"Here we are," I said, stopping at the end of the driveway. My mother's car was here. I guess she wasn't working late tonight. Miracles happen.

Cassandra had been very quiet the rest of the way here, as if lost in her thoughts. Her expression revealed nothing about how she felt about having her back broken by a gray...and now voluntarily sharing a house with another one.

In the silence, I'd found it impossible not to think about

that gray's victim. One moment swept away by a kiss from a sexy stranger, the next feeling your life fading away to nothing. A kiss of death.

She didn't have a chance.

I swallowed past the thick lump in my throat and tried to focus on something else, anything else. I'd decided to tell my mother that Cassandra was one of my friends from school. That her parents were gone for a few days, and she was afraid to be alone.

Not perfect, but it would do. My mother would believe it. She believed a lot of things without asking too many questions.

I let Cassandra into the house, eyeing her warily as she brushed past me. She studied everything her gaze landed on as if assessing it for a future report. The bamboo blind at the window, the colorful rug by the front door. The framed photos on the walls, which no longer included my father.

My mother pretended not to dwell on the divorce, but I knew it hadn't been her decision. My father hadn't moved across the ocean *just* to work at the London branch of his law firm…he'd moved there to be with a beautiful blonde British intern half his age. He almost never emailed anymore and I couldn't remember the last time we talked on the phone.

I tried to follow Mom's lead and not dwell on things like that. But it made me understand my mother's angst.

The sight of empty wine bottles lined up to go into the recycling bin made me wince. Cassandra didn't seem to notice, but I did. There were way more this week than usual. And there were usually too many.

I wasn't the only one in the family with a growing addiction to something unhealthy.

"Sam, I'm glad you're home," my mother greeted me warmly as we entered the living room. I wasn't surprised to see that she held a large glass of white wine. On her lap was a stack of papers she was going through. She was a real-estate agent, a job she was good at and put long hours into, seven days a week. I used to complain—to myself, to her, to anyone who'd listen—about how obsessed she was with the job and making money and how she had no time for me.

Since I'd learned I was adopted, she'd tried very hard to mend our shaky relationship by making sure we spent a little time together every day. She assured me that she was a great listener if I had any problems, and that she was here for me, no matter what. And yet, there were more wine bottles by the door than usual.

Stress showed itself in different ways.

I was on edge, but knew I had to hold it together. This was the one place I could still feel like myself. Home was my touchstone for being normal.

And now there was an angel here—one who'd never even been human before. There was nothing normal about that. My mother's gaze moved to her as she entered the room.

"Hi, Mom," I said, clearing my throat. "This is Cassandra. She's a friend of mine."

"A pleasure to meet you, Cassandra. Call me Eleanor." My mother got up from her chair and came over to shake Cassandra's hand. There was a genuine smile on her face. "I'm so glad Sam's hanging out with new friends. After what happened with Carly, I know the past week's been rough."

My eyes started to sting immediately at the mention of my best friend. Mom was one of the people who believed in the "running away with a boyfriend" story. Most brushed it off as the act of a rebellious teenager. But Mom has seen me cry over this and she knew I was taking Carly's absence hard. She thought I saw it as a betrayal of our friendship.

She was wrong. It was a tragedy.

"Nice to meet you, too," Cassandra said. "You have a lovely home."

"Thank you."

Well, weren't we all pleasant and polite?

"I, um, need to ask a favor…" I began, ready to launch into my cover story. But Cassandra took over for me before I said another word. She still held my mother's hand and she looked deep into her eyes.

"I'm going to be staying here with you and Samantha for a little while, Eleanor," she said smoothly. "It's nothing to concern yourself with. Do you understand?"

My mother nodded slowly. "I understand."

I couldn't believe what I was seeing. Cassandra was using angelic influence to mess with my mother's mind. Zach and Connor could do the same thing, but only in emergencies.

"Are you girls hungry?" my mother asked, taking a quick sip of her wine. "I got home late and haven't had dinner yet. I mean, I know Sam's hungry. She's *always* hungry lately. I'm shocked she's remained so skinny with the way she eats."

This just got better and better.

"Yes." The angel put a hand on her stomach and cocked her head as if trying to sense her bodily needs. "I believe I am hungry."

"I'll order some Chinese delivery."

"Delightful." Cassandra took a seat in a La-Z-Boy recliner and leaned forward to flip absently through today's paper. "Eleanor, you say that Samantha is hungry lately. What does she eat?"

I tensed at the question, and the meaning behind it. Just because she'd also given me a pass as a gray didn't mean that she was finished investigating me. I learned over. "Not what you might be thinking."

No souls, thank you. Well, except for Colin's earlier. And Bishop's last week.

I could try to convince myself that they didn't really count. I hadn't hurt them—it had only been tiny nibbles. But it was still wrong.

However, compared to the murderous gray we'd been faced with tonight…

The thought of the glazed eyes of the dead girl with the black lines around her mouth made my blood run cold.

"You name it, she eats it." My mother fought against her grin, but lost. "I can barely keep the fridge stocked anymore."

I gave her a look. "You're so funny I forgot to laugh."

"Better keep a lid on it if you can. I might need to save my grocery money to pay for other necessities." Since she was still grinning, I assumed she was trying to be funny. She shouldn't give up her day job to become a comedian. "I'm having trouble selling a house I thought would go quickly. It's on the east side right near the city line. Huge piece of property that's been abandoned for months. Worth two million."

"What's the problem with it?" I asked absently.

Cassandra continued to scan the newspaper, and then picked up the *TV Guide* to flip through it as if fascinated. If she'd never left Heaven before I suppose all of this was new to her.

"There's a rumor circulating that it's haunted." She pulled her cell phone from her Coach bag. "Which is ridiculous. It seems perfectly normal to me."

"No mournful moans or rattling of chains?"

"Nothing. Although, with it being Halloween in a few days, you'd think that might be a selling feature." She laughed at this, then left the room to call the Chinese restaurant.

Ghosts in abandoned houses. I wondered if that was even possible—if ghosts really existed.

Not my problem. I had enough to worry about without adding to the list.

When the food arrived, and the house began smelling like Chinese food—which was, in a word, divine—Cassandra had a big grin on her face.

"My first meal here," she told me. "It's incredible."

My mother gave her a strange look. "You kids and your diets."

Cassandra scanned the dishes as I piled a plate for myself high with food. "What is that? A ball of chicken? Ingenious!"

Later, Cassandra gleefully experienced an hour of television, while I could barely sit still. I wasn't sure what I should do right now, but I felt like sitting here doing nothing was an incredible waste of time. That gray tonight reminded me how much trouble I was in.

I wouldn't become like that. I wouldn't lose my mind again like I had with Colin. I wouldn't hurt anybody.

I had this under control.

Stephen was still somewhere in this city. I would find him. And he would damn well give me back my soul before it was too late. My future was still bright and sparkly.

Well, maybe not sparkly. But definitely bright.

When it was time for bed, my mother showed Cassandra the upstairs guest room where she'd be staying.

"Thank you, it's perfect," Cassandra said, putting a hand on her arm. "Listen, I've been thinking about this all night, Eleanor. I'd like you to do something for me."

"What?"

She gazed into my mother's eyes. "I think you should go on vacation somewhere really nice. You can leave tomorrow morning. Any work you have can wait until you get back. Do you understand?"

I gaped at her, stunned silent that she was using angelic influence on my mother again.

"Yes, I understand." My mother nodded. "My goodness, a vacation. What a wonderful idea! It's been so long—I don't think I can even remember the last vacation I took. I think it was Florida, four years ago. Remember that, Sam?"

"I…uh, remember. But…are you sure this is a good idea? A vacation right now?"

"No, it's not a good idea." She stroked her honey-blond hair back from her face. Her eyes sparkled. "It's a great idea! I'm going to Hawaii. I've always wanted to go there. I'll take a surfing lesson…and lie on the beach and read a book. Thank you, Cassandra. Such a wonderful suggestion. Will you be all right here without me?"

Cassandra nodded. "We'll be fine."

"I'm going to go pack!" My mother kissed me on my cheek, then hurried off in the direction of her bedroom. I waited for her door to close before I spun around to face the angel.

"Just who do you think you are?"

Her eyebrows went up. "Excuse me?"

"You think you can just influence people to do whatever you want them to do? Like it's nothing?" Every decision that had been made, taken out of my hands, forced upon me—this was the final straw. I wasn't just going to smile and nod and try to be easy to get along with so nobody saw me as a threat. This was totally unacceptable.

She looked at me as if confused by my reaction. "It's better this way. Having her here puts her in danger. You must realize that, don't you?"

Of course I realized that. I wasn't stupid. "I'm not saying you're wrong."

"Then what's the problem?"

"It's just…not cool," I sputtered. "You're new around

here—a guest! And this is my house…and my mother! You don't get to make the rules!" I turned away and went to my room, slamming the door behind me.

Immediately, I felt like a petulant child who'd just thrown a temper tantrum. But I couldn't help it. I tried to be on my best behavior and fit in, to not make any trouble, even when my life was falling apart. But she'd pushed me too far.

Cassandra had succeeded in making me feel utterly powerless. And that, in turn, made me realize I had no control over anything in my life.

I sank to the floor next to my bed and pulled my knees close to my chest. The three full plates of Chinese food I'd eaten sat heavily in my stomach, threatening to come back up.

Cassandra pushed open my bedroom door a couple minutes later. It wasn't a big surprise that she didn't knock first.

I looked up at her, guarded. "What do you want now?"

She pressed her hand against the door frame and looked awkward about coming all the way into my room. Again, her assessing gaze swept over my furniture, my vanity, my discarded clothes that hadn't hit the hamper. I might get straight As, but I wasn't what anyone would describe as the neatest person in the world.

"It's been a difficult evening," she said. "For you, for me. For all of us. I also sensed a dynamic between you and the other members of the team that perhaps I've disrupted in some way."

I stared up at her, trying to process the strange way she spoke. "You're a bit of a Vulcan, aren't you?"

She looked confused. "A…what?"

"A Vulcan. It's a *Star Trek* thing. Emotionless aliens who like to talk very proper."

Her frown deepened. "I'm not an alien. I'm an angel."

I sighed. "An angel who's never had a chicken ball before."

"Which was delicious. And the red dippable goo they came with?" She beamed. "Amazing."

"If you say so."

She came all the way into my room and sat on the edge of my bed. She looked at me very seriously. "I know you don't like me."

"I never said that." Not in front of her, anyway.

Her shoulders sank. "That gray this evening. He hurt me… and he hurt you. I thought I could handle it, but he defeated me easily. Too easily."

"It wasn't your fault. Grays aren't normally like that. He was a total freak of nature." One that scared the hell out of me, to say the least. I was glad he was dead and he couldn't hurt anyone else.

"That demon had to save me." She shuddered. "And he said I have a nice ass. How crude."

"That's Roth."

"Is he…" Her brows drew together "…as horrible as he seems?"

I was about to agree with that statement wholeheartedly, but then I thought about it. "I don't know. Demons are supposed to be evil and horrible. I don't like him. He's a jerk, but he's part of the team. He's doing his thing. And he did save your butt." I thought about what little I knew about Kraven. "Demons who've been humans before…they have stories behind them. They're not a hundred percent bad. At least, I don't think they are. I mean, I guess they did some really bad stuff when they were alive in order to become a demon. Right?"

"I'm sure they did."

I remembered Zach's story about the good deed with the drowning kid, and that giving him the chance to become an angel. I figured it would be the exact opposite—a bad deed—

to become a demon. "It's bizarre, really. Because, as far as I'm concerned, demons should be totally evil to the core."

That was one of the things that freaked me out the most. How you couldn't tell who was a demon and who was an angel. How similar they looked. Only their imprints confirmed what they really were.

"In the beginning," I continued, "I assumed Bishop was a demon by the way he handled that dagger of his."

"Yes, he does have a way with the Hallowed Blade."

My ears perked up at this name. She'd called it that before. "Is that what it's called?"

She nodded gravely. "All angels of death are assigned one."

I blinked. "Angel of…what?"

She glanced down at me sprawled on the floor. "Angel of death. Bishop is one of Heaven's assassins, which is why he's one of the few officially authorized to carry such a dangerous blade."

"Oh." I could barely find my voice.

"Didn't you know this about him?"

"No. It—it hadn't come up." It was a whisper. I couldn't manage much more than that. A piece of information like this was enough to knock the breath right out of me.

"That's why he was chosen to lead this mission. His record shows that he doesn't hesitate when it comes to—"

"Killing," I finished for her, feeling sick inside. "The ritual…and dealing with the grays…"

She nodded. "If his departure hadn't been tampered with, I have no doubt that the grays would all be…" She trailed off and looked at me sheepishly. "Of course, I'm sure an exception would still be made for those who don't feed and whose souls still exist intact. Somewhere. He wouldn't have just killed you indiscriminately just because you're, well…one of them."

I swallowed hard. "I hope you're right."

Bishop's mission here in Trinity required someone with the right instincts. No hesitation. It had always made my blood turn to ice, seeing him at work. That determined, emotionless expression that came over his face just before the blade met its mark.

I'd known Bishop was dangerous, but…an actual angel of death?

Holy hell.

"I should rest." Cassandra stood up and moved toward the door. "Tomorrow I need to get a fresh start."

"Cassandra…" I said, my voice still barely audible. "Can I ask you a question?"

"Of course. What?"

I took a deep breath and looked right at her. "What's the real reason you were sent here?"

A shaky smile formed on her lips. "I'm here to lend a hand to the team during this difficult mission. Why else? Good night, Samantha."

"Good night."

She left, but not before I'd managed to get a small glimpse of her thoughts. It was another one of my newly uncovered talents. I could read a demon or angel's mind…if they weren't actively trying to block me. All I had to do was look into their eyes and concentrate hard.

Cassandra lied. She wasn't here just to help the team. She had her own mission, an entirely separate one.

I really wished I knew what it was.

It took me hours before I finally drifted off to sleep. My head was a horrific mass of nightmares about evil grays and dead girls, before they finally parted for something much more pleasant.

A dream about Bishop.

He was seated across from me at a small wooden table in the middle of a wasteland—a cracked, dry desert that stretched as far as the eye could see. There was nothing in sight to the horizons all around us. The sky was a flat, pale gray, like a coating of paint.

"Where are we?" I asked.

"Good question." He wore black. Black jeans, black T-shirt. The darkness only made the color of his eyes stand out more— like sapphires.

What Cassandra had told me about his job in Heaven was so far in the distance now I couldn't remember the details. I knew it had disturbed me, but at the moment it was the last thing on my mind. All I felt was happy. Happy to see him. Happy we were alone—no matter where this was. "I'm dreaming right now, aren't I?"

"You are." He smiled—an easy smile that made my heart do an automatic flip.

"So this isn't real? Not some sort of mind meld?"

"No. Just a dream. *Your* dream."

I looked down at myself to see I wore a fancy red dress, gauzy and big and silky, like a ball gown. I'd never worn anything so extravagant in my entire life.

"You're beautiful," Bishop said.

My gaze snapped to his. "It's just the dress. It's not me."

"You're wrong. It is you." There was something in his eyes that made me believe he meant it. "I wish I could kiss you right now."

"You *can* kiss me here." If this was just a dream, then nothing I said or did counted. I liked the idea of that—total freedom. "Normally in my dreams…we do more than just kiss."

His brows went up. "Really."

I nodded, fighting a smile.

"You want to do more than just kiss me, Samantha?"

"Maybe I do." My heart pounded. The endless bravery I normally had in my dreams seemed to be escaping like sand sliding through my fingers. "But there's a problem."

"What?"

"There's a severe balance of power missing in this…whatever this is between us. I know hardly anything about you. You know everything about me. I have no power over you at all."

"Wrong. You took part of my soul. You know I'm drawn to you like nothing I can control, which is why I've tried—and failed—to stay away. Even when I do keep my distance you can still see through my eyes whenever you want to."

This was another little skill I had. After I'd kissed Bishop and taken part of his soul, there were the odd times I got flashes of what he saw—even if we were nowhere close to each other. I couldn't read his mind or feel his emotions, but I could see through his eyes.

"It's not whenever I want to," I said. "It's totally random."

"You underestimate yourself. Your power. But I'm not surprised. This game has barely begun."

"Game?" I frowned. But then my gaze moved to the table between us. I hadn't even noticed what was on it before. It was a chess board with white and black pieces. "Are we playing a game?"

"We seem to be."

The pieces were already in play, not all lined up at the edges. Bishop was playing the white pieces, and I was playing the black ones. He'd already taken one of my pawns. "But I don't even know how to play chess."

"Then you need to learn. And you need to learn fast."

The next moment, he stood up and swept the board off the table. The pieces went flying in every direction.

I got to my feet, alarmed. "Bishop, what are you—?"

He didn't let me finish my sentence. He grabbed the front of my dress and pulled me toward him, crushing his mouth against mine.

My thoughts fell away as he kissed me—and I kissed him back. Now *this* was more like my normal dreams about Bishop. Passionate, reckless, total abandon. Incredible.

No hunger to ruin the moment. No ravenous need to devour his soul.

Just his lips against mine with no consequences. No punishment. Only pleasure.

When our lips finally parted and I opened my eyes, there was a coldness in his gaze that betrayed the scorching heat of the kiss.

Cold as ice. It was the look he normally got just before he—

I gasped as he sliced the dagger into my chest. I scrambled back from him, collapsing to the ground. Grasping for the hilt, I pulled it out with a pained cry. My blood was difficult to see against the red dress, but it flowed, pulsing out with every beat of my heart.

I gasped for breath. "I trusted you."

"No, you didn't." He stared down at me sprawled on the cracked, dry ground. His dark brows were drawn tightly together. "You never did."

I fell all the way backward, struggling to keep breathing. All I could manage was a small shriek when Cassandra appeared behind Bishop. He didn't see her.

He didn't see the golden dagger in her hand.

She slashed it across his throat in one smooth, violent motion. His hands flew to the wound as the blood began to gush. A moment later, he fell to my side.

The roaring vortex of the Hollow opened up—even here. It was the last thing I saw before I died.

And the last thing I felt was Bishop grasping hold of my hand.

I woke up, gasping for breath. My sheets were soaked with sweat. I felt the strong urge to bolt from my bed and start running as fast as I could somewhere, anywhere. But I forced myself to stay right where I was.

Bishop was an angel of death. One of Heaven's assassins.

Cassandra hadn't been lying when she'd told me this. I believed her. This piece of the puzzle fit really well, even if it revealed a terrifying picture.

He'd killed me in my dream tonight.

It was what I feared would happen in reality, no matter how much I tried to deny it, even to myself.

But I was different. Bishop and me—we were connected on a deeper level. Even though I didn't know anything about his life before he became an angel, or his life *as* an angel, I had to trust my gut when it came to him. And my heart.

Because I *did* trust him.

Heart and gut didn't lie—at least, not at the same time. They *didn't*.

chapter 8

I might be seventeen years old, but watching my mother leave for the airport in a taxi still made me choke up like a little kid.

"Call me if there are any problems." She gave me a big hug in the driveway. I clung tight to her before finally letting go. "I'm sure you and Cassandra will be fine here without me, but no parties, okay?"

I just nodded, my throat tight.

I hadn't said a word to try to stop her. Even though I hated how Cassandra had magically coerced her to leave town, I knew it was for the best. She'd be safer away from here for a week. And she was so excited about the trip, how could I spoil it for her?

There had always been something stopping her from taking this dream vacation. A husband who didn't like to travel (unless it was permanent, and in the direction of his new girlfriend), a kid who always had anxiety attacks on airplanes (that was me—I hate being trapped in small spaces, especially three miles above the ground), and then a job that barely allowed her any time off.

So I was happy for her. Really.

But standing there, watching the taxi drive away down the street, the realization that I was really alone sank in deep. Even though we didn't always get along so well, she represented my normal life. And soon she'd be five thousand miles away.

"I need to go," Cassandra told me after I went back inside, out of the cold, and ate a big breakfast of eggs, toast and Pop-Tarts. She gleefully had some cold Chinese food and more red goo.

She wore clothes she'd borrowed from me this morning. Just because an angel arrived ready to do her mission—whatever that mission really was—didn't mean she packed a bag. Even though she was a few inches taller than me, and had a bigger chest, my clothes looked good on her. It was annoying how good they looked, really.

"To the church?" I asked.

"Yes."

"I'll come with you." I had to get out of here. I couldn't keep dwelling on what was wrong with my life—I had to do something to fix it. Also, I needed to see Bishop. I wanted to ask him about what Cassandra told me—him being an angel of death. I wanted to know why he'd never told me this before. Maybe that could help stop nightmares like the one last night.

"No, I think it's best that you stay here." She put her dishes in the sink. "Let the professionals handle this problem."

I blanched. "You think I'd get in the way?"

"I just think it would be safer if you stayed here. Take the day to rest and reflect. I'll let you know if we learn anything."

"Rest and reflect?" I repeated, dumbfounded.

"Exactly. Have a lovely day." Without another word she was gone, out the front door. I watched through the kitchen window as she walked down the driveway and disappeared around the corner.

Rest and reflect? Seriously?

wicked kiss

Needless to say, there was very little resting. Lots of reflecting, though, as I thought and overthought everything over the next couple of hours.

Even without being around anyone to trigger my hunger, I still felt it pushing in at the edges, gnawing on my control like a dog with a bone. Taking part of Colin's soul last night had barely satisfied me for a couple hours.

It scared me—especially with too much time to think and nobody around to distract me.

I flipped through the newspaper only to see another article about two more mysterious deaths in the city. Police were stumped. There was no cause of death that could be determined, no sign of murder or disease. It was as if the victims had just stopped living. The only clue that the deaths were connected was the strange black lines around their mouths.

I forced myself to stop reading the article and flipped to another about three teens who'd committed suicide on Friday night. They didn't go to my school and I didn't recognize the names, but it also sent a chill through me.

There was no good news in Trinity to be found today, it would seem. It wasn't just me who was in trouble in this city. Everybody—even those not touched by the supernatural—was at risk.

Studying was my strong point. It got me good grades. It should be able to help me get the answers I needed to help myself and other people at risk right now. I went on the internet and searched for more information about nexi, the spawn of angels and demons.

I found nothing helpful. At all.

After a full half hour of staring at the screen, a scream of frustration rose in my throat, but I forced it back down and tried to think rationally. Who my birth parents were was something I had no control over. I needed to refocus my energy and attention on what I *could* control: my goal of finding Stephen and retrieving my soul. I'd deal with what it meant to be a nexus after I did everything I could to fix my immediate problems, lose my hunger and have the chance to be close to Bishop (or anyone else, for that matter) without...difficulties.

I grabbed the landline to call Stephen's house, which was only two doors down from my own. My cell phone had taken up permanent residence in my nightstand drawer. Grays had a weird supernatural vibe that messed with the signal and made phones like that completely useless to me.

His mother picked up. I shakily asked if she'd heard from him lately and where he might be. She had no information for me—and yet again, she said she was sorry. This wasn't the first call I'd made to the Keyes residence in the last week. I'm sure his mother thought I was obsessed with her son. I was. But not for the reason she might think.

Discouraged, I hung up after saying a hurried goodbye. I stood in the center of my bedroom, my fists clenched at my sides, feeling utterly helpless and alone.

I hated feeling that I had no control over my life anymore.

Cassandra told me to stay home and let the "professionals" handle this. Well, I'd decided I wholeheartedly disagreed. I would go to the church and get my answers, even if it was just to grill Bishop about his mysterious past.

Just as I'd pulled my coat on and started for the front door, the phone rang. I almost ignored it, but something drove me to pick it up.

I picked up the phone. "Hello?"

"Samantha."

I froze. He'd only said my name, but I knew the voice. My grip on the receiver tightened. "Stephen?"

"I need to talk to you."

My words tripped over themselves in a hurry to escape my mouth. "Where's my soul? Where's Carly's soul?"

"I have to see you in person." There was a short hesitation. "Look, I know you hate me…"

I had to slump down in the nearest chair since my legs gave out. "I just want to be normal again." The words bubbled up my throat before I could hold them back. I knew very well that it couldn't ever happen. Even if I wasn't a gray, being the secret daughter of an angel and a demon had made me abnormal from the day I was born. It didn't matter that I'd only recently learned the truth.

"Meet me at the Trinity Mall," he said. "On the fourth floor by the railing. It's busy there today so you don't have to worry about me doing anything threatening, if that's what you're afraid of."

I stood up and pressed my back against the wall for support. "Everything about you is threatening, Stephen."

"Don't bring one of your new friends."

"Why wouldn't I bring all of them? You're the bad guy here, remember?"

"I'm not as bad as you might think. We're the same. We should be on the same side."

My grip tightened on the phone. "I'm on my own side. Nobody else's."

"Then you should want all the information you can get about what's to come. Meet me there in an hour."

He hung up.

I stared at the phone before I finally placed it back on its base.

I'd been searching for him for a week and had come up with nothing but air. If Stephen didn't want to be found, then he wouldn't be found. But now he wanted to talk to me.

On his terms.

My first instinct was to find Bishop, but if Stephen saw him with me I knew he'd leave and I'd never see him again.

I had to get my soul back on my own. Put the lid back on this box and keep it there. Then I'd be able to leave the city again, get past the barrier. Other people's souls—including Bishop's—wouldn't drive me crazy with hunger. Everything would be better.

I could still fix this.

The Trinity Mall. Not my favorite place in the city.

Over three hundred stores on four levels, it was a shopping mall slash tourist destination. Trinity was huge enough to have a few malls, but this was the crown jewel right in the heart of downtown. I used to love coming here with Carly, shopping for hours on end, and having lunch in the food court downstairs, back when we both had regular-size appetites. We'd still gorge on the food—hamburgers, Chinese food, souvlaki, French fries, you name it. She'd complain about her slow metabolism and grumble about how I never gained a pound. I'd tell her she looked fine—because she always did whether she realized it or not. I should have told her how much I envied her curves.

But then I ran into some trouble here. After my parents' divorce was finalized six months ago, I went on a bit of a shoplifting spree. Or, as my guidance counselor put it, "a cry for attention."

It was never much, just enough to give me a rush of excitement that I was getting away with something. That I wasn't being perfect, or good, or coloring inside the lines like everyone had told me to all my life. Instead of focusing on being a perfect student and getting all As, I got a lipstick. A scarf. A leather wallet. I knew it was wrong even as I shoved them in my pocket or under my shirt. I didn't try to justify it as something I needed that I couldn't afford. I could afford it. My father felt enough guilt over the divorce and his move across the ocean that my monthly allowance, written on checks with his gold-stamped law firm logo in the corner, were so big I didn't even need to apply for part-time jobs. I mean, I couldn't buy a car or anything major, but for the necessities of life, I could get what I needed.

Getting caught had been mortifying in so many ways. No charges were laid, but my humiliation was witnessed by several kids from school. The cop had been a jerk to me, treating me like a total juvie and a spoiled brat. I'd sat in the back of a cop car for an hour, and only through sheer will had I avoided having the anxiety attack I always got in enclosed spaces. I'd closed my eyes and breathed in and out, pretending to be somewhere, anywhere else.

My penance for my short life of crime was to do some community service. I worked in the kitchen at a local mission and had the chance to interact with people who really had it bad while I had never appreciated how good I had it. I had a home, a roof over my head and a mother who loved me. I'd met homeless people who had nothing and nobody.

It was the most important lesson of my life. Be grateful for what you have, since it can be taken away at any time. Sometimes fate steps in to pull the rug from beneath your feet whether you're prepared or not—and we all fall differently.

I now regretted my month of shoplifting, and not just because I'd been caught. I knew it was wrong and I'd done it for stupid reasons. Not that there was ever a good reason to steal.

But I still hated this mall. I usually shopped at the one on the north side of the city. Took longer to get there, but at least the floors weren't tiled with my shame.

Past Macy's and a lineup of other stores that at one time would have been calling my name were the escalators up to the fourth floor. I wasn't a fan of the elevators due to my claustrophobia. I didn't even like wearing turtlenecks.

At the moment, I didn't need any more anxiety than I already had.

The railing curved in a circle around the open center of the fourth floor and looked down into the main floor food court a hundred feet below. A massive chandelier of crystal birds hung from the glass ceiling, a piece by some artist that had cost a ton of money when the mall opened twenty years ago. When the sun from the skylights hit it just right—it was magic.

I gripped the railing and gazed down nervously at the food court. Despite my big breakfast, my stomach grumbled. Sundays were a busy day at the mall. There were thousands of people here, and I swear I sensed the press, the heat and the scent of every one of their souls.

I couldn't stay here for very long. Already, I felt the need to escape.

"You're here."

Stephen's voice bit through my concentration and I tensed, turning slowly to see him leaning against the railing six feet to my left.

This was real. He was here. I'd finally found him.

Or, rather, he'd found me.

Stay calm.

But that was a losing proposition. I couldn't be calm around Stephen Keyes.

A very short time ago I thought he was the hottest guy I'd ever seen, in Trinity or anywhere else. Black hair, cinnamon-colored eyes with a slight exotic slant to them thanks to his Hawaiian-born mother.

Stephen only dated the most beautiful girls. I never expected to be one of them. I preferred to admire him from afar and keep my heart safe from being trampled on. But…then he kissed me. And he'd hurt more than just my heart.

For a fleeting moment, I'd honestly thought the boy I'd always had a crush on had been into me. Instead, he'd been on assignment for my aunt to remove my soul and free my nexus abilities so they could be used for her gain.

I had no interest in someone like Stephen who would lie to me, use me and steal something so valuable from me. And I never would again. While Bishop had sworn to help me, and I did believe he meant it despite my many doubts and questions about him, the only person I completely trusted was the one I saw in the mirror.

My grip on the railing tightened painfully as a group of teens moved past, way too close, the scent of their souls brushing into my orbit of hunger.

"So here we are," Stephen said.

"That's close enough," I said when he got four feet away.

He stopped. "I'm not planning to hurt you. I'm not the one who carries around a sharp golden dagger, remember?"

"No, you're the one who helped my aunt nearly kill me."

"I don't think she would have killed you." There were dark shadows under his eyes, which made it look as if he hadn't slept in days. I'd noticed the same circles under my eyes this morning, thanks to my nightmare-induced tossing and turning. "Besides, she's gone."

A stomach-churning image of the Hollow grabbing hold of my aunt after Carly had stabbed her with Bishop's dagger flashed through my mind. "Are you upset about that?"

He gave me a grim look. "No."

I didn't want to take my attention off him in case he disappeared in a puff of smoke. This is what I'd wanted. I'd searched the city for him for a week and now he was standing right in front of me. "I don't want to talk about my aunt, Stephen. I'm here for one reason and one reason only."

"Your soul."

"And Carly's. Give them back to me."

He looked down at the food court, his jaw tight. "Look at all of them. It's hard to believe they have no idea what's happening in Trinity right now. Right in front of their eyes. Humans." He said it with barely contained disgust.

He was trying to change the subject. I had to stay calm and not make any huge demands. He had all the power here, but I didn't want him to know that. "You're human."

"I was."

"Now you think you're more than that?"

He didn't answer my question. His gaze flicked to me. "You were already more than human before this."

I tried not to grimace. He knew I was a nexus, thanks to Natalie. My little secret that nobody was supposed to know. "Other than the hunger, I don't feel any different than before."

Stephen studied my face, as if searching for some clue there. "You will."

I still gripped the railing as if it was the only thing keeping me from tumbling over. "No, I won't."

He shook his head. "Things are changing…ever since Natalie's been gone."

"Is this another recruitment speech or a warning?"

He snorted a little, and I could have sworn he looked a bit nauseous.

I frowned. "Are you all right?"

That earned me another dry laugh. "Do you really care about my well-being, Samantha?"

My hands were sweating as I forced myself to stay calm and not start shrieking demands. "You wanted to talk to me. So talk. What's changing?"

He kept his eyes forward, not looking directly at me. "It wasn't like this when Natalie was still around."

"What?"

"It starts with the cold. Like…worse than normal. Worse than the cold we feel from not having a soul. And the hunger…" His expression tightened. "You can't ignore it even if you try. It's there…a constant need that doesn't leave for a second, driving you to feed from someone…anyone. And it doesn't get satisfied when you give in to it…it—it just gets worse."

I think I stopped breathing. This wasn't what I'd expected him to say—not at all. "What are you talking about?"

He swallowed, and when his gaze met mine I swear I saw fear there. "Stasis."

I shook my head. "What's stasis?"

When he wrenched his gaze from the food court to look at me again, there was something in his eyes that scared me. Something bleak and defeated.

Stephen was afraid.

This realization chilled me right down to my bones.

"Feeding—kissing someone—it makes you feel better for a little while. But…it doesn't stop what's going to happen. We're changing, Samantha. You will, too. We lose our minds, our control. Everything."

I started to tremble. He was talking about the zombie grays. "But—but that's what happens to the grays that feed too much. Natalie warned us to control ourselves or we'll end up like that. But if we don't feed, it won't happen. Right?"

"It's different now. She didn't know. We go into that state and…then we come back out again. That mindlessness, it's only the beginning." He didn't say it like it was a good thing.

I stared at him, trying to understand, but then with a sickening feeling it all clicked into place for me. "Oh, God. The gray from last night…"

"What?"

"He was different." My words were barely audible. I tensed up as more people closely brushed past us. "He—he was stronger, more powerful, and…and *evil*. Like, he had no…" I gritted my teeth before I managed to continue. "Like he had no soul."

Stephen didn't mock me and tell me this was a stupid thing to say—that of course a gray had no soul. Instead, his expression only grew more grave. "That's right. Any morals, any compassion we have left—after stasis, it's gone. Stripped. Soulless, completely and totally."

I took this in and worked the disturbing information over in my head. "I thought you were already like that."

He let out a humorless snort. "I've changed from how I was before, but not completely. Not like what I've seen in the past few days."

I clasped my hands tightly to keep them from shaking. "So this guy—he was one of the zombies, and then he…then he came back from that?"

He nodded.

I couldn't speak for a full minute, just staring at him. "Why are you telling me this? Why did you want to meet me here?"

He looked at me steadily. "Because it's my fault you're like this. I wanted to warn you."

There was a big part of Stephen that had been changed forever by becoming a gray, one that could be manipulated by Natalie to do bad things on her behalf—but he wasn't completely changed yet. There was still some part of him that remained the same Stephen that I'd had a crush on.

He was afraid of what was to come. For himself…and for me.

I fought to find the words to speak. "How long before it happens?"

He didn't speak for a moment. "All I know is—it's coming, Samantha. And I don't know how it'll go for me."

My stomach clenched. "What do you mean?"

"Stasis either evolves you into something dark, something evil—worse than anything I ever could have imagined." He hesitated. "Or…it kills you."

chapter 9

Stephen didn't start laughing and tell me he was just messing with me. He was totally serious. This horrible situation didn't have a happy ending, a slow fading of the hunger like my aunt had suggested, and a return to normal life.

It had a death sentence.

I grabbed hold of his sleeve as my numbness over his deadly proclamation faded and panic set in like somebody lighting up a firecracker inside me. "You need to give me back my soul...and Carly's, too. Please, Stephen, before it's too late."

His expression turned stony. "You mean before I change. Or die."

I dug my fingers into his arm as he began to pull away from me. "Stephen—"

"Oh. My. God. You have *got* to be kidding me right now, right?"

My stomach sank at the sound of the familiar voice behind me. I didn't have to turn around. I knew who it was.

If I had a nemesis, Jordan Fitzpatrick was it. She was a drop-dead gorgeous redhead, and an aspiring model. We went to the same school.

She hated me. And the feeling was completely mutual. I

didn't like coming face-to-face with her in public places since she never held back on her opinion, especially when it came to me. Sometimes I could take it and throw it right back at her. But other times words could hurt me, even if they weren't sticks and stones.

Did I mention that Stephen was her ex, and he'd broken her heart?

While still reeling from the horrific news Stephen had shared with me, I turned slowly to see Jordan standing there with her best friend and trusty blond sidekick, Julie Travis. Julie was another one who wasn't thrilled by my continuing existence—and vice versa. Julie was the reason that Colin and Carly had broken up over the summer. She'd slept with him while he'd been drunk at a party.

It wasn't all Julie's fault, of course. Colin was at least fifty percent to blame. But still. If anyone hurts my friends and has zero remorse about it, then that's a nice shortcut to getting on my hate list.

Julie shot daggers at me through her eyeballs for standing here in the middle of the mall talking to Stephen Keyes. She still considered him Jordan's property. Jordan, however, didn't even glance at me. Her attention was fully fixed on Stephen.

"You," Jordan began shakily, as if grappling for the right words. "I—I didn't even know you were back from university."

He didn't speak for a moment. He appeared to be stunned, his face pale. "I am."

"You haven't replied to any of my texts."

He averted his gaze, instead choosing to look at the crystal birds above us. "I thought we dealt with this, Jordan. It's over between us."

"Oh, you made that clear in your email, don't worry."

I already knew he'd dumped her via email. That was cold.

Jordan swallowed hard. "I guess I don't feel like I should be blamed for wanting to know the reason why." Finally, I received a withering look of death. "Or maybe I do know."

Here we go.

Stephen flicked a glance at me before returning his attention to her. "It's not what you think."

"Isn't that what they always say in the movies? Pathetic. No, I think it's exactly what I think. You're interested in Samantha, the town klepto."

I winced at that. But at least she didn't call me a slut this time.

When Stephen kissed me at Crave, people saw it. But they hadn't seen a monster devouring a victim's soul. They thought they'd just witnessed a hot kiss.

News got back to Jordan through the grapevine while she was still dealing with the heartbreak of being dumped in such a cold, impersonal way. I couldn't totally blame her for being angry. I would have been hurt, too, if the guy I really liked was seen kissing somebody I disliked so much.

Still, Jordan's high school drama didn't trump my life-and-death struggle. I needed time with Stephen to convince him to give me my soul back before it was too late.

"We're just talking," I told her as calmly as I could.

Sounded so harmless: just talking.

Only it was a subject that had the potential to destroy not only mine and Stephen's, but the lives of every single person in Trinity if we didn't find a solution.

"I don't really care what you do." Jordan said in that way that made it clear that she *did* care very much what Stephen did and with whom. "Damn it."

Her eyes became glossy and she angrily wiped at them.

Tears of pain, no matter who they were from, had a way of

working their way under my skin and directly to my heart. She wasn't just being a bitch. She was genuinely hurt over this.

Something flashed across Stephen's face just before he turned away from her.

Anguish.

Stephen hated hurting Jordan like this. I'd had a hunch that he'd broken up with her at the same time he'd been turned into a gray by Natalie, and it wasn't because he'd been romantically interested in my aunt.

No. It was because he loved Jordan and he didn't want to hurt her.

Damn. I didn't want to feel bad for two people I hated. But I did, anyway.

"I can't be here right now." Stephen turned away.

Jordan grabbed his arm. "You're running away? Just like that? So typical."

He yanked his arm away from her. His breathing had quickly become more labored. She'd entered his orbit of hunger. I was very familiar with how out of control he was feeling right now.

An impossible-to-ignore need for him to kiss her; heart pounding, hunger rising, but knowing the kiss would hurt her.

Torture was definitely the right word.

Stephen spun around and their eyes met. This time he caught her in his arms and pressed her back against the railing.

"I told you to stay away from me, Jordan." But he said it in that sexy, come-hither kind of way, which would make a lot of girls just want to get that much closer.

"I wanted to." A tear actually slipped down her cheek, and she angrily swiped it away.

"Jordan, come on," Julie urged. "We should go."

But instead, Stephen took hold of Jordan's upper arms and

pulled her to him. His focus had narrowed to her lips. He was going to kiss her. And she was going to let him.

It was like watching a scary soap opera.

I couldn't let this happen. I grabbed Stephen's arm and dug my fingers in hard. "Don't even think about it."

Clarity came across his clouded expression and his brows drew together. He staggered back from the both of us, swearing under his breath.

"I mean it, Jordan. Stay the hell away from me," he growled.

She inhaled sharply, disappointment skittering across her flushed face. "I hate you!"

"Good. That helps." Finally, he turned and began walking rapidly away.

"Wait, Stephen!" I started to run after him.

Julie stepped into my path to block me. "Where do you think you're going?"

"Get out of my way." I shoved her out of the way and scanned the immediate area to locate Stephen, but I couldn't see him anywhere.

He was gone.

My one shot to talk to him, to explain why he needed to help me. And now he'd disappeared into the crowd in five seconds flat.

"Damn it!" I had more questions than I had to begin with. And absolutely no answers. How was I supposed to find him now?

"You need to stay away from Stephen," Julie warned me.

I glared at her. "And you need to mind your own business."

Jordan let out a shaky sigh and rubbed her eyes, succeeding in smearing her mascara. "I'm going to forget him. This time for good. He doesn't deserve me."

"You're right," Julie agreed. "He doesn't."

I kept frantically searching the crowd of faces, but his was nowhere to be seen.

"I hate you and Stephen," Jordan snapped at me. "I wish I'd never met either of you."

I tore my gaze from the crowd to meet her furious expression with one of my own. The pain was still raw enough in her eyes to deflate my anger just a little. "You might not believe this, but sometimes when things seem horrible, they're actually a good thing. Trust me, Stephen isn't—"

Snap!

Suddenly, I wasn't in the mall anymore; I was at the church. And I was looking at Cassandra and Kraven, both lit from the bright light entering through the beautiful stained-glass windows.

I saw them through Bishop's eyes.

"I don't want to talk about this," he growled.

"She kissed you?" Cassandra gave him a look of sheer disbelief. "Why didn't you tell me this last night?"

"It's not important." Bishop sent a quick glance at Kraven, who gave him a smug look in return, his arms crossed over his chest. "Got something to say? Or have you said enough for one day?"

"Sorry, had to be honest with Blondie here." The demon glanced at Cassandra. "I know it takes a lot of my little brother's energy to stay away from gray-girl, especially when he gets crazy."

"She's dangerous to you now," Cassandra said with concern. "If she was to drain your soul completely…a fallen angel or exiled demon can't exist without a soul in the human world. You would die."

Bishop didn't flinch at this confirmation. "I have it under control."

"I'm surprised that you got to know her well enough to learn of her supernatural gifts. As a gray, I would have thought you wouldn't have hesitated to kill her. Your reputation as one who does his job to the letter precedes you."

"Bishop didn't sense her grayness right away. All he sensed were those big, brown eyes of hers. And she might be short, but she's got

a killer set of legs." At whatever dark look Bishop shot him, Kraven shrugged. "What? It's the truth. Funny, though. Always thought you liked blondes better than brunettes. Or…wait. Maybe that was me. I forget."

"I sensed there was something between you," Cassandra said, "but I wasn't sure what it was."

Bishop didn't reply for a moment. "I'm affected by her."

"Duh," Kraven said. "The fallen angel falls hard for one of the monsters he's supposed to put a dagger into. It's textbook, really."

"It's not that. It's my soul—because of what she is, it binds us. And the kiss only made it worse. This is—it's nothing more than a simple inconvenient addiction."

Even though I was only observing this, his words felt like someone had reached into my chest to tear out my heart.

An inconvenient addiction.

Was that really all this was?

"Inconvenient, definitely, but there's nothing simple about this." Cassandra came forward to touch his shoulder gently. She gazed up into his face. "I can help you. I want to help you."

He didn't pull away from her as she rubbed his arm. "I can handle it. You don't have to be concerned."

"Us, concerned?" Kraven's lips quirked. "Personally, I'm all for you two hooking up again. I'd like to see what happens when the rest of that soul's sucked out of your mouth. Oh, and you should probably keep in mind that some other places she might want to put those pretty little lips of hers might be a problem, too."

Bishop's glare shot to the demon. "Shut your mouth."

"I should be telling you the same thing."

"Be quiet, both of you," Cassandra snapped, clearly frustrated. "Honestly, how do you get any work done while squabbling so—"

Snap!

I was back at the mall and I staggered away from Jordan

and Julie, bringing a hand to my forehead. They were both staring at me.

"What was that?" Jordan asked sharply. "Did you just have a mental meltdown or something?"

"I—I'm fine."

She pushed her fingers into her hair to yank her long bangs back from her face as if they were annoying her. "I didn't ask if you were fine. I don't care if you're fine. But you just checked out for a moment there. Blank city."

I barely heard her. I was reliving what I'd just seen through Bishop's eyes. He denied to both Kraven and Cassandra that he felt anything toward me more than an inconvenient addiction.

Between speaking with Stephen, losing him in the crowd, and then overhearing the conversation between the angels and demon, I could barely remain vertical. Even though I was in the middle of the mall surrounded by people, I'd never felt so scared and alone.

An inconvenient addiction.

He was an angel of death who'd been alive for…I didn't even know how long. I knew nothing about him. All I had were words. And those words were giving me no comfort today. None at all.

"You are a very beautiful girl." A woman with a clipboard approached us.

I forced myself to look at who was talking and to whom.

The middle-aged woman with long auburn hair and blue eyes, wearing a black designer suit, swept her gaze over Julie.

Julie pressed her hand against her chest. "Me?"

"Yes. Let me take a look at you." The woman grasped her chin, tilting her head from side to side. "Exquisite. I'm a modeling scout. I think you might have what it takes."

"Really?" she said with excitement.

"Yes. My name is Eva. And you?"

"Julie. Julie Travis."

Eva took her hand and squeezed it. "A pleasure to meet you, Ms. Travis."

She handed Julie a card before she walked off, sending a casual glance over her shoulder at me and Jordan as she went.

Julie beamed. "Can you believe that? A modeling scout thought I was exquisite."

"It's probably one of those agencies that charges a lot of money for your portfolio and don't do much else," Jordan said.

Julie gave her a sharp look. "That's not nice."

"I'm sorry, but it's true. I mean, it's just the mall. Do many people usually get discovered here?"

"You're mad that she didn't even notice you."

"I'm already signed with a real agency in Manhattan. I don't need some Trinity-based agency to represent me."

"Whatever. It's not like she gave Samantha a card."

"I don't want a card," I said.

A strange tingle went down my arms, like an unseen breeze. I frowned and glanced around to see what caused it, but there was nothing.

Stephen said that just before stasis, the cold increased. But this wasn't cold...more like a bit of electricity charging the air.

Weird.

Jordan gave me an appraising look. "She's way too short. I mean, look at her. She's practically a hobbit."

I'd had more than enough of these two for one day. "I'm leaving."

I had to find Stephen. I'd do another sweep of the mall first. Maybe he hadn't left yet.

I couldn't believe I lost him so easily. When I'd been close—so close.

"Don't let me stop you," Jordan said, then added, "freak."

It was on the tip of my tongue to say something cruel or

cutting to her back, but I stopped myself. I flicked a glance at Julie, no longer paying attention to our standoff. She gazed over toward the food court.

I tried to breathe normally. "I know you're not going to believe this, Jordan, but I'm not seeing Stephen. We're not together in any possible way. I'm not interested in him."

Her lips thinned. "Like I care who you might be interested in."

"I think you care too much."

"And I think you're an idiot."

"Nice." I rolled my eyes. "You know, sometimes pulling your head out of your own ass helps improve your clarity. You should try it sometime."

I was sympathetic to her pain, but I refused to be *completely* defenseless here.

"It sucks," Julie said.

Jordan glanced at her. "What does?"

"Everything. My life, it's just so depressing."

Jordan eyed her. "Join the club."

"Sometimes—" she sniffed and dragged her hand under her nose "—it all gets so overwhelming. Like today. I felt good when I got here. I felt good until just a moment ago. And now I feel...so sad...."

"Stupid Stephen," Jordan said. "He put everybody in a bad mood."

"You know how much I hate seeing you so hurt over that jerk."

Jordan flicked an uncomfortable glance at me, before returning her gaze to Julie. "Let's talk when we have more privacy, okay?"

Julie let out a shaky breath and turned to face us. Her eyes were filled with tears. "You shouldn't let him get to you, Jordan. You shouldn't. He doesn't deserve you."

"I know."

"No, you don't. It's just like me and…and Colin.…" Her bottom lip wobbled.

"You're not into Colin, are you?" I asked. I wanted to leave, but I couldn't while she was in the midst of this impromptu meltdown.

"I didn't think so, but now that I think about it." She inhaled shakily. "Just another example of someone I thought wanted me who only wanted to use me."

"We were going to forget about that," Jordan said pointedly.

"I can't forget! And—and now with the modeling agent and you saying how ugly I am."

Jordan gasped. "I never said you were ugly!"

"You said that a real modeling agent wouldn't want me. Wouldn't care about me. That I am so ugly that nobody wants to be my friend. I know it. It's been like this all my life. It's why my mother left us."

Jordan and I exchanged a worried glance. This was going from bad to worse.

"Relax, Julie. Seriously." She held her hands out. "Let's go get a coffee downstairs and chill out. It's been a stressful day, but there's no reason to freak out."

Julie was crying now. I just stared at her in shock. I hadn't heard any rumors that she was unstable in any way, but this was definitely unstable behavior, to say the least. And her massive mood change seemed to have come out of absolutely nowhere.

"Sometimes," Julie said in shaky bursts, "I hate life. Everything about it. It's too hard. I wish I was dead."

"Don't say that. Come on…" Jordan reached her hand out.

Julie just shook her head. "Goodbye."

Before we could do anything, say anything, or even make a move toward her, she took hold of the railing…

And threw herself over the edge.

chapter 10

Jordan's ear-piercing scream sliced through me like a knife. I raced to the railing to look over with horror. Julie had crashed onto a food court table and now lay there, her limbs at awkward, unnatural angles.

"Oh, my God," I whispered, my throat closing. I couldn't believe what I was seeing, what I'd just witnessed happen right in front of me.

Chaos swept through the first floor, through the whole mall. Screams and cries of horror filled the air, and a rush of bodies swarmed around Julie.

"Why?" The anguished word wrenched from Jordan's throat as she gripped the railing next to me. "What happened? Why would she do that?"

I couldn't speak. And nothing I said would help this make any sense.

I stayed with Jordan as we hurried downstairs, but it was too late. The fall had killed Julie. The ambulance attendants confirmed she was dead. Jordan started to sob, and she clutched onto me tightly as if she needed something—anything—to anchor her.

Making everything that much worse was the fact that down

here, so close to the swell of people who'd witnessed Julie's suicide, my hunger didn't let up for a moment. My heart pounded, and I put some distance between myself and Jordan and everyone else as soon as I could, trying to think. Trying to rationalize what happened.

I failed.

Nothing could explain this. Nothing could make it better.

The police arrived and asked Jordan some questions.

"I don't know why she did it." Jordan's words were raspy, her face tear stained. "She was fine. All day. All week. She wasn't upset or anything. But she—she just lost it."

The police officer took her statement, then they took mine, which was basically the same thing. A teenager had committed suicide in public.

I didn't like Julie, but I never would have wished for something like this to happen to her.

It wasn't right. Seventeen was way too young to die.

Jordan was in shock. She'd stopped talking and just started to tremble. I directed her away from the food court and into an alcove of the mall. She pressed her back up against the wall and called her father to come pick her up. She was in no shape to drive home.

I gave her the bottle of water I had in my leather bag. She took it from me with shaking hands and took a sip. She didn't complain that it was room temperature.

"It's my fault," she said, her voice hollow and broken. "She was so happy about the modeling agent. I felt bad about Stephen so I had to bring her down. And—and this happened."

She'd sunk down to the floor, her long legs pulled tight up against her chest. I braced my shoulder against the wall. My hunger swirled the longer I stayed in this busy mall, but I couldn't just abandon her here. Not like this.

"It's not your fault," I assured her. But really, I didn't know

116

what had triggered Julie to end everything in such a horrible, final way. "Was she depressed? Like not just today, but maybe clinically depressed and on medication?"

"No." She frowned. "I mean, I don't think so. She never said anything to me." She drew in a ragged breath. "I didn't even know she was still into Colin. I should have known. She was my best friend."

My heart clenched for her. "Is there anything I can do?"

Finally, this seemed to break through to her. Her brows drew together and she looked up at me through red, puffy eyes. Her perfectly applied makeup was only a memory now. Her gaze hardened. "It's probably your fault this happened."

I stepped back, my stomach souring. "You know I had nothing to do with that. I barely knew Julie."

"You stole Stephen from me. And now my best friend is dead." Tears streamed down her cheeks. "Anything else you want to destroy today?"

My face burned from her words as if she'd struck me, but I refused to hit back. Not this time. "I'm sorry she's gone, Jordan. I know how much you cared about her."

There was nothing I could say to make it better. It looked like I could only make it worse by staying. So I left.

If I'd seen any signs of what was going to happen—what Julie was going to do—I would have done whatever it took to stop her. But as the moment played over and over in my mind on my way home, I couldn't think of any clues to what triggered her mood change. One moment she was fine, the next she was suicidally depressed.

Like a switch had been flicked in her head.

Every time I closed my eyes I saw her falling over the side of the railing, like a song on repeat. Over and over.

Between Stephen's chilling revelations of what was to come for grays, to eavesdropping on Bishop's conversation about inconvenient addictions, to Julie's suicide, I couldn't deal with anything else right now. I especially couldn't handle being around anyone who triggered my hunger.

I went directly home and locked the door behind me, dropping down to the floor, and finally released the sobs I'd been trying so hard to hold inside.

For the rest of the day, I did my best to avoid the world. It was my new hobby. It served me well for six hours of solitude. However, the pizza delivery guy had smelled much better than the pizza had, which was so unsettling I barely managed to eat more than half the pizza.

Mom called to say she'd arrived at her fabulous resort in Honolulu, and was going to start exploring immediately. Even long distance she sounded every bit as thrilled about her spontaneous trip as she had here. Angelic influence had some serious staying power. I missed her, but I told her to have a good time and not to worry about me.

After the call, I distractedly flipped through *Catcher in the Rye,* our current read in English. I'd read it before, so all I really had to do was refresh my memory.

It was late when Cassandra got back. The angel went directly to the refrigerator to get herself something to eat—more Chinese food leftovers.

From the kitchen doorway, I warily watched her prepare a plate. She looked over her shoulder at me, and her eyes narrowed.

"You didn't tell me you kissed Bishop," she said. There was accusation in her tone.

I cringed. "Good evening to you, too."

She put her plate down and spun to face me, her eyes flashing with blue light. "Do you know how dangerous that was?"

wicked kiss

Her words were harsh and unexpected. My eyes filled with tears.

"I'm sorry," she said, her brows drawing together. She drew closer to me. "I'm sure you know it's dangerous. I don't have to tell you."

"I didn't know he had a soul at the time. Neither did he." Not much of an excuse, but it was true.

Her frown remained as she studied me. "You're upset."

I inhaled shakily and ran my hand under my nose. "You could say that."

"Why?"

"Oh, let me think." I tried not to sound sarcastic, but failed. "I'm a soulless monster you and your buddies have the authority to knife in the heart at any given moment." I chose not to share what I'd learned from Stephen—or even that I'd seen him. Not yet. And not with her. "Other than that, I—I witnessed somebody kill herself today."

Her face blanched. "Kill herself?"

I nodded. "It was terrible. Right in front of me. She jumped to her death."

Her mouth worked, but nothing came out for a moment. "Just like that. No warning?"

"No."

I tried to swallow past the lump in my throat.

"Where were you?"

"The Trinity Mall. I'm sure it'll be in the paper tomorrow. Probably already on the internet tonight." I shivered.

She opened her mouth as if to say something, but then closed it. Her grave expression didn't change. "I'm sorry you had to witness something like that. You've had to deal with so much."

All I could offer was a meager shrug. "I just wish I could have stopped her."

"Some things can't be stopped."

Cassandra didn't touch her food, instead throwing it in the garbage as if she'd lost her appetite. I wasn't sure what to make of her change in mood.

"I'm going to bed," I said. It was late. I was tired. And whether I liked it or not, I had school tomorrow.

"You need to stay away from him," she said as I turned to leave the kitchen.

I froze and looked over my shoulder at her. "Who?"

She just looked at me patiently. "Bishop's mind isn't working right because of his fall—because of the burden of his soul. He tries very hard to ignore this and do his job anyway, but if he was fully lucid, he'd see the risk of being anywhere near you."

I grappled for something to say. "I don't want to hurt him. It's the last thing I want."

"If you're not careful, that's exactly what you'll do."

There wasn't anything else to say, or nothing that came immediately to mind. I escaped to my bedroom with thoughts racing, and a sick feeling in the pit of my stomach.

After failing to get any real answers out of Stephen, I was at a temporary loss with my plan of action. I'd have to look for him. Maybe he'd contact me again.

Maybe, maybe, maybe.

Too many maybes.

Tomorrow was Monday. I had school bright and early. I hadn't given up hope so much that I planned to start cutting classes. Going to school represented my continuing hold on my future—and that I had a future to hold on to. Despite any drama I faced outside of McCarthy High, I'd keep up my grades so I could go to my first choice college next year. One day, my life would be far outside of the Trinity city limits.

It *would* happen.

I sat at my vanity table and brushed all the tangles out of

my long, wild mane of hair. I planned to get it cut to a more manageable length so I wouldn't always have to pull it back into a ponytail, but I hadn't gotten around to it yet.

I stared at my reflection for a long time, trying to see some sign of the supernatural in my eyes. I knew it had to be there, since I had enough of it swirling around inside of me, but they looked the same as always. Brown. And currently filled with anxiety.

The room was stifling. I'd cranked the heat when I got home and despite my constant chills, I desperately needed some fresh air. I went to the window and pushed it open, inhaling deeply. It made me shiver, but the cold October air helped clear some of the fog from my head.

Then I turned to my bed and grabbed the sheets—but I froze in midpull.

After staying at a low level ever since getting back home from the mall, my hunger suddenly surged to the forefront. My breath caught and held as I sensed his presence.

"You shouldn't leave your window open," Bishop said. "Anyone might be able to get in."

I spun to face him, my eyes wide with shock at what I was seeing. But there he stood, framed by moonlight near the open window.

A gorgeous, blue-eyed, six-foot tall angel of death was standing in my bedroom.

I grappled for something to say, anything at all. My pulse raced. "How did you…" I gestured at the window behind him, my gauzy curtains fluttering with the cool breeze. "This is the second floor and there's no ladder or tree out there."

My flustered reaction made him smile, an expression that shot right to my heart. "I have a few hidden talents."

His gaze lowered to my clothes—or, rather, lack of them. My cheeks started to burn. I certainly wasn't naked, but a snug tank top and a loose pair of sleeping shorts weren't exactly modest.

I fought the urge to cross my arms over my chest. It wasn't like I had that much to cover. "Why are you here?"

It sounded much ruder than I meant it. Seeing him gave me a wild inner thrill that I tried to cover, especially after my conversation—or *warning*—with Cassandra earlier. Seeing Bishop alone like this was dangerous. It triggered my hunger like nothing else in the world.

He shouldn't be here and he knew it, too.

But here he was anyway.

Bishop wrenched his gaze back up to my face. It took him a moment to say something, and the weighted silence stretched between us. "I wanted to check on you. Make sure you're all right."

I sent a quick glance over my shoulder at my closed bedroom door. "Be quiet or Cassandra will hear us."

He didn't come any closer to me. He stayed by the window, which helped me keep most of my head together. "She knows what happened…between us. Did she tell you?"

I nodded. "But I already knew."

His gaze met mine directly as he studied me, frowning. Then clarity crossed his expression. "You know, I'm really not thrilled with this handy eavesdropping skill of yours."

I bit my bottom lip. I was so cold that goose bumps had broken out over my bare skin. I crossed them, shivering. "I can't control it. It just happens."

He turned to the window and closed it. "What did you hear?"

A thousand different emotions bubbled inside me and I wanted to force them down and keep my game face on. Pretend that nothing affected me. Too bad *everything* affected me lately. My analytical and detached view of the world around me had dropped away, leaving me completely raw and vulnerable.

Bishop affected me. Sometimes I forgot how much, when he wasn't this close to me, but he did. His scent, his presence, his warmth—everything called to me across the six tiny feet separating us right now. I wanted to close that distance, throw my arms around him and kiss him passionately. It was a need like eating, sleeping—a primal drive I couldn't ignore.

I gripped the baseboard of my bed, digging my short fingernails into the smooth wood, and tried to stay calm. "You said that this…what you feel for me…it's an inconvenient addiction." I looked at him directly. "And yet here you are at midnight in my bedroom. Not smart."

His expression tightened. "I wish you hadn't heard that."

"Doesn't matter," I lied. "Today—it's put a lot of things into perspective for me." I took a deep breath. "I talked to Stephen."

Bishop was next to me in a heartbeat, taking hold of my arms. Electricity sparked between us, making me gasp. Making *him* gasp.

He swore, and let go of me, taking a shaky step back. "You talked to Stephen. When? Where?"

"He called me. I met him at the mall."

"Why didn't you find me?"

"Because I knew if he saw you he'd bolt." I tried to maintain my control, but it was difficult. "I wanted to convince him to give me back my soul."

His expression was tense. "And did you?"

"I think it was possible, but…we were interrupted. He told me stuff, Bishop." I'd kept this from Cassandra, but Bishop needed to know. "He says that super-gray yesterday—that's what's happening to everyone. That grays go through a stasis— they turn zombie, but it isn't permanent like we thought. It's just a stage. When they come out of it they're stronger, smarter and totally sociopathic. If they don't come out of it...they die." Panic clawed at my chest as I related this horrible information. "It's one or the other. Stephen wanted to warn me."

I studied his reaction to this. It wasn't filled with surprise, more like grim acceptance. "You already knew this, didn't you?" I asked.

"I didn't know for sure."

"Well, now you do." Another tremble went through me, and not just from being cold this time. "It's going to happen to me."

He shook his head. "No, it's not."

I let out a small snort. "You sound so certain I almost believe you."

He raised his fierce gaze to mine. His eyes glowed with a soft blue light in the darkness of my room. "You're different, Samantha. You're not like the others."

"I don't know if who my birth mother and father is will have much to do with this particular outcome."

He clenched his teeth, anger brightening the celestial energy in his eyes that held an edge of madness. "It has *everything* to do with it. And you need to keep fighting, keep resisting. You're not like the other grays."

"Is that why you came here? To test me? To see how controlled I am?" My voice trembled. "Because I hate to break it to you, but I'm not. Not when you're this close to me."

"I had to come here."

"You *had* to?"

"Yes."

I looked at him directly, raising my chin. "Then remember, when I attack you, you've only got yourself to blame."

chapter 11

My words of warning didn't seem to panic him. "Are you planning on attacking me, Samantha?"

My cheeks burned to admit it, but it was the truth. I shrugged. "Think it, say it. That's how I've always been. Maybe I should keep more of my thoughts to myself."

Despite the intense gravity of our discussion, there was now a small smile playing at Bishop's lips, which only worked to draw my attention there. "You're very honest. Very open. I like that."

"One more thing we don't have in common. I'm an open book. You're…closed with a lock and key."

The smile disappeared completely. "What else did Stephen tell you?"

I'd hit a sore point. We could discuss grays and death and souls all night long, but any mention of his secrets and he shut down. Typical. "Not much. Like I said, we were interrupted." My voice caught. "A girl killed herself at the mall. Right in front of me."

His dark brows drew together. "What? Who?"

I shook my head. "It's not related to Stephen or anything.

She was fine, then she got really depressed, like zero to sixty. Then she…" I drew in a ragged breath. "It was horrible."

His expression was grave. "I'm sorry you had to see that."

"Life and death, Bishop. It can change in a heartbeat. Any second. Any moment. It can all be taken away. I never realized that before, but it's true."

He drew closer again. "Not to you. You're going to have a very long and very happy life. I swear you will."

The fierce way he said it nearly made me smile again. "Money-back guarantee?"

"Absolutely." He searched my face. "There's something else troubling you tonight. What is it?"

I *was* an open book. I might as well not close the cover just yet. I looked up at him, taking in his height, feeling his very overwhelming presence filling this room. He studied me as if both fascinated and wary of what I might say next.

"You didn't tell me you're an angel of death," I whispered, my voice suddenly hoarse.

His gaze darkened. "Cassandra told you."

I nodded. "I should have guessed. I mean, the way you handle that dagger…"

"She shouldn't have scared you."

"Scared? Me? To find out you're one of Heaven's assassins?" I turned to face my vanity. I could see him behind me in the shadows, watching my reaction. "I did have a dream you killed me last night."

"Stupid dream."

I shrugged a shoulder, studying my reflection. Loose, my hair was long enough to reach my waist, and hung over my shoulders. "Maybe it was a vision of the future. I have those, you know. Sometimes."

"It was just a nightmare. Nothing more."

"So it's true. You're not denying it. You are an angel of death."

There was a short pause. "I am."

My heart skipped a beat at the confirmation. "And if they pull you back to Heaven and reverse your fallen status, that's what you'll continue to be. An angel given the task to assassinate threats against the human world, against Heaven itself—threats like my aunt."

He nodded. "That's right."

"Or…like a gray you have an inconvenient addiction to."

This was met by silence for so long that I wasn't sure if he'd answer me. But then, "You say whatever's on your mind, but sometimes you need to listen with more than just your ears. Words aren't always that reliable."

He'd succeeded again in confusing me. "What does that mean?"

Bishop held my gaze for a moment in the surface of the mirror without speaking. "I came here tonight to give you something. A gift."

I blinked at the sudden change in subject, my heart pounding. I turned to face him directly. "What is it?"

He reached under his shirt and pulled out an object wrapped in leather. He unwrapped it slowly to reveal the contents.

I tentatively drew a little closer to see it. It was a gold dagger, smaller than the one he had, which was the better part of a foot including the hilt. This was more the size of a steak knife, but with a wavy blade tapering to a sharp tip. A ruby was set into the ornately carved hilt.

"It's absolutely beautiful," I breathed.

He nodded. "It's something I got at the Trinity museum. They have no idea what it's really for or how rare it is. The metal—it's gold infused with steel, but it has an old spell on it."

My gaze shot to his. "Like a magic spell?"

"Yeah." His lips curved at my amazement. "There is magic in this world, Samantha. You must realize that by now."

"I've been trying to enjoy what little denial I still have left."

He held the small dagger in his hand, and I couldn't resist reaching toward it to run my index finger along the hilt, the carving rough against my touch. When I touched his warm skin, that familiar shiver of energy sparked between us, making my breath catch.

"This dagger can do damage to a supernatural. It won't kill an angel or a demon, but it will hurt them more than a regular knife would."

I pulled my hand back, alarmed. I sat down on the edge of my bed. "Why would I need something like that?"

"For protection."

I searched for the right words. "But we already know I can zap them if anyone threatens me."

"You need to be touching them to do that and they can't be actively blocking you. There are too many factors in play. A good sharp dagger, however, doesn't need anything but the right opportunity to use it. I'm not saying you'll need it, but I'd rather know you have it just in case."

I tried to process all of this. "You said it's from the museum. You mean, you—you stole it?"

He looked down at it before looking at me again. "Borrowed. Without permission."

That earned a full smile from me, albeit a shaky one. "Bad angel."

He laughed softly. "Sometimes rules need to be bent. So will you accept it?"

I studied the small dagger again. It was so incredible. And I swear I could feel a hum of otherworldly energy coming off it—much like I did with Bishop's Hallowed Blade. "I'll accept it."

"Good. Then stand up." When I did as he asked, he knelt down in front of me. "The sheath can be strapped to your thigh. It's the best way for you to conceal it."

"Awesome," I managed. "I'm going to have a concealed weapon at the ready. I could work for the mob."

I inhaled sharply as he attached the sheath to my bare right thigh, and pulled the straps tight. His fingers slid over my skin, sending an uncontrollable shiver racing through me.

He glanced up at me, his gaze darkening. He had to be able to hear how loud and fast my heart was beating.

I cleared my throat. "Thanks, I think?"

"You're welcome." He didn't pull away from me immediately, keeping his hands pressed against my skin, circling the leather sheath. "Try not to lose it, though. It's kind of priceless."

"Noted." I struggled to breathe normally.

As he rose slowly to his feet, he trailed his hands along my sides, stopping at my waist, an inch of bare skin between my shorts and top. The shiver of energy raced between us.

This was different than him being close to me in public. This—all alone with no one watching us. It felt even more dangerous.

At this point, I couldn't have pushed him away even if I'd wanted to. And I definitely didn't want to. His spicy scent sank into me. The warmth of his touch, normally enough to chase the cold away, burned right into my skin.

His expression tensed as he looked down to where his hands grasped my waist. "Touching you…even knowing you're a nexus…I still don't understand why it helps bring such clarity to my mind. Why it feels…"

"Feels?" I could only manage a whisper.

His gaze met mine. "So good."

I let out a hoarse laugh, throaty and nervous. "Maybe for you."

He let go of me abruptly and stepped back. The cold returned like a bucket of ice water had just been poured on me.

I shook my head. "I didn't mean it as a bad thing."

"Of course you did. It *is* a bad thing." He raked his hand through his messy hair. "I forget too easily. I'm making this worse for you. Cassandra's right—so are the others. It's better if I stay away. I don't know why I can't."

"Inconvenient addiction," I reminded him shakily. My hunger raged like a caged beast inside me, even with him now more than an arm's reach away from me. I fought hard to keep it locked up.

"Yeah." He watched me from the shadows of my room. "Very inconvenient."

I sat down heavily on the side of my bed and touched the leather sheath of the dagger. It was light in weight, barely noticeable. I focused on the carved hilt, running my fingers over the ruby, feeling its tingling power across my skin—its *magic*. It was a pure magic. It had no darkness in it. That much was reassuring.

Bishop stayed silent. My only indication that he hadn't left was my ever-present hunger pains, currently holding steady at a level eight. And a half.

"How long have you been an angel of death?" I asked quietly.

"Long enough."

Frustration rippled through me and I looked directly at him. I couldn't hold it in any longer, all the questions that rose up in my throat. "How long since you died? Since Kraven died? Did you die at the same time? Why is he a demon and you're an angel? You said you killed him and sent him to Hell. Did you know that would happen? Is that what made you an angel? Was it some sort of Heavenly test?"

He turned to the window, placing his hands flat on the pane as he looked outside to the street. His shoulders were tense. "I can't talk about these things."

"In general? Or just with me? I don't understand why you refuse to tell me *anything* about yourself that might help me understand you better. No wonder I have nightmares about you." Then I was the one who swore, before covering my face with my hands.

Bishop was beside me in a moment, kneeling down on the floor next to my bed and taking my hands in his to pull them away from my face. His expression held deep torment.

"I don't keep truths from you to hurt you."

"Then why?"

His brows drew together. "I just can't talk about it. You need to trust me."

"I want to."

"I know you rely on your head a lot of the time. You're smart. You look at things from that standpoint. That studying and getting good grades is the only way there is to understand things. But some things can't be spoken aloud. Can't be studied. The truth won't tell you about me." He swallowed hard. "Trust your heart."

"My heart is a bit of a liar."

"No, it isn't." His grip tightened on my hands enough that I finally looked at him. Our eyes met and held. "It knows the truth even if you don't realize it yet."

He was so close, too close. Again, I didn't pull away. I couldn't.

"You could have given me that dagger anytime," I whispered. "Why now?"

His lips curved to the side. "Maybe I wanted an excuse to visit you alone in your bedroom."

That coaxed a very small laugh from me, and despite my better judgment, I entwined my fingers with him. I didn't stop looking in his beautiful blue eyes—eyes I dreamed about every night, even apart from disturbing nightmares. Most of my dreams about Bishop were very good ones.

I slid off the side of my bed so we kneeled face-to-face with each other. I released his hands so I could slide my hands up the front of his chest, his skin warm through the thin barrier of his T-shirt. My thoughts were falling away with each second that passed.

Dangerous. Too dangerous. Cassandra was right.

I needed to kiss him.

This is why he'd come here. All joking aside, all gifts, and information and horrible days pushed away.

He'd come here tonight so I would kiss him. So I could satisfy his inconvenient addiction to me—even if that meant I might take the rest of his soul.

Bishop's hands tightened at my waist and he pulled me closer to him, close enough that I could feel the rapid pulse of his heart against mine. His eyes glowed an intense blue. I was lost in those eyes as I slid my fingers over his jaw, cheeks, temples and up into his dark hair, so soft to the touch.

My lips were only a whisper away from his...

Snap!

The night's cold, so cold I can see my breath. My hand shakes as I clutch the torch.

"I can help," I insist, feeling useless just standing here.

"No, you stay up there," James says. "You can't see a damn thing, anyway."

"Go to hell." I glare at him, but have to admit the outline of my brother's familiar form is blurry—only his golden hair is recognizable

to me, lit up like a halo from the torchlight. Dark and light—that's what Kara calls us. Total opposites.

I'd never admit that what the doc told me yesterday has put a deep, shaking fear into me—so much that I couldn't sleep a wink last night. If I go blind I'll be useless to anyone, especially myself.

It doesn't take James long before he finds the body. It's a fresh grave. At this time of the year, it's best to get to them quickly or the ground freezes up, making it impossible to snatch anything until the spring thaw.

I throw the torch to the side and help him pull the coffin from the ground, ignoring his protests. It's hard work and both of us are sweating buckets by the time we're finished. I grab the crowbar and get to work on the lid. The woman was rich and insisted on being buried wearing her jewelry. How stupid. Can't take it with you—that's what Kara says. But we'd be more than happy to take it from you.

"Damn. Look at that rock," I say, squinting at the egg-size jewel on her necklace.

"I know. She knew how to live."

"And now she knows how to die. Paper says she choked to death on some fancy food at a party." I peel the jewels from her wrists, fingers and neck, and toss them in my canvas bag. "What about the body?"

James twists the small gold cross at his throat, his expression turning thoughtful. "We're taking it, too."

I hate this part the most. Stealing jewelry is fine. Stealing bodies… I'd never get used to it. "Let's leave her this time."

"Leave her?" James frowns. "You know Kara will be furious if we don't do exactly what she says."

"Do we always have to do what Kara says?"

Frown forgotten, a typical grin creeps across my brother's face. "You always do, kid. Anything she asks and then you beg for more. Why should this be any different?"

"Ass." His comment earns him another glare, even if it's true. I

*hated when he called me kid. I'm fifteen now, just turned. At six-
teen, my brother thinks he knows everything.*

*Stealing bodies to sell to the medical school is the least that Kara
asks of us in her grand schemes. Her goals have grown much darker
now that she's joined that new club of hers. She claims it's going to
give her all the power she ever wanted—by tapping into the occult.*

*I don't believe any of that. I'm too busy to waste my time chasing
fairy tales. I'd leave that kind of nonsense to her.*

*She isn't with us tonight. She's with her new friend as they at-
tempt to summon a spirit from the beyond.*

What a waste of time.

*Fingers of dread crawl over my flesh as I look down at the dead
woman's face. I hate graveyards. And tonight feels worse than normal.*

"Something wrong?" James asks.

"I don't trust her."

*"Who, Kara? That makes two of us." James's grin holds. "Don't
worry, kid. We're in this together, you and me. Till the end."*

I nod, reassured. "Till the end."

*"She gets the body, we get the jewels. We'll scrape together enough
to get your eyes fixed or get the best goddamned pair of specs in the
whole—"*

Snap!

Bishop got to his feet and staggered back from me across
my bedroom until he hit the wall.

"What—?" he began, his brows drawn tightly together.
"What did you just do?"

I didn't get up from the floor. Instead, I stared at him, my
eyes wide. "I don't know."

And I didn't. When I normally had my mind melds with
Bishop, I saw through his eyes—but I was still *me*. This time,
it was different. I *wasn't* me. *I* wasn't there. It was all Bishop—
his thoughts, his emotions, his everything.

"What did you see?" he asked quietly.

I had no idea what it would have felt like for him. He didn't usually realize when I had my "normal" peeks into his daily life. But this time he did.

"You and Kraven…" My breath came quicker. "You were grave robbers. A woman, her body—you were going to sell it to a medical school. She had some jewelry, too, you were going to sell. You were fifteen, and your eyes…I think you were going blind."

His face paled. "You saw my memories."

I stared at him, then nodded. Silence stretched between us. All I could hear was the sound of my heart hammering in my chest as I slumped back on my heels. The throw rug was my only protection from the cold wood floor.

"That is a very dangerous talent you have, Samantha." He said it softly, but I'd never heard him say anything with more of a dangerous edge to it. It made goose bumps break out over my arms. "Don't do that again."

"I wasn't trying to do it. It just happened." I swallowed hard and looked down at my hands until I summoned my courage again. "Who's Kara?"

When I looked up, my window was open again.

Bishop was gone.

The cold air blew in, chilling me to my bones, even as my hunger began to fade.

chapter 12

I think I got about an hour of sleep that night. If that.

My brain worked overtime, trying to process what I'd seen. What I'd learned. Focusing on Bishop's memory was good for one thing, though—it took my mind off Stephen. Off Julie. Off my own problems.

Since Bishop's eyes were bad back then, I hadn't gotten a very good glimpse at anything, but I could tell this much… based on the clothes the dead woman wore, the jewelry, how Kraven was dressed…

It was a long time ago. But *how* long?

Seeing this memory brought forth another thousand questions that now needed answering. But nobody was willing to answer them.

All I knew was that he and Kraven had been grave robbers. Bishop had been fifteen, and Kraven, sixteen—so approximately three years before they died. They worked for somebody named Kara, who they didn't trust—a woman who was getting into the occult. That didn't bode well for what I knew about their futures.

It had been disturbing, but it hadn't made me loathe Bishop

or fear him. I didn't know why he wanted to keep his past from me so badly that he wouldn't even tell me his real name.

After I forced myself out of bed, had a shower and got dressed, I saw Cassandra downstairs. I half expected her to know about Bishop's midnight visit, as if she might have some kind of angelic intuition about this sort of thing, or felt the spark of energy between us that still, hours later, made my skin tingle.

The angel gave me a weary look. "I'm still tired."

"Join the insomnia club," I said, nodding at the cupboard. "Coffee's up there."

"Will that help me?"

"Probably not. But it'll feel like it does for a little while. My mother swears by the stuff to get her through a long day. I think she's one of Starbucks's best customers."

Cassandra got the canister of coffee down and looked at it, confused. Finally, I took it from her and helped make a pot of coffee, then fixed it for her like my mother would—heavy on the cream and sugar.

She sipped from the mug gingerly, then gave me a smile. "I like it."

"Hooray." I sat down at the kitchen table after grabbing some toast and peanut butter—the pieces piled high on my plate to help stave off my constant hunger. I had a cup of coffee, too, even though it wasn't my drink of choice. Then I gave the angel a guarded look. "So off to do your mission today?"

"Of course."

"The mission with the others or your supersecret one?"

She blanched. "I don't know what you're talking about."

I shrugged. I wasn't prepared to tell her I read her mind the other night. At least, a small piece of it. It would raise too many questions I didn't want to answer right now. "If you say so."

Cassandra's real agenda for being sent here wasn't my concern—at least, I didn't think it was. Today, I had to get my bearings again. I had to find Stephen. I'd been so close at the mall yesterday—I had to find him before…

I took a gulp of the hot coffee and swallowed it down.

If he went through stasis, if he turned into a total sociopath instead of only a part-time jerk…

Then I was in serious trouble. Without my soul I was next on the list to either turn evil or die.

My attention was again drawn to the blond angel standing nervously by my kitchen sink. She gripped the counter behind her. Her skin was pale. This wasn't the warrior I'd seen kick Roth's ass on Saturday night. Something was wrong with her.

Concern welled inside me. "You okay?"

She blinked, as if my voice summoned her out of her deep thoughts. "Oh, yes. I'm fine. Of course I am."

"You seem a little distracted this morning."

"Sleep is important. I failed to get enough."

"That's all it is?"

She brought her coffee mug to the table and sat down across from me. "It's different here. I—I feel different from when I'm home. The sleeping is one thing. The need to eat is another."

"Okay." She was starting to worry me. "What's wrong, Cassandra?"

Her blue eyes raised to mine. "Emotions. They're… troubling."

"In general, or *your* emotions?"

"Mine." She swallowed hard. "It's like a sensory rush—a wave crashing over me. Too much all at once. I can barely process it."

"Is that because you're one of the hosts?"

She nodded. "It would be different for one who was once human. They'd already have experienced all of this. But for me…" Her cheeks reddened. "I need to be focused while I'm here. It's so important that I don't get distracted. But…it's proving to be a challenge. Especially when I'm around him."

Him.

My grip tightened on my coffee mug. The hot liquid burned my fingertips through the ceramic, but I didn't let go. "I'm not following."

I wasn't sure I wanted to follow if she was talking about Bishop. Jealousy poked its pointed head up and glanced around with a sour look on its face.

She forced a smile. "Forget it. It's nothing."

Was she trying to say she was falling for Bishop? That being around him made her feel things—confusing things?

My chair made an unhappy squeaking sound as I pushed back from the table. "I need to go to school."

Cassandra looked alarmed at the suggestion. "Do you think that's wise? A school would be filled with human souls. It could be dangerous for you."

"Yeah, well, if I don't go I'll start failing my classes. You have goals, I have goals. Sometimes those goals are different."

I didn't know what was up with Cassandra's melancholy angel act, but I knew it had something to do with Bishop.

The thought tied my stomach up into unpleasant origami shapes that looked a lot like two angels in love.

McCarthy High was only a few blocks from my house, its expansive grounds covered in big trees and grassy lawns, although the leaves had fallen from the trees by this time of the year and the lawns weren't quite as green as they were when school started early last month. Winding paths led to the football field and the parking lot. This was my fourth year here. I was a senior. A veteran. I knew this place like the back of my hand. And I could tell when something was different, even if it took me a second to realize what it was. When I saw it, my stomach sank.

The flag out front was at half-mast.

The news about Julie's suicide was public knowledge.

Holding tightly on to my control, I weaved through the crowded halls toward my locker. I couldn't help but overhear the talk about Julie. Mostly people were shocked, overwhelmed, upset. Some were openly crying and consoling each other, those who knew her well enough to call her a friend. However, I overheard two girls being snarky, making snide comments like "some bitches deserve to die."

I sent a withering look in their direction, which they barely noticed.

Then I banged into a guy from my afternoon history class, Noah—the one planning the big Halloween party. He gave me a slow smile. I forced a shaky one, too, even though his soul made it difficult to think. Orbit of hunger. Bad.

"Hey, Sam," he said. "Looking good this morning."

I eyed him warily. "If you say so. I guess lack of sleep becomes me."

He laughed drily before sobering. "Sucks about Julie, but I know she would have wanted me to go ahead with my plans. You coming to my party on Wednesday night?"

"Going to try my best."

"Wear something sexy," he suggested, before he disappeared down the hall.

Hmm. Let me think about that. Was I going to Noah's big Halloween party? *No.*

Would I be wearing something sexy even if I did? *Definitely not.*

The problem—one of the many problems—with being a gray is that I gave off this...*vibe.* Maybe it was the same vibe that messed with my cell phone. It made me more appealing than usual. Even at five-foot two, with brown hair, brown eyes and what I considered average looks, I now got hit on daily.

I'd never been so popular with boys as I'd been since I lost my soul. It was a moth and flame situation. Get too close to me and you're in danger of getting torched.

Every one of these boys, like Noah, would be happy to volunteer as my victim—would be thrilled to let me kiss them, all so I could take their soul to satisfy my hunger.

Just the thought of it made my stomach clench—not with disgust, but with the desire to feed. The toast this morning hadn't even made a dent in this ongoing problem.

It's getting worse. I didn't want to admit it, even to myself, but it was true. Stephen said that the cold and the hunger increased when we were close to stasis.

It was getting close. All I could do was ignore it with all my willpower and do everything I could to figure things out before it was too late.

Even though this reminder of my dark side made me want to flee the school immediately, I forced myself to go to my first class—English. Colin sat directly behind me. He was already there. There were dark circles under his eyes. Seemed to be a common fashion statement this week.

I didn't meet his eyes, but I noticed his shoulders tense as I drew closer. He didn't say anything.

At least he was here. It was a worry I'd had ever since he'd kissed me on Saturday night. I was certain I hadn't taken much, not enough to really hurt him. But I hadn't been totally sure.

I froze as he leaned forward, his edible scent growing impossible for me to ignore.

"I'm sorry about Saturday night," he whispered. His breath was hot on the back of my neck. "I was drunk. I shouldn't have kissed you."

I shook my head. "Forget it."

"I heard you were with Julie when she..." His voice broke off. "When she fell."

I glanced over my shoulder at him, and nodded. His expression held deep pain.

"People are saying she did it because of me," he whispered.

I shook my head. "That's not true. Don't blame yourself."

"Why would she do something like that?"

"I wish I knew."

That was when our English teacher, Mr. Saunders, started class. He pushed the thick glasses he always wore, which magnified his eyes to twice their size, back up on his nose.

"Like I said on Friday—" Mr. Saunders's back was to us as he wrote on the whiteboard. "We have a quiz today on *Catcher in the Rye*. I hope you all finished reading it over the weekend."

There was a quiz today? I didn't remember him saying anything like that on Friday. Didn't matter, though. I'd read the book before. English was one of my best classes. No worries.

Catcher in the Rye was one of those books that seemed really simple on the surface—almost too easy to read. But it had layers and layers of depth to uncover if you were willing to do the work.

I tried to focus on the test, but it was difficult. My mind kept wandering all over the place. Still, I finished with twenty minutes left to go before class ended.

Someone knocked on the door and Mr. Saunders answered it. After a moment, he looked in my direction.

"Ms. Day?" He peered at me through his thick glasses. "You've been summoned to the guidance counselor's office. You can finish tomorrow."

"I'm finished already." I got up uneasily and dropped my test at his desk, casting another glance toward Colin, who watched me from the back of the class, expressionless, before I left the room.

I'd spent a lot of time in Ms. Forester's office during my shoplifting fiasco. She'd tried to make me feel comfortable about pouring out my soul about my parents' divorce. About my *feelings*. And I did, to an extent, even though it made me uncomfortable to sit in an office and discuss emotions with someone I barely knew, who had a box of tissues at the ready for the tears of her students.

"You wanted to see me?" I asked Ms. Forester when I saw her. The door to her office, which was opposite the principal's office, was ajar.

She beckoned to me. "Come in, Samantha."

Ms. Forester was young, pretty, still in her twenties, with long, dark hair swept back off her face. She wore tight blouses and slim pencil skirts a couple inches over her knees, which *I* didn't appreciate, but plenty of boys did.

I tentatively entered the small office and immediately saw a familiar face in one of the two chairs opposite the counselor's desk.

Jordan was here, too. And the look she sent me was sharp enough to kill.

chapter 13

Jordan tore that sour look away from me and twisted a long piece of red hair around her index finger. "Ms. Forester, I told you this isn't necessary."

"I think it is," the counselor said calmly.

At least I knew what this was about. Jordan and me—we were bound forever by the horrible, tragic moment of Julie's death. Jordan had composed herself well, now wearing a mask of indifference. However, it didn't reach quite as far as her eyes, which still held that sharp edge of pain I'd seen there yesterday.

I wanted to dislike her as much as I always had, and, really, she hadn't given me any reason to change my opinion about her. But my heart still ached for her loss. I knew far too well what it was like to lose a best friend—to lose Carly. At least I still had a sliver of hope that she might be found again. But Julie was gone.

I forced myself to sit down in the chair next to Jordan. "This is about what happened yesterday."

"Yes." Ms. Forester's expression was grave. "I thought it would be a good idea to talk to you both together. Immediate grief counseling is essential when a close friend passes so suddenly. I didn't want to waste any time before I let you both know I'm available to you whenever you need me."

"Samantha wasn't Julie's friend," Jordan said tightly. "I was."

Ms. Forester's gaze moved to her. "But she was there with you when it happened. You said so yourself."

Jordan inhaled shakily. "That's right."

I waited for her to blame me in some way for what happened, like she had yesterday. But she didn't say anything like that.

Damn. I hated this so much. I hated that something so real, so brutal had happened. Before, with all the supernatural struggle I'd experienced, I expected bad things around any given corner—but this…it was real. And I couldn't make sense of it. I couldn't rationalize someone doing that to themselves. Losing hope in mere minutes.

"Jordan's right, I wasn't Julie's friend," I said softly. "But what happened…I don't understand it. Why would she do something like that?"

"I don't know," Jordan whispered. "I swear she wasn't depressed before. She never even mentioned Colin. I shouldn't have said the thing about the modeling agency. She was pretty enough to be a model. But I didn't know she even wanted that."

"It wasn't your fault," I said.

That earned me a sharp, guarded look, but instead of saying anything she just frowned at me.

"You two can help each other," Ms. Forester said, nodding. "Friends need to come together in times of grief."

"We're not friends," I said.

"Definitely not," Jordan agreed.

Ms. Forester flipped through the folders in front of her, gazing down at the small lines of handwriting. "Samantha, you're friends with Carly Kessler, right? She recently left town.

Not in the same tragic way as Julie did, but it's still an unexpected loss."

The mention of Carly was like a sucker punch to my gut. "It was."

"Don't ignore your feelings. Be real and work through them. It's the only way to deal with these emotions." She shook her head. "I wish I could do something to help these kids before it comes to this. It's the fourth time since Friday a student has taken their own life."

My gaze shot to her. "Fourth time? The fourth suicide?"

She nodded grimly. "Marville High had three deaths on Friday. There have been several others in Trinity in the last week, too."

I remembered the newspaper article. "Three friends. They all died together. But why?"

"I don't know. All I do know is none had any documented history of depression or anxiety. Teen suicide is too prevalent already, but this recent rash makes me wonder if something's happening to push them to take this horrible step. Perhaps it's an online bully or some other trouble we're not hearing about. I hope not. I hope no one else is headed for the same fate."

"Me, too," I whispered.

When Jordan and I were finally dismissed, with Ms. Forester's cell phone number in hand in case we felt we had no one else to talk to, I worked through it in my mind. Four suicides in less than a week—and many more before that in the city. The four I knew about were students, but none were known to be depressed.

"It doesn't make sense," Jordan said in the hallway, voicing my thoughts. "Julie was fine. I spent hours with her yesterday and she was *fine*."

I remembered the moment when Carly was swept away from me, taken by the Hollow. I'd completely lost my mind with grief and panic, scrambling to get her back—and if it hadn't been for Bishop I would've been lost, as well. At that moment I would have done anything to save her.

"I'm so sorry," I said shakily.

She looked at me strangely. "You really mean that, don't you?"

"Of course I mean it."

"Something bad is happening in this city." She got a far-away look in her green eyes. Then she pulled something out of her small Burberry bag and showed it to me. It was a business card for DMM: Divine Model Management. "Remember the modeling scout who stopped and talked to us? She touched Julie just before she went all crazy."

"And?"

"And…" She frowned hard. "I don't know. I just get this gut feeling that she had something to do with this. Julie was fine, she was happy, and we were planning a trip together over winter break. You don't make plans for the future if you're thinking about killing yourself minutes later. Do you?"

What a bleak thought. But I had to admit it was a valid point. "I don't know."

She shoved the card back into her bag. Her brows were drawn tightly together. "It has to be something else. The modeling scout—when she touched Julie…it was like she drained her happiness away and left only misery behind. So much that she couldn't deal. Maybe…maybe the same thing happened to the other girls who killed themselves, too. Maybe it's all connected."

I stared at Jordan, who seemed to have morphed into a tall, redheaded Nancy Drew. "That's crazy."

She hitched her purse strap higher on her shoulder. There was a wild look in her eyes. "Is it? It's like that kissing mob I've been hearing about. I'm sure I saw one of them—I saw him kiss a girl and when he was done and ran away, she looked wrong. Like he'd hurt her by kissing her. I thought it was only my eyes, but she was all glazed and weak, before she snapped out of it. And I swear for a second she had these weird black lines around her mouth—like the ones that some dead people have been found with."

"Where was this?" I asked evenly, heart pounding.

"At Crave." She eyed me. "You're not giving me a look like I'm crazy. Do you think it might be true?"

"I don't know." The fact that Jordan had seen anything like that had completely thrown me off. Up until now, I'd basically assumed everyone was somehow fooled in this city and didn't realize there were dark things lurking around the corner.

But that was irrational. Of course some people would notice something amiss. Especially those who were hypercritical. That would definitely be Jordan.

"And then there's Stephen," she continued, as if she didn't particularly care it was *me* to whom she was spilling this info. "I mean, I don't know exactly, but there's something bizarre going on with him. He tells me that it's over, but—he got this look in his eyes yesterday…" She shivered. "I know he doesn't mean to hurt me. I *know* it. I need to see him again."

As much as I desperately needed to find Stephen again, he and Jordan coming face-to-face was a bad idea. I didn't think she'd survive another confrontation without triggering his hunger past the point of no return. "Not a good idea."

She glared at me. "I forgot for a second that you were drooling all over Stephen."

Just when I started to let my guard down around her she had to unsheathe her claws and draw blood. "That's not true. Look, Jordan, I know you don't like me, but you have to trust me on this. Stephen is bad news and you need to stay far away from him."

"I forget. Why am I even talking to you right now?"

She walked away before I could say anything else.

No, the two of us would definitely *not* become friends. Ever.

The rest of the day was a blur. I couldn't concentrate at all. I kept going through what Stephen had told me about stasis, what happened with Bishop and the thought that the modeling agent could have somehow stripped away the happiness from Julie so much that she had to kill herself.

But, no. That couldn't be it. What happened to Julie was a tragedy, a senseless tragedy. That was all it was.

If nothing else, school was a distraction. Because when I got home, there was nothing to keep my mind off my problems.

After a couple hours of feeling shut out and hopeless, the walls began to close in on me. I couldn't stay here and do nothing while everyone else was doing something.

I decided to go to Crave again. It was a good enough place to restart my search.

At just after seven o'clock I left the house and walked two blocks toward the bus stop at a clip.

"Going somewhere?"

I'd noticed him already, but he'd stayed silent and I'd tried to ignore him, hoping he'd go away.

"Out for a walk," I replied tightly.

Kraven picked up his pace to walk next to me. "I'm stalking you. I know you like that word."

"Suits you."

"A job's a job."

The bus came along right when I arrived at the stop and I got on it. Kraven followed close behind me.

I took a seat at the back, as far from the handful of passengers as I could get. The demon took a seat across from me.

I eyed him warily. "Bishop's busy tonight?"

"Giving Blondie his full and undivided attention. Jealous?"

Something inside me tightened unpleasantly at that. "Why would I be jealous?"

He casually stretched his arms across the seats and leaned back. "Oh, no reason, I suppose. True love dashed into the rocks below the cliffs of Teenland. It's a heartbreaker. All I can do is witness it and shake my head sadly."

I ignored the commentary and fell silent for a few minutes, staring out the window as the city lights rushed past. Finally, I couldn't take it any longer. I twisted in my seat to look at him. "What's the latest on the gray situation?"

"About five-two, never smiles. Quite miserable, really."

I glared at him. "Other grays. Not me."

He waved a hand flippantly. "Totally under control. In that 'hard to find, we have no real idea what we're doing, we're going to be stuck in this city forever' kind of way. Heard you witnessed a suicide yesterday."

I cringed. "At the mall."

"Friend of yours?"

"Acquaintance."

"You don't seem too broken up by it."

"I'm broken up." My throat thickened. "Nobody should go that way."

He shrugged. "I'd like to push a few people off a high cliff if I had the chance."

"Like Bishop?" I asked, watching him carefully for his answer. In the memory meld I'd seen how close they once were. That was probably my biggest surprise. By the way they interacted now, I would have thought they'd always been enemies.

Kraven had been willing to do anything to help Bishop restore his sight. And I believed at that time he'd meant every word.

He rolled his eyes then moved his attention to the road zipping past outside the bus window. "I can think of a few other choice ways he should go. But we're one big friendly team right now, aren't we? All for one, one for all."

"Are you?"

That earned me a look. "Someone's rather combative tonight."

"Didn't expect the company. Feel free to go back to a reasonable stalking distance when we get off this bus."

"We'll see."

I stopped talking for another couple minutes. "Can I ask you a question?"

"You can ask. I might not feel like answering."

My grip tightened on the strap of my leather bag. "How long ago was it that you and Bishop were grave robbers? A hundred years ago? More?"

His head whipped in my direction and for a second, his amber eyes glowed red in the half darkness of the bus. "Somebody's been doing a little research."

It was enough of a reaction to let me know I'd struck a nerve. I shifted in my seat and the vinyl squeaked. "You don't seem ashamed."

"Should I be?"

I almost laughed. "I just accused you of being a grave robber. Yeah, I'd think you'd be ashamed of that."

"Dead people." Kraven shrugged. "What do they need that they're buried in? We needed it more."

"You were poor?"

He didn't answer for a moment. "Let's just say we were underprivileged." He went silent, studying me curiously. "How did you learn about this, anyway?"

"I have my ways."

He snorted. "So cryptic. I'd normally appreciate that if I wasn't slightly uneasy about you knowing stuff about my past."

I'd struck gold when it came to serious information about the brothers. I couldn't stop digging now. "You and him… you got along well. You wanted to help him fix his eyes."

The amused look faded from his face. "Nearly forgot about that."

"Did you help him?"

"Can he see now?"

I twisted a finger nervously into my hair, loose around my shoulders tonight since I'd taken it down from its tight ponytail the moment I'd gotten home. "I figure him being an angel kind of fixed any previous problems."

"You figured that, did you?" There was now a sour note in his voice.

I lowered my voice. Even though we were far from the people at the front of the bus, it still made me nervous that anyone might overhear. "I know he killed you, but it doesn't make sense. Why would he do that? You two cared about each other."

His jaw was tight and he stood up from his seat as the bus came to its next stop. "Anyway. This conversation's over."

I followed him off the bus, quickening my steps to keep up with him. I wasn't letting him get away now. "He killed you and sent you to Hell. He told me that much. I saw his memories last night, like I was reading his mind—saw them, experienced them. Then he freaked out and left."

He stared at me over his shoulder incredulously. His legs were long enough that if he really wanted to put distance between us and escape me, he could. "I just bet he did."

"It was when he was only fifteen. You two worked for someone named Kara. You sold the cadavers to a medical school, but you kept the jewelry to sell to help fix his eyesight. And you…" I strained to remember what I'd seen. "You wore a gold cross around your neck. Makes me think you were religious."

His expression was now a mirror image of how Bishop looked at me last night after the memory meld. "I'd stop talking now if I was you, gray-girl."

Stop? But I'd just gotten started. And I was on a roll. I had to keep pressing. There was something here—some connection I knew was vital. "Bishop changed his name to show how much he wanted to forget the past. Kraven's your last name, isn't it?" I was guessing now, but I knew I was right. "James is your first name. Just because you go by your last name doesn't mean that you're forgetting who you were. You remember. Come on, tell me something. Anything."

"Why?" There was the faint echo of pain in his voice. "So you can understand *him* better? Sorry, I'm not really in the mood to help pave your way to true love, sweetness."

True love? Maybe in my wildest dreams. But I'd never been a dreamer, I'd always been a realist. Even now. "You're kidding, right? He's an angel who's been around for years and years. He's an angel of *death*—an assassin. How could I ever seriously think somebody like him would be interested in me beyond his…inconvenient addiction?" It hurt to say it out loud, even if it was the truth.

"Interesting choice of words."

"I mind melded with him yesterday and heard everything. If he feels anything for me, it's the result of his soul's bizarre bond to the gray that attacked him."

"He did say something like that. Nice and neat explanation, isn't it? But if you think that's all it is between you two crazy kids, that should be freeing, right?" He groaned. "You have bigger problems than whether or not my little brother holds a torch for you. Way bigger if you don't find that missing soul of yours."

I stopped walking and looked around, trying to pinpoint my location. "Where are we?"

It wasn't as densely populated here on the east side of the city as it was closer to my house downtown. This wasn't the stop I would have gotten off at to go to Crave. We'd gone farther than that—I hadn't even realized I'd missed my stop until now.

However, I did see something I recognized. On the lawn of a huge house on a large lot we were walking past was a for-sale sign with my mother's name on it.

"House for sale," Kraven said, watching me check out the property. "Looks expensive."

"I wonder if this is the house," I said, staring at it through the iron gate at the end of the driveway. "My mother said she can't sell it."

Suddenly, I gasped as a wave of hunger crashed over me, stronger than anything I'd ever felt before. It was enough to make me drop to the ground, hard enough to bruise my knees. I couldn't find my breath. I reached up to grasp one of the iron bars to keep me from collapsing completely.

Kraven eyed me cautiously. "What's wrong with you?"

"I can't…" I struggled to breathe properly, to think, but I couldn't. I shook from head to toe. It was as if there was something inside me, a ravenous beast that wouldn't let me think or feel anything but emptiness, hunger, stretching wide and cavernous—never full, never satisfied. What I usually felt was only a pale version of this.

If I didn't feed soon, I was going to die.

It was the only clear thought I had.

Was this what Stephen warned me about? Was this stasis?

I was moving, but not through any choice of my own. It took a second for me to register what was happening. Kraven had picked me up, thrown me over his shoulder and was rapidly running away from the house. He didn't put me down again until we were a couple blocks away, near a line of stores.

I stood on shaky legs next to a small Italian restaurant. Through the glass windows, a few tables with red tablecloths were clearly visible—people eating, drinking wine, enjoying themselves.

It helped to move away from the house, but not as much as I'd like it to. Some people walked by us, moving toward the entrance to the restaurant—two of them, a man and a woman. When Kraven let go of me I immediately made a move toward them, not able to control myself.

Kraven grabbed my arm and held me firm until they disappeared inside.

I think I hissed at him. Like an angry snake.

"Nice," he said as he pulled me around to the side of the building where nobody in the front could see us. "See? This is what I expected with you being all gray. But no, you normally have to be all innocent and nonthreatening. Makes it difficult to do my job."

"Are you going to kill me?" I gasped for breath. "You better. Because I'm so hungry right now I know I'm going to attack somebody. I can't control this."

"Yeah, right. I'm going to kill you for having a momentary burst of crazy. If I did that, my little brother would carve your initials into my spleen before he cut my head off."

I pressed my hands to my temples. The pressure was intense and the hunger came in crashing waves, one after another. I could barely stay on my feet.

I whimpered. "I hate this. I hate it so much."

"Yeah, me, too." He didn't sound happy. Then he grabbed hold of my arms and pulled me against his chest. "Oh, hell. This worked before, so maybe it'll work again."

The next moment, his mouth was on mine.

chapter 14

Don't ask me how it worked, but it did. Something about kissing the demon, going through the motions of feeding from him, managed to fool my inner monster. Made it believe it was getting what it wanted.

Kraven's grip twisted into the front of my coat to hold me still. My arms were slack at my sides. He had to hunch over to make up for the difference in our heights.

I kissed him back as if I had no choice. I didn't. This wasn't a conscious decision, it was one of necessity. And slowly, slowly my mind began to clear.

His hands slid around to the small of my back and he pulled me up tighter against him. My eyes were squeezed shut, but I couldn't even try to pretend that I was kissing anyone else. Kraven's scent was unique to him—a pleasant spicy musk with undertones of smoke, like he'd been hanging out near a campfire for a few hours. He was the same height as Bishop, the same build, but they were so very different, so very—

Snap!

I was scanning the streets, looking for something.

No, wait. This wasn't me. It was Bishop. I was seeing through his eyes, but it wasn't a memory this time. It was now, and all I could do was observe, not feel what he was feeling. He flicked a glance at Connor, who was crouched on the sidewalk nearby.

"That was close," Connor said, turning his copper-colored eyes in Bishop's direction.

"Too close. Damn Hollow isn't working right anymore." Bishop looked down at the dagger he held. It chilled me to see that the blade was coated in blood. He'd just killed something. A gray that was no longer around; the Hollow must have opened up and taken it already.

Connor rose to his feet, scrubbing a hand over his shaved head. "Either it works to snatch them away, nearly taking us, too, or it doesn't open up at all. Why?"

"Don't know. Wish I did." Suddenly, Bishop's breath caught. "Go find Zach."

Connor looked at him with alarm. "What is it?"

"I sense her. She must be close."

"Who? Are you talking about Samantha?"

Bishop nodded. "She needs me."

"I didn't think that location link between you worked anymore."

"Sometimes it does. Like now."

Connor's gaze grew wary. "You know what Cassandra said. You should stay away from Samantha."

"I don't care what Cassandra said. Go. I'll catch up later." He didn't stay to argue. He took off at a run, scanning the streets, looking for something.

Looking for me.

He had this...ability...to find me—from the first moment we touched. The others didn't. It was a trait unique to Bishop. I wondered if it had to do with his particular job in Heaven. That made sense. An assassin needed to be able to track his prey.

I knew it didn't work so well all the time, especially when he got confused. When things got in the way of his concentration. When I was too far away.

But sometimes...it worked perfectly.

He was closer than I thought. Only around the corner from the house with the iron gate. He breezed past it, not looking twice in its direction.

Two more blocks up the street and Bishop staggered to an abrupt stop.

He saw me. And I saw myself through his eyes—it was a jarring sight. I was up against a side wall of the Italian restaurant, my arms tightly around the demon's shoulders, clinging to him as he kissed me.

I didn't remember grabbing hold of Kraven like that. But I guess I had.

Keeping his attention on us, Bishop quickly closed the distance, reaching forward to grab—

Snap!

Kraven staggered back from me and spun around to face the wrath of his brother. I wiped my mouth with the back of my hand and braced myself against the wall of the restaurant. I was dizzy and weak, barely able to stay on my feet. Barely able to process what just happened.

"What the hell are you doing?" Bishop's words held deadly malice. His narrowed eyes glowed bright blue. But he finally shoved the dagger in his grip into the sheath on his back.

For a second there—based on the murderous look he'd given Kraven—I'd been positive he'd completely lost his mind and was about to slice it through his brother's chest.

When I inhaled again, my hunger returned—and it was totally focused on the angel this time. I felt his warmth from where I stood, propped up against the wall. I fisted my hands at my sides to keep from automatically reaching for him. Kraven's kiss was enough to take the edge off, but the desire was still there.

I needed more time to get my head together. I squeezed my eyes shut and tried to calm myself.

"Um, what am I doing?" Kraven began, more maddeningly amused than concerned by the angel of death glaring at him. "My *job*, of course. Why? Whatever did it look like?"

"Your job, huh?" Poison dripped from the words. But when Bishop turned to face me, the anger slipped from his expression. "Are you all right?"

"What?" I blinked at him, stunned. It was the last thing I expected him to say after his furious arrival.

He touched my face, stroking the long, dark hair back that had fallen across my forehead. That breath-catching tingle of electricity flowed between us immediately.

"Oh, give me a break," Kraven said drily. "I wasn't forcing myself on her if that's what you're thinking."

My cheeks began to burn as I remembered Kraven's lips against mine.

"What happened here?" Bishop asked sharply.

"I had to kiss her. Obviously." The demon leaned a shoulder against the wall nearby. "She was having another soulsucker meltdown like at Crave the other night."

I was shaking now. "Please, Bishop..."

His breath caught. "What is it?"

"I'm sorry, but...you're too close to me right now." My brain was growing fuzzy at the edges. My vision narrowed on his mouth.

He swallowed hard, his Adam's apple jumping as he did. He slid his hands to my arms, gripping them firmly. His gaze sank into mine and he was close enough that I could feel the rapid beat of his heart. It was just like last night in my room. Dangerous.

But there was one six-foot-two difference tonight.

"Uh-oh. I think you've caught him in your spiderweb, gray-girl. Allow me to lend the hapless fly a hand." Kraven grabbed the back of Bishop's shirt and yanked him backward and out of my orbit of hunger. His warmth disappeared in an instant, and the cold rushed in on all sides.

There was still a spark of something unhinged in Bishop's eyes—something uncontrollable. Then he swore under his breath and raked a hand through his messy mahogany hair as he looked away from both of us.

"Exactly," Kraven said, nodding. "Best keep you two crazy kids apart."

Bishop glared at Kraven before his expression cooled. "Want to tell me what's going on here?"

Still weak and shaky, my legs finally gave out and I slid down the wall all the way to the ground. But at least I could think again. "You missed the part where I nearly attacked somebody a minute ago. I'm losing it, Bishop. Little by little. And it scares the hell out of me."

His gaze, now guarded, moved back to me. "What are you doing out here tonight?"

I let out a shaky breath. "I couldn't just stay home and wait for other people to solve my problems. I'm looking for Stephen, of course. Luckily, Kraven was keeping an eye on me when my control took a nosedive."

An unpleasant smile cracked through his expression and he shot a withering look at the demon. "My big brother, so attentive. Especially when it comes to you, Samantha."

Kraven spread his hands. "I'm here to help."

"Let's try this again." Bishop held his hand out to me, and I eyed it wistfully and warily. "It's okay. I'm better now."

"Really?" I chewed my bottom lip as I took his hand and let him pull me to my feet. He let go of me immediately, regretfully, and tore his gaze from mine to look at his brother again.

"Ah, that charming look of death," Kraven said. "I know it well. But, really, you shouldn't be jealous over a simple kiss between me and your girlfriend. You know. *Another* one."

He glanced at me. "What was that tonight? Strawberry lip gloss? I approve."

"Thank you for helping me." My cheeks burned. "Also, go to hell."

"Been there, done that."

Bishop fixed him with a steady look. "Why would I be jealous? It was so good of you to sweep in and save the day like the hero you are."

Even I recognized sarcasm when it was spread on that thick.

The problem was, it was true. Kraven had helped me. He *had* saved the day.

Bishop knew it, too. And while he might accept that it was necessary, the dark expression on his handsome face made me think he didn't like it at all.

I drew my coat closer to help keep out the chill. If I wasn't touching Bishop—which was a seriously bad idea right now—the cold of the night bit right through the fabric and sank straight down to my bones. Being that it was only October 29, it couldn't possibly be as cold as it seemed.

The cold is one of the signs of stasis, I reminded myself silently. *Just like the hunger, it's getting worse.*

I bleakly focused on the night sky for a moment, which was dotted with bright stars. No searchlights. No quests for new team members tonight.

"Blondie told you to patrol without her tonight—and she also told you to stay away from gray-girl," Kraven said, crossing his arms. "Trying to impress her with your warrior prowess and angelic obedience so you can land a ticket back to Heaven and a chance to regain your brain. Right?" He glanced at me. "For the record, he's still cutting his flawless angel skin to maintain his sanity without your magical touch. Won't last forever, though. He knows it, too."

"Bishop, no!" My voice broke. "You have to stop doing that."

He hissed out a breath. "Sometimes I have no choice."

I shivered. "What does Kraven mean, it won't last forever?"

Bishop spoke to me, but his attention was now on the demon. "Little by little my sanity's slipping away no matter what I do to try to stop it. This soul inside me…the more it takes hold of me, the more damage it does to my mind. And some damage can't be fixed."

"No." I said it firmly, even though my stomach sank all the way to the ground at this confirmation. "That's not going to happen to you."

"No?" He flicked a glance at me, his blue eyes haunted. "You don't know what it's like when the craziness grips me."

"You don't think I know what it's like to start to lose your mind and your control? We might be complete opposites in a lot of ways, Bishop, but this much we have in common. Sometimes we lose a battle. But that doesn't mean it's the end of the war. Only if we stop fighting is it really the end."

His jaw tightened. "Maybe you're right."

"Damn right, I am." My surge of anger over his fatalistic attitude had helped chase my own away. "No maybes about it. We're going to fix me and we're going to fix you. Somehow, someway."

"FYI, I'm not kissing you, too," Kraven said to him. "So you can just forget it."

I shot the demon a look. He wasn't fooling me with this nonchalant, joking facade of his. Whenever he dealt with Bishop, there was an edge to him—to both of them. Something dark lurking under the surface. Barely restrained animosity.

I continued to wipe at my mouth to remove the taste of Kraven's lips, disturbed that the kiss had lasted way longer than it had to due to the unexpected mind meld. I looked around. "Something about this area triggered me. Like, out of nowhere. I've never felt anything that horribly immediate before."

Bishop also scanned the street as if searching for clues. "And now? How are you feeling?"

"Better. Just—" I turned my gaze to his "—don't come any closer to me right now."

Something slid through his eyes then, something vulnerable, before it disappeared and his expression hardened again.

Then something else caught my attention.

A woman slowly shuffled down the street toward the abandoned house at the end of the block. She was making a mournful, whimpering sound. My blood ran cold. It sounded like she was in desperate pain.

And she sounded exactly like I had only a short time ago.

"She's a gray," I said, my voice catching.

At the house, she grasped hold of the bars of the gates and shook them, as if attempting to break them down to get to the house.

Bishop and Kraven shared a look.

"I can't go back there," I whispered. "Whatever's happening to her…it happened to me, too."

The gray was openly weeping as she clawed at the gates, her shoulders racking violently with her sobs.

"I'll take care of her," Bishop said.

My gaze shot to him. I knew exactly what he meant. And it wasn't to send her to a psychiatrist to work out her problems. A chill went through me. "But she's so helpless right now. You're just going to kill her?"

His face was tense. "I'll talk to her first. But if she's lost herself…if she's gone into stasis…we know what that means. She can't think straight."

I couldn't help it; I reached out to grab his arm. "Neither can I sometimes."

He looked down to where I touched him, his expression tormented. "You're different."

"You sure about that?" Kraven asked without any humor.

"Yes," he hissed. "So let me deal with this."

The demon waved a hand. "Be my guest."

I watched tensely as Bishop turned to walk toward the woman. He didn't reach for his dagger—not yet—but I knew he wouldn't hesitate if he had no other choice.

I wanted to have an argument for why he couldn't do this— that the woman was pathetic and helpless and needed assistance. But I knew there was no help for her. What I saw wasn't a woman who could be reasoned with, but a monster out of its mind with hunger. One who could hurt others—one who could *infect* others.

She was part of a dangerous disease that needed to be cured.

And there was a beautiful angel of death moving steadily closer to help end her illness.

But before Bishop got within twenty feet of her she cried out, clutched her head and collapsed to the ground. A scream caught in my throat as I watched her begin to literally melt right before my eyes. It was like something out of *The Wizard of Oz* when the water hit the wicked witch of the west. Smaller and smaller, she sank into the ground…until there was nothing left but a pile of clothes.

It took less than a minute.

I was trembling violently as I faced Kraven. His expression was grim, but not surprised like my own.

"That's happened before." My voice quaked. "Hasn't it?"

He nodded. "Ever since the Source was killed, this is what's been happening to some of the grays we come across. The Hollow doesn't open up for these ones—they're just gone.

Makes our jobs a hell of a lot easier, but…" He glanced at me, his lips thinning.

He didn't have to finish the sentence. As a gray, it could happen to me, too.

"Bishop briefed us on stasis," he continued. "This chick obviously wasn't strong enough to handle it."

You change or you die, Stephen warned me.

This was door number two.

That poor woman. Once she was a girl like me who'd been kissed by someone who made her heart beat faster.

Now her heart didn't beat at all.

"This proves it. We need to find Stephen tonight," Bishop said when he returned to us, his expression hard and determined. "There's no more time to waste."

Kraven scoffed. "Drop everything and try to find gray-girl's soul so she's not the next one to melt into a puddle of sludge?"

Bishop fixed him with a contemptuous look. "There's a new club I want to check out. Grays have started to hang out there ever since they realized we were keeping a close eye on Crave. I sent Cassandra and Roth there earlier to take a look."

"So let them handle it," Kraven said.

"No. We're going, too."

This was the first I'd heard about an alternate club for grays. But it made sense. Stephen needed somewhere to spend time— and he had been at Crave almost every single night since he'd returned to the city from university. "How did you find out about this?"

"From another gray."

"Why would he tell you anything?"

Bishop held my gaze steadily. "Let's just say I can be very convincing when I want something."

Kraven snorted. "Better leave it at that. Wouldn't want to disturb gray-girl's delicate sensibilities."

I stared at Bishop. "Wait. Are you saying you tortured the gray?"

"Some people need convincing before they decide to be helpful. This one was particularly unwilling to chat." He shrugged. "He talked, that's the main thing. I got the information I needed."

A shiver ran down my spine. "I'll take that as a yes."

Just when I thought I'd figured out what to expect from the angel, he threw me another curveball. And the worst thing was, I didn't hold this against him. He was right—some people needed convincing. But it still put a sick feeling into the pit of my stomach that he'd go to such extremes to help save me.

I looked into his blue eyes, wishing I could read his mind like the others.

But maybe I could. Maybe he was just *really* good at shielding—and the mind melds and memory melds were something completely different he couldn't control.

"I know you're doing this for me," I whispered. "Thank you."

His dark brows drew together and that edge of something vulnerable returned. Then that very human expression disappeared like magic and he tore his gaze from mine.

"We need to go check out the club right now," he said.

"Fine," I agreed, my tentative tone turning fierce. "And don't even think about trying to stop me from coming with you."

A small amount of humor returned to his beautiful blue eyes. "Of course you're coming. Stephen sees us, he'll make like Houdini and disappear. You're the bait to keep him right where he is."

I raised an eyebrow. "Bait, huh?"

"Bait who likes to get herself in serious trouble whenever possible."

"That would be me." I nodded slowly. "Just do me a favor... both of you..."

The demon and angel both looked at me.

"Don't kill him—even if we do get my and Carly's soul back." Putting it into words felt like I was jinxing it, but I had to say this. "He's just as freaked out by stasis as I am. Call me crazy, but if there's a way, I want to help him, not hurt him. Okay?"

Bishop blinked. "You want to *help* him."

I nodded.

"You know—" a full grin appeared on his entirely too kissable lips "—maybe I'm *not* the only crazy one here, after all."

chapter 15

"Hooray," Kraven said drily. "Another all-ages kiddie club. How exciting."

He was wrong about many things. This was one of them. The club Bishop had taken us to didn't cater to the underage crowd like Crave. Ambrosia was decidedly adult and crowded.

I'd heard of it before. Very popular, and wall-to-wall busy seven days a week. Carly once suggested we get fake IDs so we could sneak in and check it out. Since that was just after my near-arrest for shoplifting, and I'd been extremely paranoid about coloring outside the proverbial lines again, I'd refused to let her talk me into it.

Carly'd always liked chasing adventure way more than I had. I'd always, with very few exceptions, played it safe.

But nothing was safe anymore.

It was ten o'clock when we finally got there. I feared I'd get carded at the door—one of the few tests I'd inevitably fail. I knew Bishop wasn't able to do the angelic influence thing that the others could. And demons didn't have that particular skill.

But he'd figured out another way of influencing humans—one that worked nearly as well. He produced a roll of bills and paid off the bouncer. That was all it took to get a hand stamp and entrance. Money talks.

I'd heard a lot about the club, read articles about it on the internet, but it was even more impressive in person. A billionaire had bankrolled it for his Victoria's Secret model girlfriend—who was named Ambrosia—and it had that sexy, high fashion meets big bucks look. And to add to the cool factor, the most hopping part of the club was three stories belowground. I checked my coat upstairs and we descended a glass, spiral staircase studded with crystals, sparkling under the pot lights.

Downstairs, the place was packed—despite it being a Monday night. The bar was in the middle, and the huge shiny black-and-silver dance floor to the far left. It put Crave to shame. Everywhere else, in the main area and in the many more private alcoves, were plush designer sofas and chairs, as well as tables where well-dressed patrons could mingle, drink champagne and sip cocktails.

But, just like at Crave, the music pounded. It was the one thing they had in common.

"This is where you think Stephen is?" I asked Bishop. Stephen was only nineteen, not that that seemed to matter all that much, as evidenced by how easy the bouncers were to pay off.

"It's a guess," Bishop said.

There were also at least two hundred other souls here in this club. I couldn't ignore that fact no matter how hard I tried, especially after how out of control I'd been only a short time ago on the street. I fought hard to keep my focus and not let my hunger take over—my constant, invisible, inner battle.

Bishop glanced around our immediate area. "Where did Kraven go?"

I looked over my shoulder and spotted him almost immediately. The golden-haired demon was impossible to miss, even in a crowd. "By the bar. He's getting a drink."

"Typical. He's always preferred getting drunk to working."

I looked at him, surprised. "Demons can get drunk?"

He raised an eyebrow. "He used to be human."

"So did you," I reminded him, and was rewarded with an immediate tensing of his expression. It was almost amusing, really. He was like Pavlov's dog. Ring a bell, the dog salivates. Mention his past, Bishop gets grouchy.

"Right," he finally allowed. "Well, some things don't change. Alcohol and other drugs still affect us. If we're not careful."

"Maybe he wants to drown the memory of…what he had to do to me earlier."

There was no humor in his eyes anymore. Instead, there was a flash of something much darker. "That kiss?"

My cheeks burned. "Yeah, well. He doesn't like me."

"He likes you more than he likes me. He hates my guts."

"You think he still holds it against you that you killed him and sent him to Hell? Shocker." I honestly didn't mean it to sound as smart-ass as it came out. But there it was.

"Let's keep looking for Stephen," Bishop said tightly.

I deflated. My confidence came and went, really. Right now, it went. "Sorry, but you're the one who gave me that enticing piece of information and now you want to pretend you never said anything."

He studied me for a moment, expressionless, then a grin finally tugged the side of his mouth. "You are bound and determined to learn my deepest, darkest secrets, aren't you?"

"*Determined* is a good word. Obsessed might be another one."

His smile only grew, the expression working like an arrow shooting straight into my heart. "Obsession can be a dangerous thing, Samantha."

My gaze moved to his lips. "Don't I know it."

He wrenched his attention from me to scan the club, and then turned around to face me full-on. "Am I too close? I'd rather not make this difficult for you."

I swallowed hard, ignoring the constant hunger being near him brought forth. "It's always difficult when I'm close to you."

His jaw tensed, and he turned away. "Then I should give you some space."

"I didn't mean it like that. It's better now than it was before." I grabbed his arm, and electricity sparked between us. He tensed and turned back to face me.

Then he immediately directed me away from the crowd and off into a quieter alcove, past a translucent crystal-beaded curtain. The loud music still blared from the live band and I couldn't even make out what the lead singer was singing, but it was slightly muted here, giving the illusion of privacy.

"Bishop, last night when I saw your memory…" I began. I had to get this out. It weighed on me like a two-ton elephant sitting on my chest.

"Let's forget about that." His attention moved to something over my shoulder, but I think he was simply trying to avoid eye contact.

"But that's just it—I don't want to forget it. I know you think I might have seen something that you didn't want me to see. That somehow it's going to make me dislike you or fear you. But you're wrong."

He gave me a wry look. "Then I guess you didn't see nearly as much as I thought you did."

"Why can I do that?" I whispered, my voice hoarse. "I know I can do the mind-meld thing, but it's not like I can control it."

"You're a nexus." He moved closer so he could also speak quietly in case we were overheard. The song had ended and the band slowly eased into the next one. The buzz of conversation beyond the curtain swirled around me. "You have a strange power over the ethereal and the infernal. That includes me. Add that to the fact that you took a piece of my soul… well, that gives you certain powerful abilities."

As much as I'd love to be someone who just readily accepts every mind-blowing thing that has happened to me over the past couple of weeks, I wasn't that girl. The less I thought about my birth parents and what that meant—and I honestly didn't know exactly *what* that meant—the less freaked out I got.

"I don't feel so powerful," I said, swallowing hard. "I don't know why anybody would even be concerned with someone like me. There's no way I could throw anything off balance."

"I think you underestimate yourself."

Bishop was still too close to me, and his warm, spicy scent made it nearly impossible for me to concentrate. "Have you ever known of another nexus?"

"They're rare, but yes. Once, years ago, I met one."

"What happened?" I asked, breathless.

He met my gaze. "I killed him."

I gasped. "Oh, my God."

His brows drew together and he watched me, as if wary of my reaction to this jarring statement. "You always say that you're the one who doesn't hold anything back and I'm the secretive one. But I don't want this to be a secret. I need you to know this, now that you're aware of what my job was."

I worked it over in my mind, trying to reject it, but I knew I couldn't. "So it was an assignment for Heaven—this nexus was bad. A real threat."

He nodded, his jaw tight. "This is exactly why I know you're different."

"Why?"

He surprised me by giving me a small grin. "That you even

have to ask me that proves it all the more. You know that a nexus—while very rare—can't access their powers while their human soul covers up what they really are."

"Yeah. Natalie told me that. That's why she had Stephen remove mine."

Something unpleasant crossed his expression at the mention of my aunt and Stephen. "The nexus I dealt with removed his soul through dark magic. *Blood* magic."

I gulped. "I'm guessing that doesn't involve magic wands and fairy dust."

"Not even slightly. He knew what he was doing, and was willing to sacrifice other lives in the process. Your soul was taken against your will and now you're actively fighting to get it back."

"I am a fighter."

"Don't I know it." His lips quirked.

"This is why you don't want the others to know about me, isn't it? Because if Heaven or Hell found out the truth—you'd have to kill me, too."

Any humor vanished from Bishop's expression. It was more than enough to tell me I was right. "Like I said before, Samantha, you can't let the others know what you are. You won't like the results."

He began to turn from me to return to the main club, but I grabbed his arm hard. That familiar charge of celestial energy flew between us—so powerful this time that I swear I saw literal sparks. He froze before he glanced at me again.

I held on to him tighter. "You know, you really piss me off sometimes."

He didn't pull away. "Excuse me?"

I hissed out a frustrated breath. "Seriously. You refuse to tell me anything about yourself, except these frustrating bits and pieces. And then when we start talking about something important, you want to turn away and ignore me. But you're still the only person who wants to protect me. That means something to me."

Yeah, something big. Way too big to wrap my head around.

"I'm not the only one. Kraven proved tonight he's more than up to the task of filling in when I'm not around." His words were tight. "You really don't think he likes you? I saw the way he was kissing you—tonight *and* Saturday night. Maybe you should think again."

Kraven didn't like me. At all. The two times he'd kissed me—that was only because there wasn't any other choice. "Now you're being ridiculous."

This earned a short, humorless laugh. "Not many people have ever called me ridiculous before. But okay. Don't let him fool you, though. The brother I knew—that one you might have seen in my memory—is long gone. He's a demon now. Just because he's able to play the part of a charmingly sarcastic Boy Scout now and then doesn't mean he isn't dangerous."

"I guess you have that in common."

"You're right. We do."

"But you're an angel, not a demon. I know that means you're good, even if you don't totally believe it yourself. If you tell me more about your past, I won't hold it against you. I swear I won't, Bishop."

His brows drew tightly together. "Why do you want to know so badly?"

"I just do." I couldn't tell him the truth. I couldn't tell him that I wanted to know because every single time I saw him I fell that much harder for him. He might feel the need to protect me, he might feel *something* for me, but in his mind it was all due to his soul and my hunger. And that hadn't been proven otherwise.

But for me, I knew it was different. Hunger and heart—

they weren't the same thing, no matter how hard he tried to justify it and explain it away.

No matter how he might have looked at Cassandra, or how much they had in common with each other, he didn't look at her in the same intense way he looked at me.

The way he was looking at me right now.

He hissed out a breath. "We don't have time for this right now."

I sent another furtive glance toward the main club through the beaded curtain. I couldn't see Kraven anywhere. And Stephen wasn't around, either. I knew we needed to be out there right now, but I had to do this. I had to know the truth.

"Let me see your memories. You don't even have to tell me about them—maybe you can just show me. We can try."

"Samantha, you need to stop being so concerned with my past and be more worried about your future." His jaw tightened. "And make sure you keep that dagger on you at all times. No matter what. Do you have it tonight?"

I shrugged. "Maybe."

He glared at me. "You're seriously the most stubborn person I've ever met. You know that?"

I glared back. "Ditto." Then I froze as he pressed me back against the wall and slid his hand down my side and over my thigh. "What are you doing?"

"Checking something."

My heart slammed hard against my rib cage and the delicious scent of him, of his soul, was slowly driving me crazy. He was so close. And his touch, even if it was through my jeans, not against my bare skin, had helped shut off my senses to everything around us—no music, no voices, no crowd, nobody else—only this moment.

"Good," he whispered as his fingers trailed over the weapon and sheath hidden beneath my loose jeans. "Although, it'll be too hard to access quickly unless you start wearing short skirts."

I struggled to breathe normally. "Is that a request?"

"A suggestion." His now-heated gaze locked with mine and held. "Damn it, Samantha. It wasn't supposed to be like this."

"Like what?"

"You were not supposed to be part of my problem."

On the surface, word for word, it almost sounded like an insult. But the way he said it, low and throaty…me being problematic for an angel of death—it was the sexiest thing I'd ever heard in my entire life.

My hunger swirled around me, ever tightening like a cool silk scarf binding me in place. Everything else faded into the background—my future, my survival, the safety of everyone in the city, even the fate of my best friend trapped in the Hollow.

I didn't care about anything else.

Only Bishop.

"Kraven's right." His breath was warm against my cheek. "When I'm this close to you…it's like being a fly trapped in a spider's web. I can't seem to free myself."

"I want to kiss you right now." I was completely unashamed by the truth spilling from inside me. "So much. It's driving me crazy."

He didn't reply; he just nodded slowly, his gaze fully fixed on my lips.

"I won't take it all. I can stop myself before it's too late." My hunger turned me into something other than myself, other than the shy and awkward kid who'd only allowed herself crushes on a couple of guys before. The girl who shielded her heart to keep it from being broken. The one who looked in the mirror and still only saw a skinny girl with long, wild hair and barely enough chest to stuff in the smallest bra on the rack.

But Bishop had never looked at me like I was that girl. He

looked at me like I was something amazing. Something beautiful beyond words. Something he wanted more than anything or anyone else.

And, at the moment, with the sounds of Ambrosia now only a distant echo, I knew he was every bit as lost as I was.

He drew closer, closer until finally…finally, his lips brushed against mine.

chapter 16

I literally groaned with pleasure to be able to touch him, to taste him. Bishop's breath was so warm, so sweet. I wanted more…

"Please," I whispered, staring deep into his blue eyes. "Bishop, please—"

Snap!

It's done.

The knife in my hand clatters to the ground. The blood wells beside his body. He stares up at me as he gasps for his last breath. He stares at me as if looking at a stranger instead of his own brother.

"Why would you do this?" he whispers. "Why?"

"Because you had to die today." I would think I should feel something at this moment, some form of regret, but I feel nothing. Nothing at all.

"You know what happens to me now. Don't you care?"

"No, I don't."

"What did she promise you? What's your reward?" The pain in his gaze that I would surprise him like this, that I'd stab my own brother in the back without warning, is deeper than his physical pain.

"Goodbye, James." I turn from him toward the door.

"You'll burn for this, you stupid son of a bitch."

I glance over my shoulder to see the shadows already rising up to claim him. "No. You will."

Snap!

Bishop staggered back from me, his eyes wide. I pressed the back of my hand to my mouth, stifling a scream.

"What did you—?" he began, but then his words broke off. There must have been something in my eyes, some shock and horror, that stopped him from asking what I'd seen.

"Stay here," he said sharply, averting his gaze. "I'm going to search the club for Stephen."

He knew I'd seen another memory of his past, but I didn't think he knew which one in particular. Any memory, according to Bishop, was an invasion of his privacy, of his mind. And it could lead to jarring revelations.

He was absolutely right about that.

The next moment he was gone. My mind cleared a fraction at a time, but I trembled as I pressed up against the wall.

When I had the memory melds, it was as if I *was* Bishop. I saw what he'd seen, I heard what he'd heard. I felt what he'd felt.

But it was different this time. Something had been very wrong with him.

Watching Kraven die in that memory had shaken me more than anything I'd faced because the person who killed him was the one person I'd quickly come to care about more than anyone else.

And the more I learned about Bishop, the more shaken I became.

Someone who'd done something so horrible, who'd murdered his own brother in cold blood…how was he given the chance to become an angel?

Out of the corner of my eye, I saw someone pass by outside the beaded curtain. My breath caught.

It was Stephen.

Without waiting another second or thinking about it first,

I hurried after him, trying desperately to keep him in view through the mass of people.

I finally caught up to him by the stairs, catching his arm. "Stephen!"

He spun to face me. His face was pale, his eyes wild and unfocused. "What are you doing here?"

"I came here to find you." I turned to frantically scan the club for Kraven and Bishop, but they were nowhere to be seen.

"Leave me alone." He pulled away from my grip and started up the stairs. I followed after him. My head still swam from the memory meld, but there was no possible way I was going to let Stephen out of my sight now that I'd found him again.

Bishop was right about him being here. Now all I had to do was convince him to help me. I'd been so close at the mall yesterday, I knew it. I'd seen it in his eyes. Witnessing his fear about stasis had changed something inside me when it came to Stephen. For so long now I'd blamed him for my misfortune, for my hunger and troubles. I still did. But he wasn't totally the villain I'd made him out to be—unrepentant and evil to the core. He was just somebody else in over his head, dealing with the ramifications of his own bad choices.

There had to be a way to help him, too. Being a gray had changed him, but not completely. I'd seen the way he looked at Jordan yesterday. How I knew he wanted to protect her, even if he chose to do so by being a standoffish, passive-aggressive jerk.

There was still good in Stephen. And I was going to give him another chance to prove it to me.

"Where are you going?" I called after him.

"I need to leave."

"You don't look so good."

Stephen glanced over his shoulder as we ascended the stairs.

It took all of my energy to keep up with his long strides. "I don't feel so good."

He was so pale, even the color of his eyes seemed faded. And he was shivering. The cold was getting worse for him, even worse than it was for me.

My throat closed. "You're going into stasis."

He didn't answer, instead quickening his steps. When we reached the lobby, I didn't have time to get my coat out of the coat check. If I did, I knew I'd lose him. Instead, I emerged with him through the doors into the night, only the thin cotton of my shirt to protect me from the chill. It would have to be enough.

He walked so fast I had to literally run to keep up with him. "You can't just keep ignoring me. Please, Stephen. You need to help me. You know you do."

Finally, he stopped walking and turned to face me when we'd gone about a block from the club. His expression was bleak. "It's too late, Samantha."

I shivered, and crossed my arms tightly over my chest to try to stay warm. "I know you're scared. If you help me, I can help you, too."

"You think so? Afraid not. Nobody can help me. And nobody can help you, either."

His words were like a slap—which was how he'd meant them. He was lashing out at me because he felt so desperate and alone. But I wouldn't let myself be put off that easily. Not tonight. "You can't lose hope."

He laughed, a dry and humorless sound that sent a fresh chill down my spine. "Natalie promised me a lot of things when she was still alive. She said it was going to be great. That nothing would get in our way. That we'd be together forever. I believed her. Mostly."

Empathy welled inside me. He'd been played by my aunt

like a fool. She'd used him any way she could. "Don't tell me you were in love with her."

"Hardly." He glared at me. "Don't you know by now, Samantha? I'm an opportunist, always have been. Natalie represented an opportunity for me to be more than what I was. I took it. In fact, I jumped at it, sacrificing everything in the process. I deserve this as my punishment."

"You're not that bad."

That earned another laugh that echoed coldly off the dark buildings surrounding us. "No, I'm worse."

"You broke up with Jordan to save her. That proves to me that there's still something inside you that gives a damn."

His laugh broke off and he sent a look at me so sharp that it almost cut. "You don't know anything about what happened with Jordan."

He started walking again, but I scooted around to block his path. The two of us were momentarily lit up by a set of headlights from a car turning the corner. It only showed me how pale Stephen was. And that even though he shivered from the cold, there was also a sheen of perspiration on his forehead. He looked sick.

"Maybe you're right," I said. "Maybe I'm just guessing. But I saw something in your eyes at the mall. You don't like hurting her. I'm not saying I get it. I mean, to me Jordan's a total bitch. But maybe down deep—maybe with *you*—she was different. Maybe she saw the real you, and vice versa. Maybe it was true love."

"Shut up." His voice shook. "It's over—everything is. I'm going into stasis and right now I need to be anywhere but here."

When he moved again, I literally shoved him back a step. "Stop. Just stop. My friends…they can help you. I'm serious."

He didn't look at me, he looked at the ground by my feet.

Michelle Rowen

"Yeah, right. They can help by putting a knife through my heart." He rubbed his forehead as if his head ached. "I still have just enough self-preservation to want to crawl off somewhere private if I'm going to die tonight. I don't want to be killed. If that makes me a coward, then fine. I'm a damn coward."

With that, he pushed me out of the way.

"Stephen, don't go. Please." My voice caught.

He looked over his shoulder at me, his face shadowed by the small amount of light from the nearby streetlamp. "I'm sorry, Samantha. I'm sorry I did what Natalie told me to do. I shouldn't have taken your soul."

My eyes burned. "You can make it up to me by giving it back. Simple."

"Nothing's simple anymore. For me or for you."

Regular reasoning wasn't working. I needed to up my game. "What do you want? Protection from my friends? I've already asked them not to hurt you. They won't."

"Sure, they won't."

"What else do you want?"

"Bargaining, Samantha?" A glimmer of a cold smile played at his lips. "Has it really come to that?" Then the smile died. "I know what this is. You're trying to slow me down so your buddies can catch up. Aren't you?"

"No, I came after you by myself. Nobody else saw you."

There was no more patience in his gaze. "Goodbye, Samantha."

I clutched onto his arm, digging my fingernails in hard. "You'd really walk away, just like that? I guess I was wrong about you. You really are a selfish asshole."

He spun to face me, grabbing the front of my shirt and yanking me forward. My anger fell away, replaced by fear. He had nothing to lose right now. And there was nothing friendly or kind in his eyes. Instead, all I saw was endless pain. "You're

184

right. I am a selfish asshole. But you were also right about Jordan. I love her and don't want to hurt her. She'll be better off when I'm dead. Because this stasis? I hope like hell it kills me tonight. I don't know what I'd turn into if it doesn't."

He shoved me back so hard that I fell to the ground, twisting my ankle. As I scrambled to get back to my feet, he started running away.

I tried to pursue, but white-hot pain shot through my ankle. I whimpered out loud, limping as fast as I could in the direction he'd fled. I got as far as the next block before I realized he was nowhere to be seen.

He could die tonight from stasis and he still had my soul, and Carly's soul, too.

It was over. I'd failed.

"Damn it," I whispered, my throat closing. Hot tears streaked down my cheeks, but I furiously wiped them away. They wouldn't be any help right now. Tears never helped.

"There you are."

My gaze shot to the right. Sitting on the curb was someone I recognized immediately. Someone I'd been searching the city for, just as I'd been searching for Stephen.

"Seth!" I didn't want to take my eyes off him in case he disappeared like an elusive ghost, but I had to crane my neck to keep searching for Stephen.

He was gone.

"It's over." I inhaled sharply, raggedly, and forced back the burn of tears. All I could feel now was the pain in my ankle. I let myself drop down onto the curb next to him.

"Over? It's hardly started, beautiful star." He called me that, beautiful star, and I had no idea why. One day I'd have to ask him why that was his chosen nickname for me when I cared enough to know the answer. "One by one they'll all disappear until there are none left. But that doesn't mean it's over. Soon, but not yet."

Didn't sound like much had changed when it came to Seth. The fallen angel always talked like this—half insane homeless dude, half Yoda. I knew he saw things, important things. Visions, kind of like what I had sometimes. Somewhere deep down there was importance to the things Seth said to me.

Over? It's hardly started.

Okay. Good to know, I think.

One by one they'll all disappear.

Grays? They were disappearing, thanks to stasis. Thanks to the team's nightly patrols and Bishop's shiny knife.

Until there are none left.

A chill went through me at this. I guess I didn't need a code breaker to help figure out that hidden message.

Seth looked much the same as he had the last time I'd seen him. Of an indeterminate age—anywhere from thirty to fifty. Dark hair, shaggy, dark beard, black eyebrows. Unfocused brown eyes. There weren't many lines around those eyes, which told me he was probably on the lower end of the age scale. Possibly even younger than that.

I noticed something different about him this time.

"What are those?" I asked.

He glanced down at his arms. The sleeves of his shirt had been pushed up. On his skin were wispy lines, like a tattoo. He pulled his shirt down to cover them.

"Part of the package," he said. "Comes with the territory, I've realized. They're pretty, don't you think?"

Not really, but I chose not to comment. I wondered if an angel or demon stayed in the human world long enough, they'd gain those marks. "I've been looking for you, Seth."

"Hard to find myself sometimes. We all get lost from time to time."

"There's someone I need you to meet. Another fallen angel. He's found ways to deal with…his soul." Ways that made me queasy whenever I thought of him cutting himself. "But I need to know if there's anything else he can do, anything you tried when you first fell that helped?"

Seth grinned to show perfect, white teeth, so unexpected in his otherwise ungroomed, grimy face. "Forget him, beautiful star. He won't matter in the end. And now the time grows close—close enough to touch."

"The time for what?"

"Can't you feel how close you are?"

I shook my head. "What are you talking about? Close to what?"

Seth cocked his head and gazed at me as if mesmerized by what he saw there. "Your death, of course."

chapter 17

I reeled back from Seth in shock. "My *death?*"

"It's written all over you like a poem." Madness glimmered in his eyes. "It's your destiny, beautiful star. A necessary step of a longer journey."

The angel had managed to put my darkest fear into words and throw them out on the cold night air as if they meant nothing at all—just a random observation.

"How can I stop it?" I asked tightly.

"You can't."

"I'll fight it."

"You can try. You'll fail."

I clenched my fists at my sides so tightly that my fingernails bit into my palms. I focused on that pain, and the pain in my ankle, and tried to think, to rationalize this.

Seth was crazy.

He said crazy things.

And yet…I knew that stasis was coming for me just like with Stephen. Stasis, that dark and deadly wraith in the distance, growing closer by the day.

"Go back to your little angel and his friends," Seth suggested, standing up from the curb. "Enjoy the time you have left."

I forced myself up as well and grabbed his arm. "Wait."

I looked right into his eyes, trying to channel that part of my nexus ability that allowed me to read the minds of angels and demons. This hadn't come with an instruction manual, but it was always waiting just below the surface for me to tap into.

And…yes…I could sense something, feel something. It was there, as if shining at the bottom of a dark pool of water…I just couldn't reach it.

The others could block me if they tried hard enough. I could bust through it if given enough time. I pictured it like a tall, solid wall of ice. Ice cracked, and it could be broken.

"You spend too much time focusing on the wrong things, beautiful star. It will be your undoing. You obsess about your fallen angel, yet he's not the only one to fall, is he? The girl fell far to the ground and death claimed her, locking her in its embrace."

My breath caught. "Are you talking about Julie? Julie Travis? You know what happened at the mall? Why did she do that? Was there a reason for it?"

"There's a reason for everything." Seth glanced around our surroundings, the dark and empty street that made me think we were the only two in the city if it wasn't for the buzz of activity a block ahead, back near the club. "Something has been released here, something beyond the gray. It devours all that is good. And the lost ones wander, their numbers growing daily. They search for escape, just as we all do. But they're trapped, just like we all are. You already know this—you know more than you think you do."

I was losing him again. For a moment, he'd almost been making sense. "What do I already know? Stop playing games with me, Seth."

"Life is a game, beautiful star. One with a time limit. And it's time to accept your destiny."

"If my destiny is death, then I don't accept it."

"You have no choice."

"There's always a choice." My anger had given me the strength that accepting defeat had bled away. This time I looked into Seth's eyes with every bit of focus I possessed. He knew things. And damn it, I was going to find out what they were.

That mental wall was there, blocking my access to his thoughts and any truth he was trying to hide from me. I sensed the crack and pressed hard against it.

She's not ready yet. But she will be soon.

That was all I got before I was shoved right out of his mind and the crack in the wall closed up tight, smacking me in the face like a bungee cord. I staggered back and fell over my injured ankle, gasping with pain as I hit the ground hard. A car came around the corner, momentarily blinding me with its bright headlights as I struggled to rise to my feet and look around.

Seth was gone.

What the fallen angel had told me was like a storm pounding me on all sides. I felt battered and bruised as I hobbled back to the nightclub, shivering from the cold. I had to find Bishop and tell him what happened.

What Seth said could have been a pack of lies. Every rambled, crazy word of it. Talking to him had been a waste of my time.

She's not ready yet. But she will be soon.

Trying to figure out the workings of that fallen angel's mind would wind up driving me crazy, too.

My hand stamp worked fine to get me back into Ambrosia,

no questions asked. I retrieved my coat right away, hoping to chase some of the chill away, or at least attempt to ignore it as long as I could.

Clutching the handrail, I descended the sparkling, crystal staircase to get to the main club. Limping, I made my way through the crowd, the loud music filling my ears, the scent of the souls pressing in on me, threatening my focus.

The first person I recognized didn't see me. Cassandra zipped by, so close I could feel the breeze she created with her swift movement. Roth was right behind her. He grabbed hold of her arm and pulled her into one of the alcoves, covered by the beaded curtain. I followed, confused.

"Where do you think you're going?" Roth demanded.

"Away from you," Cassandra replied angrily. "Now leave me alone."

"Not going to happen."

"Honestly, take a hint, demon. The farther away from you I am, the easier everything is."

"Easy's boring."

"I'm here for a reason. And it's not to entertain you."

"Trust me. You're not that entertaining."

I pressed against the wall, favoring my ankle. I didn't understand why Bishop would send them here together to search for Stephen. It was obvious to me how much they despised each other.

"I swear, demon. Let go of me."

"And what if I say no?"

"Maybe I'll get Bishop's dagger and shove it through your chest. Put you out of your misery."

Roth laughed darkly. "That a promise or a threat, angel?"

"Your choice."

Enough of this. I pushed the curtain aside and looked in at them. Roth had Cassandra pressed against the wall, his hand on her shoulder. Her eyes glowed blue in the darkness as she looked at me.

"Good." She shoved away from the demon. "This is over."

He grabbed her wrist to stop her. "It's not over till I say it is."

"Let go of her!" Everything about this demon set my teeth on edge. I didn't know why Cassandra didn't kick his butt like she'd done the other night. I knew she could flatten him without barely lifting a finger.

Roth gave me a dark look. "Mind your own business."

"I'm making this my business."

He actually laughed at this. "Isn't that sweet. The gray cares about you, angel." He tightened his grip on her wrist. "Are you two besties now?"

I didn't bother trying to reach for my new knife. Bishop was right; it was too hard to access under these jeans. Instead, I touched Roth's bare arm and bust through his mental barrier as easy as cracking an egg. He must have been distracted tonight. I only channeled a low-level zap into him, but it was enough to make him unhand Cassandra and stagger back a few feet until he hit the wall hard. He let out a satisfying grunt of pain.

My gaze shot to Cassandra. "You okay?"

She stared at me. "How did you do that?"

Oops. I really didn't like the look on her pretty face. Instead of being upset over her confrontation with the jerk of a demon, she regarded me with confusion…a look that began to shift to growing clarity. As if things were slowly clicking into place for her.

More dangerous clues to what I really was.

"Forget it." I swallowed hard, averting my gaze. "I have to find Bishop."

Without waiting another second, I pushed through the curtain and scanned the dark club. Memories of what I'd seen in his mind—when he'd killed Kraven—rushed back over me with the force of a tidal wave.

It was a long time ago, I reminded myself. *Whatever made him do that, he wasn't the same person as he is now.*

It had scared me to feel the cold inside of him, his apathy for the pain he'd caused someone he loved. For a moment, I'd reeled from that horrible truth, wanting to hide my head like an ostrich and forget I'd seen anything. But I couldn't. And I knew I had to learn more to make sense of it all.

That was what realists like me did with things they couldn't wrap their heads around. They gathered information and hoped it would all fit into tidy stacks, leading to firm and resolute answers. But this didn't. And I didn't think it ever would.

I knew Bishop hadn't forgotten. And I knew it ate away at him every time he saw Kraven now. With so much bad blood between them, I didn't know how they were able to work together at all.

Who was this horrible Kara person and what had she done to Bishop to change him so much?

I made it to the middle of the dance floor, searching for any sign of either the angel or the demon, when the sound of a blood-curdling scream cut past the loud music. I wrenched my head in the direction of the ear-splitting sound, but everyone around me began moving, rushing, pushing against each other to get to the stairs.

I grabbed a stranger's arm. "What happened?"

The man's eyes were wild with fear. "Somebody just got murdered."

He slipped away before I could get anything else from him.

Horror clawed at me, and I started to fight against the crowd to get back to the dance floor. "Bishop! Where are you?"

I saw the victim first. He lay in the middle of the now-cleared dance floor, on his back, his eyes glazed. A sparkling fall of lights from the ceiling brushed his pale skin. And the all-too-familiar black lines branched around his mouth.

"Oh, no," I whispered, clamping a hand over my mouth.

A gray's victim lay dead, having been drained of his soul. And it had happened right in the middle of a crowd.

I took another step closer, but a strong hand closed on my arm, stopping me from taking another step. I spun to look, ready to fight—but it was Bishop.

"Don't get any closer," he warned. "You don't want to be involved in this."

"I already am involved." I pulled away from him, stepping back a few feet so I could try to clear my head. Even now, even with this horrible sight in front of me, being close to Bishop was dangerous—as we'd proven without a doubt earlier.

I could still feel the brief kiss we'd shared, just before the memory meld had saved him from my rising hunger.

"I need to get you out of here." His expression was grim. "Are you coming or do you have a bizarre urge to talk to the police when they arrive?"

Smart-ass. "Fine. I'm coming." I couldn't turn my attention back to the dead man who'd come here tonight to dance and drink and have fun, only to meet someone who kissed him—that exhilarating magical dark kiss that stole his soul and his life.

Kraven met us at the stairway, downing the rest of his drink in one gulp before discarding his glass. "Long time no see, sweetness. Did you have fun tonight?"

I stared at him incredulously. "Someone just got killed! Don't you care?"

He flicked a glance toward the body as he began to ascend

the stairs behind me. "And how would my caring make any difference? Still happened. Dude's still dead."

"Why couldn't you stop it?" I demanded, turning to look at Bishop as we left the club to meet Cassandra and Roth outside.

"Keep walking," he said tightly.

I held my tongue until we got a block away and turned the corner where we were sheltered from the rest of the people who'd fled the nightclub. The sound of the approaching police and ambulance sirens made me shiver. I drew my coat closer, but it didn't help at all.

Cassandra stood nearby, scanning the area. Roth leaned against the wall. Kraven had his arms crossed, his expression uncharacteristically dour.

"Well?" My attention was fully fixed on Bishop. "There were four of you in that club. A club that you said yourself is a known hangout for grays. Couldn't you have stopped that? I thought angels and demons could sense grays."

His brows drew together and he regarded me for a moment without speaking. "I was focused on looking for one gray tonight. Stephen."

"In case you need a reminder," Roth growled. "You're *looking* at a gray. She could have killed that human herself."

I gaped at him. "Are you kidding?"

"Hardly."

"Or maybe Stephen did the deed himself," Kraven suggested. "Does he swing both ways when it comes to soul sucking?"

I sent a withering look in the demon's direction. "He didn't do it, either. It was somebody else."

"How do you know that for sure?" Bishop asked, watching me closely.

"Because I followed Stephen out of the club a half hour ago." I allowed that to register for him, and his blue eyes widened a fraction. "Yeah. I talked to him. Unfortunately, he didn't want to talk to me."

"And what happened?" Cassandra asked, drawing closer. "Did you get your soul back?"

"No." I fought to keep my voice from quaking. "He's not all that interested in helping me right now. He's going into stasis as we speak. He could be dead by morning and I have no idea where he went."

"Good riddance," Roth growled.

Bishop swore under his breath, and rubbed a hand over his forehead. "I didn't even see him."

"It's over." My chest felt so tight it was almost impossible to breathe.

"No, it's not. We'll keep looking. You, however—" Bishop raised his gaze to mine again "—are going home where it's safe."

"Safe?" I sputtered. "You want me to go home where it's *safe.*"

My frustration was mirrored on his face. "Did I stutter?"

"Uh-oh," Kraven muttered. "Trouble in paradise."

"I need to help." I couldn't just go home and do nothing. I couldn't be alone and let everything close in on me. I already felt claustrophobic enough as it was.

"You can help by letting us do our job," Bishop said firmly.

"Yeah, really stellar job so far." I glared at him. "Bravo."

His lips thinned. "I know you're frustrated. It hasn't been easy. But it's not going to get any easier if we don't find Stephen."

"He's long gone." That defeat I'd felt earlier that I'd been fighting hard against was rising up off the mats, ready for another round. "It's over. My soul is gone. I'm a gray and all I feel is hunger, Bishop. It's all I am now."

"It's not all you are." He drew closer to me.

Too close. I pressed my hands against his firm chest and he froze, looking down at where I touched him. But then I surprised him by shoving him backward. "Honestly. Just stay back, would you? Are you *trying* to make this more difficult?"

"I don't know," he growled, his gaze darkening. "Are you *trying* to be a bitch?"

That comment made me let out a half gasp, half laugh of shock.

The other three watched us with varying degrees of wariness and interest. I only saw them peripherally. My focus was entirely on the angel who was currently glowering at me.

"What did you see earlier? With me?" he asked, his voice low.

He was cheating by changing the subject on me. "It doesn't matter."

"The way you're looking at me right now makes me think it does matter. A lot."

"How am I looking at you?"

"Like you despise me."

"Am I?" I didn't despise Bishop, just the opposite. My feelings toward him were very confusing, true, but I didn't hate him. I didn't think I could ever hate him.

"Oh, please," Kraven said evenly, with an extra helping of sarcasm. "Share with the class. We're fascinated by everything you two do together. Good times."

"What did I see?" I repeated, still focused only on Bishop as if he might disappear the moment I took my attention off him, like Seth had. "Just a glimpse of your past. And let me tell you, it wasn't exactly a joyride."

"A glimpse of his past?" Cassandra asked, frowning. "How is that even possible?"

Bishop ignored her, his blue eyes fixed on mine. Something much less than sane slid through his gaze then. "You wanted to learn more about my past, Samantha. I guess you should be careful what you wish for."

"We're wasting time here," Roth said sharply.

"You're right," Bishop replied, tearing his gaze from mine. Finally, I could catch my breath. "Like I said before, go home, Samantha. Now. And let me get back to trying to save your damn life."

I actually flinched at that, his words as sharp as any blade. "Don't bother. I can look after myself. What happened here—" I thrust my chin back in the direction of the club "—shows you need to focus on your mission, not on me. There are other people at risk in this city. Actually, about a million of them. I don't want to be the one you blame for failing to save them."

His gaze returned to mine, now guarded. "That's not what I'm saying."

"No, but it's what *I'm* saying." I swallowed hard, ignoring the burning sensation moving swiftly from my throat to my eyes. "I get it, Bishop. I'm an ongoing problem you need to deal with. And part of you hates me for it."

His expression tightened. "It's been a long night. You're tired."

I let out a sharp laugh. "You're right, I am tired. Of all of this. I'm tired of caring what you think about me. I'm tired of my hunger and how it draws me to you. It's a problem for me, too, in case you didn't realize that. My life was a hell of a lot easier before you came into it."

Kraven and the others smartly chose not to be a continuing part of this conversation. They'd backed off, letting Bishop and me have this standoff all by ourselves.

"Is this you being honest with me again?" he asked. "While I hold back?"

"Yeah, what a shock." I crossed my arms tightly over my

chest. "But thanks to that memory meld, now I know why you're so secretive."

His teeth were clenched together, madness sparking in his gaze. This conversation was working to unhinge the shaky hold he had on his control. "What happened back then is none of your business. Not yours, not anybody's."

My ankle still hurt from being twisted earlier; I hadn't had a chance yet to ask Cassandra to heal it. But that was the last thing I cared about at the moment.

"You win. I'm leaving," I said softly. "But can you do me one favor, Bishop?"

He didn't reply for a moment. "Of course."

"Stay away from me."

Surprise slid through his eyes. "What?"

My stomach churned, but I knew I had to say this. Too much had happened tonight. That murder victim had been the final straw. Bishop spent too much time worrying about me, and not enough time keeping everyone else in this city safe. That had to end, and it had to end tonight.

"Being around your soul…" I pushed the words out. "It's too difficult. I don't like how I feel when I'm near you. So I want you to do what Cassandra suggested, what the others think you should do, and stay away from me. I want all of you—every one of this team—to stay away from me."

"Me, too? I'm staying at your house right now, remember?" Cassandra said uncertainly.

"Except for Cassandra," I amended, glancing in the blonde's direction. "But you need to give me my space, too. I'm not part of the team anymore."

"You never were," Roth grumbled.

Bishop just fixed me with a steady look, his face tense, his eyes glowing soft blue in the darkness surrounding us. "You're so damn stubborn."

I tore my gaze from his. "Just stay away from me, Bishop. Please."

He hissed out a breath. "If that's what you really want."

"More than anything."

I started walking away, my ankle crying out with pain with every step I took. I focused on that pain, welcoming it into my life so I wouldn't start to cry for real. Or turn around and tell him to forget everything I said, that it was a momentary burst of craziness that I already regretted.

It was the right thing to do. He had to regain his focus. The sooner he did, the sooner this mission would get back on track. And the sooner he could go back to Heaven and be cured.

I wanted to think it was the gray's dead victim that had inspired this decision, but it was something earlier. Before Stephen, before Seth. It was when Bishop had let me kiss him. How he hadn't fought it. He'd wanted it as much as I had.

I could have killed him tonight, without any resistance at all.

I cared about him too much to ever want to hurt him like that.

Instead, I'd hurt him in other ways if it would keep him away from me.

I'd gone a few blocks from Ambrosia toward the nearest bus stop before I realized somebody was following me.

My shoulders tensed, but I didn't have to turn around.

"Did he tell you to come with me?" I asked tightly.

"Uh-huh," Kraven said. "I'm just a humble foot soldier following orders."

I let out a groan of frustration. "Awesome. So he's already ignoring what I asked for."

"Your charming list of demands? Yeah, well, maybe this will be a onetime thing. Wouldn't want to cramp your new girl-power lifestyle choices."

"I can find my own way home."

I started to ignore him again, but just like last time, he followed me onto the bus when it arrived. He sat in front of me, leaning over the back of the seat to eye me curiously.

"So what's up?" he asked.

I tensed. "Are you trying to annoy me?"

"Is it working?"

"Yes."

"You're grumpy. Did somebody have a fight with her beloved tonight?" He rolled his eyes. "You two are way too intense, even apart from each other. Together, it's like…ugh. Spare me the drama."

I crossed my arms, refusing to rise to the demon's bait. "It's great how you can ignore death and mayhem so well."

"It's a gift."

I shifted my gaze to look directly at him. "One acquired before or after Bishop killed you?"

That wiped the grin off his face immediately. "You really know how to bring down a fun evening. Is that your special talent? Other than the mind reading and zapping?"

"You could tell me the truth about what happened."

His smile returned, only it was colder this time. It gave me the chills. "I could. But if there's one thing you should know about me, Samantha, it's that you should rarely trust anything I say."

Only at rare moments like this did I think I was chipping past the demon's thick armor and seeing the real James beneath it all. I found that oddly encouraging. "You called me Samantha."

He cocked his head. "It's your name, isn't it?"

"Yeah. But I usually get gray-girl or sweetness."

"Two adorable nicknames."

"Two sarcastic slurs."

"Potato, po-tah-to."

And just like that, his mask of smart-ass indifference was back up. I gripped the edge of my vinyl-covered seat as the bus turned a corner. My dagger pressed against my right leg, which only served to remind me of the night Bishop visited me in my bedroom, kneeling in front of me to help strap the sheath around my bare thigh.

"I honestly have no idea what to think about you, Kraven," I said, turning my gaze to the city streets speeding past us.

His grin widened. "Are you saying you think about me? Like...in the shower, maybe?"

I shot him a look. "You wish."

"Where's a genie when a guy needs one?"

I kept looking at him, trying to see past that mischievous sparkle in his eyes to the real Kraven underneath. "I'm sorry that happened to you. Really. I know how much you cared about him."

His expression froze and something raw and pained slid behind his amber-colored eyes. "Forget it. I have."

"Sure you have."

I'd succeeded in making the demon stop talking to me just when I *wanted* him to talk. But even I knew when to stop pushing.

The bus came to a stop and I got off, favoring my ankle. I wasn't an expert, but I didn't think I'd hurt it as badly as I'd initially thought. It already felt better than earlier.

It surprised me that Kraven continued to follow me. I thought I'd more than outstayed my welcome with him tonight.

"Ready to talk?" I asked without turning around to look him in the face.

"You know, maybe you should focus on the problems you

have right now rather than look to others' problems as a distraction. It won't fix what's broken."

He knew me a little too well. "Let me ask you a couple questions."

He caught up to me so we walked side by side. His expression was so serious that for a moment I could really see the resemblance between him and his brother in the line of their jaw, the shape of their eyes, and along their cheekbones. It wasn't always so obvious. "Why? Is it because you're madly in love with him and you want to find the answers to save him, body and soul?"

His words were like a punch to my gut, hearing them spilled so carelessly out in the open. "Don't be ridiculous."

"Or maybe you want to save me." His elusive smile returned. "Maybe ever since our little experiments started you can't get me off your mind and you're dying to kiss me again. You're all—Bishop's kind of cute for an emo angel boy, but that brother of his? *Way* hotter."

I glared at him. "Who's Kara?"

"Pass." He kept his eyes on the sidewalk in front of us. "Next?"

"I think she must have done some spell to make him go crazy."

He raked a hand through his hair. "Crazy. That's a good word."

"Was she a girlfriend?" I persisted, undeterred. "Yours or Bishop's? What happened to her?"

"Next question," he hissed out from between his teeth. "Or I'm leaving."

I deflated. I didn't doubt he'd just walk away. I'd tread on dangerous territory. But what wouldn't be dangerous territory when it came to him and Bishop?

"Is Kraven your last name?"

"Yes." He gave me an unpleasant grin. "See? That one wasn't so tough."

"You said once that you and Bishop had different fathers, which is why you have different coloring. Who was your father?"

He was silent for a few heavy moments. "A man who had a great deal of money, but wasn't interested in claiming a bastard as his son. I took his last name anyway just to piss him off." His lips curved to one side and there was a dim red glow to his eyes now, betraying his fluctuating emotions. "Believe me? Or do you think I'm lying? Do you think this is some sort of interesting puzzle? That solving it will help everything make sense? You'd be wrong."

He was right about one thing. Focusing on his past helped me forget my own present, if only for a few minutes. "I'm not wrong."

My house was at the end of the block. I was limping now and he noticed, not that he said anything or offered to slow down.

"My turn," he said. "I have a couple questions for you now."

I kept my focus on my driveway. My mother's car was parked there, giving the illusion that someone was home. I'd left a light on in the living-room window. No one would guess the house was completely empty.

"You can ask," I said tightly. "I can't guarantee I'll be any more cooperative than you've been."

"Noted. Okay, so I've been thinking a lot about your special skills, gray-girl. Blondie seems to think you have supernatural intuition."

My stomach started churning nervously. "I guess that's what I have."

"Yeah, but why? That's the question. What makes you so special?" When I didn't answer him, he leaned closer so he could whisper. "I was right, wasn't I? You *are* adopted. And I'm guessing your birth parents were a little…unusual. Maybe a true case of opposites attracting, if you know what I mean? And I think that you do."

I recoiled from him. "You're wrong."

He gave me a patient look. "Lying's an acquired talent. Takes years to master. I should know. Bishop knows the truth, doesn't he? It's one of your lovey-dovey secrets. Something I'm betting my bottom dollar that he told you not to reveal to any of the rest of us. Cue dramatic music."

I needed to stay calm and not give anything away. He was just fishing, looking for information. Trying to read my expression. Kraven, despite his troubled past, was a demon. A troublemaker. He wanted to make this difficult for me. It was in his nature.

"Whatever, Kraven," I said smoothly. We'd reached my house and I didn't hesitate to go up the driveway. I stopped at the front door before I braved another look at him. "You seem to know everything, don't you?"

"Unfortunately not. But I know enough. I've seen enough." He swept his gaze down the front of me. "All that supernatural energy in such a petite body. You'd think it might burst right out of the seams."

He knew. Without even saying the exact words, without any confirmation from me, he'd figured out my secret. Bishop had put such fear into me about anyone finding out. I was frozen to the spot, unable to move.

I turned away from him to face my front door, trying to figure out a way to fish into my jeans and pull out my dagger. I reached for the waistband.

He grabbed my wrist. "You don't have to be afraid of me. And you don't have to make a pathetic attempt to reach for your little weapon. I mean, let's not get insulting here."

"I can zap you even without a weapon," I said through clenched teeth.

"You can try. But it would be a waste of time. I'm not planning on telling anyone your little secret, if that's what you're afraid of."

I turned to face him. "Maybe I don't trust you."

"Smart girl. And you're smart not to trust my brother, either. If you're not careful, he might put a knife in your back like he did with me."

He let go of me, and walked away without a backward glance. I watched until he'd disappeared into the shadows before I scrambled for my key and let myself into the house.

The demon knew my secret.

And the scariest thing was, at this very moment, that was the least of my problems.

chapter 18

Cassandra knocked quietly on my bedroom door at one o'clock when she got back to the house. "Samantha, are you still awake?"

I pulled my sheets up to my neck and tried to be quiet.

Go away, I thought. *I don't want to talk to you. I don't want to talk to anyone.*

After a minute, my ruse worked. I listened as she padded down the hall toward the guest room.

I wasn't a huge fan of hiding from the world and my problems, but tonight I would do just that.

Sleep was elusive, as it usually was lately. I drifted from one nightmare to the next, tossing and turning until I finally woke up just before six o'clock, twisted in my sheets so much it took effort to unravel myself.

I didn't try to sleep again. Instead, I got up, showered and got dressed.

I choked down a large breakfast in the hope that it would ease my hunger this morning. I didn't know how it was possible, but I was *more* hungry after I'd finished than I'd been to start with.

Increased hunger. Increased cold.

Both signs of oncoming stasis.

I wanted to hate Stephen, figuring somehow that might make everything easier, but the fear I'd seen in his eyes last night had quickly worked its way under my skin. I wished he would have let me try to help him. Instead, he'd run in the opposite direction as fast as he could.

We all choose our path to walk. Even by not choosing, we're still making a choice that will affect our lives for better or worse.

I left the house before Cassandra got up, hoping to avoid any discussions with the angel that might involve what happened last night and the topic of Bishop—because thinking about *him* right now wasn't going to help.

It was still bright and early when I got to school—my sanctuary. The place where I felt the most in control of my life. I might not be the most popular kid, not even close, but I knew what to expect. I got good grades, my teachers liked me; I felt like I belonged. Just the sight of the lockers, shiny linoleum floors and the faint hum of the fluorescent lights gave me a welcome sense of calm. At least, a small piece of it.

I stared at Carly's abandoned locker for a full minute before opening my own next to it.

"Why do you always worry so much?" she'd say when I was down or overwhelmed about something. Pick a topic, there was always something on my mind causing me angst. *"Worrying doesn't change anything. And it's a complete waste of energy."*

"Plus, it causes wrinkles," I'd add drily.

"Exactly!"

Don't worry, be happy. Yeah, easier said than done.

I slid down to the ground, pulling my legs in to hug them to my chest. Today I wore black opaque tights and a skirt that fell to my knees. Much easier access to the dagger if I needed it. I touched the reassuring outline of the gold knife through the garment. Just to be annoying, my mind immediately delivered an image of Bishop kneeling in front of me, his warm hands brushing against my skin.

I squeezed my eyes shut, tried to breathe normally and attempted to focus on what I was going to do next. Thinking about Bishop was a distraction, even on good days, and right now I didn't need to be more distracted than I already was. I told him I'd find the answers on my own. I'd meant it.

Last night, however, I'd been way more confident. Today... well, today just seemed hopeless.

Then again, Tuesdays had never been my favorite day of the week.

Someone nearby made a sound of disgust, an "ugh" that made me crack one eye open to see who was at school as early as I was.

Jordan stood in front of me with her arms crossed over her chest.

"What are you doing here?" she demanded.

"Free country, last time I checked. You?"

"I have stuff to do."

I couldn't help notice the dark circles around her eyes. Since I was certain they were from sleepless nights thinking about Julie's suicide, I chose not to mention them. I didn't like Jordan, but I wasn't that cruel.

"Stuff to do at seven in the morning?" I asked.

"I wanted to get an assignment done early."

"Good for you. Don't let me stop you."

Jordan rummaged through her purse and something fell and hit my leg. I reached for the business card and pack of gum.

"Give that to me." She thrust her hand out to me impatiently.

It was the card to the modeling agency—the one the scout had given to Julie. "Why do you still have this?"

She snatched it away from me. "Because I'm going there. I just need to drop my assignment off at first period, then I'm out of here. I'm going to find out if I'm right—that there was something strange about that woman."

I pushed myself up to my feet and looked at her warily. "Not a good idea."

Her expression only became more determined. "There's something strange going on in Trinity."

She worried me when she said stuff like this. Knowledge was power—but it could also be dangerous. And in some cases, deadly. "It's a big city. There's always strange stuff going on."

"Stranger than normal." She let out a shaky sigh and rubbed her eyes, which made me realize she wasn't wearing any makeup today. Not a stitch. For an aspiring model who prized her beauty more than her brains, this was more surprising than anything else. "It's like…I don't know, it's like I'm the only one who can see it. Everyone else goes about their days normally, like they don't realize there's something horribly wrong. But I see it. I *feel* it. And what happened to Julie, it—it just made everything more real. I can't ignore it anymore. I need to figure out the truth."

What Seth was rambling about last night, about the girl who fell—I was sure he meant Julie. But then he confused me, as he tended to do, and I'd mostly forgotten it. But still, why would he mention her if there wasn't something truly wrong about her death?

"I know you're in pain," I said evenly. "But you should calm down."

"I'm not going to calm down. Julie… She wasn't suicidal. Not at all. I keep going over and over and over it in my head. She was fine. And then something changed." Her face was etched in confusion and despair as her green eyes tracked to me. "Do you know there've been twenty suicides in less than a week? And none of them were clinically depressed."

My chest clenched at the news. "How do you know this?"

"When I want to find things out, I find things out. Nothing stops me. I talked to the police—I told them about Eva, but they don't think it's anything worth investigating." She let out a strangled cry of frustration. "So annoying! They think Julie was some kid depressed over a guy who decided she was finished living. But it's not true. I lost her. And I—I lost Stephen. I'm losing everyone I love."

Hearing her pain so acutely, with no filters, made my own heart start to ache. And she didn't even know the truth about Stephen. To her, he was just a jerk who'd dumped her with no explanation, not a guy who'd broken up with her to try to save her life. "I'm so sorry. Really. Maybe you should see the guidance counselor again. She might be able to help you."

She composed herself, rubbing her eyes, and stroking her red hair back from her face to tuck it behind her ears. "I don't need help. I need answers."

We had that much in common. The sheer determination I saw on her face worked to nudge mine back into consciousness this morning, like downing three espressos in a row.

But I worried that she was chasing her tail, and all she'd get from her frenzied search for the truth was more disappointment. "You honestly think that modeling scout did something to Julie? Like...she took away her will to live? With, like, a single touch?"

"Yeah." Jordan fixed me with a bleak, scared look that betrayed her usual calm, cool bitchiness. "That's exactly what I think she did."

Then she was gone.

I watched her walk away, part of me wanting to stop her.

If I tried, I knew I'd fail. She was bound and determined to play Nancy Drew over this mystery.

If Julie had been kissed by a gray, then I might be able to wrap my head around an outside influence changing her personality. But it wouldn't have happened that fast.

Jordan had her own path to follow, and nothing I said would have stopped her.

Part of me wanted to worry about her—the other part knew I had enough to deal with without adding this to my list. What I really needed was to find balance in my life again, even if it was only for a few hours of school. Here I was normal. Out there…I wasn't.

Bishop always talked about balance and how important it was to the universe. Well, the balance of me being a perfect student with me being the daughter of a demon and an angel, as well as a gray with the dark hunger I dealt with daily…

Yeah. I desperately needed to restore my balance. Maybe then I could figure everything else out.

Over the next two hours, the halls slowly began to fill with kids, moving to their lockers, heading for first period. Outside my English class, Kelly caught up with me, grabbing my arm before I went into the room.

"You going to Noah's party tomorrow night?" she asked, her face flushed. She was rarely early for any class, and I knew she always peeled into the parking lot with literally minutes to spare.

"Oh, right. The Halloween thing at his house?" I asked.

She nodded excitedly. "But it's not at his house anymore. He's found an even better place for it. It's going to be amazing."

"Sounds…amazing," I forced out.

"I'll email you the deets when I get them. There's literally going to be, like, two hundred people there. I'm going as

Aphrodite. Sabrina's going as a witch, which is so expected, really." She rolled her eyes, but her smile didn't fade. "You should be a cat. Like, a sexy cat."

A sexy cat. Right. Kelly knew me so well. "Great. I'll, um, think about it. Okay?"

Halloween costumes and parties...not on my priority list this week.

Kelly sped away down the hall toward her Trig class, and I entered my English class. My eyes were drawn immediately to Colin, slouched in his seat behind my desk. I approached cautiously, trying as hard as I could to ignore the hunger that grew with each step. I clutched my books and binder tight to my chest.

He looked upset, pale. I hoped he wasn't still blaming himself for Julie's suicide. He'd made some dumb choices, but he hadn't been the one to push her. She'd jumped of her own free will.

At least, I thought she had. Jordan had other ideas about that.

Jordan was right about one very important thing—there were weird things going on in Trinity right now. That was the reason Bishop and the others had been sent here in the first place. And it only made me more certain that getting him to focus on that instead of me had been the right decision. They didn't need or want my help—unless I spotted another searchlight. If that happened, I'd let them know immediately. Beyond that? I needed to stay out of their hair.

And that was exactly what I would do. Here in class.

"You okay?" I couldn't help but ask, glancing over my shoulder at Colin when I sat down.

"Never better," he replied through clenched teeth.

"Somehow I just don't believe you."

His eyes were narrowed, mean. "Oh, Sam. You always could read me like a book. You're so awesome."

"Whatever." I turned back around, my heart sinking. So I guess he'd decided to start hating me again.

It should make me happy that he'd finally learned his lesson. Stay away from Samantha Day. Still, his unexpected sarcasm felt like a slap.

He groaned a few moments later. "I'm sorry. I'm having a lousy day, okay?"

"Yeah, okay. Like I said, whatever."

I didn't want him to change his mind. I wanted him to hate me. That would make everything much easier.

Mr. Saunders walked into class right on time and glanced at the thirty students. He pushed his glasses up on his nose. "I finished grading your tests from yesterday. Congrats to those with the highest scores. For the rest of you…well, better luck next time."

Right. Our test on *Catcher in the Rye*. Part of me relaxed at hearing he'd been grading. Grades. School. And especially English, my favorite subject. They calmed me. I read everything I could get my hands on—novels, new and old, trashy and high literature. I devoured words like I devoured…

Well, not a good comparison, really.

But I loved to read. I loved how authors put words together on the page to invoke images and feelings. While I hadn't totally decided what I wanted to major in once I got to university—and I still hadn't given up hope of this possibility, no matter how bleak things got—I felt strongly that I wanted to be a writer of some kind. I'd always journaled. I'd always written short stories and poems to entertain myself.

They say to do what you love and you'll never work a day in your life.

For me, English Lit was what I loved. By far, my best subject in school.

"Ms. Day?" Mr. Saunders called my name and I rose from my desk to go to the front to claim my test. He held it out to me. "Have to say, I was disappointed."

I looked down at it.

A bright red "F" stared back at me.

There wasn't even a plus sign involved.

There had to be a mistake. "I got a—an F?"

"Maybe next time you should read your assignment. Just a suggestion." He looked past me. "Mr. Edwards?"

With that, I was dismissed. With the first F I'd ever gotten in my life. For an essay on a book I'd already read. And loved.

This couldn't be happening. I tried to rationalize it, but failed.

Yeah, failed. I failed. Big time.

I sat down heavily in my seat, still staring at the mark.

"It's only one stupid test," Colin offered from behind me. Of course he'd seen the grade. It was impossible to miss. An airplane would be able to spot an F that big and red.

But it wasn't just a test, it was a sign. The balance I'd hoped to regain by coming to school today, to get back to where I belonged and felt like I fit in…

Fail.

I tried to concentrate, but it wasn't an easy task. With Colin behind me, almost in the orbit of hunger. With others moving past my desk. With the bitter taste of the bad grade in my mouth…it all fell apart.

At nine forty-five, my hunger ramped up from a low and controllable level to a burst right off the charts.

It closed in all around me, stealing my breath, clenching my stomach.

It was no longer a question of "if" I'd feed, but "when."

I needed to get out of there as fast as I could.

Scrambling to grab my books and my leather bag, I rushed out of my seat toward the front of class, toward the door, toward escape.

"Ms. Day?" Mr. Saunders looked at me as I zipped past him. "Where are you going? There's still fifteen minutes left in class."

"Cramps!" I announced shakily. "Horrible, nasty menstrual cramps! I need to go!"

He grimaced and waved a hand, while some of the kids in the front row snickered. "Then go."

I escaped to the bliss of the empty hallway, headed toward my locker, no longer tormented by the thirty souls pressing in on me. I needed a few minutes to get my head back together. To think clearly again.

"Samantha!" Colin called after me.

Oh, crap!

I searched the long hallway, looking for the best route to make my escape. My heels clicked against the shiny linoleum. I needed air. I needed to get out of there completely. I needed to finally accept that my life was not what it used to be while I tried to pretend that it was, even for a couple of fleeting hours here today.

I'd been fooling myself.

I didn't belong here in my so-called "normal" life. And I didn't belong with Bishop and the others.

I was an outcast.

I wiped the tears from my eyes and kept walking toward the nearest exit.

"Sam!" Colin grabbed my arm to bring me to a halt. "What's wrong?"

I turned to face him and shoved him hard against his chest to push him away from me. "Stay back."

He had the nerve to look at me with concern. And here I thought he hated me. I wished that were true. "The look on your face when you left class… I was worried."

"I have cramps," I offered weakly.

"Which is really gross, but I don't think it's the truth. You're upset about something."

I hissed out a breath, studying his face as he, again, was stupid enough to come closer to me. My hunger swirled, a raging tornado inside of me ready to take down trailer parks and wreak havoc with anything that got in its path.

"You hate me," I reminded him. "I hurt you."

"What happened to Julie made me realize something—life is too short. I can't hold a grudge. I know you don't like me, not like I like you. But we're friends, still, right? You're my friend no matter what happens."

"You followed me from class. You always do that."

"I wanted to make sure you're okay." His breathing had increased. He'd taken hold of my arm again. Despite his words of understanding, there was something in his gaze…something lost.

I knew what it was. A gray's victim sought the gray who'd kissed him. It was an unavoidable trap. Even my harshest, coldest words wouldn't be enough to keep him away from me forever.

I looked down at where he clutched my arm. "When will you ever learn, Colin?"

"I know you don't mean to hurt me. Just like with Julie— I didn't mean to hurt her."

His scent was too much to bear. I couldn't deal with this. I needed to go.

"Colin…"

He took hold of my other arm. "Just give me a chance, Sam.

One chance. I think I'll go crazy if you never kiss me again. Please. Just once. One kiss."

"Fine," I whispered.

Then I pushed him up against the lockers and crushed my mouth against his.

chapter 19

I'd lost the fight a minute ago, but hadn't realized it till now.

No, that was wrong. What was I saying? I felt it. I knew this was coming from the moment he followed me out of class. He asked for this. He wanted it. Even now he groaned against my lips as I began to feed on his soul.

As I kissed Colin, all I thought of was Bishop. It was his kiss I craved more than anyone else's. The only one I dreamed about, fantasized about, wished for, hoped for. Bishop's mouth against mine—after he whispered that he loved me, despite our problems, despite everything that threatened to keep us apart.

He was an angel of death and had been for a long time. He only looked eighteen, but he'd existed for much longer than that. How could I ever think I could be something more to him than a problem to solve, or an inconvenient addiction?

I didn't think. I'd hoped.

And I'd lied shamelessly last night. I didn't want to stay away from him. No matter what—

Snap!

The entire team was gathered in the church.

"It's a problem," Connor said. "I've been looking into it and I'm sure this is it. All the recent suicides—they're connected. There's a

demon loose in the city, one who escaped the Hollow. Like the Source of the grays fed on souls, this demon feeds on hope and happiness and the will to live. It drives these kids to kill themselves."

"You're sure about this?" Cassie asked, her beautiful face tense as she listened to Connor's speech.

He shook his head. "Hell, no. I'm not sure about anything anymore." Connor usually had a quip or a joke for anything, but today he looked pained. Concerned. "But I think I'm right. The suicide rate in Trinity has skyrocketed over the past week. This demon is getting hungrier and it needs more and more to sustain it."

"Then we need to find it." Bishop rubbed his forehead. "Damn. My head—it's killing me."

"You okay?" Cassandra asked.

"Trying my best."

"Who cares?" Kraven mumbled. He leaned against a nearby pew next to Roth, his arms crossed over his chest.

"You're working too hard," Cassandra said, ignoring the demon. "Did you get any sleep after staying out all night looking for that gray?"

"I got enough."

"I doubt that. Not if you're feeling this way. I know you're having trouble concentrating." Her expression hardened. "And would you stop doing this?" She pressed her hand against his torso. He flinched.

"It's none of your business what I do."

"It is my business. Show me. All the way this time."

He looked at her for a moment without making any moves. Then he peeled his shirt off completely over his head.

"Where are my five dollar bills when I need them?" Kraven said drily. "Just do me a favor and leave the pants on, okay?"

Roth said nothing, but gave Bishop a dark look. Something in the demon's eyes went beyond regular distaste.

Bishop looked down at himself and the deep cut bisecting his abdomen. "It's the only way I can keep my mind clear."

"You could get Samantha to help you," Cassandra said, her brows drawn together.

Bishop shook his head. "She made it clear. She doesn't want to see me again. And it's for the best."

Snap!

I hadn't stopped kissing Colin, but the jarring mind meld had managed to give me back a fraction of my normal clarity. I tasted his soul as I devoured it, saw it in my mind—a ghostly shimmering ribbon—little by little, leaving him and entering me. Feeding me. I'd nearly taken all of it when I managed to push back against him and break off the kiss.

He slid to the ground. I hadn't taken it all. Not all.

But I'd taken most of it.

I stared down at him with horror. Black lines branched around his mouth and he looked dazed and pale. He made a sickly wheezing sound as he gathered his breath. Immediately, I wanted to go back for more and it was by sheer will alone that I stopped myself.

The lines faded and he pushed at the floor, trying but failing to stand. "What happened?" He looked up at me. "Sam, why do you look so upset?"

"Are you okay?" I choked out, tears streaming down my cheeks.

"I think so. A little dizzy, but otherwise…"

"I'm sorry."

"For kissing me?" A small smile appeared on his lips. "No reason to apologize for that. It was amazing."

I just shook my head, wiping at my tears. He seemed okay, now after two kisses. Did a soul grow back or could someone survive indefinitely with less than a whole soul inside them?

"I need to go."

"Where are you going?"

"Away. Now."

"I'll come with you." He looked so lost, so alone—like he had nobody. My heart wrenched, but it didn't change anything. I needed to put distance between us, for his own good.

"No, just…no, Colin." I ran away from him straight to my locker where I dropped off my books and grabbed my coat. I left right after that, bursting out into the morning air. I was going to miss the rest of my classes. At that moment, I didn't care.

I'd lost it. And the worst thing this time—or *competing* for worst thing—was that my hunger hadn't been sated even a bit. I wanted more. Something was changing inside me, making this even worse than it had been before. Before I could control myself, unless I was in extreme conditions. But now…my control was slipping away at breakneck speeds.

If it hadn't been for that mind meld, I would have taken it all. And that would have either changed Colin into another gray…or it would have killed him.

I ran away from the school for a half mile before I finally stopped, bracing my hands on my thighs, and took deep choking breaths of cold air.

I'd told Bishop to leave me alone. Nobody had been watching me, lurking in the shadows. Nobody was here to stop me. They were all at the church, dealing with other problems.

I'd never felt so alone in my entire life.

But I couldn't go home, which was exactly where I wanted to go.

After what I'd heard in that mind meld, I knew I had to go downtown. I had to find Jordan. She'd left school to find the model scout who'd touched Julie, inspecting her as a potential model. After that, Julie's mood had plummeted. Jordan thought that the woman had something to do with that— that her touch had messed up Julie's mind and driven her to kill herself.

Eva might be an anomalous demon who'd escaped from the Hollow—just as Natalie had. Instead of souls, she fed on good emotions, leaving only the bad ones behind. All the suicides in the last week could be because of her.

And Jordan was going to confront her.

I had to do something. I couldn't stand back and let her get hurt.

I checked the phone book to find Divine Model Management. Then I hopped on a bus to get downtown as fast as possible. I entered the building, scanning the area for any sign of Jordan, but she wasn't there.

The agency's office was on the fifth floor. I considered leaving, going to the church and trying to find Bishop to tell him, despite my harsh words—and his—last night. This wasn't personal. This was business. And I knew he could do something about it. Beyond that, I missed him more than I thought possible. Seeing through his eyes in the mind meld only made that fact impossible for me to ignore.

However, Jordan didn't have that kind of time. I had to do this on my own.

I took the elevator up to the fifth floor. The agency was large, with dark hardwood floors, lots of glass and silver. The logo was on the wall in large, shiny letters.

"Yes?" The receptionist greeted me from behind the tall, red desk.

"I'm looking for…" I scanned the waiting room, but nobody was here except for me. "Eva?"

"What's your business with her?"

I scanned my mind for a lie good enough to get me past this gatekeeper. "She gave me her card at the mall, told me to stop by."

The receptionist's gaze moved over me skeptically. I did my best not to look guilty or like I was a big liar.

"For our petite division?" she asked.

I could pretend to be an aspiring model. Sure, I could. "Um, yeah."

She still didn't look all that convinced. But she picked up the phone and pecked in a couple numbers. "Eva? There's a…" She looked at me. "Name?"

"Samantha Day."

"There's a Samantha Day here to see you. Says you gave her your card?" There was a pause, and the receptionist looked at me. "She doesn't remember you, but she says to go on in. Third office to your left."

My mouth went dry. "Okay, thanks."

I walked down the hall nervously. I had to remember that I wasn't helpless here. I was a nexus, and if she was a demon then I could deal with her. I'd read her mind to get the truth. I could defend myself with my zapping ability. And the skirt made accessing my new knife a lot easier. I slid my hand over its reassuring shape.

I stopped at the door, which opened in front of me. The woman I'd seen at the mall gave me a once-over. She was definitely middle-aged, with auburn hair, paler highlights and, although I was no expert on the subject, she wore a designer suit that easily could have been featured in a Vogue spread.

"I didn't give you a card," she said. "I remember everyone."

"Where's Jordan?" I asked, my throat tight. I wasn't playing this game any longer than I had to.

She frowned. "Jordan?"

"Jordan Fitzpatrick. Redhead. Way taller than me." Although that might not help pinpoint someone in a place like this. "Was she here earlier?"

"Oh, right. Jordan." She shook her head. "I was very sorry to hear what happened to her friend. Your friend, too, right? Such a shame."

wicked kiss

"Was Jordan here?" I asked again, firmer. I swept my gaze over her from head to foot. It was so hard to tell if she was a demon. I couldn't exactly ask her to lift up her blouse so I could see her imprint. And she wasn't making direct eye contact with me.

She patted her hair in its perfect chignon. "She stopped by earlier, but she's gone. Wanted to ask me a couple questions. Seemed so upset. Poor kid. I tried to help, but I couldn't do much, I'm afraid. Look, Samantha, I'm very busy. I'm about to head out to do a sweep for new talent. We're looking for girls for a last-minute show at the Trinity Mall this weekend. It could be a onetime thing for you to try it out."

"Modeling?" I eyed her warily.

She looked at me curiously. "Well, of course. This *is* a modeling agency."

"I'm not a model." Last time I checked, super short and lacking model looks seemed to be a big deterrent in that particular industry.

Her curious expression turned confused. "Then what are you doing here?"

"Looking for Jordan."

"Right. Well, she's gone. I figure she'd headed to school."

I moved a little so I could look into her eyes. Deep into them. And I accessed that part of me that allowed me to read the minds of demons. It was part of what made me dangerous as a nexus—the unspoken truths of a demon…or an angel… could be used against them. The secrets of Heaven and Hell lay just behind their gazes. That was what I'd use to find out who she was, what she wanted and what had really happened with Jordan.

However, there was one problem.

I couldn't read her mind.

225

And there was no wall there to stop me. There was just…
nothing.

She wasn't a demon. She was human.

A man walked down the hall.

"Joe," she called to him, moving to the doorway. "Listen,
it was a great breakfast meeting. Let's do it again soon, okay?"

"Sure thing, Eva." He grasped her hand and shook it firmly.

She didn't devour his emotions, leaving him a suicidal
wreck. Of course not. This woman was one hundred percent human.

Jordan was wrong. She must have figured that out herself
and headed back to school.

I let out a huge, shaky sigh as relief washed over me.

"I have to go," I said.

"What about the show?" Eva asked.

"I'm not interested, sorry." I escaped from Divine Model
Management as fast as I could. My heart pounded hard, but
my previous anxiety lifted. I'd honestly thought something
bad had happened to Jordan on her search for the truth.

While she wouldn't have gotten the answer she needed, my
nemesis would still be breathing. Who knew I was so concerned with her well-being?

With a lighter heart and renewed optimism that this was a
sign of better things to come, I headed to the bus stop, turning at the corner up ahead.

"Samantha," a familiar voice greeted me.

My breath caught and I pivoted to see Stephen standing
there, as if waiting for me.

"You…" I managed, shocked. Seeing him gave me a rush
of conflicting emotions—happiness that he was still alive, and
wariness…that he was still alive. He'd been so sure last night
had been it for him, that he'd been going into stasis, that he'd

convinced me, too. "You're okay. I thought last night… I—I thought I'd never see you again."

"Yet, here I am." He drew closer. He wore a knee-length black wool coat that matched the color of his hair. His cinnamon-colored eyes scanned the street before they fell on me. A few cars went by. "I have something for you. Something you need. And it's time I gave it to you."

My soul. He had my soul and he was finally going to give it back to me!

"Thank you, Stephen," I said, my throat tight. "Where is it?"

"This way." He nodded to a car around the corner, parked at the side of the curb.

I followed him, still wary, but hopeful. He opened the passenger-side door and pulled out a wrapped cloth. I drew closer to see, my heart pounding.

"Is that my soul?" I whispered.

He unfolded it and I waited to see what was inside, but it was only a cloth. And it smelled strange.

I frowned. "What is that?"

"Like I said, it's something you need." Then he grabbed me, his arm an iron vice across my chest.

I fought back immediately, shrieking as he pressed the cloth over my mouth and nose. I scrambled under the edge of my skirt to grab the dagger and pull it free from its sheath, and then tried to stab Stephen with it. He caught my wrist before I could make contact. His grip tightened until a lightning bolt of pain wrenched through my wrist and I heard a sharp crack. My cry of pain and fear was muffled by the cloth, and the dagger clattered to the pavement.

He was strong—so strong. He'd broken my wrist like it was nothing more than a twig.

Michelle Rowen

All I smelled were harsh chemicals. I kept fighting against him for a few moments longer before darkness welled up all around me, dragging me down, down, down…

chapter 20

Chloroform.

I was sure that's what Stephen had on the cloth. I'd only seen it in movies before. Now I'd experienced it in full Technicolor unconsciousness.

I wasn't sure how long it was until I started waking up. As soon as awareness began swirling around me and I peeled my eyelids open a little, the cloth was at my mouth again. I barely had a chance to struggle or summon a scream before darkness welled up.

This happened twice more before I finally came to full consciousness. My head ached. The world around me was blurry. My chest hurt when I inhaled raggedly and hoarsely, followed by a dry, wheezing cough. My broken wrist throbbed.

I lay on a hard floor in a small, dark room—small enough that my claustrophobia kicked in immediately and my heart began to race. There was a tiny window near the high ceiling that let in enough light to tell me it was late afternoon. I tried to breathe, in and out, and may have let out a small moan.

Apart from my headache and wrist, the next pain I felt was sheer, unadulterated hunger.

"Finally. Thought you were never going to wake up."

I blinked several times until I finally shifted my gaze in the direction of the voice—also the source of my current hunger.

Jordan was crouched next to me.

"Get back," I croaked out.

She shifted backward to give me some space. It helped a little.

"Where are we?" I managed. "What are you doing here?"

Her expression was pinched as she looked around. "Where we are? No idea. Some room with a locked door. What am I doing here? I'm guessing it's the same reason as you. You didn't come here of your own free will." A bit of her bravado slipped away and I could see the fear in her green eyes. "I thought you were dead."

I rubbed my head with my good hand. "And you're disappointed that I'm not?"

"Don't be stupid. Of course not. I don't like you, Samantha, but I didn't want you to die. There's been enough death this week." Her voice quavered. "What the hell is going on?"

The room was no more than ten square feet. I hated being in enclosed spaces so much. It made me feel trapped. Now I was *literally* trapped. "How long was I out?"

"A day and a half."

I forced myself to sit up. "A day and a half?"

"It was yesterday morning when I was brought here. You were brought in an hour later. And then...all afternoon. Night. Day again...it feels like forever. He threw in a water bottle and a couple energy bars. I saved one for you."

I sat up completely. My head throbbed with the effort and I brought my knees up in front of me, hugging them to my chest as I tried to sort things through. I pressed my right hand against my chest. My wrist was definitely broken.

Panic and anger swirled inside me at the thought that Stephen had kept me unconscious for a day and a half.

Locked in a basement with Jordan.

I looked at her. "We need to get out of here."

"Gee, what a fantastic idea. I hadn't considered that before." Her sarcasm dripped. "The door's locked. And it's made of metal. There's no way out. I already broke three nails trying."

"What about that window?" I looked up at it.

"Do you have a secret identity as Spider-Man I'm not aware of? Besides, you're small, but that window is still way too tiny to squeeze through."

I struggled to get to my feet. Jordan tried to help me but I flinched away from her.

"What is wrong with you?" she snapped.

My stomach clenched as I tried to get control of myself. It took a second. "Trust me, you don't want to get too close to me right now."

"You are so weird."

"Yeah, I'm weird. But take my word for it, okay? Stay back." I got to my feet on my own and turned in a circle. It looked like a storage room, cleared of any storage so the room was completely empty. Just white walls. Ceiling-set lights. That small window. Two trapped girls. "Do you have a cell phone?"

"Oh, my God!" she exclaimed. "My cell phone! I could just call someone for help." She glared. "He took it away from me, of course. First thing he did."

I scowled at her. "You're not helping."

"Why is Stephen doing this?" Her earlier smart-ass tone had been replaced by raw pain and confusion. "Why would he do this to me?"

"Maybe you should have left him alone."

"Nice. And let you have him?"

A cold line of perspiration slid down my back. Being in this tight spot with no idea how to escape was starting to freak me out. "Believe me, I don't want him. There's only one thing I want from Stephen and it's definitely not his body."

Jordan's bottom lip wobbled. "He's a monster."

"Did he kiss you?" I asked with alarm when the thought occurred to me. At her look of confusion, it took all I had in me not to reach forward and shake her. "Did he?"

Her eyes sparked with fury. "No. He was too busy knocking me unconscious to do any making out. Not that I'd ever kiss him again after what he's done to me. Bastard."

"Good."

"Oh, I see. You're the only girl that psycho can kiss now. Is that it?"

"Save your jealousy, Jordan. It's not helpful right now." I went to the door, pressing my left hand flat against its smooth, cool surface. There was no handle or lock on this side, only flat metal.

Then I started to pound on it. "Stephen! Let us out of here!"

Jordan grabbed my shoulder. "What are you doing?"

I literally shoved her away from me. Her soul was like a tempting second skin she wore, and the last damn thing I wanted to do right now was lose what little control I had left and attack her. "What did I tell you about not getting close to me?"

She frowned deeply. "Stephen said the same thing to me when he brought me in here."

"He did?"

"Yeah. I figured he just doesn't like me anymore."

"I think he might like you *too* much," I mumbled. Then I pounded on the door again until my left fist hurt. It was a very sharp reminder that my nexus abilities did not extend themselves to super strength, at least, not when a demon or an angel wasn't involved. No, a big metal door was more than enough to keep me trapped. And my only ability as a gray was my current and growing need to devour Jordan's soul.

It was my worst fear come to life. No way to escape my hunger. What happened with Colin would only be foreshadowing if I didn't find a way out of this room.

"Stephen's one of them," Jordan whispered.

She wrung her hands anxiously. "The ones who hurt people, who can absorb their energy somehow. It weakens them—can kill them. The murders in the paper, the ones where the victims have no sign of trauma, only those strange lines around their mouths. The police don't know why, but I do. I saw it before, and Stephen's one of them. He's got us in here and he's going to kill us."

I looked at her, stunned that she figured it out—even if she had no idea what she'd figured out. "I don't think his plan is nearly as simple as killing us."

"You're not looking at me like I'm crazy. Why aren't you freaking out?"

My heart was going a thousand beats a minute, but I was doing everything I could not to let it show on the surface. "I am freaking out, believe me."

"I checked out the modeling agency. But—but that woman…"

"She wasn't the reason why Julie killed herself," I finished. "I know. I checked her out, too."

She looked shocked. "You did?"

"Yeah."

"Why?"

"I was trying to make sure you didn't get yourself killed."

The mix of surprise and gratitude in her eyes both froze off quickly. "That wasn't smart. Since now we're going to die, anyway."

"Yeah, well, you're welcome. And we're not going to die.

Stephen, he…he has another reason for keeping us here. And I think we're going to find out what it is very soon." There was the sound of a lock turning and the door began to creak open. My mouth went dry with fear. "Like…right now."

I staggered back from the door and, for the first time since I came to, felt for the knife at my thigh. Only the leather sheath remained.

"Asshole," I muttered. He'd broken my wrist when I pulled out the dagger to defend myself. Of course he hadn't given it back.

Stephen entered the room and closed the door behind him.

He studied us each in turn before casually leaning against the wall. "So we meet again."

I eyed the door, knowing it was my only escape. The key must be in his pocket. "Planning to knock me out again?" I asked icily.

"Not right now. Maybe later."

"You need to let us out of here," Jordan said, her voice breaking.

I watched for his reaction to her, and was surprised to see there wasn't one. His face remained cold and impassive.

"You're not going anywhere. Not yet."

"Start talking," I snarled. "What do you want?"

"What makes you think I want something?"

"Basic deduction. You dragged both of us here and locked us up. You haven't hurt Jordan."

He shrugged. "I knocked her out. Didn't get to the chloroform in time. Had to slam her head against a cement wall. I'm sure that hurt."

I glanced at Jordan to see her flinch at the reminder. I finally noticed that there was dried blood along her right temple. I narrowed my eyes at Stephen. "What is wrong with you? Why would you do that?"

He held my gaze steadily. "Sometimes you have to make tough decisions."

I grabbed his shirt with my left hand, furious now. "Let us out of here."

He eyed my grip on him before he smirked. "Nah."

Then he took hold of my shirt, balling the material in his grip, and shoved me backward with inhuman strength. Jordan's scream pierced through the small room as I went flying backward and hit the wall. I fell flat onto the ground and lay there dazed and gasping for breath.

Grays didn't have strength like this. The super-gray who'd broken Cassandra's back had. The realization made my blood run cold.

"You've gone through stasis." I forced out the words as I tried to sit up.

"My evolution was quicker than I thought it would be." Stephen towered above me, his cinnamon-brown eyes glinting. When I tried to get up, he pinned my shoulder to the ground with the heavy sole of his shoe. "Don't make me hurt you more than I have to. Stay down."

I didn't take direction very well. I struggled, but the pressure only increased as he shifted his weight to my collarbone.

"No angels here to heal you. I suggest you don't move unless you want me to break some more bones, Samantha. For what I need from you…you don't have to be in one piece."

I stopped struggling. He leaned over and yanked me up, slamming me into the wall hard enough to knock my breath out of me.

"Let go of her!" Jordan shrieked. She was fighting him now, clawing at his arm. But, while she was tall, she wasn't any stronger than a typical seventeen-year-old girl. Not compared to something like Stephen.

He shoved her away from him. She stumbled and fell to the ground.

Stephen glared at her. "Stay down."

He had me raised off the ground, my feet dangling. While he hadn't broken any bones this time, I'd definitely sprained my shoulder. The pain only fueled my anger and helped my claustrophobia take a backseat.

"Does it make you feel like a man to beat up two girls like this?" I asked. "You're a pathetic lowlife. You always have been."

His hateful smirk returned, making his handsome face very ugly. "Wrong. I'm an example of the highlife, the best yet. Do you know what it feels like after going through stasis? I thought losing my soul was a good thing in the beginning. It gave me confidence all of a sudden. It made girls look at me more than they already did—and every one of them wanted me. That extra something we have, it's to draw our victims closer. Gives us a chance to feed. And they like it, even when you're draining every last bit. You know that, right?"

I didn't say anything. He didn't need the confirmation.

"It tastes better now, taking a soul," he said. "And we take the whole soul, every time."

Repulsion shot through me. "Now when you kiss them, you can't change them into another gray. You kill them."

He laughed. "Stupid humans, milling about this city. They think they're the top of the food chain. But they're not. Why can't you get it through your head, Samantha? You're one of us. You're part of the new order."

"Oh, my God. The new order? What is this, some sort of gray power thing? You're sick."

"You'll feel differently after you've evolved to the next level." He raised an eyebrow at my blanched look. "You know it's inevitable, don't you? You must feel it drawing closer by the hour."

His words made me ill. I kept quiet, hoping that my glare would suddenly turn into something capable of killing him where he stood.

"Stasis is like a wave in the distance, taking its time to arrive," he continued, "but when it gets closer you realize it's more like a tsunami. Natalie thought the less we fed, the more it stayed at bay. But it's just the opposite. The more you feed, especially closer to stasis, the more you delay it, but it's not forever. When it gets here you'll lose yourself completely. There's no other choice."

His words sent a fresh ripple of jagged fear through me. "You lost yourself?"

Stephen nodded. "Monday night. At Ambrosia. I lost it. I had to get out of there. Funny thing was, I left so I wouldn't hurt anyone. Once you lose it, you don't care about meaningless things like that. All you think about is feeding. And your victims? They're *still* drawn to you, even in that mindless state. Easy pickings. I fed a lot that night. And I woke up the next morning better than ever."

"What are you talking about?" Jordan demanded. "I don't understand any of this. What the hell are you?"

"I'm the future. Your future." He looked at her. "You called me a monster before, but I'm way better than that."

She gaped at him. "You can take someone's soul by—by *kissing* them?"

"That's right."

Her shocked expression soured. "That sounds *really* lame."

He gave her a cold smile that didn't reach his eyes. "You'll change your mind."

Stephen was still in love with Jordan. Don't ask me how or why, but he was. I'd seen it at the mall. That was my confirmation. Even though he'd gone through stasis, there was still something there when it came to his feelings toward the redhead.

She had a soul. She was close to him right now, trapped and vulnerable. And yet, he didn't make a move to feed on her because it would kill her if he did.

That meant something very important to me.

"Stop this, Stephen." He still held me effortlessly against the wall as if I weighed no more than a teacup Chihuahua. With his increased strength, he could break my spine with the smallest twist. And he could do the same—or worse—to Jordan.

His eyes narrowed. "I don't want to stop. This is it, Samantha. This is what I've been waiting for all my life. My reason to exist."

"And what reason is that? You're stuck in this city like all the others. You're trapped as much as I am in this room."

He cocked his head. "Natalie said that you have the power to cut a hole in the barrier with your boyfriend's dagger."

My stomach clenched. I'd hoped he'd forgotten about that little hypothesis, my aunt's quest to escape from Trinity so she could spread her evil far and wide. "She was fooling herself. I can't do that."

Stephen glanced at Jordan again, who hadn't gotten up from the ground yet. "Samantha's the daughter of a demon and an angel. That gives her special powers that I need."

"Shut up." Any mention of what I was put me into immediate panic mode as if the words themselves had power.

He grinned. "It's a secret, though, so shh. Don't tell anyone."

Jordan's eyes widened. "Oh, my God. Are you serious?"

My gaze shot to her. "Don't listen to him. He's a liar."

Her face was so pale her freckles stood out more than they

normally did. "Demons and angels...but those things don't really exist."

"Wrong," Stephen said. "They're prowling the city right now, on a hunt for things like me. Although, I'm pretty hard to kill now. Nearly impossible, really." He raised an eyebrow. "Haven't come to rescue *you* yet, have they, Samantha? Thought they'd taken you as a pet."

Bishop had found me when Kraven was forced to kiss me. But his tracking ability wasn't reliable anymore.

Did he even know I'd been missing for a day? Had Cassandra noticed the house was empty, or had she thought I'd gone to bed early again last night and left first thing this morning?

I'd told Bishop I wanted nothing to do with them, and with him. And he'd agreed to give me my space. To say I regretted our last conversation would be a monumental understatement.

I did need him. And I wished desperately he was here.

Mostly so he could kick Stephen's ass and introduce him to that handy golden dagger of his.

My empathy toward Stephen Keyes was at an end.

"What do you want with us?" I demanded, trying my best to remain calm when I felt anything but. "Or did you just want to talk to us all day?"

He looked over his shoulder at Jordan again, who was finally pushing back up to her feet. "Every soul I take makes me stronger. Strength means power. Power means I can have anything I want—become a true leader, respected and feared. But the others like us...they bore me. Most are too weak to survive stasis, anyway."

I glared at him while holding my injured wrist protectively against my chest. "Too bad. You can have everything, but you're all alone. Boo hoo. Maybe you should buy a goldfish to keep you company."

Jordan reached for something on the ground—a loose brick

I hadn't noticed before—and slowly crept up behind Stephen. My breath caught as she swung it forward to bash him in the head, but he turned just in time and yanked the brick out of her grip. Then he grabbed her throat and slammed her up against the wall directly beside me.

Too close. I couldn't be this close to someone with a soul right now. From the claustrophobia, to the pain, I'd become too weak. Hunger crashed over me and I literally whimpered.

Stephen's expression shifted to one of victory.

"See, Samantha? You can pretend to be all high and mighty and above these earthly needs, like someone worthy of hanging around with Heaven and Hell's best. But at your core, you're exactly like me. And it won't be long before you change to something much more interesting. We'll get along better then."

"What?" Jordan choked. "Samantha's not…"

Stephen smiled. "Yes, she is. I made her myself. I took her soul in a kiss that she was begging me to give her. She's wanted me since she wasn't much more than a kid. Right, Samantha?"

"And now I want to kill you," I growled.

He laughed at this and the sound sent a shiver racing down my spine. "I took her soul because her demon aunt asked me to. I actually felt bad about it at the time. Just a kid."

I tried to kick him, but his grip increased on my throat. Jordan's, too, since she let out a hoarse scream.

"Don't hurt her," I managed.

He didn't loosen his grip on either of us. "You want to know my plan? It's this. I'm going to leave you two alone for a while. It won't be very much longer before you can't hold back, Samantha. You'll take Jordan's soul, and you'll take it all."

"What?" My throat closed with horror at the suggestion.

His cheeks tightened. "If I did it myself, I'd kill her. And I want her to live. I want her to be…improved. There's room for both of you at my side in the new world if you survive stasis."

He flung both of us to the side and went to the door. "I'll check on you later."

He left.

I scrambled to the far corner of the room, which still wasn't far enough away from Jordan to help clear my head.

I thought Jordan was crying for a moment, but when she pulled her hands away from her face, she looked mad as hell.

"Explain to me right now what the hell is going on here!" she demanded.

I tried to breathe shallowly as possible as I gave her a bleak look. "What part don't you understand?"

"All of it!"

I studied her for a moment, her furious expression, the sparking anger in her eyes. "I think you understand more than you realize."

"What does this have to do with Julie's suicide?"

"Honestly?" I thought about it. "Nothing, directly. But in a way, everything bizarre that's going on in this city is related."

If Connor had been right in his hypothesis about the new demon in town, everything bad going on in Trinity was related to the Hollow and how it had become a two-way swinging door, rather than Heaven and Hell's dumping ground. It had a case of bulimia now, purging what it had once swallowed down.

Jordan raked a shaky hand through her long, tangled red hair. "I thought I was going crazy, but it's all true. Stephen's a monster. And you're…you're a monster, too. Was he lying about that?"

I swallowed hard. "Depends on your definition of monster."

She glared at me. "You're one of these things that can steal a soul with a kiss."

My chest tightened. "Afraid so."

"And Stephen's the one who changed you into one of these things."

"Yes."

She inhaled shakily. "He kissed you, but he won't kiss me."

My eyes narrowed. "Don't sound so disappointed. Believe me, this is *not* something you want. It's horrible. This hunger, it's…the worst thing I've ever dealt with."

I'd already given in to it three times. It couldn't happen again or I knew I'd lose myself completely.

She hesitated. "But you're something else, too. Your parents…"

"My *birth* parents, you mean." I chewed my bottom lip. She knew, so there was no reason for me to try to keep denying it. "I didn't know the truth about myself until very recently."

"What does it mean?"

"Only that I'm more confused about my personal identity than ever before."

She paced in small lines, back and forth, her arms crossed over her chest. "Doesn't that trump the whole gray thing? Isn't that some sort of power that you can draw from to help you?"

I wished it was that simple. I really did. "What I am underneath, it's got nothing to do with this. It's like they're separate things. Who my real parents are isn't going to make anything easier."

Her skin had paled to a ghostly white. "And now Stephen wants you to infect me."

I pulled my knees up to my chest and started to rock myself. My mind flashed back to kissing Colin in the hall, how I'd had zero control then when I'd always been able to stop myself before. What happened to Stephen—it was going to happen to me. Soon. Or I was going to drop dead like that woman in the street the other night who'd disintegrated before my very eyes.

"I don't know how long I can deal with this, Jordan. I'm losing it. It's scaring the hell out of me."

She got to her feet and took a couple steps closer to me. Before I knew it I'd risen to my feet as well, unconsciously drawn to her soul.

"You're *not* kissing me," she said uneasily, holding up her hands to try to keep me back.

"Trust me, Jordan, you're the last person on earth I'd ever want to kiss. And it's not just because you're a girl. I'm sure Stephen would rather change you himself, but if he kisses you he'll—" I swallowed hard. "He'll kill you."

"Stephen…" she whispered, then shuddered. "Have you kissed anyone?"

I nodded. "Two."

"And did you kill them?" she asked breathlessly.

"Not yet."

She started to tremble. "Oh, my God. This isn't happening."

My vision was narrowing by the second. Jordan had stepped away from me, but the scent of her soul was driving me crazy. I watched her like a wolf might watch a small, scared rabbit in the forest.

She attempted to look brave and assured. "Just…try to control yourself. You're stronger than this!"

My thoughts were spinning away from me like the tornado in *The Wizard of Oz*. I tried to grasp onto them before they all blew away. Then something important occurred to me. "Wait. I wasn't hungry when I was unconscious. It's only when I'm awake."

Her eyes were wild, panicked. "You want me to knock you out?"

I nodded crazily. "Do it."

And then Jordan disappeared and all I could see was her soul—shiny and tempting. The cure to my pain, the answer to my hunger. She scrambled for something as I drew closer, closer. Then I grabbed her shoulder, my right hand still useless, and pulled her closer.

She screamed, and swung something toward me.

Sharp pain slammed through my head as she successfully rendered me unconscious.

My head was screaming when I woke up this time. But along with the pain, a shaky clarity had returned.

My hunger, however, hadn't gone anywhere.

"If I hit you again you're going to get a concussion," Jordan warned. "A fractured skull. Or a clot. Or an aneurism. Or…something really bad!"

I groaned, and looked across the room at her crouched in the opposite corner, clutching the brick tightly. "Or maybe I'll get amnesia and forget all about this."

The pinprick of light through the tiny window told me it was still day—but the sunlight was fading. I hadn't been out for long this time. One of the fluorescent lights set into the ceiling flickered now, as if ready to go out completely. It cast spooky shadows through the room.

"He hasn't checked on us again," she said, casting a furtive glance at the door.

"He will."

"When?"

"When it's done. When you're changed. When I've…fed." The words tasted as bad as they sounded. There was a security camera up in the far corner I hadn't noticed before. I gestured at it. "He's watching us."

Jordan moved into the camera's line of sight and gave it the finger. "Screw you, Stephen! I hate you for this!"

"Ditto," I murmured, then cringed. "Ow, my head."

Her expression now was fierce and determined. Her anger toward Stephen had given her some extra strength. "Stay right where you are. I'll use this again."

I flicked a wary glance at her and her brick. "Feel free. But that's only a temporary answer. My hunger…it's worse than ever. I need to feed."

"Not on me."

"I don't think there's going to be a choice soon. If I go into stasis here…a brick's not going to stop me." I fought to come up with a plan of action, but I was tired and weary, hungry and in pain. I didn't want to give up, but I was worried my strength wouldn't last much longer.

"What about those angels and demons Stephen mentioned? You know them?"

"You could say that."

"Where are they?"

"Not here."

I longed for Bishop to come bursting in here in a blaze of glory. I'd never been the damsel in distress type, the girl who dreamed of a guy sweeping in to save her in the nick of time like they did in corny movies. Besides, if I looked at this objectively, I *wasn't* the damsel in distress in this situation—Jordan was. I was the scary thing hiding in the shadows ready to leap out and devour her.

"I always knew," Jordan whispered.

I stayed in the opposite corner to her, a good ten feet away from the orbit, wishing it would make things easier. "Knew what?"

"That there were things bigger than me in this city. Supernatural things. I always believed." She actually smiled, a pained, scared expression. "My mom, she likes to go to psychics for readings. Does it every week. I think she does it instead of going to a shrink. With a psychic, she can blame all of her problems on otherworldly activity. But I don't think she really knows it's all real."

"But you do."

She hugged the brick to her chest as if it was a comforting teddy bear. "I felt it. I always thought I was a little bit psychic. Like, with ghosts and stuff. Nobody believed me when I was a kid, so I stopped talking about it. It faded to nothing for ages. Lately, though, it's been getting worse."

Something about what she said felt important. Really important. "Since when?"

"The last few weeks."

I pressed up against the wall. If Jordan really had psychic abilities, they'd been triggered back into action at about the same time Bishop and the rest of the team had come here and the barrier was put in place to keep all supernaturals contained in this city-size zoo. "Jordan Fitzpatrick, psychic medium to the stars."

She laughed drily under her breath. "You would not believe how much some of them can make. And I'm sure most of them are total frauds."

"I'm sure."

She blinked and her smile faded quickly. "I loved him."

I didn't need a map to keep up with her sudden change in direction. "I know you did."

Her eyes grew glossy. "When he dumped me, I didn't understand. I thought it was because he was in university and I was still in high school. But I thought what we had...even though we hadn't dated for very long—I thought it was real. I fell for him so fast. He was so wonderful, but then I knew he had secrets he didn't want to share with me. I tried to learn the truth, but all he did was push me away."

I went totally silent. It was like she was talking about me and Bishop. "Some secrets can be scary."

"Stephen didn't scare me. Not then. He does now. He never did anything to hurt me before. Even when…I guess he was changed. I thought he was cheating on me. And the stupidest thing was I would have forgiven him. I would have taken him back, even after I heard he was seen making out with…" She looked at me, and clarity shone in her green eyes. "That was the time. When he kissed you. That's when it happened."

I nodded, the lump in my throat too thick to swallow past.

"That jerk," she snarled. "He should have told me! I could have helped him before it got this bad. And now he's out there killing people? He's a killer, Samantha. The boy I love is a killer." She looked at me strangely. "Why are you crying?"

"Damn it." I pushed away the tears streaking down my cheeks with my good hand. I hadn't meant to let myself weaken like this, but it happened. The more she talked about Stephen, the more I thought about Bishop and how much I cared about him even after witnessing some of the horrible moments in his past.

She looked at me with an incredulous expression. "I seriously need you not to flake out on me right now."

I shook my head, which had begun to cloud up again. I couldn't pull myself out of this hole I'd found myself in. It was only getting deeper. "I can't concentrate."

Her expression only grew more fierce. "You can. Now, just figure it out. From the sound of it, you're oozing supernatural energy from your pores. You're half demon and half angel, which is completely ridiculous, but I'm going with it, anyway. So figure out a way to get us the hell out of here so I don't have to bash your brains in."

My thoughts raced, and again I kept coming back to Bishop and that connection we had—how he was able to find me, even if it was unreliable lately. But I still had mind melds with him, as strong as ever. "There's only one way I can think of. I need to contact somebody."

"No cell phone, remember?"

"No, not by phone." I closed my eyes. "I—I think there could be another way. But it might not work. In fact, I'm pretty sure it won't."

She let out a frustrated snarl. "Stop being such a damn pessimist and start trying."

Words to live by, courtesy of Jordan Fitzpatrick, my high school nemesis.

In my dream about Bishop, the one where we were playing chess before things got disturbingly homicidal, he'd said something to me—that I could control our mind melds. I hadn't believed it at the time since they were so random, so unpredictable. They came out of nowhere like being flattened by a truck.

Then something Jordan said tweaked something in me. She'd said I was half demon and half angel. But this wasn't totally accurate. I was the *daughter* of an angel and a demon. I was a nexus. I was the connection, the center point, the combination of the energies of Heaven and Hell.

If you asked me, that sounded way more powerful.

I'd always doubted this power, taken what came to me when it came. Seeing the searchlights was something I didn't control. It just happened. Zapping the demons and reading their minds took effort. Other times it was effortless. If they didn't fight me…it was effortless.

But maybe *I* was the one making things difficult.

I was certain my mind melds with Bishop were because I'd taken part of his soul—and it was still inside of me. That's why I could see his memories if I looked in his eyes. Bishop's soul was a bridge between us and had been ever since the kiss we shared. I needed to find that bridge and walk across it.

And I needed to do it right now.

chapter 21

I focused on that piece of Bishop that was always with me. The memory of our kiss. The warmth of his touch. The deep and endless way he looked at me, even when I was frustrating him and vice versa.

His soul, the thing that had caused him so many problems, was beautiful—a ribbon of silver that stretched outward from me to a point in the distance I couldn't see.

And this I saw with my eyes *closed*. I'll admit it was bizarre, but I wasn't going to second-guess myself. It was real. It was him. I knew it.

I held on to that ribbon of silver like a rope and let it guide me to him. I didn't fight it, I didn't force it. I just let it happen.

"Hurry up," Jordan urged.

I pried open one eye with annoyance. "Would you give me a—"

Snap!

"*—has to be somewhere in the city.*" *Bishop paced back and forth along the sidewalk. Dusk had fallen. Tall buildings surrounded him—glass, concrete, steel. Out of the corner of his eye there was traffic visible on the road, rush hour as everyone headed home from their jobs.*

He was right downtown, a nameless street I was sure I'd been on a million times before.

"Or she's dead," Roth said from nearby.

Bishop turned on him. "Shut your mouth."

Whatever look was on Bishop's face earned a dark glare in return. "I'm sick of shutting my mouth."

Bishop cast a glance over the rest of them—all were present, Roth, Cassandra, Kraven, Zach and Connor—watching the angel with varying degrees of wariness, uncertainty or disdain.

He fixed his attention on Cassandra. "Take Roth somewhere out of my sight."

She approached Bishop, her expression cautious. "We're all worried about her, you know. When she didn't come home last night—"

"You should have told me immediately, not waited until today."

She winced at the harshness of his words. "She wanted us to leave her alone. I didn't think—"

"That's right. You didn't." He brought his hands up to his face to cover his eyes, hunching over a little. "Not thinking...can't think... can't keep it together. My head, it's messed up, more and more."

"Come on, Bishop," Zach said. "You're strong. You have this. We believe in you."

Bishop snorted at that, a dry, humorless sound—a trait he shared with his brother. "This soul." He took his hands from his face and clawed at his chest through his black T-shirt. "It's destroying everything."

"So make yourself bleed again," Kraven suggested. He was the farthest away, leaning casually against the glass door of a building. "If you need someone to hold the knife, I'm happy to help."

"Why would you say something like that?" Connor snapped. For the one who usually had all the jokes and quips, he was uncharacteristically pissed off.

Kraven shrugged. "Sheesh. Don't get your panties in a bunch, sunshine."

"Doesn't help anymore. Nothing helps. Only…her." Bishop fisted his hands at his sides as he turned a furious glare on his brother.

Kraven raised his eyebrows. *"Why do I get the look of death? It's not my fault gray-girl went AWOL."*

When Bishop swore, there was a harsh, insane edge to his voice that scared me. He was seriously losing it. And the more crazy he sounded, the more our connection began to get staticky, like a TV station with interference. *"I need to find her. Can't find her, can't sense her—not like I used to. Where is she?"*

Cassandra tentatively moved closer and hugged Bishop against her. *"We'll find her. I promise we will."*

Bishop looked beyond the blonde angel to Roth, who looked back at him with open animosity, his eyes glowing red in the fading light of dusk.

So supportive, that demon. It made me want to kick him as hard as I could in his demon crotch.

Zach and Connor stood together to Roth's left, both watching Bishop with tense expressions.

"What do you need us to do?" Zach asked. *"Name it."*

"Help me find her."

Zach frowned. *"How?"*

Roth let out an exasperated groan. *"Enough already. We need to hunt grays. And in case you're forgetting, we have that other demon in town doing his best to make your precious little humans off themselves. Remember that?"*

Cassandra paled and she drew a shaky hand through her hair. *"He's right. We do need to keep focus. I'll go with Roth and patrol. You and the others keep searching for Samantha."*

Bishop didn't reply for a moment, but his gaze was unflinching on both Cassandra and Roth. *"Fine. Go."*

They didn't hesitate. With a final searching look from the angel, and an unpleasant one from the demon, the two ran down the street to disappear around the next corner.

It was a hopeless feeling, watching this and not being able to do anything.

But wait…maybe I was underestimating how much I could do. I'd taken hold of that piece of Bishop's soul to lead me here—that had been intentional.

Maybe I could intentionally communicate with him.

"Bishop!" I sent his name through the razor-thin connection, along that silvery ribbon that joined us.

He brought his hands up to his head, his breath ceasing completely for a moment.

"This is ridiculous," Kraven said. "Pull yourself together. What do you want us to do, boss? Speak now or forever hold your tongue."

"I thought I heard…" Bishop whispered. "No, it's impossible."

I kept watching, now stunned. Had he heard me?

"What is it?" Zach asked, drawing closer, concern in his green eyes.

"I thought I heard…her. Calling to me."

Zach and Connor exchanged a look.

"Bishop!" I said it louder, my heart pounding. "It's me. I'm here!"

"Oh, give me a—" Kraven began.

"Quiet! I need to concentrate. I need to clear my head so I can know if this is real."

"And how are you going to do that?" Kraven asked.

Bishop yanked the dagger from his sheath and held it against his bare arm.

My view of what he saw flickered in that moment of craziness. For a second, I feared I was losing the connection completely.

Connor grabbed him before he made the cut. "Don't do this!"

Bishop pushed him back. "I have to. It's the only way."

Horror crashed over me. "Don't you dare cut yourself!" My scream wasn't delivered out loud. It was fully internal and my words sped along the ribbon that joined us. It was the same one that allowed me to see through his eyes—a metaphysical television cable.

The blade stilled.

"It's her," he whispered.

"Bishop…" Zach said cautiously.

I couldn't believe this was really happening. He heard me!

"Samantha?" Bishop said hoarsely. "Is that really you?"

A million thoughts and questions raced through my mind about how this was possible and what it all meant. But none of that mattered right now. "I swear, Bishop, if you cut yourself again I'm going to kill you!"

He snorted softly, still half-uncertain. "This is incredible. Where are you?"

"Oh, boy," Kraven said, coming into Bishop's sightline to peer at his brother curiously. "He's definitely gone completely off the deep end this time."

I did what I usually did when it came to the demon and ignored him. "Stephen grabbed me yesterday morning. He has me in a locked room, but I don't know where."

"How can you do this? How can I hear you in my head?"

"Now he's talking to himself," Kraven said, bemused.

"Shut up," Zach snapped at him. "You're not helping."

Kraven rolled his eyes. "Whatever. He's crazy, that's all. Don't you see that?"

God, he was so frustrating. "Tell James I told him to shut the hell up."

Bishop snorted. "He'd just talk more."

The image I saw through Bishop's eyes went staticky again, it flickered to black, to white and then back to normal. "I don't think this is going to last much longer. Bishop, listen to me. I got to you from that piece of your soul I took—it's still inside me. It's what our bond is, why I can see things. It works both ways, I'm sure of it. So you need to find that, too. You have to follow it."

"I'll do it. I'll find you. I swear it."

"Hurry, though. I—I don't have much time."

"What do you mean?" His voice turned harsh and raw. "Did that son of a bitch hurt you? I'm going to kill him."

"Stephen locked me in a room with someone—someone with a soul. Please, you need to find—"

Snap!

The thread connecting us disappeared and my mind returned fully to the small, locked room. My eyes popped open.

"What are you doing?" Jordan demanded. "Do you really think meditation is going to help us right now?"

I sent a look at her across the room. "You sure better hope so."

So strange, but just being in Bishop's head helped to bring me some much-needed warmth. The whole time I'd seen through his eyes I didn't think once about the previous memory melds, not once. I wasn't afraid of him. All I felt when I'd been in his head was that warmth. He wasn't the same person now that he'd been back then.

I'd told him I wanted him to stay away from me. He'd believed me, even though I'd never told a bigger lie in my life.

"Now what?" Jordan asked, the anger fading from her voice.

I swallowed hard. "Now we wait."

I concentrated on the sound of my heart beating, but I lost count at a thousand. My stomach growled. It was so empty after being locked in here for so long. Food might help a little; the more I ate the better I felt. But not enough.

Something hit me and I opened my eyes to look down at the energy bar that had pinged off my leg.

"Eat it," Jordan said.

"It won't help."

"Eat it anyway."

I ate it. And then I tried to come up with a Plan B. Because with every minute that ticked by, my resolve and my control were slipping away like the sand in a very scary hourglass.

My chills returned and my arms broke out in goose bumps. I crossed my arms over my chest and tried to keep from shivering.

I could figure this out. I had to use my brain, which had rarely failed me before—not including the F I'd received on my English test. I'd assumed I knew enough. One can't assume. One had to know for sure, because guessing could lead to failure.

I could *pretend* to take Jordan's soul. Stephen would see through the camera and he'd come in. I'd use Jordan's brick to knock him out. Yeah, that was a plan.

A really lousy one.

"Come on, brain," I mumbled under my breath. "Start thinking."

Sadly, it wasn't cooperating today. A full hour had gone by and Bishop wasn't here. We were stuck and nobody was going to rescue us.

"I don't like the way you're looking at me," Jordan said uneasily. "I swear, if you come anywhere near me, I'm clobbering you."

She scrambled to her feet as I moved closer to her. My wrist and shoulder were still in pain, but it was a distant echo now. My hunger had steadily moved to the forefront, impossible to ignore. Impossible to fight.

"I can take you," she managed shakily. "You've never intimidated me before. I mean, look at you. You're the size of a hobbit."

Normally, I'd resent that. I wasn't the size of a hobbit. Five-two wasn't *that* short, but compared to statuesque aspiring models like Jordan…

Size didn't matter. Not in a case like this.

I'd made it across the room, so close now that she gasped

and raised the brick over her head, ready to smash it down at me like she had before.

But this time I stopped her, snatching the makeshift weapon away like taking candy from a very tall baby. It was time to end this. Stephen had won. And once this was over, when he came in here after watching me devour his girlfriend's soul through that security camera and turning her into a gray, I was going to kill him.

My vision blurred at the edges as I reached for her.

And then the door burst inward.

"Get them apart," Bishop instructed sharply. "Now."

There was no argument. The next moment, I was wrenched away from Jordan. I fought hard against the very strong person who held me.

"Missed you," Kraven growled into my ear. "Glad to see you're still in one piece, gray-girl."

My struggling only made my wrist and shoulder hurt worse, but I was still in a daze, unable to focus on anything except my hunger. "Let go of me!"

"As hot as it would be to see you kiss another girl, I'm going to have to decline your request."

Only Bishop and Kraven had entered the room. Zach and Connor were nowhere to be seen. My breath came fast and shallow, my attention now focused on Bishop. He scanned Jordan, checking if she was okay while she cowered in the corner, staring at the rest of us in shock.

Then his gaze moved to mine. And locked.

He was so beautiful, it took my breath away. And even though I'd only been apart from him for a short time, every fiber of my being reached out to him.

"Samantha…" He began moving closer to me, as if hypnotized by whatever he saw in my eyes.

"What the hell are you doing?" Kraven growled.

I managed to slip out of the demon's grip bonelessly, dodging him as he tried to grab me again. Bishop and I moved toward each other, meeting in the middle of the room. I didn't hesitate for a second. I wrapped my arms around him as he pulled me against him and crushed his mouth against mine.

From the broken-down door to the kiss, it had all happened in a matter of seconds.

The taste of his lips only ignited the fire inside me more. I burned for him—I always had. And his mouth on mine... it was perfection.

But I didn't have a chance to kiss him longer—or to start to feed. Kraven was there, grabbing me by the shirt to violently yank me back.

He looked disgusted. "You two *are* a couple of addicts, aren't you? Pathetic. Get away from her. I mean it."

Bishop made a strangled sound, as if he was fighting the urge to kiss me again with every ounce of strength he had. The way I was feeling right now—this utter abandon—I knew I'd take it all.

Bishop might be going steadily crazy, but he was still sane enough to listen to his brother.

He gave Kraven an agonized look. "Do it. Just do it and get it over with."

I didn't know what he meant. I still saw the world through that gray daze, those with souls in the room brighter and more beautiful than anything else.

So hungry, please...

But the one who didn't have a bright and beautiful soul captured my face between his hands and forced me to look at him instead of the dark-haired, blue-eyed angel.

"Third time's a charm," Kraven mumbled. Then he kissed me bruisingly hard, forcing me to remain still with one hand now gripping my long hair, the other circling my throat.

No…I want Bishop…not Kraven, not…not…

But I only fought it for a moment. Then my thoughts cut off and I was kissing him back every bit as hard as he kissed me. My hunger slowly, *very* slowly this time, began to ease. My arms slid over the demon's shoulders to cling to him, otherwise I knew I'd collapse to the floor in a heap.

I *had* to kiss him—there was no choice for me. It was the only way I could regain my control.

Bishop grabbed Kraven's shoulder. "Enough."

Finally, the demon broke off the kiss, leaning back a few inches to look into my eyes. "Are you back?"

I nodded, holding his gaze. I stared into the depths of those amber-colored eyes. Same shape as Bishop's. Different face. Similar lips. Different kiss.

She's okay. But barely this time.

Kraven's thoughts. His walls were down, so I could piece through his mind. I didn't know what I was looking for until I found it.

She doesn't hate me. She can say she does, but she doesn't. No girl kisses like that if she doesn't like it. He hates it so much, hates that I have this power over her. He hates that I can taste her when he can't. She could fall for me. She's halfway there already. And when she does…such sweet revenge. I can watch him suffer before I finally shove that dagger through his heart.

chapter 22

I broke our gazes and stumbled back from him.

A frown creased Kraven's brow, as if he didn't expect this kind of reaction after such a seemingly passionate kiss.

"What's wrong, sweetness?" he asked, his frown deepening.

"Don't kiss me again," I whispered. "Ever."

A glimmer of clarity lit in his eyes. And the next moment his mental wall crashed down, locking me out.

I turned to face Bishop standing there rigidly, his jaw tense. Then I threw my arms around him. His heart pounded against mine as his grip tightened around me.

"I told you I'd find you," he said.

I nodded, currently speechless. That had been close. Too close. I reached down to take his hands in mine, feeling that incredible electric spark between us. He let out a quiet groan as he squeezed his eyes shut, and I knew his clarity was returning.

But, just like mine, it wasn't at one hundred percent anymore. Not even close.

He opened his blue eyes, which held much more sanity than had been there before. He cupped my face between his hands, his skin warm against mine. His thumb moved over my bottom lip and his expression darkened.

He hates that I can taste her when he can't.

Kraven thought that a minute ago, and by the look on Bishop's face he might have been right.

"So let me guess," Jordan's voice trembled out from her corner, where she was currently huddled in a tight ball. "These are the guys you called here through that meditation thing you did."

With effort, I tore my gaze from Bishop's to look at her, relieved that she seemed unhurt. "You got it. Jordan. Meet Bishop and Kraven."

"What *are* they?"

"Helpful Boy Scouts," Kraven said, cocking his head. "Well, look at you. Almost dinner for our gray-girl here."

The demon offered her a hand, but she ignored it and shakily rose to her feet on her own.

"Back off," she snarled.

Kraven just looked at her blandly. "Charming."

Along with my restored clarity, my anxiety returned. I gestured at the security camera. "Stephen probably saw you get here and escaped."

"He didn't escape," Bishop said.

My eyes widened. "Did you—?"

"Come on. Let's get out of here." He led me out of the room. The door had been ripped right off its hinges. Bishop noted my stunned observation of this. "I'm stronger than I look."

I was breathless as we moved away from my previous prison. Jordan silently trailed after us, but she was recovering and her gaze was watchful and fierce. Jordan might be a lot of things, but she didn't take well to playing the victim.

Kraven was the last to leave the room. I faced forward so I wouldn't have to meet his eyes again.

Now I knew for sure that his breezy exterior was only a

mask he wore to throw people off. Underneath, he was every bit as dark, scary and devious as I would have expected a demon to be. His murderous, vengeful thoughts had chilled me down to my bones.

His hate for Bishop had been palpable. It made my skin crawl, even now.

"Kraven wants to kill you." I said it loud enough for only Bishop to hear.

His jaw was tense. "I know."

"You do? What are you going to do about it?"

He kept his attention fully on the dark hallway before us. "Let me worry about my brother."

Easier said than done. I already worried, even before I'd read Kraven's thoughts. But what I'd seen in Bishop's memory—that betrayal of one brother by the other in such a brutal, final way...I couldn't say Kraven's desire for vengeance wasn't justified.

Still, I truly believed what had happened back then had other causes. Bishop may have done the horrible deed himself, but he'd been used by someone or *something* else.

Kraven didn't know that. Or if he did, he still blamed Bishop solely for what happened.

I followed Bishop up a flight of stairs, through another torn-open doorway and then we were outside. The cold bit into me, but I welcomed the fresh air. The cool breeze made me shiver. The sky was dark now. Clouds covered the stars and moon.

As I always did at this time of the day, I scanned the horizon for any sign of a searchlight. But there was nothing to be seen.

"Stephen!" Jordan gasped.

My gaze shot to where she was staring in shock—the super-gray himself was being restrained by Zach and Connor. Connor held Stephen's arms tightly behind him, while Zach pressed the golden dagger to Stephen's throat.

He hadn't escaped.

Stephen's gaze tracked to us and narrowed.

"They got to me before I changed your girlfriend." I couldn't keep the outrage from my voice. He'd try to force me to do such a horrible thing. He'd knocked me out and imprisoned me for more than a day.

I was surprised that instead of anger or rage in return, he just looked grim.

And was that...raw disappointment I saw in his eyes?

Some super-gray. For a sociopath, he seemed to have a lot of emotions to sort through.

Maybe love is the hardest emotion to destroy, I thought.

Oh, please. Give me a break.

"Why, Stephen?" Jordan's voice quavered. "Why would you try to hurt me like that?"

"I never wanted to hurt you." He struggled against Connor's grip on him, nearly breaking it.

"Hold still," Connor snarled.

Zach's gaze flicked toward me and his green eyes warmed a fraction. "Glad you're okay, Samantha. I was worried about you."

I let out a shaky laugh. "That makes two of us."

"Move again," Bishop warned Stephen, "and we'll kill you."

Stephen fixed him with a wry look. "But then you won't get Samantha's soul back. Are you willing to take that chance?"

Bishop's expression only turned colder as he drew closer to the gray. "Where is it?"

Stephen snorted. "Wouldn't you like to know?"

Bishop slammed his fist into Stephen's stomach.

I slapped my hand over my mouth, unprepared for the sudden show of violence.

Stephen barely flinched from the hit. "That kind of tickles."

Jordan paced in short, frantic lines, wringing her hands. I

swept my gaze over the building where Stephen had locked us up. It was an abandoned warehouse in an industrial section of town, and we now stood in an empty parking lot. I never came here, so I didn't know precisely where we were. Beyond the warehouse, a half mile away, I could see the lights of the city.

"Hit him again," Kraven suggested. "And don't hold back this time."

Bishop glared at Kraven over his shoulder. "I wasn't."

"If you say so."

As Bishop was about to do just that, I found myself at his side, grabbing hold of his arm to stop him. He looked at me with surprise in his blue eyes.

"What are you doing?"

"I don't want to sound like an after-school special here, but violence isn't the answer."

He looked down at my firm hold on his arm, his muscles tensing under my touch. "Let me do what I have to do."

"He won't talk until he's ready, no matter what you do to him."

"We disagree about that."

I snorted softly. "Wouldn't be the first time."

Bishop gave me a wry look. "So what would you suggest? He's gone through stasis. He's different now, worse than before. And after what he did to you…" The madness sparked in his eyes again, despite my continued grip on him. "I want to tear him apart."

"Samantha, you're hurt," Zach said, then looked at Kraven. "Cover me."

Kraven switched places with the angel. Connor still held Stephen prone from behind, and Kraven now gripped the gray's throat. "Don't move. I'm not nearly as nice as the rest of these boys. And I haven't ripped out any throats lately."

I didn't think he was bluffing.

Bishop's brows had drawn together at Zach's words. He scanned my face. "Is he right? Are you hurt?" He hadn't noticed how I'd been favoring my right wrist, but now his attention dropped to it and his eyes glowed blue. "It's broken. That bastard broke your wrist."

The craziness growing in his gaze worried me. "Relax. That's the worst of it."

"I could try to heal you. I'm sure I could do it. I'm stronger than I was before, but I—I just need to concentrate."

"No, Bishop," Zach said sharply. "In your current state, healing would take every last ounce of life energy you've got left. And then some. I'll do it."

Every last ounce he had left? Not a good idea then.

I glanced over at the other angel. "My shoulder, too. And, uh, while you're at it, I'm dealing with a bit of sprain in my left ankle."

Zach glanced at Bishop warily before he shifted the golden dagger under his arm, and placed his hands on me, sending his momentarily painful healing energy through my injuries one by one to heal me up as good as new.

"Better?" he asked.

"Much. Thank you." I was relieved the dull throbbing pain was finally gone.

Bishop fisted his hands at his sides and his gaze returned to Stephen. "I strongly suggest you help us out here."

"Or what?"

Bishop sent a frustrated glare in my direction. "Being nice isn't working."

"That was nice?" I cleared my throat, half amused at his minor attempt at calm negotiation. "Believe me, I'm not suggesting we give him a free pass, but beating him into a pulp isn't going to get my and Carly's soul back. We need to learn more about stasis, too. I don't think it turns a gray totally evil."

"Could have fooled me," Bishop replied.

"Yeah, well, Stephen's still in love with Jordan."

Jordan gasped. "He's…what? How could he feel anything for me with the way he's treated me?"

Zach had returned to grip Stephen's shoulder and hold the dagger to the gray's chest. Kraven moved back a few feet to give them space.

"I'm right, aren't I?" I said, focused on Stephen now. "What you felt before, it's stronger. But it's more obsessive now. More crazed." I swallowed hard. "Still, you're not completely lost."

He laughed, a dry sound. "You're right. I'm just a friendly puppy. Have your friends let me go and we'll talk it through over coffee. All is well."

"Stubborn, though," I said, glaring. "We can do this my way, Stephen. Or we can do this Bishop's way. My way hurts less."

The breeze picked up. And a strange crackling energy slid over my skin, making me shiver.

"What was that?" Jordan gasped. "Did you feel that?"

"Feel what?" Bishop asked.

"That sensation." She frowned deeply, her expression haunted. "I felt that at the mall, I swear I did. Samantha, that was the same feeling I got just before Julie lost it."

I stared at her. She'd felt it, too. Now I remembered that I *had* felt something at the mall, but hadn't thought anything of it at the time.

"What is it?" I asked, my voice hoarse.

There was fear in her eyes. "I don't know."

"You need to kill me," Stephen whispered. "It's too much. I've hurt too many people."

I whipped my head in his direction. He'd slumped a little in Connor's grip, like he was losing his strength.

"What game are you playing now?" Bishop said carefully. "You *want* me to kill you?"

"He'll do it," Kraven said, his arms crossed. "If you say pretty please."

Stephen drew in a shaky breath. "They can't see me. Nobody can. It's like I don't exist. But I do. I'm here. I was there for so long, but now I'm back and all it does is hurt. He never should have let me out."

I inhaled sharply. "Look at his eyes. They're not right."

Stephen's eyes were normally a cinnamon color, a medium rusty-brown. Right now they were glazed over with a sheen of white.

"Do you see me?" he whispered.

I flicked the briefest of glances at Bishop to register his confusion matched my own, before I returned my full attention to Stephen.

But this wasn't Stephen. Not right now. Clarity dawned for me, growing brighter with every second that ticked by.

"I see you," I said firmly. "What do you want?"

"I want it to stop."

"What is this?" Bishop asked. "What's going on?"

"This…I'm sure it's the new demon," I said. "The one that escaped the Hollow. The one driving people in Trinity to kill themselves. That's who you are, isn't it? Somehow, someway, you're able to drain the will to live from those you touch." Realizing this made me want to run in fear. But I stood my ground.

Stephen's spooky eyes stayed on me. He nodded, his expression etched with despair. "Yes. But you're wrong about one thing…I'm not a demon."

When I drew closer, Bishop caught my wrist, keeping me from taking another step. He, like everyone else present, regarded Stephen now with shock.

"What are you, then?" Bishop asked.

He drew in another shaky breath. "I am...I *was*...an angel."

Bishop's eyes widened. "An angel?"

Zach and Connor exchanged a surprised look, but they didn't budge an inch. Jordan shivered a few feet to my right, and Kraven watched all of this with interest. He rarely looked surprised about anything that ever happened, even the shocking stuff.

For me, I was stunned by this revelation. Stunned speechless, in fact. If my aunt had been an anomalous demon that hurt people, that made a twisted kind of sense. She'd been a *demon*. But an angel...

They were supposed to be the good guys.

"How did this happen?" I managed to say.

"I was expelled from Heaven," the angel speaking through Stephen explained. "The soul inside me, it drove me crazy. It was torture, every day I existed here in the mortal world. I wandered, trying to find a place for myself, but there was nothing but pain and misery. Finally, I couldn't take it any longer. I had to end my suffering. I—I set myself on fire, hoping the flames would purge my pain. That death would give me silence and peace. The Hollow claimed me."

"That was stupid," Kraven said without emotion at this horrific tale. "A fallen angel or an exiled demon can't kill him or herself with fire. Or a bullet. Or a hungry shark. That soul inside you takes on a life of its own and retains your consciousness, even if the body's been destroyed." His lips thinned. "But I suppose you've already figured that out, haven't you?"

Stephen's face held endless misery. "I have nothing left except my hunger. When I move through those here in this world, it gives me temporary relief."

"But you're hurting them," I said, my throat tight. "You have to stop."

He nodded. "Tonight I will ease my pain once and for all. It's why I'm here. Why I was released from his kingdom. I do what he tells me."

"What who tells you?" I asked.

"The only one that matters. The only one that knows the truth." His eyes locked with mine. "You know, but you don't. You can't see, not yet. But you will. You will see everything like I do. Like he wants you to. Soon, very soon."

I shivered.

Bishop met my gaze and his expression was bleak and haunted. This was a fallen angel, just like him, one whose soul had driven him insane. But this angel had chosen suicide as his only way out, which only made things worse.

He composed himself quickly and turned away from me to face Stephen again. "What do you mean? What are you going to do?"

Instead of replying, Stephen let out a strangled moan and dropped to his knees. Connor and Zach finally lost their hold on him and seemed uncertain of what to do with this most recent development.

"Bishop?" Connor asked.

"Don't touch him again," Bishop warned. "Not yet."

Stephen's eyes lost the opaque sheen and returned to their normal color. Again, I felt that strange crackling sensation slide over my skin. It made my heart race knowing it was caused by a bodiless fallen angel with a touch of death.

I exchanged a look with Jordan, who was rubbing her bare arms. She'd felt it, too.

"That was seriously freaky," she said, her voice trembling.

Jordan was what Cassandra originally thought I was. A human with supernatural intuition. She saw what others didn't. She sensed the invisible. She saw the unseen.

I guess we did have way more in common than I'd originally thought.

"Too much pain," Stephen groaned. "Make it stop. Please, make it stop."

My gaze shot to him as he crawled toward Zach, reaching a hand up beseechingly. "I hate what I've become. I hate that I hurt her. I'm sorry, Jordan. I'm sorry for everything. I want it to end. Please, kill me."

"Stephen, no!" Jordan gasped out. "What's wrong with you?"

"The angel—" I grabbed her arm to keep her from moving closer to him. "He took Stephen's will to live—just like what happened with Julie. Bishop, do something! He's going to hurt himself!"

Connor and Bishop both moved quickly to grab Stephen and they pulled him back up to his feet. But now Stephen, loose from being restrained, used that super-gray strength of his to fight, shoving Connor with enough force that he flew back, landing hard on the pavement.

"You're not hurting anyone else tonight." Bishop grabbed the back of Stephen's shirt.

"Kill me then," Stephen begged.

"Sorry. It's not that easy." Bishop slammed the gray into the wall of the warehouse hard enough to knock Stephen out. He sent a look in my direction and raised a dark eyebrow. "Too violent for you?"

I fought to breathe normally, and repressed a nervous laugh. "I'll allow it."

The barest of smiles moved across his lips. "I've wanted to do that for a while."

"Go team," Kraven said drily. "So what happens now? When he wakes up? Do we have a suicidal gray on our hands?"

Bishop shook his head. "My bet is it passes. The will to live, happiness in general, is not a measurable entity. It's an emotion, a mental state. It's possible when he wakes up he'll be back to normal. We'll take him to St. Andrew's and monitor him."

Stephen was incapacitated. Jordan and I had escaped. Any broken bones had been healed.

We were lucky. It really could have gone much worse than this.

"I'm so sorry. It was my fault." Zach shook his head. "I had him, but he slipped away from me."

Connor had pushed himself to his feet. "I'm fine. A couple bruises. Nothing to worry about."

"Yeah, forget it," Bishop said. "He was possessed. You're lucky he didn't attack you, too. His strength is off the charts."

"But I'm the one with the dagger." Zach looked down at the golden weapon in his grip. "I should have been the one to stop him."

"Like I said, forget it."

"I can't. I can't forget it. It's always this way. I have potential, but I don't live up to it. My father told me that once. Nothing I did ever impressed him. Nothing." He let out a shaky sigh. "He was ashamed of me. It made me ashamed of myself. I hated him so much. I—I can't believe that hate didn't turn my soul dark and heavy. There were times that I wanted to kill him."

I'd completely stopped breathing. "Zach...the angel...did it touch you, too?"

He turned his anguished gaze toward me. Tears began to streak down his cheeks. "It doesn't matter. I can't do this anymore. It's too much. I thought I was strong, but I'm not. Trinity is doomed. We were set up to fail. Do you know what happens then? The city will be destroyed—wiped off the face of the earth because I failed. I have nothing to live for. Nothing!"

"No, Zach! Don't!" I screamed.

But it was already too late.

Zach turned the dagger toward himself and plunged it into his chest.

chapter 23

There was nothing we could do to stop him.

"Zach!" I screamed again, but the sound of my voice was swept away by the thunderous roar of the Hollow opening up.

Zach dropped to his knees.

"I'm sorry," he said, before collapsing completely.

"What—what is that?" Jordan shrieked. "What's going on?"

"Stay back." I held out my arm to block her from coming another step closer. Panic shot through me as Bishop started moving toward Zach. "What are you doing?"

He met my eyes, his expression grim. "The dagger."

Oh, God. The Hallowed Blade…it was still in Zach's chest. And the Hollow was reaching out for him with its fingerlike tendrils of darkness.

Bishop was ten feet away from Zach. I was farther back, but even I felt the powerful suction.

My throat hurt, and I realized it was because I was screaming. Losing Zach like this was bad enough, but Bishop was risking everything to get the dagger back.

"Leave it!" I yelled. "Don't get closer to him!"

But Bishop rarely did what I wanted him to do.

I hated that dagger, an instrument of death that had taken

Zach and was about to take Bishop, too. I started to move closer to stop him, but Jordan held tightly to me to keep me back.

Bishop made it to Zach's body and didn't waste a second before pulling the dagger from the dead angel's chest.

The very next moment, the Hollow's dark fingers wrapped around Zach's body and snatched him back into the horrific, swirling vortex.

Then it reached out for Bishop. He struggled against its pull as those smoky, black tendrils moved around his wrists, his chest, his throat.

"Bishop!" I screamed.

Suddenly, Kraven was on the move, nearly too fast to see. For a second, I was terrified he was going to shove Bishop all the way into the Hollow. I let out another strangled cry. Connor appeared at my side to help Jordan hold me back and keep me out of the vortex's pull.

But instead of pushing him, Kraven tackled Bishop hard and rolled them both out of range.

The Hollow didn't disappear; instead, it swiveled as if on an axis. When I was lined up in its sights, it stopped. I swear it stared at me—a hurricane of darkness.

I stared back as my heart thundered in my chest. I couldn't have looked away if I tried.

So close now. Can you feel it? I will need you soon—sooner than I thought. Prepare yourself, Samantha. He can't save you. Only I can.

The words sounded hollow in my head, loud and clear, but empty and devoid of emotion. And a sudden, terrifying realization froze me in place.

This thing, this horrible *thing,* had a mind I could read. It was sentient.

And it knew who I was.

I couldn't keep looking at it. I forced myself to tear my gaze away toward Bishop and Kraven, who scuttled away from the Hollow's roaring mouth.

A moment later, it began to swirl smaller and smaller, until it disappeared completely. The roaring sound vanished, but the echo of it still rang in my ears.

The five of us stood in the warehouse's empty parking lot in stunned silence.

Zach was gone.

Bishop was at my side in an instant, pulling me into his arms.

"What just happened?" Jordan demanded. "Am I going completely insane?"

The next moment, Stephen began to come to. He groaned and lifted his head. Kraven swiftly moved toward him, pulled the groggy gray to his feet, then whacked his head off the wall again. "Stay down."

We'd saved the monster, but lost an angel.

Walking next to Kraven, Connor carried Stephen fireman-style over his shoulders as we made our way back to St. Andrew's. Jordan trailed silently next to me, sending scared, but annoyed looks at me every few moments. Bishop was to my right, his solid presence something I needed for strength right now, even though we weren't touching.

No one said anything. We were all in shock.

Standing between two people with tempting souls, I struggled against my hunger, which had begun to increase again to a level impossible to ignore.

The misery must have been clear on my face.

"How much longer?" Bishop asked quietly.

He didn't have to clarify that he meant my stasis. That had to be what the voice in my head had also meant, although I didn't know what or who it was, only that it scared the hell out of me. "I don't know."

"Guess."

I swallowed hard. "Not long."

He swore under his breath. "When Stephen wakes up again, I will get your soul back."

I tensed. "By hurting him."

"I'll do whatever it takes." He said it so firmly that I believed every word. The cold that had worked its way into every part of my body thawed just a tiny bit to know he was willing to go to extremes for me.

But I didn't say thank-you. I couldn't thank him for an offer to torture somebody for information, even if it was to save my life.

Once we returned to the church, the reality of losing Zach set in. Grief clawed at my chest, but I fought to hold back any tears.

Also the fact that I'd been held captive for a day and a half was catching up to me.

"I need water," I said. "My throat's so dry."

"There's a bathroom at the end of that hall." Bishop nodded toward the back of the sanctuary.

With a sweeping glance over the group, including Jordan, who didn't meet my gaze, leaning against the pews in the darkened church with its high ceiling and stained-glass windows, I slipped away to freshen up. I desperately wanted to eat, drink and have a shower. Not necessarily in that order.

The halls were dark, but I found the bathroom easily. I pressed my hand against the smooth, cool door and pushed it open. The electricity might not work in the church, but the water did, which was a relief. I scooped handfuls of it from the tap to my mouth, until my thirst faded.

I heard something and stopped drinking, raising my gaze

to look at my reflection in the mirror above the sink. I saw a very pale girl with dark, tangled hair and haunted brown eyes.

The sound I heard was low voices from nearby. I immediately recognized them as Cassandra's and Roth's.

I left the bathroom and moved farther down the hall to the end, where there was a small secretarial office, its door slightly ajar.

"You have to stop this," Cassandra said.

"You think it's that easy?"

"It has to be. There's no other way."

"You're wrong."

"Then you're delusional. I didn't come here for this. I never wanted this."

"That makes two of us." Roth's words were sharply edged with annoyance.

"I hate you."

"Yeah, I hate you, too."

What were they arguing about now? Cassandra despised the demon as much as I did, but constant squabbling wasn't going to help anybody right now.

They'd gone silent, but then I heard a quiet moan. My heart skipped a beat. If he was hurting her...

I pushed the door open all the way, ready to interrupt like I'd done at Ambrosia the other night.

Then I stopped when I saw them, and my mouth fell wide-open in shock.

They weren't squabbling. And he wasn't hurting her.

They were kissing. Passionately.

I must have gasped loud enough for them to hear, because they broke apart so fast it was almost comical. Cassandra's hand flew to her mouth and her gaze shot toward me.

Guilt flooded her expression.

"This isn't what it looks like," she managed.

Roth glared at me defiantly. "Yes, it is."

She sent him a withering look. "Shut up."

I hadn't just seen things. They *were* kissing. Mouth to mouth. A demon and angel were *kissing*.

Roth met my surprised gaze full-on, and I sank into his mind like butter. He was currently wide-open, his walls one hundred percent down.

Damn angel. Why does she make me feel this way? I'm so screwed.

From the look on Cassandra's face, the feeling was mutual. They were falling for each other.

And here I'd been absolutely sure she was into Bishop with her touchy-feely-healy ways. Boy, was I wrong about that.

Normally, and despite my animosity toward Roth, I might think this was cute. But I knew the rules that forbade demons and angels from being together like this. I was the result of such a relationship—and it had destroyed my real parents. It had killed my birth mother.

My thoughts must have been written all over my face, because Roth swore. "Influence her to forget this."

Cassandra shot him a look. "I'm not doing that."

Now she has a problem using her angelic influence—which, for the record, I didn't think would work on me, anyway. Before, however, with my mother and her impromptu trip to Hawaii, she'd had no second thoughts about taking the easy way out.

They were afraid I was going to tell on them. But doing that would doom them, just like telling anyone my secret about being a nexus would potentially doom me.

I knew all about keeping dangerous secrets.

"I won't tell anyone." It was the first thing I'd said since entering the room.

"How can we trust you?" Roth asked tightly.

"You'll just have to." Honestly, though, if I'd read anything malicious in his mind all bets would have been off. But he liked her. He didn't want to, but he did, anyway.

Roth, the hateful demon, had emotional layers. Who knew?

"Where have you been?" Cassandra suddenly demanded, coming toward me to grab my arm. "We've been so worried about you!"

"I'm fine now," I said, swallowing hard. "But you need to know something. Something bad."

I told them about Zach. Roth's expression hardened, but Cassandra's eyes filled with tears.

"No," she whispered. "It can't be."

"But it's not a demon like you all thought," I said, my voice hoarse. "It's an angel. One who feeds on happiness and the will to live with a touch. It happened to Stephen, too. We don't know how he'll be when he wakes up."

"This is terrible. I didn't know it would be this bad." Cassandra drew a shaky hand through her long, pale hair.

I looked at her, confused. "What do you mean? It sounds like you knew it was an angel."

She nodded gravely. "I've been searching the city for her."

"Her?" Roth said, every bit as surprised as I was about this. "Why didn't you tell us?"

"I've been trying to find a solution to this problem myself, but I've failed. I was about ready to share the details of my true mission with the rest of you."

So Cassandra did have a secret mission after all. And it was to find the bodiless angel who'd escaped from the Hollow.

"I wish you'd told us earlier," I whispered, my throat tight.

"Me, too." She blinked back tears.

They followed me down the hall toward the office at the far end where Connor had tied up the still-unconscious Stephen, the ropes tight at his wrists and ankles. Bishop and Kraven stood nearby. I lingered at the doorway as I filled Bishop in

on everything—everything *except* Roth and Cassandra's secret romance.

Jordan stood next to me, her attention fully focused on
Stephen. She slanted a glance at me as I watched her carefully. "What?"

"Don't you want to go home?"

"Not yet. I need to know what's going on here." She
blinked. "And nobody's kicked me out yet."

"So Blondie's an angel with secrets, huh?" Kraven said,
rolling his eyes. "How utterly shocking."

He had his smart-ass mask firmly in place. The fact that
he'd saved Bishop from the Hollow hadn't come up since it
happened. It was one of many elephants in the already too-
small room.

Roth thrust his chin at Stephen. "Why didn't you just kill
this loser?"

"Because he has Samantha's soul," Bishop said with a look
toward me. Our eyes met. He was holding on to his sanity
with both hands tonight, but I could see it was a struggle. I
wanted to help him, but I held back. Since I was a large part
of the problem right now, the least I could do was stay out
of the way.

"So what do we do?" Connor asked.

"We deal with this," Bishop replied. "Then we go out and
find a way to stop that angel."

"And how do we do that if it doesn't have a body to kill?"

"Simple," Roth said. He was making an excellent attempt
at not looking at Cassandra at all, even though she stood right
next to him.

"Simple?" she said with disbelief. "How can you say anything about this is simple?"

His jaw tightened, but he still didn't meet her eyes. "Sounds
like the angel sometimes possesses a body before it feeds. That's

when it'll be at its most vulnerable. We can kill it with Bishop's dagger." He finally glanced at her, giving her a half grin. "Not simple, but fairly brilliant. Don't you think?"

She didn't comment on Roth's brilliance.

But I would. "That's a terrible plan."

Roth glanced at me, his eyes narrowing. "Why?"

"Because you'd have to kill a human—or whoever the angel is possessing. That's called murder."

He just stared at me. "Bishop, could you muzzle your pet, please? She's getting all moral on us."

I spun to face Bishop. "You can't possibly think this is a good plan."

His expression was grim. "It's not a good plan. But it may be the only one we have that will work."

I felt the color drain from my face. "You're serious, aren't you?"

"Yes, I'm serious. That angel's driven at least two dozen people to their deaths, including Zach. If it takes the sacrifice of one innocent in order to save an entire city, then that's unfortunately what will have to happen." His harsh expression softened just a little. "Try to understand."

I wanted to argue, but I couldn't find the words. It was a horrible plan, the worst ever, but I couldn't think of another way to end this. And I didn't want more people to die because of that angel's hungers.

"This is so messed up," Jordan blurted out. "Everything I hear is seriously blowing my mind. Are you all for real? You're literally making Samantha look like the only sane or smart one in this room right now."

Coming from Jordan, that nearly sounded like a compliment.

"Red's mouthy," Kraven said. "Could be a problem."

"What are you going to do?" I challenged him. "Kill her, too?"

"Don't give me any ideas, sweetness."

Then Stephen grunted, low and weak. He was waking up. Everyone's attention shot to the restrained super-gray. He raised his head with effort and blinked open his eyes. There was dried blood on his forehead from where he'd hit the wall twice.

He scanned the five of us, lingering on Jordan, before he ended with Bishop. "Change of scenery, I see?"

Bishop had already drawn the dagger out and I eyed its sharp edge with trepidation. "Time to talk, Stephen."

"I like talking. When I feel like it."

"Wait," I said. "Stephen, are you better now?"

His forehead furrowed. "Better than what?"

"Before, you were so depressed. You wanted to die." His confused look told me everything I needed to know. "You were right, Bishop, the effects of the angel's touch fade if given enough time."

"Good to know." Bishop was silent for a moment. "You and Jordan need to wait outside now."

I turned a dark look at him. "And let you do your thing?"

His blue-eyed gaze remained neutral. "That's right."

"Your way of dealing with problems kind of freaks me out, Bishop."

"We're going to have to agree to disagree on this subject. There's no time to argue."

Stephen snorted. "Are you defending me, Sam? That's so nice of you."

I spun to face him, anger heating my cheeks. "I should let him carve you up. You haven't done a damn thing to earn my trust or respect. Everything you've done has been to hurt me. To hurt Jordan."

wicked kiss

His expression shadowed. "I never wanted to hurt her."

"Are you serious?" Jordan sputtered. "You knocked me out, you kept me prisoner. You nearly had a hobbit feast on my soul. What do you call that? True love?"

He stared at her incredulously. "Yes, actually. I did all that so we could be together again."

I stared at the two of them, realizing that Stephen really did this out of love for Jordan. This was one seriously twisted romance I was witnessing.

Jordan let out a frustrated shriek, spun around and stormed out of the room.

"Go with her," Bishop advised.

His shoulders were tense as he clenched the dagger. His body language showed his stress more than his even expression did. He didn't want me to see what he had to do to save my life.

How many times have you hurt someone to get what you want? I thought. *How many have you killed on your missions for Heaven?*

I couldn't read his mind, but I knew the answer would probably scare me very deeply.

Still, I didn't budge from my spot.

Bishop groaned. "Samantha, you have to be difficult, don't you?"

"Don't let him hurt me, Sam," Stephen said tightly. "I did it all for love. You get that, don't you?"

I believed he did. And I also believed he was manipulative enough to use my sympathy for that weakness against me.

Bishop wasn't filled with patience tonight. He sheathed his dagger, then took me by my arm, sending a shiver of electricity racing across my skin. He then directed me out of the office and back into the sanctuary where Jordan had fled to.

Cassandra joined us.

Bishop nodded toward Jordan. "Can you help with her, Cassandra?"

The angel nodded, and approached the redhead who watched her with a tense, guarded expression.

"What do you want?" Jordan asked sharply.

"Look at me." Cassandra smiled when Jordan did what she asked. "You need to go home now. It's been a difficult ordeal for you, but it's over. Everything is okay. You don't have to worry. Everything you've seen tonight, all the strange and confusing things that have scared you—you're going to forget them. They'll be like nothing more than a fading dream."

Jordan blinked. "What are you, crazy or something? Get away from me."

Cassandra cleared her throat. "Um, it usually works much better than this."

"You're losing your edge, Blondie," Kraven said. He'd also left the office, and now leaned casually against the back wall of the church.

"What are you doing out here?" Bishop asked.

"I follow the drama. It's entertaining. Besides, Connor and Roth have Mr. Tall, Gray and Devious under control. Don't get your feathers ruffled."

I inhaled sharply as Bishop took my arm again. I'd been trying my best to ignore it, but his soul was doing crazy things to my head right now.

"You need to leave," he said firmly.

"I can't."

"I can't think when you're here. And I need to be able to think."

The events of the night swirled around me, making me dizzy. So much had happened I couldn't process it all, but I didn't want to leave. I slid my hand down my leg to feel the leather sheath strapped to my thigh.

Suddenly, I remembered what it had held.

My eyes bugged and I grabbed the edge of Bishop's shirt. "Bishop…Stephen, he took my dagger earlier. He probably still has it."

Clarity shone in his eyes, then he turned from me and stormed out of the sanctuary and back to the office. The rest of us followed.

Connor lay unconscious on the floor near the wall, which now bore an angel-sized dent. Roth lay on his back, gasping, the familiar, small golden dagger protruding from his throat.

The wooden chair the super-gray had been seated in was now in pieces.

Stephen had escaped.

chapter 24

Cassandra let out a strangled cry and rushed to Roth's side. She pulled the dagger out and immediately set to work at healing him.

Kraven went to check on Connor, but thankfully he was already starting to regain consciousness.

"I'm sorry," I whispered, my chest so tight it was hard to breathe normally. "I forgot all about the dagger. I should have said something earlier. Now he's gone."

Bishop turned to me, and I expected to see anger in his eyes that I'd been so thoughtless, but there was nothing like that. There was frustration there, but it wasn't directed at me.

"No." He took my hand and squeezed it. "You've been through a lot. You didn't forget on purpose. This isn't your fault."

"Sure it is," Kraven said.

Bishop sent a glare at him. "Actually, if you'd stayed in here this could have been avoided."

"Or I could be the one with the knife sticking out of me." He shrugged. "Maybe you'd like that."

"Maybe I would."

"Ouch."

The anger fell from Bishop's gaze as he turned from his brother and, if you asked me, it was as if he regretted his harsh words. He kept my hand in his like he needed the contact to keep his mind clear.

The longer I was near him, the *less* clear my head became.

"Connor, take Jordan home and make sure she stays there," Bishop instructed, his voice tight.

"Can't," Jordan said. "I have plans tonight."

He looked at her with surprise. "You were kidnapped and imprisoned in a locked basement storage room by your obsessed boyfriend for nearly two days and you have plans?"

She glared at him. "I have a social life, you know. There's a huge Halloween party tonight I can't miss. I spent a ton on my costume."

Bishop gave me an exasperated look, which almost coaxed a smile from me despite everything that had gone so horribly wrong.

I shrugged. "She says she has a costume."

"I'm Cleopatra," Jordan said, as if that explained everything. She cocked her head. "Wait a minute. I think I'm remembering something important." Then she inhaled sharply. "When Stephen first found me, before he knocked me out, I told him about the party. He seemed…interested in going. As if it might make him feel normal again. He said we could go together." Her eyes moved back and forth rapidly as if she was remembering the moment in detail. "I mean, obviously he was just playing games with me, trying to get closer so he could grab me. But still, maybe he'll show."

"Where's this party?" Bishop asked, his voice measured and almost too calm.

"It's Noah's party." Jordan looked at me. "You're invited, too, right? He has the hots for you, FYI."

I cleared my throat. "Yeah, well, the feeling isn't mutual."

"Gray-girl's curious charm doesn't seem to be lost on many," Kraven drawled, amused. "Hobbits are hot."

"It's not at his house," I said, remembering what Kelly told me in the school hall yesterday. "He found another place?"

"Yeah, an abandoned house in a private area on the far east side of the city—at Oak and Peters. Thinks it'll add a spooky touch. Figures it might be busted, but that's supposed to make it more exciting." She crossed her arms. "I'm going."

I watched Bishop carefully for his reaction to the stubborn redhead. "Connor, like I said, take Jordan home safely. What she does after that is entirely up to her." He shifted his gaze to his brother. "Kraven, go with Roth to this party and keep an eye open for our gray friend. Connor can meet you there later."

"And if we see him?" Connor asked.

"Detain him. Any way possible."

Connor's eyes narrowed and there was a hard set to his jaw. "With pleasure."

They didn't wait. They left, Jordan sending a glance back toward me, but no goodbye. It would have been easier for her if the angelic influence had worked. Whatever made her different, that gave her the supernatural intuition, had prevented her from being influenced.

She would remember everything she'd seen, everything she'd learned.

It was dangerous information for a seventeen-year-old. I should know.

When they left, Bishop looked at Cassandra. "You'll go with Samantha back to her house. Wait for her outside the church, all right?"

"All right." Cassandra glanced at me, then left the two of us alone.

"And where will you go?" My chest clenched at the thought of saying goodbye to him again.

"The others want me to stay away from you. I think we've already proven how dangerous it can be when we're too close."

I swallowed hard. "Yeah, very dangerous. So where are you headed?"

He held my gaze. "To your house."

My brows rose. "What?"

He snorted softly at my surprised reaction. "I honestly don't care what anybody says, I'm not letting you out of my sight right now. Understand?"

I just nodded, stunned he was even suggesting this. He could have easily let Cassandra take me home and joined the others at the house party.

But he wanted to stay with me.

He took hold of the small dagger now lying on the top of the empty wooden desk. He wiped the blade on his jeans to clean it of Roth's blood.

"I believe this is yours." He handed it to me. When I took it from him, our fingers brushed against each other.

I returned it to its sheath under my skirt. "Thank you. I'm sorry about what happened—"

"Don't apologize. And Kraven's wrong. It wasn't your fault. What Stephen did to you…" His expression darkened. "I could have killed him for that."

"Killing isn't always the answer."

"I know that."

I swallowed hard. "I saw you kill Kraven. In your memory."

He turned away, but I caught his arm.

"It wasn't you," I said firmly. "It couldn't have been. There has to be some other explanation why you'd do that."

When his gaze met mine again, this time it was stormy. "It's funny, you seeing that memory."

I laughed this time, a dry, humorless sound. "What's so funny about it?"

"Because…a lot of the details are a blank for me. But I guess, somewhere in my head it's all still there, crystal clear." His brows drew tightly together. "What happened with Kraven… he was my brother. We had our problems, sure, but—I remember the cold certainty that came over me that night. The knowledge that he had to die and that his soul was bound for Hell…but—" he rubbed a hand over his mouth and looked away from me "—I don't know why I couldn't stop myself from killing the one person who ever gave a damn about me."

I stared at him. This was the confirmation I'd been looking for. "You can't remember why you did it? Seriously?"

He gave me a wry look. "It doesn't excuse what I did."

"But in a way it does. It tells me you weren't yourself at the time."

"But I still did it. Nobody else. You saw that yourself."

I tried to figure it out, but failed miserably. "No matter what you might have done, you're still an angel. Your soul was not dark and heavy enough to become a demon, so as horrible as it was, it must have been the right thing to do at the time. You told me yourself—killing Kraven and sending him to Hell is what helped you become an angel. There has to be a reason for that."

"There was." He inhaled deeply and let it out slowly. "There was somebody on my side. Somebody who put in a good word for me—somebody who also sent people to Hell whenever he got the chance."

"Who?"

He searched my face as if waiting for me to recoil from him with disgust and horror over all of this. But I'd been in training lately to handle a lot of bizarre stuff. I could handle more. I was like a pack mule for supernatural craziness now.

"My father," he finally said.

I blinked with surprise. "Your father?"

He nodded slowly. "Just like your birth mother—my father was an angel. That got me a chance when otherwise I know I would have been damned."

"Your father was a—an *angel*." Maybe this pack mule's back wasn't as strong as I originally thought.

"Yeah. Let's just say, my mother had widely differing tastes when it came to men." He shook his head, his expression shuttering as if he'd realized he'd said far too much. "Come on, I'm taking you home."

I needed more time, more information. But he'd put an end to it. Quite honestly, I think this was the most I'd ever gotten out of him. While mind-blowing, I considered it serious progress.

We caught up with Cassandra, and together we headed back to my house. Once there, it felt very strange to have Bishop come in through the front door. It seemed like such a mundane thing for someone like him to do.

Entrances through bedroom windows, however...

"I'm starving," Cassandra said immediately. She hadn't said much on the way here, keeping quiet and looking pale. Now that her secret was out, her real mission, I had no idea what was going on in her head. When I'd met her eyes to try to find out more by reading her mind, I'd found that her walls were up—solid and impenetrable.

She disappeared into the kitchen, leaving Bishop and me alone.

"Are we going to the party tonight?" I asked.

"No. The others have it under surveillance. We'll go back to Ambrosia and look for Stephen. Someone there has to know where he is."

His gaze moved over everything in the foyer, from the

throw rug, to the coatrack, to the framed pictures of me and my mom.

"Pretty boring stuff," I said, embarrassed by the level of mundane he was able to witness in such a small space.

His attention moved to me. "Hardly. I find everything here...very interesting."

My face felt warm. His soul was hard to ignore right now, as was my hunger, but I hoped I had a decent lock on it.

The calm before the storm, I thought. *Gets better before it gets worse.*

Such a pessimist.

No, a *realist*. There was a big difference.

"Earlier, you said that you didn't want to let me out of your sight," I said cautiously.

He didn't take his eyes off me for a moment. "That's exactly what I said."

"There might be a slight problem with that plan."

"What?"

I took my coat off and threw it on the coatrack like I'd done hundreds of times before. "I need to take a shower."

He raised an eyebrow. "Okay. Well, make it a fast one and I won't have to check on you."

"Fastest ever." I turned away from him before he could see me blush and rushed up the stairs to the second floor.

Before I hopped in the shower I quickly checked voice mail. There was a message from my mom about how much she was enjoying her vacation. Another one from Kelly confirming the new location for Noah's Halloween party and how she hoped I'd be there, even though I'd been missing in action lately. No calls from the school. I'd missed the better part of two days, but they hadn't checked up on me yet. For all they would have known I was sick at home. It was a big relief.

When I hung up, I heard my bedroom door open, and I repressed a smile.

"It's only been five minutes. You're already checking on me?" I turned to the door, surprised to see Cassandra standing there, not Bishop.

"Are you all right?" I asked, concerned by how upset she looked.

She shook her head. "I didn't mean for any of this to happen."

I swallowed hard. "Care to be more specific? There's a lot happening."

"With the angel I was sent to find. How much damage she's done—how many lives she's destroyed after escaping the Hollow."

"That's not your fault," I assured her.

"Feels like it is."

I moved toward her and took her hands in mine and squeezed them. "No, it's not. It's her—she's disturbed. Really disturbed. And this—it's the only way she can cope. Can you think of any way we can help her without having to kill somebody she possesses?"

"I keep trying to find another way. I don't know."

"Can we talk to her? Can we reason with her?"

"I hope so." She blinked, her eyes glossy. "But I'm not just upset about that. It's…Roth, too."

I watched her carefully. "What about him?"

"I can't explain how I feel. Before, I—I could barely even tolerate being in the same room as him. He annoyed me so much. And normally, I'm very even tempered! I am praised for my calm and professional manner. Always!"

"I'm sure you are," I agreed without hesitation.

"He's become a distraction. He's the reason I haven't been able to concentrate on my real mission as much as I should."

Her forehead furrowed, but then her expression relaxed a fraction. "What am I saying? Am I seriously trying to blame him? It's not his fault. But he's…a great inconvenience to me."

I couldn't help but laugh just a little. "Yeah, that's usually the way it is with boys—no matter who they are."

Cassandra's eyes snapped up to mine. "When he kissed me for the first time last night I slapped him. Really hard. But all he did was laugh at me before kissing me again. And *that* time…"

"That time you kissed him back," I finished for her.

"He's trying to make me look like a fool," she whispered, her expression agonized. "He doesn't really like me."

"Wrong. He does." No reason to play games here. "I read his mind. I saw that he's confused—just as confused as you are—but there are real emotions at stake here…for both of you. Nothing simple, nothing neat, but it is real."

This confirmation didn't seem to make her happier; if anything, her expression became only more miserable. "That's even worse than I thought."

My chest grew tight and I hugged her. "Don't worry. Nobody has to know you're breaking the balance rules with him. I swear I won't tell anyone. You're safe."

"It's not that."

I leaned back. "Then what is it?"

She wiped her eyes. Then her gaze rose to meet mine again. "Wait. You can read minds, too? Is that like what you did with Bishop—how you saw his memories? How can you do that?"

I thought she already knew this. Letting more of my secrets out of the bag—even though I hadn't considered *this* one a secret—made my heart start racing. "It's just more of that supernatural intuition," I said evenly. "I think Jordan's got the same thing going on."

She studied me a little too closely and I could practically

see the wheels turning in her head. Her eyes widened with shock. "Samantha...are you a nexus?"

I stopped breathing. "What?"

"It would explain everything, actually. I'm not sure why I didn't consider it before. But...if that's true...how could you be a gray, too?"

I fought to stay calm and look confused instead of panicked over this hypothesis. "I don't know what you're talking about. I'm nothing special. Just a messed-up kid who has a minor bit of sixth sense going on."

Her strained expression didn't ease off. "Sure you are. Or maybe, just maybe, we're both in way more trouble than we'd like to admit."

I swallowed hard. "Maybe."

She didn't keep grilling me on the subject. She left, closing the door softly behind her. I sat down heavily and stared at myself in my vanity mirror, trying to harness my racing thoughts. Even up here I still felt Bishop's presence downstairs. My hunger swirled, making it difficult to catch my breath.

Now Cassandra knew my secret, too.

I jumped in the shower and tried to let the scorching hot water—a relief after being locked in that basement for so long—wash my cares away. Didn't work in the slightest. I got out in record time.

It wasn't until I turned on my blow-dryer that I had the vision.

I didn't have many of these. But when I did have them, they flattened me with their intensity. This one wasn't an exception to the rule.

Like a waking dream with the intensity of a hurricane. The images shifted, sliding, turning so I could barely see anything properly.

It was a house—a big house with tons of kids there wearing masks and costumes. They milled about, drinks in hand; making out, talking, having fun. Music blared all around.

I also sensed the mind of the angel—the bodiless one. Somewhere else. Somewhere close. She wasn't like the others—the team of angels and demons I'd come to know. She was different. The essence of what she once was distorted like a reflection in a funhouse mirror, turned monstrous, feeding on joy and hope to keep her own misery at bay. She knew doing this was draining her victims of the will to live. It filled her with despair, but she couldn't stop. Survival and hunger were this angel's only remaining motivations.

She was as wretched as she was terrifying.

She felt drawn to this house. It was like a bright beacon lighting her way through the dark city.

And when she arrived she would find so many kids who were filled with life and joy…

It would be an incredible feast for her.

The vision shifted, like metal twisting after a car wreck. It was after—bodies strewn around the house, lifeless, blood everywhere, it smeared the walls and oozed out onto the carpet and hardwood floors.

Noah's Halloween party had turned into a mass suicide.

The vision ended and I staggered back, my head splitting in pain. It knocked me right to the floor. Immediately, I scrambled to get up, finished getting dressed and raced downstairs as fast as I could.

Bishop looked at me with alarm from where he stood, still in the foyer, this wild girl who'd practically flown down the stairs with still-damp hair.

"What's wrong?" he demanded.

I explained as quickly as I could what I'd seen. Cassandra appeared, her arms crossed. She'd heard me. Neither of them told me not to worry, that it was only my imagination.

"Has it already happened?" Cassandra asked shakily.

I shook my head. "No, but it's going to."

"A vision of the future." She eyed me warily. "Do you have these often?"

"Thankfully, no." My last one had been a vision of the city being destroyed and sucked into what I now knew to be the Hollow. I didn't remember it with perfect clarity—I think it was a way of my mind rejecting the sight of such an apocalyptic disaster.

But the future *could* be changed. Neither of my horrible visions had to come true.

"We're leaving," Bishop said firmly. "Right now."

"I'm coming, too," I said just as firmly.

He met my gaze. "Yes, you're coming, too."

Looked like I was going to Noah's Halloween party after all.

chapter 25

"We can take my mom's car," I said, grabbing the keys before I left. "But I can't drive."

"Why not?" Cassandra asked.

"No license. I've been meaning to get around to it."

"I can drive," Bishop said, taking the keys from me.

"You have a license?"

"Well…not technically. But that's never stopped me before."

"Good enough for me." I climbed in the backseat. Cassandra got in the passenger side. "Just—promise me not to hurt the car."

"I'll try."

"Try, like, really hard. Despite dealing with angels, demons and otherworldly death vortexes, you haven't seen my mother when she's angry."

"I could grab a different car," he offered. "I've hot-wired them before."

"Stealing cars," I said under my breath wryly. "Why am I not surprised?"

"I preferred to think of it as borrowing." He flashed me a wicked grin that made my heart race even faster before he turned the key in the ignition and pulled out of the driveway.

I didn't want to think about how this night would end, but I knew that everyone at that party was currently at risk. If we didn't do something to stop the bodiless angel, it would be a massacre.

As we neared the house, I felt the harsh stirrings of my hunger. It cramped my stomach. "Wait. Don't get any closer."

Bishop must have heard something in my tone that alarmed him. He pulled up to the curb and backed up twenty feet. "Better?"

"Yeah, a little. This house—it's the same one where I had a hunger freak-out before. When I was with Kraven." I recognized the neighborhood immediately. Even from where we were—a block away—I could see my mom's real-estate sign out front.

This was where the Halloween party was being held.

"What is it?" Bishop asked. "What's triggering your hunger here?"

"I don't know. Although...maybe..." I got out of the car when he and Cassandra did, sending a wary gaze down the street.

"What?"

"It's stupid, but my mother said this house is haunted. That's why she was having a hard time selling it. Maybe I can sense the ghosts? Does that make any sense?" Noah had arranged for his Halloween party to be held in an allegedly haunted house. If I was my normal, everyday self I would have thought that was really cool.

"We'll check it out. You—" Cassandra gave me a concerned look "—wait here by the car."

I hated that I'd have to hang back and not be a part of this, but with the way that house made me feel, I knew there wasn't any other answer.

Something else approached from the shadows nearby. It took a moment for me to realize it was Kraven.

"Good party," he said. "You're missing all the fun."

"You took Jordan home?" Bishop asked.

"I did. She's a charmer. And by that I mean she's a total bitch."

"But she's safe."

"Debatable. She's already here at the party—must have gotten into her costume in record time. I gave her the evil eye when I saw her ten minutes ago, and got the middle finger in return. Like I said, charming." He swept a glance back toward the house. "I know this is a problem area, based on gray-girl's reaction the last time we were here." He eyed us. "Why are you here?"

"I had a vision," I explained. "The angel that killed Zach is coming here."

"Visions." He raised an eyebrow, scanning me. "Right. Forgot you could do that. You're like a veritable toolbox of supernatural handiness, aren't you? No wonder my brother doesn't want to see you dead. Yet."

There was something off about him, but I wasn't sure what it was. Something crueler and ruder than normal.

"What's your problem?" Bishop asked, a hard edge of unpleasantness in his tone.

This made Kraven laugh. The cold sound shivered down my spine.

"My problem. You know, I've been thinking a lot about what's happened earlier tonight. Crazy stuff, right?" He glanced at each of us in turn. "I keep coming back to the moment I saved your ass, brother."

I had wondered if they'd forgotten about that. I sure hadn't. The moment when Kraven saved Bishop from being swept into the Hollow right after Zach was burned into my brain.

Bishop studied him with his arms crossed over his chest. "If you have any problems with me, we can deal with them later."

Kraven shrugged. "Nah. I want to deal with them now."

I looked at Bishop to get his reaction to this; there was a look of deep annoyance on his face. He turned to Cassandra, and unstrapped his sheath and dagger from under his shirt, then handed it to her.

"Go," he said. "We'll catch up to you. Survey the party and see if there are any problems. If there are, you know what to do."

Cassandra flicked a glance at me, her gaze worried...and there was something else there. An edge of sheer determination and resolve.

She was good at her job. This was what she'd been sent here for—to deal with this lost angel. After that, I knew Cassandra would be able to focus on helping the guys with the continuing gray situation—as well as dealing with whatever was going on with her and Roth.

The sooner this bad angel was destroyed, the better. I just hoped Cassandra would be able to think of a way to reason with her.

She walked right up to Kraven, who was blocking her path.

"You going to give me a problem right now, demon?" she asked tightly.

"No, Blondie, you're not my concern tonight. Go flutter away where you're needed. I think Roth's already in the house. I'm sure he'll be thrilled to see you."

Something in the way he said it—that all-too-familiar mocking edge to his words.

He knew about Cassandra and Roth.

The demon knew too much for his own good.

With a glare that showed that she might be thinking the

same thing, Cassandra took off at a run in the direction of the party house.

I drew my coat closer to block out the chill. I assumed Bishop would want me to wait in the car while they checked out the house, but I wasn't ready to crawl back inside yet.

It was so cold tonight—like below zero. At least, that was how it felt to me.

Increased cold, increased hunger.

I blocked out the sound of Stephen's voice from inside my head. I wasn't like him. I wasn't. My birth parents were very special. I was special, too. I would be different.

I would not lose hope.

"So here we are," Kraven said, his arms crossed. He moved slowly toward us, his gaze locked on Bishop in a chillingly predatory way. "You, me and your little girlfriend. Or is she? I'm getting confused. You can't kiss her. She's basically one of the things we're fighting against here in this city that will keep us trapped for as long as she's still breathing. Being around you is torture for her. I wonder what the appeal is. Frankly, I can't see it."

"Are you going to whine all evening or get to the point?" Bishop asked.

"Whatever. I do sort of get it, you know. You're addicted. She's addicted. It's kind of adorable, if you're into junkies. Won't end well, I can guarantee you that."

"If I wanted your opinion, James," Bishop said unpleasantly. "I'd beat it out of you."

Kraven smirked at him. "Noticed that you got rid of the only weapon in this city that can kill either of us. Did you do that on purpose?"

"What do you think?"

"I'm going to vote yes on that. You're afraid I'm going to kill you."

"More like the other way around." Bishop looked at me. "You should go back home."

"And miss this brotherly standoff?" I said. "Not a chance."

Nope. No way was I missing out on this. After what I'd seen, what I'd heard, and the way my imagination was working overtime to put it all together, I wanted to know more about them. Both of them.

Kraven laughed again coldly. "You haven't fooled her completely, you know, with your angelic sparkle. She knows there's bad blood between us."

"I could have spotted that from a mile away," I told him. "Even without a glimpse at some of Bishop's memories."

Bishop cringed at the reminder that I'd seen bits and pieces of his very sordid past.

"Bishop," Kraven said, rolling the name over his tongue with distaste. "I never asked. Did they give that painfully insipid name to you or did you choose it yourself?"

Bishop stood there, unflinchingly. "They gave it to me."

"New identity, new existence. You think you can forget who you were? Like it's that easy?"

"Trying to."

"It'll never happen."

"You saved me tonight, Kraven. Don't say you were trying to push me into the Hollow. Because you weren't." His jaw tightened. "That means something to me."

Kraven scoffed, his attention turning to the Italian restaurant a block up the street where he'd kissed me the other night to help me deal with my hunger. "It would have solved a lot of problems to see you take a nosedive in there. It was a knee-jerk reaction to save your ass, nothing conscious about it."

When Bishop turned away from him I saw an edge of pain slide through his gaze that made my heart wrench. Whatever he tried to make either of us believe, Kraven still had the power to hurt him with words.

"Enough of this," Bishop growled. "We don't have the time. We have to get to that house and stop a group of kids from committing mass suicide. Understand? What happened to Zach isn't going to happen to anyone else."

"If I'd let the Hollow take you," Kraven continued as if he wasn't paying attention to a word Bishop said, "then I wouldn't have been able to witness your continued suffering."

Bishop looked at him. "Is that what you want? To watch me suffer?"

Kraven's lips thinned. "That's what I've wanted ever since you sent me to Hell and got a first-class elevator ride up to Heaven as some sort of shining champion."

"You think it was that easy for me?"

"I don't give a damn how easy it was."

"What the hell is wrong with you? Both of you?" I snapped, unable to keep it inside any longer. I usually said what was on my mind without too many filters. Tonight wasn't going to be the exception to the rule. "You could have had this out with each other for the last three weeks, but you wait till now? Why now? Why here?"

Kraven glared at me. "Because I saved him tonight and it pissed me off. That's what I used to do, you know. Save his ass when he got into trouble. And he thanked me by shoving a knife into me when he knew I was already on Hell's shortlist."

"Don't try to pretend you were a good guy, James," Bishop said darkly. "You weren't."

He snorted. "Nah, I was as badass as they came back then. But I was also young and stupid. I didn't even get a chance to try to redeem myself for the things I did. I might have succeeded."

Bishop hissed out a breath. "Whether you believe this or

not, I wish I could go back and change what I did." Again, he averted his gaze from his brother as pain slid through his eyes.

A small muscle in Kraven's cheek twitched. His dark gold hair had fallen into his eyes and he swiped it back. His amber eyes held the same pain I saw in Bishop's. "Like I'd believe a damn thing you say."

"It's the truth. Believe it or don't believe it. Right now, I don't care. There are bigger things to deal with in this city tonight than our feud."

"Feud?" Kraven snapped. "You think this is as simple as a feud?"

Bishop straightened his shoulders and wiped the pain from his face before he turned to Kraven again. "It's ancient history."

"Doesn't even bother to apologize," Kraven said, flicking a glance at me. "How do you like that? Total son of a bitch."

My chest felt so tight listening to all of this, I could barely breathe. I understood Kraven's outrage, and I also believed that Bishop regretted what he'd done. "You two need to talk about this later."

The demon shot me a dark look. "And here I thought you were drooling to learn the truth about my brother. Maybe you're scared to know it now. Might change how you feel about the two of us. Might make you like me more."

"You don't even give me a chance to like you," I snapped. "Before you go and say something to make me hate you again."

"Ouch."

"But…I know there's still good in you, Kraven," I continued, forcing myself to stay calm. "You proved that by saving Bishop earlier."

He rolled his eyes. "Oh, bite me, sweetness. Seriously." Then he returned his gaze to Bishop. "By the way, I know she's a nexus."

My stomach dropped.

Bishop froze. "What?"

"Angel and demon parents. I think you've been acquainted with nexi in the past as one of Heaven's lapdog assassins. Killing them, anyway. Not whispering sweet nothings in their ears."

Bishop's expression darkened. "You don't know what you're talking about."

"So I guess that makes three that should be put on your kill list, right? A dangerous angel-demon hybrid like sweetness here, and two rule-busting renegades like the romantically inclined Cassandra and Roth."

Bishop stared him down. "Are you finished running your mouth?"

"Oh, I'm just getting started."

Bishop stormed toward Kraven, grabbed him by his shirt and slammed him down on the hood of my mother's car hard enough to make me shriek. "No, you're definitely finished. It's over. I've tolerated you long enough. Your hate has made you blind—you keep us from getting to that house and helping those who need help because you're so consumed by your own self-pity. You destroy anything you touch—just like old times. I see that now. You haven't changed a bit."

"Screw you," Kraven spat out. "What do I care what you think? You're crazy. You're losing it."

"How about this, James? Make a threatening move toward Samantha and I will kill you. And this time there won't be any deals or rituals to resurrect your sorry ass again."

I couldn't help but agree with the demon. Bishop had every right to be angry with him, but there was something erratic about his behavior now, something crazed flashing behind his gaze. Something dangerous.

"Bishop, let him go," I said, my voice shaky. "Please. We don't have time for this."

When he looked at me, Kraven shoved Bishop back from him.

"You think you can kill me? Not if I kill you first. You can't even handle being leader as it is. You can cut yourself up as much as you like, you can hold hands with gray-girl all day long, but soon it won't help. You're going to be completely bat-shit insane soon, no matter what quick fix you have in place. And I'll be happy to sit back and watch the show with popcorn in hand."

Bishop's fists were clenched at his sides. "I've felt guilty for killing you all this time. When I saw you for the first time in that alley with no memories…knowing I had to stab you…"

Kraven's eyes glowed red in the darkness, betraying his anger, his pain. "You did it without any hesitation. Both times."

"You don't know what's going on in my head."

"I don't want to know. I hate you."

Kraven grabbed Bishop's shirt and slammed him against a brick wall so hard that the surface cracked. Bishop shook it off and launched himself at the demon, grabbing him hard. They started to fight in earnest now, years of anger and pain built up to overflow tonight. Two immortal beings raging against each other, able to hurt, to draw blood, to break bones, but not kill each other. Not without the dagger.

"Stop it," I growled. "Both of you."

It was so cold I swear my skin was turning to ice. My hunger hadn't stopped for a moment. It had only increased, doubling every minute, even though we were far enough away from the house that it shouldn't have bothered me, and there was enough distance between me and where Bishop and Kraven were fighting.

My heart pounded faster and faster. My breath came so quickly I thought I might hyperventilate. A wash of darkness moved across my vision.

I let out a harsh cry and collapsed to my knees. The world spun—reminding me of the one time me and Carly did vodka shots before a house party to give ourselves courage, but ended up violently ill instead. But this was worse—much worse than that. I clawed at the pavement, breaking my already short nails.

"Samantha—" Bishop was at my side a moment later. There was a bloody gash on his forehead.

I moaned, then dragged in a ragged breath that hurt my throat. "No, don't get close. Too close. Too much. So cold, Bishop. It's so cold. Please…"

Kraven stood nearby. His face was bleeding, too. "You know what's happening to her. You know what this means."

"Be quiet," he snarled.

"It's time. Don't wait to see what happens to her next— or how much she'll suffer. Put her out of her misery now." Instead of joy in the demon's tone, there was dark certainty. He didn't say this to be cruel. This was something they'd discussed before.

What to do when I finally went into stasis.

"I thought you actually gave a damn about her," Bishop said tightly. "Guess I was wrong."

Kraven shot him a look of disdain. "Suggesting a quick, clean death, rather than melting on the sidewalk? Rather than seeing her turn into a total sociopath? Yeah, you're right. Guess I don't give a damn."

Bishop swore. "Go to the party. Find the others. Help them. Stop that angel any way you have to."

"Wait. What about…I can kiss her again if it'll help."

"It won't help. Not anymore."

"But—"

"No. You'll never kiss her again."

Bishop picked me up in his arms as if I weighed nothing more than a feather and cradled me against his chest. Then he turned away from Kraven and began running down the street in the opposite direction. I could barely lift my head to see Kraven still standing there watching us get farther and farther away, a bleak look in his amber-colored eyes.

He knew the same thing I knew—whether I lived or died, this was the end for me.

chapter 26

Kraven had put it perfectly. Tonight, I would either die and fade away, or I would go into a zombielike state. And if I survived, I would come out the other side totally evil.

A living nightmare.

I'd rather die than be like that.

This was happening too fast. It had been drawing closer and closer, but I'd really started to believe I was different. I'd believed the lies.

I wasn't different. I was a gray. And I was terrified of what was to come next.

Bishop came to a townhome and kicked the front door. The lock splintered the frame as it swung open. It was all dark inside. Nobody was home. He carried me inside to the living room where he gently placed me down on the sofa.

I twisted. It wasn't pain, really. But something bad was happening to me. The cold and hunger combined to make me numb as it burrowed into me—a caterpillar creating its cocoon. My vision went blurry and my skin turned to ice.

"What can I do?" Bishop asked harshly. "What can I do to help you? I need time to find Stephen. To get your soul back. It's not too late."

I just shook my head back and forth. It *was* too late. It was happening, and it was happening now. "Stephen said the only way to hold off stasis—would be to feed."

"When did he tell you this?" His voice turned angry. "Why didn't you tell me?"

Whatever was inside me moved through my limbs to my fingers and toes, making everything numb and cold. "Doesn't matter anymore. I wouldn't do it, anyway. I won't hurt anyone like that—not again—no matter what."

"You should have told me anyway, Sam. Damn it."

He never called me Sam. Always Samantha. More formal—even though I loved how he said my name. "But I can't feed. I can't—"

Then, suddenly, his mouth was on mine. I let out a cry of surprise. He kissed me hard and deep, gathering me in his arms so much that he raised me right up off the sofa.

This is what I'd dreamed about—Bishop's lips on mine as he kissed me with total abandon.

But it wasn't supposed to be like this.

"Feed," he whispered. "Come on. Feed on me, Samantha."

His heart beat fast against my own weakening pulse. I still sensed his soul, I still craved it more than anything else, but there was a wall there, muting it, closing off my access to it—even if I'd wanted to take it. My heart wrenched at the thought of hurting him. But if he'd done this before, I wouldn't have had any choice. I would have lost control and destroyed him forever.

I had control now. But there was a very good reason.

No, scratch that. A very *bad* reason.

"It's too late," I whispered.

"No." His voice caught and twisted. "I won't accept that."

"I'm dying."

"No!" He got up and kicked the coffee table, sending it

flying across the room and splintering into the wall. Then he fell to my side again, his expression agonized. "Take my soul. Take all of it. I don't care. I can't lose you."

When he crushed his mouth against mine again and kissed me so hard and desperately, my lips felt bruised.

But nothing happened. It was a while before he finally relented.

My voice was strained and barely audible. "Do your job. Take my life. End this. Don't let me become like Stephen."

"I'm not giving up on you."

Tears streaked from the corners of my eyes. The horrible cold pressed in on me on all sides, despite Bishop's warm touch. Icy fingers sank into me, freezing me from the inside out. "You've killed things like me before. Why is this any different?"

"Because *you're* different." He reached down to clutch my hands in his. His brows were drawn tightly together above eyes that blazed bright blue. "You're better than this. You don't realize how strong you really are—not yet. You've only just started to know what you are. You're amazing. And you can fight this." His voice was broken, raw. "I can try to heal you, Sam. Stay with me!"

As he spoke, his voice had grown fainter and fainter. I wanted to reply. I wanted to tell him that I loved him. I didn't want to leave him. I wanted to be with him, now and forever. Despite everything, despite my fear over his past, despite it being such a short time since we'd met. Despite the secrets and lies...

I loved him.

But there was nothing he could do to save me.

My vision...my world...faded to gray.

Then to black.

Then to white.

And then...uh, blue.

Blue?

Yes. Blue. With fluffy white clouds.

There was something at my back. Something hard. I pressed my hands down to feel hard sand.

Where was I? What just happened?

"Are you going to lie there all day or what?"

I recognized the voice, but it was a moment before I could put a name to it. I pushed myself into a sitting position and looked around to see that I was in the middle of a wasteland, just the one from my dream about Bishop...where he'd kissed me and then killed me.

I swiveled until I saw Seth sitting nearby at a table, looking at me.

"You," I said, confusion crashing down all around me. "I... uh...what's going on?"

"You died, that's what's going on."

I slowly got to my feet, turning around in a slow circle to take in the endless desert that stretched out all around me. The sky was the same flat gray I remembered from the last dream. And it was warm—I hadn't felt this warm outside, or in, since my soul was taken. At least, not unless I was holding Bishop's hand.

"I'm dreaming right now. But how can I dream if I'm dead?" I whipped back around toward him. He looked different from the last time I saw him. Cleaner. Better groomed. His dark beard was trimmed short, not long and scraggly. Now I realized he was at least ten years younger than I always thought he was. If he was even thirty I'd be surprised. "What are you doing here?"

"In your after-death dream?"

"Yeah."

He shrugged. "I guess you wanted me here."

I studied him, trying to figure out what didn't seem right. Then it clicked. "Wait. You sound totally sane."

"I am sane here." He glanced around. "Other places, not so much."

I looked down at the table he sat at to see that there was a game of chess set up. "I've dreamed about chess before."

"You were playing it?"

"Yes, I mean, I think so. But I don't know how to play chess. Checkers, now we're talking. But chess is complicated."

"You're right. It's very complicated." He waved a hand. "It's your move, by the way. I've been waiting a very long time for you to get here."

I sat down across from him and looked at the board before meeting his brown eyes. "How can I play if I don't know how?"

"You know more than you think you do."

"You said that to me before, but seriously, I don't know."

"Then I'll teach you. Be happy to. Only…" He glanced around. "We don't have much time left."

"I'm dead." I said it flatly, shocked that the idea of it didn't trouble me as much as I thought it might. Just like before, I still felt numb. "And I'm dreaming."

"You are."

Maybe it was because I felt better here. More whole. There was no hunger, no cold. But still, there was something missing. Something that felt empty in my chest.

Bishop. My hands began to tremble and I pressed them tightly together. "I can't stay here."

"First, make your move." He nodded at the board.

One piece glowed with a soft blue light, drawing my attention. "What's that piece called?"

Seth looked down the board. "That's the bishop."

My breath caught. When I put my hand on it I felt it hum

pleasantly against my skin. The piece knew where it wanted to go; all it needed was my help to get there.

I pushed it forward two spaces. "Is this okay?"

"Yes." Seth smiled, leaned forward, and made his move, knocking over my bishop with his piece. He snatched it off the board and placed it to the side. "Check."

"Check? What does that mean?"

His lips curved. "It means I'm winning."

I blinked at him. "Why am I dreaming about you, Seth? Why now?"

"Time for you to go." He stood up from the table and the chess board shimmered away so there was nothing left on the table. A moment later, there was no table, either.

My panicked gaze shot to his. "But where can I go if I'm dead?"

He drew closer and patted my cheek. "It won't be much longer now. Angel, demon, light, dark. Even gray. Their destiny is already decided. Soon. Very soon."

"But I don't understand."

"You do. You just don't want to yet."

"Wait, I don't—"

But then the wasteland slipped away. Seth vanished. And everything went black again.

A moment later, my eyes shot wide-open and I sat bolt upright, gasping for breath.

I was in the dark living room again, on the couch where I'd died. I frantically searched the shadows to find Bishop.

He was there. Sitting with his back against the wall, his eyes glazed. Only the light from the moon and streetlamp shining through the window allowed me to see him.

"Bishop…" I began.

"Couldn't save you, couldn't heal you. You died in my arms."

Michelle Rowen

"I'm not dead."

He shook his head back and forth. "I hear you, but you're not here. Memories haunt me now—like they always have. Always, forever. I'm okay with that, when it's you. Haunt me, Samantha. Haunt me till the end. The very end."

His voice was low and hollow. The sound of it sent a chill straight through me. And his words, his tone—he'd completely lost his mind.

My heart broke for him, for his pain, knowing that I was the one to cause it.

"Couldn't save you," he muttered. "Couldn't save you. It was too late. I failed you. I failed you and now you're gone."

My body ached as I gingerly pushed myself up to a sitting position.

"I'm not dead," I said again, stronger this time.

When he laughed, the sharp sound cut through the dark room. "Saw you die. Watched you die. You're gone and now you haunt me." He inhaled raggedly and squeezed his eyes shut. "Damn it. Damn it, damn it, damn it."

I shakily got to my feet and moved toward him. He opened his eyes and looked up at me as I approached. The devastation mixed with glazed insanity in his eyes tore me up inside.

I crouched next to him. When I reached out to him, he cringed away from me, and averted his gaze toward the window.

"Bishop." Fear made my throat so thick it was nearly impossible to speak. "Look at me."

I didn't accept that he'd completely lost it. He believed that he could save me right until the moment it was too late, so I wasn't giving up on him. I didn't think I'd ever give up on him.

I wasn't losing him. Even if he'd already lost himself.

"I wanted to save you," he whispered.

316

"I know." I moved closer to him until I was only inches away. "And now I want to save *you*."

I grabbed his face between my hands and kissed him.

Electricity sparked between us, visible sparks—but it didn't hurt. It felt good. It felt better than it ever had before.

This was pure magic.

I was meant to kiss Bishop like this.

His tense muscles finally began to relax. I thought he would pull back, but instead he pulled me hard against him and deepened the kiss, holding nothing back.

I'd always mocked those movies where the characters kissed like this—such passion, such desperation between them as if they would die if they stopped.

I wouldn't be mocking them anymore. No way.

When Bishop finally pulled back a little, there was surprise in his wide, blue eyes—but the fog of insanity had lifted.

Relief filled me. It hadn't been too late—for either of us.

"You're alive," he managed.

"I am."

"You kissed me."

"I sure did."

"And—" his brows drew together with confusion "—you're not sucking my soul out through my mouth. Although, with a kiss like that it would have been very worth it."

I couldn't help but laugh nervously. "This is going to sound really strange, but I think part of me stayed dead. That *was* my stasis. And I didn't survive it."

Confusion crossed his gaze. "You're very lucid for a zombie."

I didn't understand any of this, but I knew there were two outcomes to stasis. Death or total evil. Unless this was one big illusion, this was neither. "Luckily, I'm not a zombie. But... the gray parts of me *did* die—the hunger, the chills."

Clarity shone in his gaze. "If you weren't a nexus, the rest of you would have stayed dead, too."

"I think so." I nodded, stunned. "But I'm back."

He pressed his fingertips to my throat to check my pulse. I definitely had one. He shook his head. "So I'm completely insane now. That must be it."

"Nope, you're not. Trust me. But we can't argue about it any longer. We have to get to the party. The team needs their leader."

Bishop took my face gently between his hands, touching me as if he couldn't believe I was actually here, with a heartbeat, back from the dead, not a zombie, and I could be near him without his soul making me crazy.

"This is completely unbelievable to me," he whispered.

He didn't say it in a "this is a miracle! Hallelujah!" way. More of a "what's the catch?" I'd been thinking the exact same thing, which helped dampen my joy of being finally relieved of my gray hunger.

"Kind of too good to be true, isn't it?" I said quietly.

"Kind of." He nodded gravely.

Bishop might be many fantastical things, and we might have next to nothing in common, but at his heart he was a realist just like me. My resurrection was not exactly textbook. Even I knew that. Especially with that after-death dream starring Seth, the fallen angel.

I quickly shared that with Bishop. "Do you think it was just a dream?"

He studied me. "Knowing you, Samantha, I honestly don't know."

As the numbness wore off, the realization that I'd literally returned from the dead—which I'd been for at least twenty minutes according to the wall clock—set in.

I was back, with no hunger, no cold, and I'd allow myself to feel joy at that.

The gray part of me had gone into stasis and she'd died twenty minutes ago on that couch.

The rest of me had come back for more. With a sore chest and bruised lips—and grateful as hell for both.

Together, Bishop and I left the townhome and raced down the street to get closer to the abandoned house—which, at the moment, was definitely *not* abandoned. Noah must have gotten word that it was haunted and decided that would make it a cool new location for his Halloween party. The iron gates were open enough to squeeze through. Some kids were out on the front lawn smoking. Everyone was in costume.

Well, not everyone. I'd been a bit preoccupied to think of something cool to wear.

The most important thing? Everyone was still alive.

My chilling vision had shown a massacre. The aftermath of the bodiless angel's carnage. It hadn't happened yet. Which meant we still had a chance to stop it.

"Are you okay here?" Bishop asked. "I know this place gave you problems before."

"I'm fine," I said, shaking my head. "Whatever it was…it's not an issue anymore."

"Good." Still, his expression was guarded and watchful as he studied me, as if waiting for something bad to happen. For my head to start spinning, or an alien to burst out of my chest.

It might be Halloween, but I sincerely hoped that my personal horror movie of the night was now running its end credits.

It was crowded here—to put it mildly. The furniture was covered in plastic dustcovers, but that gave it an appropriately eerie feel. Kids milled about. Music blasted from the speakers. There had to be more than a hundred kids from school here, elbow to elbow. Costumes of all kinds—scary, sexy, funny. Some kids wore masks, others makeup.

Seemed like a great party, actually. In another life I would have probably enjoyed myself, if I'd been ignorant to the dangers lurking close by, ready to destroy absolutely everything and everyone.

Yeah, that knowledge put a bit of a damper on potential fun.

Connor caught our eye and waved at us from across the room near the stairs. We went right to him. His gaze was alert, and there was none of the humor I was used to seeing on his face. It had disappeared after Zach's death.

He'd lost his best friend tonight.

"Nothing," he said, shaking his head. "Standard teen fare. Some underage drinking and some weed, but nothing supernatural. And no sign of our friend, Stephen."

"The angel's not here yet," Bishop said.

Connor stared at him. "The angel's going to be here?"

"I guess you haven't run into Cassandra yet."

"No, not yet. Big party. Roth's around here somewhere, too. We're ready for anything." He glanced at both of us before turning his attention to the crowd. "What's the plan, Bishop?"

"When and if the angel arrives, we need to isolate it. Get it away from the other kids."

After it possesses someone, I thought. The thought still made me ill, but even I had to admit that we were running out of options.

Was one dead kid worth the lives of a hundred?

Someone caught my eye. Jordan, in full white-and-gold Cleopatra costume and black wig, was quickly making her way down the stairs from the second floor as if she was being chased.

"Bishop," I said, "I have to find out what's wrong with her."

He caught my hand, but not hard enough to stop me. I might have lost my hunger, but the shiver of energy between us when we touched hadn't gone anywhere. "Be careful."

I nodded, then without another word, I threaded my way through the crowd of costumed kids and met her at the bottom of the stairs.

She didn't even notice me until I caught her arm. "Jordan, what's going on?"

She froze and looked over her shoulder at me. Her face was pale as a sheet of paper, despite her eyes heavily circled in black liner. "You're here."

She didn't say it as an insult, just as an observation.

I grabbed her hand. She didn't immediately pull away. Her skin was cold as ice. "What's wrong?"

"I had to be here tonight. Socially, I mean, I couldn't miss it. But I didn't know…" Her breath came in rapid gasps.

"Know what?"

"I didn't know about…the ghosts."

I stared at her. "Excuse me?"

"This place is haunted. Like one hundred percent total hauntage."

My eyes widened. The rumors were actually true about this house? "You can feel that?"

She nodded. "It wasn't too bad when I got here. Just a low hum for me. But then some girls broke out a Ouija board upstairs and—*bam*. She—she spoke to me." Her eyes were glossy. "I *know* it was her."

"Who?"

Jordan met my gaze. She looked equal parts terrified and stunned. "Julie."

A chill shot down my spine. "Julie?"

Her forehead screwed up into a frown. "I mean, I know she—she's gone…but she's *here*. And I—I had to get away."

I'd been stunned into utter silence. This was why I couldn't approach this house before. As a gray, my hunger had been triggered into overdrive.

Ghosts were disembodied souls. And this house was filled to overflowing with them.

I scanned the party. I couldn't sense anything now, but Jordan could. She was the one with supernatural intuition.

What was wrong with this place? Why were so many ghosts here? Why was Julie still here?

There had to be a reason, and I had a strong feeling it was vitally important.

"Show me," I said, clutching Jordan's arm. "Show me on the Ouija board right now."

chapter 27

Jordan gaped at me. "Are you nuts? I'm not going back up there."

If there were actual ghosts stuck in this house, there was a reason for it. And if they were disembodied souls, then they might be able to point me in the direction of the angel. They might even help me communicate with her so no one else had to get hurt. "I thought Julie was your friend."

She grew even paler and her freckles stood out even more against her white skin and black Cleopatra wig. "The others weren't taking it seriously. They think it's just a big, stupid joke. But it—it scared me."

"Of course it did."

"I felt her, Samantha. I felt her…presence. And I felt others, too. What is this?" she asked, her shaky voice betraying her fear. "Why can I feel these things? Am I going crazy?"

I really hated to say this even though it was true. "Because you're special."

That earned me a glare that cut through her bleak expression. "Shut up."

"I'm actually being totally serious right now." I exchanged a glance with Bishop across the crowded room. I pulled Jordan with me back up the stairs. She didn't resist this time. From higher up on the stairs, I spotted Kraven over by the stereo speakers. He was drinking something out of a red plastic cup and he looked morose. His gaze flicked to me and his brows shot up.

Yup, still alive, I thought. *Shocker.*

It had been his suggestion that Bishop put me out of my misery. Part of me hated that he'd done that, the other part knew he'd meant it to help end my suffering.

Even *I'd* begged for death at one point.

We found the room where three girls I recognized from school were gathered around a Ouija board. Then looked up at us. "Oh, you're back," a blonde said. "Good. It's not working anymore without you."

Jordan looked at me as if for guidance.

I tried to stay calm. "You need to ask Julie why she's still here. Why all of them are."

"Because they're ghosts," she replied. "Duh."

"No. I mean, I don't know much about this, but to me a ghost sticks around because it has unfinished business. If there are a bunch of them, all stuck in this house, there has to be a reason." I'd dealt with angels and demons; I couldn't let the thought of ghosts freak me out. Still, it was incredibly unnerving to think there might be spirits all around us, watching and waiting. But for what?

Jordan finally nodded and sat down and looked at the other girls. "Get out of here."

"But it's our board," the blonde whined.

Jordan sent a razor-sharp glare toward her. "*Now.* I'm not asking again."

She had a natural way about her that was incredibly intimidating. This time, I appreciated it. The girls fled the room, leaving us alone in the musty-smelling room. The sound of the blaring music downstairs made it difficult to concentrate, but when I closed the door it helped muffle it a little.

Jordan looked up at me from the floor as she settled in front of the Ouija board. "Just so you know, I'm doing this for Julie, not because you asked me to."

I nodded. "Noted."

She eyed me. "You seem different tonight than you were earlier."

I sat down across from her and pressed my hands against the smooth wood floor. "I died a little while ago. Went to a dream dimension and had a bizarre chat with a homeless fallen angel."

She stared at me. "You're being serious right now, aren't you?"

"I am."

"Dead."

"On arrival. But I'm back. And I'm not a gray anymore."

There was more confusion, but then hope lit up her eyes. "Does that mean that Stephen can be cured, too?"

My throat tightened. "I don't think so. It was something bizarre that only happened to me."

The hope disappeared from her green eyes and they brimmed with tears. "So he's not going to get better. Ever."

I could empathize with what it was like to lose someone you loved—for them to slip out of your grasp no matter what you tried to do to save them. It hurt like hell, even if they weren't literally dead.

"I'm sorry," I said.

At that moment, I honestly meant it.

"I'm losing everybody." She drew in a ragged breath. "But if I can help Julie…"

She placed her fingertips on the Ouija board pointer.

"Do you need me to do that, too?" I asked.

She shook her head. Her forehead furrowed as she concentrated. "Julie, please come back. I'm sorry I ran before. Are you still here?"

I swear the room grew a few degrees colder. The fine hair on my arms rose.

The pointer slid across the Ouija board to YES.

A shiver went down my spine.

Jordan's gaze shot to mine.

"Why is she still here?" I asked, my chest tight.

"Why are you still here?" Jordan repeated shakily.

The pointer moved toward the alphabet, picking out a letter at a time.

TRAPPED

"How many are there?" I whispered. "That are like you?"

Jordan didn't need to translate this to the spirit world before I had my answer.

HUNDREDS

Horror slid through me. Hundreds of ghosts were in this house.

"What's trapping you?"

BARRIER

"Oh, my God." I inhaled sharply. "The barrier that's around the city? The one that keeps supernaturals inside?"

YES

"What barrier?" Jordan asked, looking directly at me, her brows tight together.

"Don't worry about it."

"Don't worry about it?" Her voice turned sharp. "It's trapping my best friend's spirit inside so she can't go to Heaven. I'm going to worry about it."

She made a good point. Besides, Jordan already knew way too much about what was going on in the city. She may as well know about the barrier, too.

"Why did you pick this house to be in?" I asked.

NEAR BORDER

And then...

THIN BARRIER HERE

I racked my mind to figure out what Julie meant, then it suddenly came to me. This house was very close to the city limits. It was only a block away. Therefore it was close to the edge of the protective barrier that trapped all supernaturals inside. Here, the barrier must be thinner than anywhere else. The ghosts—everyone who'd died since the barrier was created—had been drawn here collectively. "What happens when you try to go through the barrier?"

PAIN

A violent shiver raced through me. "I'm sorry."

HELP US

"I wish I could."

HELP US

My chest tightened. "I don't know how."

ONLY YOU CAN

Jordan gave me another dark look. "Why aren't you helping them? I mean, you've taken the crown as Miss Supernatural right now. Can't you do anything?"

The pointer moved again, picking out letters almost faster than I could follow.

IT'S HERE

Jordan looked down as Julie answered a question we hadn't even asked.

"What's here?" she asked breathlessly.

DEATH ANGEL

"Do you mean the one that made you..." I didn't want to say it out loud. Julie didn't need a reminder that she'd been driven to kill herself. "Can you see it?"

SO SAD

That would be it. It was here. Panic gripped me. "What does it want?"

PEACE

"How can I stop it without hurting anyone?"

CAN'T

"But what if..." I'd tried to work it out in my head. If the angel was a bodiless thing that could possess people, that meant it was basically like a soul. Grays consumed souls. Could a gray, one who hadn't gone through stasis yet, consume this angel and leave the human body it inhabited intact?

Jordan took her hands off the pointer for a moment to adjust her black Cleopatra wig. The point began to move all by itself.

We watched in stunned silence as it pointed to a letter at a time.

RUN

It was only one word spelled out on a board, but it held an urgency that couldn't be ignored. I got to my feet so fast I got a head rush.

Jordan grabbed my arm. "Do you feel that?"

A familiar tingling sensation moved down my arms.

I swallowed hard. "Yes."

I couldn't feel the ghosts, the souls that were trapped here—not anymore. But I could still feel the presence of the angel.

Jordan grabbed my arm as the door pushed open. I steeled myself for what would greet us on the other side.

It was Bishop.

Relief swept through me immediately at the sight of him, but Jordan's fingers dug painfully into my skin.

"His eyes," she hissed.

My gaze shot to Bishop again to realize that she was right. I didn't automatically notice it in the shadows, but there was an opaque glaze to Bishop's eyes.

Terror clutched my throat. "No."

"He was looking for me, wasn't he?" he said in a flat monotone. "That's why you're all here. You want to stop me."

"Don't do this," I managed. "Let him go right now!"

"Fallen. Soul is jagged, pained, so very damaged. Mind filled with disappointment, sadness, endless regret. He does not make me feel better. But he holds tight onto me and I can't be free again to feed here on all these lovely girls and boys filled with joy and light. There is very little light left within this angel."

Bishop's face became strained, as if he was fighting against this possession. His teeth clenched. "Stay away, Samantha. Don't get close to me like this."

With that he turned and began moving rapidly away from the room and down the stairs.

"Stay away?" Jordan repeated. "*He's* the one who came up here. I mean, was that rude or what?"

I grabbed her arm. "Call the police. Report this party so everyone will get out of here safely. Nobody else has to get hurt tonight. And whatever you do, don't come near us again. Okay?"

She just stared at me, seemingly on the verge of arguing. But then she nodded. "Okay."

I didn't waste another second. I followed after Bishop, terrified of what would happen next.

This angel had driven Julie and Zach to suicide. She'd nearly done the same to Stephen. And many of the souls trapped in this house would be due to her deadly touch.

I couldn't let that happen to Bishop, too.

Why was she possessing him? Out of everyone in this house she had chosen him? How was that even possible?

It didn't matter. This was happening. And I had to do anything I could to stop it.

I grabbed Kraven as he passed in front of me.

"You going to tell me what happened, or should I guess?" he asked, cocking his head. "You look like you've recovered nicely."

"Bishop's possessed. Get the others. Meet us outside."

His frown deepened. "What are you—?"

"Just do it!" I screamed at him, before pushing past him and running after Bishop.

He walked slowly, as if his legs were fighting every step. Finally, we were a full block away from the house before he stopped and stood there, his back to me. I stuttered to a halt.

"Bishop…" I began.

"Damn it, Samantha, I told you not to follow me." He sounded angry, his voice drawn tight to the point of breaking.

A sob rose in my throat. "I'm not leaving you like this."

"It's dangerous."

"Yeah, well, maybe you should have thought of that before you let yourself get possessed."

"It happens through touch. I saw a kid get possessed and I grabbed him. I was going to bring him outside to get him away from the others. But it transferred to me and now it's trapped. Kid's okay. The angel wasn't in him long enough to do damage. I can hold it. Better in me than somebody else." He hissed out a breath. "Let me figure this out."

"Great. You do that." I tried not to panic more than I already was. "Okay, figured it out yet?"

"Let me go," he said, his voice quavering. It wasn't him now; there was a tonal difference, one that scared me. It was the angel who was now speaking. "You can't restrain me forever."

"I can damn well try," Bishop said through clenched teeth, as if talking to himself.

"She gives you happiness—this girl. So many good emotions to choose from when you look at her. I can taste it—all of it. I can leave you broken and raw and begging for death. You know what it's like to be fallen and anchored to something that mutes your ties to the celestial. To be discarded from the place you considered home. You gave them everything and they gave you nothing in return."

Yes, this was a fallen angel. One who'd been driven completely insane thanks to her soul. Perhaps this was all she was now—that unnatural soul given a life outside its destroyed body. An echo of pain and misery that had no choice but to loop around again and again on itself.

My empathy for her was dampened by how many people she'd harmed since escaping from the Hollow. But maybe she could still be reasoned with. She had been an angel—that meant something to me. It represented goodness and light.

No matter what Bishop had done in his human life, he was an angel. And no matter what this angel had done after she'd fallen, that didn't change what she was at her heart.

At least, I really hoped it didn't.

I approached slowly. "Please don't hurt him."

Those glazed eyes moved to me. "I can't help what I do. I hurt those who have what I don't. And all I want is more."

"Yes, you can help it. You can stop this."

"I want peace. I want silence. But death is not an option for me. I tried to die before. I failed."

Bishop's eyes were glazing more. It was now hard to tell what color they normally were.

"What can I do to help you?" My voice twisted with desperation.

"No help. Too late. This body…" He held his hands up before his face. "I could get used to this. He said I could live again if he released me."

"Who said that?"

"Soon," he whispered. "Soon you'll know everything. But

I want to live again now. I want my pain to end now. I can't wait any longer."

"The only way you can live is by destroying the lives of others." It was Kraven speaking behind me. My heart pounded so loud in my ears I could barely hear him. "You can't do that. Not with him, anyway."

"Brothers," the angel said. "You and he are brothers. You care for him."

He shrugged a shoulder. He still had his red cup in hand and he swirled its contents. "Wrong. Actually, I hate his guts. But if anybody's going to destroy his angelic life, it's going to be me, not you. So hands off."

"He's mine. And you can't stop me. Neither of you can."

I glared at the deadly angel who possessed Bishop, anger shoving past my fear. Nobody had any idea how to deal with this creature, apart from sticking the golden dagger through its borrowed chest. Well, this particular chest wasn't going to be sacrificed like that since I had grown extremely fond of it. They'd have to kill me first.

I approached, placing one foot in front of the other.

"Gray-girl, what the hell are you doing?" Kraven growled.

"I'm not a gray anymore," I told him. "That part of me dropped dead earlier. The rest of me crawled back to life."

His brows drew together at this blunt statement. "I thought there was something different about you now."

No, I wasn't a gray. But I was still a nexus. I still had the powers of Heaven and Hell that had been dormant inside me for seventeen years. And I already knew I could repel angels and demons who threatened me.

This angel might not have a body, but I could try my best to repel it, anyway. Repel it all the way back to the Hollow.

I grabbed hold of Bishop's wrist.

"Samantha, don't!" It was the real Bishop who said this, and his voice held panic.

I looked deep into his glazed eyes. "Let me try. Let me—"

Snap!

I stand on the platform, waiting for my fate. The weeks I spent in that small, stinking hole have prepared me to embrace this. Still, my legs feel weak and ready to collapse beneath me.

I'm afraid to die. So afraid.

Below, dozens have gathered to witness my execution. Some look up at me with grim expressions, others with pleased ones. Justice had finally been done in their eyes. Someone has put an end to this monster.

Maybe they're right.

"Do you have any last words?" the priest asks me, clutching his leather-bound Bible to his chest.

"No," I mutter.

"Do you wish to be absolved of your sins?"

"No."

"But in God's name—"

"I don't believe in God. Now go away, and leave me to die."

I expect outrage at my blasphemous words. But they're true. My brother was the one who clung to religion to give him strength in times of weakness. Not me.

I spot a man in the crowd I met two months ago—one who told me lies and made me empty promises. I hate him almost more than I hate Kara.

"Let me ask you one more question on behalf of your father," the priest says. My gaze snaps to him, since that's the man I was just looking at. "You agreed to something he proposed. Do you still agree?"

Two months ago I was out of my mind. The edges of my memories are fuzzy at best. I'd drunk bottle upon bottle of absinthe, hoping to erase those memories and ease my pain. It worked very well—at least, when it came to the memories.

"What difference does it make anymore?"

The executioner nudges the priest out of the way so he can loop the noose around my neck. The rough rope tightens painfully around my throat.

"Do you still agree?" the priest asks.

"Yeah, whatever you say. Now get lost."

"Your particular talents will be valued even more now that they've been honed to a sharp edge."

"Go to hell," I mumble.

He makes the sign of the cross to bless me and steps back.

I refuse to close my eyes. Instead, I stare out at a crowd that hates me. That wishes me dead.

Despite the fear that rises in my throat and chokes off my breath, I feel the exact same way. There's no one here whom I want forgiveness from. No one here to give a damn about me or that I give a damn about in return. My choices have led me to be alone today, only three days after my eighteenth birthday.

I wish forgiveness only from James.

He's the only one I miss.

I killed him. I sent him to Hell.

Now I'm certain, despite any foolish promises made by the man who claims to be my father, I'll be joining him there.

Finally, the executioner pulls the lever. The platform drops out from beneath my feet and I fall.

My death is not fast. My neck doesn't break.

Instead, I slowly strangle while the crowd cheers. They rejoice in every moment of my pain and suffering until, finally, death rises up to claim me...

Snap!

I staggered back from Bishop so violently that I tripped over my own feet and fell to the ground hard on my butt. In the distance I heard the sound of police sirens. Jordan had made the call like I asked her to and they'd arrived to break up the party.

I barely heard the sound. Barely saw the flashing lights to the far left.

I just sat on the ground and stared up at Bishop.

I'd seen his execution. I'd experienced it as if I was him.

The hopelessness he'd felt. The raw pain and loneliness. The shame.

He wanted to die that day.

But just like what happened to me earlier, he hadn't stayed dead.

His eyes were still glazed white. I hadn't been able to repel the angel. All I'd done was see another piece of Bishop's past. More pieces of his puzzle. A corner piece that snapped into place painfully and with effort.

"I can let you go," the angel spoke through him, squeezing Bishop's eyes shut. "But you must let me feed."

"No," Bishop gritted out in reply. "You won't hurt anyone else. It's over."

"Then we're at an impasse. You're mine. I will take your body over completely. Soon you will stop fighting. I can still feed through a touch. I can take the joy of others and make it my own. He promises me that I will be more powerful than ever before."

Cassandra and Roth finally approached, with Connor trailing after them. They each looked grim, their attention on Bishop. They knew what was going on without getting a recap.

Bishop's glazed eyes widened with surprise as he looked at the blonde angel. "You."

Cassandra came to a stop a few feet away, shaking her head sadly. "I tried to find you before this. You hide very well."

"I didn't know you were here."

"Would it have made a difference to you?"

"I don't know."

Tears slid down Cassandra's cheeks. "You have one chance, Marissa. Only once chance. Go back to the Hollow. Leave this city in peace. You've caused enough destruction."

Bishop shook his head. "I can't do that. He released me. He won't take me back so easily. I don't want to go back."

"All a damn distraction," Connor mumbled, loud enough only for me to hear. "What's his game? Where the hell is he hiding?"

I glanced at him. Who was he talking about?

"I hoped it wouldn't come to this." Cassandra's voice broke. "You have no idea how much."

"You abandoned me," the angel whispered. "My sister. You left me to fall and never tried to help me."

"You were damaged," Cassandra said, wringing her hands. "I knew that. There was nothing I could do for you anymore."

"Sister?" I managed. "She's the one you mentioned to me? The one created at the same time as you?"

She glanced at me and nodded. "That's right. We were like sisters. But there was something missing with Marissa. A lack of joy. Her depression only grew. It caused her to rebel against orders she was given. Finally, she'd done too much damage to be forgiven. They burned a soul into her and sent her to the human world. It wasn't all that long ago."

"Forever," the angel whispered through Bishop's lips.

"No, not forever." Cassandra's beautiful face was etched with sorrow. "Oh, Marissa. Why are you hurting people? Can't you stop?"

"The more I take, the more I want—but there's no end to it. Please help me, Cassandra. Help me."

"I will help you." Cassandra approached Bishop.

"What are you doing?" Roth growled at her, catching her hand.

"What I was sent here to do." She glanced over her shoulder at him before she pulled her hand from his grip, her expression filled with both regret and determination. "My mission."

She reached out and touched Bishop's arm.

chapter 28

I nearly screamed. Cassandra didn't know what that meant. She didn't know a touch was what transferred Marissa to a new victim.

Or...maybe she *did* know.

The transfer happened with a violent gasp from Cassandra, and Bishop fell to his knees. When he looked up, his blue eyes were clear again.

Cassandra's were now glazed.

"Cassie!" Roth reached toward her, but she stepped out of his reach.

She shook her head and held up her hands to stop him from getting any closer. "No, Roth. I have to do this. I have to control her. Only I can. She trusts me. Don't you, Marissa? You know I want the best for you." She smiled. "I can hear her in my head. She feels better now."

"I have a plan," I blurted out, knowing I had to do something, say something. "If you can hold on to her long enough... and if we can find Stephen, then maybe...I—I honestly believe he's not completely evil. He still loves Jordan. He could help us. He could use his hunger for good this time—and it wouldn't kill you since you're an angel."

To the left, the police were supervising the breakup of the party. All the kids, still in costume, were scattering. Running past us, but not even looking at us.

"Cassandra, no!" Bishop suddenly roared.

My head whipped in her direction to see that she now had Bishop's golden dagger out of its sheath and clutched in her right hand.

"Cassandra!" I managed. "What are you doing?"

"Stay back," she said as we all collectively took a step toward her.

I exchanged a panicked look with Bishop. His face was tense, his expression strained.

"What the hell do you think you're doing with that?" Roth growled.

"You approved this plan, Roth," she said through gritted teeth. "Remember?"

Clarity sparked in his gaze. "This is different."

Tears streaked down her cheeks. "It's not. This was the plan all along. I knew it might come to this—worst-case scenario, but unavoidable. I hoped I'd find another way, but I now see there isn't one. I can't let her hurt anyone else. I'm sorry."

Roth's eyes widened. "Don't do this. Please."

A small smile played at her lips. "I would have liked more time here, with you, but—" she swallowed hard "—there's no other way this can end."

She didn't wait another second. She thrust the dagger into her chest—a horrible mirror image of what Zach had done. Only Cassandra did this of her own free will.

"No!" Another scream tore from my throat.

"Cassie!" Roth lunged toward her to grab the knife, but it was too late. She yanked it out and threw it to the side just before she fell to her knees, her expression filled with pain. He

Michelle Rowen

collapsed right in front of her, grabbing hold of her shoulders. "What have you done? Why would you do this?"

Anything else he said was swept away by the Hollow as it opened wide.

"I'm sorry, Roth," she whispered. "Forgive me."

She kissed him a moment before the Hollow reached for her and yanked her back into its wide vortex of a mouth, right out of Roth's arms.

Roth shoved himself back up to his feet and stared at the vortex as if stunned and transfixed. "She isn't dead." His voice broke. "Not yet...she was still breathing!"

"Bishop—do something! He's going to—" But I couldn't finish my sentence in time.

Roth began to run toward the Hollow as if ready to jump in after Cassandra.

Bishop grabbed for him and yanked him back just in time. Roth turned around and slammed his fist into Bishop's face.

"Let go of me! I have to save her!"

"No!" Bishop yelled back at him. "We can't lose you, too."

Roth struggled hard, but Kraven was also there to help restrain him, and Connor, too. It took the three of them to pull the demon back from the Hollow.

A few horrible moments later, the vortex closed and silence fell.

Cassandra was gone. She'd saved the city from the bodiless angel. Her sister. And the full truth about her real mission was one that broke my heart.

It was a suicide mission from the moment she arrived—and she'd known it all along.

Roth believed she was still alive when the Hollow took her, but I'd seen that dagger. The Hallowed Blade—the only weapon capable of killing an angel or a demon—hadn't missed her heart. She was dead.

340

Roth fell silent and still. Finally, the others let go of him.

"Roth," Connor said uneasily. "I'm sorry. I had no idea that you and Cassandra…"

"Shut up."

"Let's go get a drink," Kraven suggested. "A real one. None of this kiddie stuff."

"No. Leave me alone. All of you." He turned the darkest glare I'd ever seen on the rest of us.

"You cared for her," Bishop said. "We all did."

He scowled. "I don't know what you're talking about. Stupid angel getting in all of our ways. I'm glad she's gone."

Without another word, Roth shoved his hands into the pockets of his jeans and started walking away.

I didn't need to read his mind to tell that he was lying. His anguish was written all over his face.

Bishop picked up the dagger from the ground and stared at the blade for a few moments of silence.

"What now?" Connor asked, his voice grim.

"Patrol," he said simply. "You and Kraven head out. I'll meet you back at the church later."

For once, and despite their earlier fight, Kraven didn't say a word against him. With a last look at me, a thousand questions in his eyes, he followed Connor down the street until they disappeared into the shadows.

I watched them walk away, again wondering what Connor had been talking about before about distractions and games. Who was hiding? What did Connor know?

I felt Bishop take my hand, and the shimmer of electricity between us worked to snap me out of my semidaze. I looked at him, our eyes locking.

"I thought that angel had you," I whispered. "I thought I was going to lose you, too. At that point, I was okay with it going into somebody else, anybody else, if it meant you'd be all right. But Cassandra...I didn't want her to die..."

"Me, neither." His jaw was tight as he squeezed my hand. "Come on, I'll take you home."

All I could manage was a nod.

It was so strange returning home after the events of the past couple days. My familiar house seemed oddly unfamiliar to me. Like the person who once lived here all her life had moved far away. Or died.

There was something waiting for me on the doorstep. A brown envelope. I picked it up to see that my name was written on it with black marker.

I exchanged a tense look with Bishop. "What do you think this is?"

"Open it," he said.

I tore open the envelope and pulled out the contents: a small, plain, gold locket on a long chain and a note.

"What does it say?" he asked.

It didn't say much, but what it said stole my breath. I held it out to him so he could read it, too.

Samantha,
This belongs to you. Consider it my payment for helping give me the chance to escape. Be normal again. One of us should get that chance.
—Stephen

Bishop touched the locket in my hand, his gaze rising from the note to mine. "It's your soul. It's contained inside this locket."

I could barely speak. "I helped give him the chance to escape? Did I really do that?"

He shook his head. "It's not your fault. You didn't want me to hurt him. You didn't want me to kill him. I guess he considered that a debt to be repaid."

Stephen still had Carly's soul, but was this the proof I was looking for that Stephen wasn't totally evil now? Or was he a super-gray who liked to have a clean slate to work with?

I stared down at the locket. It was what I'd wanted all this time—to have my soul back. To find some semblance of normalcy in my life again. To escape the supernatural craziness I'd been plunged into as much as I possibly could.

"So I get rewarded after everything and Cassandra has to sacrifice herself? It doesn't seem fair. Not even close."

Bishop watched me, studying my face as if looking for clues to some mystery there. "Cassandra knew what she was getting herself into when she arrived. What she did was very brave… and incredibly stupid. I wish she'd told us everything. Together we might have been able to find another way to end this."

I thought of how she'd felt toward Roth. "She kept secrets. Sometimes secrets are dangerous."

His gaze sought mine. "Sometimes secrets are necessary."

"She and Roth were falling for each other."

"An angel and a demon falling dangerously in love—just like your parents."

I blinked hard as I thought of how they'd ended—nearly exactly the same as Roth and Cassandra, but nobody had been there to hold Nathan back from following Anna into the Hollow. "Would you have tried to keep them apart if you'd known earlier?"

"Oh, I already knew." At my look, the barest glimpse of a smile played at his lips. "The way they started looking at each other…well, it was obvious."

I let out a shaky breath. "They would have been torn apart if others found out—just like my parents were."

"Maybe," he allowed. "Or maybe the all-important balance can have some exceptions to the rule. Maybe what happened with Cassandra and Roth—with your parents—needs to happen a few more times before those barriers can start to be broken down."

My head swam as I thought about that, about barriers breaking down, and I stared at the locket for another moment. Then my gaze shot to his. "You are kind of brilliant, do you know that?"

He cocked his head. "What do you mean?"

My heart pounded. "Incredibly brilliant! The barrier. It *can* be broken. Julie was right. I can help her and the others."

He turned me to face him, his expression confused. "What are you talking about, Samantha?"

I slipped the locket into the pocket of my jeans and grabbed his hand. "We need to go back to that house."

"The party's over. It got raided, remember?"

"I know, but—my mother told me it was haunted. That's why she couldn't sell it. Well, she was right. It is haunted. And all those ghosts—those trapped souls—I think I know how I can help them."

chapter 29

We took my mother's car back to the east side of the city to where Noah's Halloween party had been held. The house was now empty, litter scattered over the front lawn.

I glanced down the street toward the exact spot where Cassandra had been taken away. In the beginning, I'd had so many conflicting feelings about the angel, but now all I could remember was how much she loved Chinese food and the red goo.

"You probably think I'm completely crazy right now," I said to Bishop as we got out of the car and walked a block down the street to where I could see the barrier. In most spots it was invisible, but here and there it showed itself as a translucent silver mesh that stretched up over the city like an opalescent bubble.

Bishop looked up at the barrier, his arms crossed over his chest. He then sent a wry look in my direction. "Completely? No. But maybe a little. It's okay, though. I could use the company."

I held my hand out to him. "I need your dagger."

He eyed my outstretched hand, studying me as if trying to

figure out a riddle. Clarity shone in his blue eyes. "Now I *do* think you're crazy."

"I have to try."

Bishop hesitated another moment before he finally nodded. "Don't just try."

He pulled out the dagger and handed it to me hilt first. It felt heavy in my hand—and not just its weight. This knife had killed Cassandra, Zach and countless others.

A similar dagger had killed my birth mother seventeen years ago.

With whatever supernatural abilities I had with being a nexus—the same power that allowed me to read the minds of angels and demons—I could also read this dagger's energy, which hummed up my arm. This wasn't just metal. It was magic.

It felt similar to the imprint of wings on the backs of the angels and demons. This was not of this world. Here it looked like a dagger, but it was so much more than that.

This, most definitely, was a physical representation of death itself.

But I didn't want to kill anyone with it. Tonight, I wanted to help them.

Bishop already knew what I was going to attempt. He'd heard my aunt demand it of me—and then tortured him to push me to do it. It was one of the many reasons Bishop believed nobody should learn about my secret identity.

Because I might be able to do things like this.

With both hands, I brought the blade up to the surface of the barrier. I glanced at Bishop.

"Concentrate," he said, nodding. His eyes glowed blue in the darkness surrounding us. "You can do it."

I took a deep breath and returned my attention to the barrier, to the also now-glowing dagger, and brought the weapon downward in one slice. A shimmering line of golden light appeared where I'd made the cut. It gaped open and a whoosh of warm air blew my hair back from my face.

"It worked," I whispered. The golden light grew brighter and brighter, sparking with fireworklike intensity. Bishop drew me back, his arm around me as we stared up at the breached barrier.

My aunt was right. I *could* do this.

The thought both excited me, and scared the hell out of me.

Here, close to this kind of magic, created with the powers of both Heaven and Hell, I could feel the ghosts. I wasn't clairvoyant—or whatever Jordan really was. But I knew when the spirits sensed the opening in the barrier. I felt them move past us like a cool breeze. I felt their joy at being free.

"Do you feel it?" I whispered.

"Yes. I feel it." His arm tightened at my waist, his attention fixed on the barrier itself.

Everyone who'd died in the city since the barrier had been put in place—they'd all been trapped. They'd gathered in the abandoned house, waiting for the time that they could escape. That time was now.

I turned to look at him as something very important occurred to me. "Could you leave, too? You could go right now. Out of the city, away from the barrier…Heaven could pull you back. Could heal you."

He studied the torn barrier, the edges glowing with visible light. "It's not that easy for me now."

"Why not?"

"The mission's not over yet and I know I won't even be on their radar again until it is. With this soul in me, I'm basically invisible to Heaven. So I'm not leaving—not this city, not this problem and not you." When I opened my mouth to argue, his gaze grew tense. "No arguing. My decision isn't going to change. Got it? I'm not going anywhere till this is over."

I blew out a breath. "Stubborn."

"Remind you of anyone?"

"Yeah, your older brother."

He snorted at that before his expression shifted to one that was more wary. "You can't tell anyone about this."

"Kraven already knows what I am."

"He doesn't know this. This is our secret. Promise me you won't tell him."

"One more secret?"

"It's important."

I nodded, my throat tight. "Fine. I promise."

We kept watching until the cut in the barrier resealed itself a minute later. The souls had been released to find their way to the afterlife.

We, however, were still stuck inside until further notice.

Once we got back to my house, Bishop lingered by the front door, as if uncertain if he should come all the way inside.

"I need to meet up with the others," he said. "And you need to rest. It's been a hell of a couple of days."

I nodded. "Understatement. Major understatement."

But there was something I needed to get off my chest first, something I wouldn't let be buried in the silence between us. Bishop was the one who was amazing at hiding secrets—not me.

"I saw your execution," I said quietly.

His gaze shot to mine. "What?"

"When I touched you...when you were possessed. I saw you. You were hanged." I swallowed hard and looked at the floral area rug my mother had bought to warm up the otherwise cold front foyer. "You thought you deserved it. And when it happened, it took a long time before you died. I felt what you felt. It was horrible."

His expression darkened and he turned away from me. "Samantha, I really wish you hadn't had to experience that."

I moved closer to him and grabbed his arm. "All of those bad things back then. You keep them so close to you, that's why they're so vivid. There's so much about you that you won't tell me, but…"

"But what?"

I took a deep breath and let it out slowly. "But I think I have you figured out."

He snorted softly. "You have, have you?"

"I'm not afraid of you, despite everything I've seen and learned. I know you, Bishop, and you're kind of amazing."

He looked away again, but I grabbed his face and made him look at me. "And whatever happened in the past? I don't care about any of it. Who you are now, what you do and how you look at me. Those are the only things that matter. To hell with everything else."

His gaze searched mine. "I thought I'd lost you tonight."

My throat hurt too much to swallow. "Ditto. But I'm alive. And so are you. We both got second chances."

I finally let go of him and paced nervously to the door, then back.

He watched me, his expression wary again. "What is it?"

I'd been thinking about this ever since I got Stephen's note. Ever since we went to the barrier. I knew it was the right thing to do.

"I want you to have something," I said firmly. "I want you to hold on to it for me, because I don't trust anyone else with it."

"What?"

I pressed the gold locket into his hand—such a small object for what it carried inside. Bishop looked with shock at the chain now hanging from his grip.

"I realized two very important things tonight."

He tore his confused gaze away from the locket to meet mine. "The first?"

"That I can't have my soul back. Not yet, anyway. What's been happening here in Trinity is bigger than me. Bigger than any of us. And now with Zach and Cassandra gone..." My voice broke. "Well, you guys need as much help as you can get. I won't be able to access my nexus abilities if I have a soul again. I won't be able to help you if I'm just a human."

Bishop stared down at the gold locket as if stunned I'd give such a thing to him. "What's the second reason you're giving me this?"

A smile tugged at my lips and I gave him a small shrug. "I guess I'm a sucker for symbolism."

His gaze met mine again and there were so many questions and doubts in his blue eyes, but he didn't give voice to any of them.

"So?" I ventured when silence fell between us. "Will you take it? Will you keep it safe for me until I need it back?"

Finally, he nodded, then pulled the chain over his head, tucking the locket underneath his shirt. "I promise to take very good care of it."

"Thank you."

The smile he gave me then made my heart swell so much I thought my ribs might break. But it felt good. Really good.

He slid his fingers into my long, tangled hair and drew me closer so he could kiss me. Electricity shivered between us, and I swear I could see sparks, even though my eyes were closed. I felt them, that's for sure.

It felt so good to kiss Bishop with nothing at risk except my heart.

chapter 30

There was a demon waiting for me in my bedroom.

He reclined on my bed with his arms folded behind his head.

I froze in the doorway.

"What are you doing here?"

"Rough night, huh?" Kraven said.

"Get out of my bed."

He grinned. "I like how that sounds. Your bed. Me in it."

"I swear, Kraven. Don't mess with me right now."

He sat up and glanced around at the room. "It's a bit frillier and pinker than I pictured for you, but not bad. I could get used to this."

He was messing with me. I decided not to feed the troll by making any more demands or stomping my feet like a child. Instead, I stood there with my hands on my hips, glaring at him.

"Ouch. I can feel that all the way over here." He swung his legs over the side of my bed and stood up. "Saw my little brother take off a minute ago. No sleepovers planned with your beloved? Sad, gray-girl. Very sad. Oh, wait, you're not a gray anymore, are you? You went through stasis, though. I know that. I saw it with my own eyes. You were in bad shape. And then—*boom*—you're all better."

I spread my hands, trying my best to ignore his taunts about Bishop. "I died. I came back."

He studied me carefully. "As what, exactly?"

"As myself. Nothing else. I feel fine."

"Not evil?"

"No."

"Too bad. Evil can be fun." He moved closer to me, cocking his head as he watched me. It made me extremely uneasy about being alone with him.

I slid my hand down my right thigh so I could feel the outline of my dagger. "Don't even think about trying to hurt me."

He let out a quick laugh, one of surprise. "You really think I'd do that?"

"I don't know what you're capable of."

"You're right. You don't."

"It's been a rough night, Kraven. I want you to leave."

"We lost two angels tonight. Zach—I actually liked that guy." His expression darkened. "He didn't give me any problems. Shouldn't have died. Then little Miss Secret Mission. She should have told us the whole truth from day one."

"Why? Would you have helped save her?"

He didn't reply to that. "Roth is MIA."

"He liked her. A lot. They were falling for each other."

"Roth's a dick. You really think he's capable of feeling anything for anyone?"

"I do." I said it with certainty. I'd seen the look in his eyes when she'd been wrenched out of his arms. There was no doubt in my mind that his feelings toward her were completely real.

"And you think my brother feels the same way toward you?"

I glared at him. "It bothers you that I like him."

"Like? Not love? Was it his *love* that brought you back from death?" He said it mockingly. "Do you two have a Romeo and Juliet thing going on? The deadly angel-boy falls for the hybrid chick who, in another life, he would've been commanded to kill. Adorable, right?"

I looked into his amber eyes, but couldn't break through the walls he had up. Frankly, I wasn't in the mood for a glimpse at his tortured mind tonight. Despite the ability he had to press my buttons, knowing what I did about him made my heart hurt. "I'm sorry for the pain you feel when it comes to him."

His flinch would have been barely noticeable if I hadn't been looking for it. "I feel nothing for him."

"Wrong. You hate him for what he did because you once loved him more than anyone else." I let out a shaky sigh. "You have a right to feel that way."

His jaw tightened. "Permission from you to hate my brother. Gee, I feel all tingly inside."

"You trusted him and he betrayed you in the worst way possible. I don't know what you've been through in however many years it's been since you died—"

"Was killed," he corrected me.

"Tonight I saw another one of Bishop's memories. His execution." I swallowed hard. "I heard his thoughts. I saw what he saw—I felt what he felt. He was broken by what he'd done to you. And he paid the price for it. He missed you. You were the only one he wanted forgiveness from."

That snarky edge faded from his gaze. "Really."

I nodded.

The remainder of his humorous mask fell away. "You can tell me whatever you want—whatever you think you saw. Doesn't change a damn thing. And it doesn't make it true."

"You tried to save him twice tonight. I think down deep you still care about him."

"Is that what you think?" He moved closer and backed me up against the wall. I looked up at him, commanding myself not to show fear as his eyes began to glow red.

I nodded again.

I waited for him to say something else on the subject, but instead, he twisted a long piece of my hair around his finger. "So you're a nexus." His lips curved. "I know you won't admit to it in so many words. It's enough that I know it's true."

I pushed his hand away from me. "You don't know anything about me."

"Wrong. I know enough. I know in the three kisses we shared that you weren't only kissing me because you had to. You liked it, too."

My cheeks heated. "You're dreaming."

"And now you can kiss Bishop again without being in danger of sucking both his soul and his life out of him. Right?"

This was ridiculous. I was giving him way too much time to try to manipulate me. "Get to your point, Kraven. I know you have one. I'm tired and I want to go to bed."

"Is that an invitation?"

"Only if you're delusional."

His smile grew and his eyes went back to their usual amber shade. "Sweetness, you can deny it all you want, but you do feel something for me. I know it."

"You're right, James." I said his real name to see if it would get a reaction. It did. He didn't like it, but he didn't correct me this time. I slid my hands slowly up his chest and he froze, his brows drawing together. I placed my hands on either side of his face. "I do feel something for you."

His lips curved to the side. "I knew it."

I studied his handsome face, that glimmer of victory already in his eyes that I was about to admit to something that would cause Bishop pain. "I feel pity for you."

That cockiness vanished in a heartbeat and he stepped back from me so fast it was as if I'd been set on fire.

"Save the pity for someone else," he said, his voice now cold. "Besides, you can lie to yourself if you want to, but I know the truth. I see it in your eyes."

"Yeah, right. You are delusional. Rinse and repeat. All you want to do with me is make Bishop jealous. I read your mind, remember? I saw that darkness in there. That vengeance you're jonesing for. But it's not going to happen."

"Whatever you say, sweetness." He looked away, toward my window, as if shielding his expression from me long enough to gather his smart-ass mask back up. "My brother gave you a gift—that little dagger of yours. Nice and shiny. I have something shiny to give you, too. That's why I came here tonight."

I didn't ask what it was. I just stood there waiting, my fists clenched at my sides.

"A name," he said quietly, that glint of mischievousness returning to his face. "Adam Drake. And a year. 1878."

My heart started to pound harder. "Who is that?"

"Use that little computer of yours." He nodded at the laptop on my bedside table. "Do a little digging. You might find some interesting details."

I turned away from him, my head swimming. When I looked back again, Kraven was gone.

Immediately, after closing the window, I went to my laptop. I almost decided to forget the whole thing and put what he'd said out of my mind forever. But then, with shaking hands, and a slight hesitation, I went ahead and searched the name and date—Adam Drake 1878.

It got a couple direct hits. And a picture.

Adam Drake…was Bishop.

It was Bishop's real name, the name he wouldn't tell me no matter how many times I'd asked.

My hands trembled as I clicked through to an obscure web article and I read it quickly, my stomach tying itself into knots.

Adam Drake was eighteen years old when he was hanged in New York in 1878. He was in a group of grave robbers and body snatchers who worked for Kara Drake. His mother.

Kara was his *mother.* Kraven's mother, too.

Adam had killed his brother, James, nineteen years of age.

And he'd also killed twenty-five other people. With a dagger.

James had been his first victim.

These pieces of Bishop's puzzle clicked into place and left me stunned and sickened as I stared at the grainy black-and-white photo.

Bishop had been a serial killer.

And I'd just freely given him both my heart and soul.

chapter 31

Despite everything I'd experienced, everything I'd learned, and how long it took me to finally fall asleep...I slept. Hard. And I had no dreams to disturb me, good ones or bad ones.

When I woke, I glanced at my alarm clock to see I hadn't even slept in. It was seven o'clock.

Seven o'clock in the morning on the day after my death.

I got out of bed and glanced at my reflection in the mirror, surprised in a way to see that nothing about my appearance had changed. I looked exactly the same as I had yesterday, or the week before, or the month before any of this had happened.

My mother had left a voice mail for me. She said her Hawaiian vacation, as awesome as it had been, was nearly over. She'd be home the day after tomorrow, Saturday, and she couldn't wait to see me.

In a daze, I showered and got dressed just as I would on any other Thursday morning. I had toast and peanut butter for breakfast.

Something was off, though. I stood there in the kitchen for a moment, my hand pressed against my stomach.

"Oh, no. No, it can't be," I whispered.

I was still hungry—but it wasn't for food.

It had to be my imagination. I wasn't a gray anymore. I *wasn't*. But there was only one way to find out for sure.

I went to school and found him in the halls exactly where I expected him to be.

Colin glanced at me as I tentatively approached. "Hey, Sam. Not ditching today? Where have you been all *week?*"

"Around." *Kidnapped, held captive, trying to stop an angel from going postal at a Halloween party.* "Look, I—I'm sorry about what happened on Monday."

He grimaced at the reminder of our last kiss. Emphasis, I sincerely hoped, on *last.* "You know, I think I'm finally going to take a hint. I can't deal with it, Sam. You push me away and tell me you're not interested in me, but then the next moment you're all over me. It's not cool. I deserve to be treated better than that."

"I totally agree. You deserve way better that I've been treating you lately." I forced myself to step closer to him, into the orbit of hunger, and studied his face.

He watched me warily. "So what are you doing *now*?"

"Testing something." I waited for the desire to kiss him to grip me, for whatever remained of Colin's soul to pull at my control like a baited hook like it always did.

But there was nothing. I sensed nothing from Colin or anyone else in the halls.

Nothing!

A smile burst forth on my face and I threw my arms around him to give him a tight hug. He didn't hug me back.

"Nobody likes a tease, Sam. I'm not interested in any more of your games."

I let go of him immediately. "Sorry. I, uh, I'm really sorry, Colin. For everything. I hope we can still be friends."

That lost look he used to have when around me was gone. He wasn't irresistibly drawn to me anymore. More tangible proof that I was finally free—and so was he. "Yeah, sure. Just…no spontaneous hugging, okay?"

I nodded. "Okay."

We went to English and I sat there, face forward, trying to pay attention. Despite my lousy grade the other day, school was supposed to be my oasis. My touchstone. My way of feeling normal. This was what I'd clung to recently to keep from totally falling apart.

Unfortunately, it didn't work so well anymore.

I tried to ignore this mysterious new hunger inside of me, this strange gnawing emptiness, but it was next to impossible. If it wasn't for food—or *souls*—then what the hell was it?

At lunch, I searched the halls and the cafeteria for Jordan, but she was nowhere to be found. I asked some of her friends where she was, worried she might have gotten into more trouble last night after the Halloween party or worse, fallen back into Stephen's clutches. They confirmed that she'd texted this morning that she'd definitely gotten home safely after the raid. And that her father was furious with her for disappearing for two days without any explanation and then immediately taken off, in full Cleopatra gear, to a party.

"She'll be grounded till she's forty," one girl said with a malicious grin.

She was probably right.

All day I tried very hard not to think about what I now knew about Bishop.

His name. His past.

All the people he'd killed that had earned him a date with a noose more than a century ago.

I already knew he was an angel of death, but this—it felt worse. It felt dark and evil and unredeemable.

There had to be more to it. In fact, I had no doubt there

was. But still, why couldn't *he* have been the one to tell me any of this instead of his vengeful brother?

After a full school day where the most dramatic thing that happened was witnessing two kids have a screaming break-up fight in the hall by my locker, I went home and let myself inside, locking the door behind me.

Part of me wanted to go see Bishop, but the other part was too chicken to face him.

"Pathetic," I grumbled. "Some super powerful Heaven/ Hell hybrid you are, hiding your head like an ostrich when things get scary again."

Fine, I was pathetic, but I wasn't an ostrich. I just needed a little more time to process all of this.

Everywhere I looked around the house today, especially as I tossed out the remainder of the Chinese leftovers, I saw Cassandra.

She had secrets she wouldn't tell anybody, too, when maybe we could have helped her deal with them. I wondered if that was an angel thing.

I missed her more than I ever would have thought possible.

It was after six and getting dark outside when the sound of someone pounding on my front door yanked me straight out of my memories. I approached the door cautiously, peeking outside past the bamboo blind to see who it was.

Red hair. Green eyes. Furious expression.

Reluctantly, I opened the door.

"I really hate you," Jordan informed me.

"Good to see you, too."

"You've ruined my life, do you know that? *Ruined.* My father thinks I'm some sort of lying juvenile delinquent since I won't tell him where I was. He threatened to send me to live with my mother. I do not want that. Like, ever. She ignores me way better from a distance."

She seemed paler today, making the scattering of freckles stand out that much more on her nose. "Are you all right?"

"Stellar. Really stellar, thanks so much for asking." Her glare was like a laser beam cutting through my skin. "You?"

"Super duper." I pushed the door open wider. "Do you want to come in?"

"No." With a glower, she brushed past me as she entered the house. I scanned the driveway where both my mom's car and Jordan's—a Mercedes sports car I knew her mother had bought for her—were now parked, and the street beyond to see that no one else was lurking around before I closed the door. "You took off last night during all the drama and I didn't see you again. What happened with that angel dude? What happened with the ghosts? Is Julie okay?"

"Everything's..." I grappled for the right words, but found myself at a loss. "Everything's a bit better today, I think. Julie's spirit is free. She's not trapped here anymore."

Something hard in Jordan's eyes eased off just a little at that and they grew glossy as she turned away from me. "I felt like something happened. I—I sensed it last night when I got home. After the raid. Like a pressure had eased through the entire city. That's why I'm here. I needed to know. I wanted to forget it, forget you and your creepy friends, forget Stephen, but I can't. And that pisses me off."

Jordan definitely had some supernatural insight going on. This was only more proof. "Feel better now?"

"Yeah, just peachy, thanks." She glanced around. "Where's your mom?"

"Hawaii."

"Convenient."

"You have no idea."

Jordan didn't speak for a moment, her arms were crossed

so tightly that it looked painful. "Is he really evil now? Like, forever?"

It was kind of obvious she was talking about Stephen. "I don't know."

She groaned. "A lie would have been awesome."

"Sorry. Yeah, he's going to be great. Just like shiny new, no problem at all."

"You're a terrible liar."

"So I've been told."

"Where's your freaky angel guy? The one with the blue eyes to die for. Isn't he keeping you under close watch anymore?" She didn't wait for me to answer as she checked herself out in the full-length hallway mirror. "What's his deal, anyway?"

"Who, Bishop?" I twisted a finger tightly into my hair. "Oh, you know. Grave robber from the nineteenth century, serial killer, murdered his brother in cold blood. Now he's an angel of death with a soul driving him completely insane, and his brother's a demon specializing in vengeance and snark. Boring story, really."

Jordan gaped at me. "Okay. And I thought I was in serious trouble when it came to *my* love life."

"Don't worry, you are." Now I crossed my arms over my chest. "You know, we could get the two of them together. Bishop's soul is destroying him…Stephen *needs* a soul. A nice swap-o-rama might just do the trick."

Her eyes widened. "Do you really think—?"

"I was being sarcastic."

Her shoulders slumped. "Damn."

I eyed her. "Why are you really here, Jordan?"

"Honestly?" She sighed. "I didn't know where else to go. My father's going to be furious that I took off again without saying anything, but I don't think I could be in any more trouble than I already am. So here I am, seeking out the one person in the city who I actually have something in common with. Crazy, right?"

"Pretty crazy," I agreed. And as crazy as it sounded, I was glad she was here. "Are you hungry? I could order something."

She raised an eyebrow. "You and me hanging out on a Thursday night? Who would have thought?"

I actually laughed at that. "Not me, that's for sure."

As I turned toward the kitchen, the vision that slammed into me was more powerful than any other I'd ever had. It knocked me right off my feet and I hit the ground hard, my short fingernails clawing at the hardwood floor.

Powerful. But familiar.

A city in darkness, melting and draining away like water in a bathtub—falling into a dark hole in the center of everything. People, thousands and thousands of them, trying to run away but getting pulled into the vortex. There was no escape.

It was a parking lot—a wide and empty one next to an abandoned grocery store with a broken sign. Everything and everyone was drawn here like a magnet. Nobody could escape from the swirling and greedy mouth that devoured everything it could as if there was no end to its hunger.

Bishop was there trying to help. To save everyone, including me. I reached for his hand as he yelled my name, but he was swept away from me before I could touch him.

Why was I still there? Why wasn't I being taken, too? My feet were planted firmly on the ground as I watched this all unfold—this disaster beyond my worst nightmare. The end of the world. My world.

All of it being taken into the Hollow's open and endlessly hungry mouth.

"Why not me?" I screamed at it. "Why aren't you taking me?"

The Hollow answered in that deep, dark voice I'd heard before inside in my head. "Because you are me. We are the same. And I need you—I can't do this without you."

Every word it spoke turned my blood to ice. "Who are you?"

"You already know who I am."

The vision ended as if a door had slammed in my face and I found myself crouched on the floor, shaking. Jordan was next to me, staring at me with fear and confusion.

"What. The. *Hell?*" she managed. "What the hell was that? Did you just have a seizure or something? Should I call 911?"

My throat felt so raw I knew I must have screamed here, as well. "A vision. I get them sometimes because of what I am."

"A total freak of nature?"

"Yeah." I was that, but it didn't make what I saw any less true. So what was it? A vision of the future? What future? When would it happen? And how could I stop it?

The Hollow was sentient. I'd already figured that part out. But what did it mean when it said that we were the same?

And what did it mean when it said that I already knew who it was?

Something I hadn't thought about since last night came back to me in a rush. After everything that had happened since, I'd all but forgotten it.

It was something Connor said while we were trying to deal with the bodiless angel.

"All a damn distraction. What's his game? Where the hell is he hiding?"

Only I'd heard him, but there was something in his tone…

Connor knew something the rest of us didn't.

Since he was an angel, I wasn't terribly surprised he was keeping important secrets from us. But this secret couldn't remain that way. Whatever he knew, *I* needed to know, too.

I looked at Jordan. "Mind giving me a drive somewhere?"

I half expected her to say no, roll her eyes and take off without another word—unless that word was an insult. But

I'd come to learn that if there was anybody full of surprises, it was Jordan Fitzpatrick.

"Sure," she said, nodding firmly. "Just tell me where."

Hard to believe it had only been a day since the last time I was at St. Andrew's. Felt more like forever.

I swiftly checked the sanctuary and the rooms along the hall at the back. Jordan trailed after me as I explored.

"Notice that I'm not grilling you right now," she said. "But I would love to know what we're doing here again. I don't like this place."

"I'm looking for somebody." Distracted, I moved through the church trying to sense something, feel something.

Ten minutes later, the door squeaked and I spun around to see the angel in question had returned to his perch.

"Hey, Samantha," Connor said when he spotted me. "Good to see you. Bishop's not here, he's out patrolling. Roth's still missing. We also got information that there are next to no grays left in the city and he's trying to confirm it. Most dropped dead after stasis."

My mouth went dry. "Next to no grays left? Seriously?"

"As far as we know, it's just your pal, Stephen, for sure. The guys tell me you're all cured." He eyed me with curiosity. "You're no longer hungry for souls, right?"

No, I was hungry for something, but it wasn't for souls. "That's right."

"Well, good. I mean, I'm not promising anything, but if Stephen's the only one still breathing, that means we're close to finishing this mission." He glanced to my left. "Jordan, you're back."

"Unfortunately."

"Too bad that memory wipe didn't work last night. Everything would be a lot easier then, huh?"

Her eyes narrowed. "Yeah, maybe. For *you*."

Jordan was making friends all over the place with that charming personality of hers.

I was busy reeling from the possibility that Stephen might be the last gray in the city. The team had been patrolling for more than two weeks trying to take care of the gray problem. But to think that it was close to being over...

Of course, Carly would still be a gray, too.

Carly...

I shoved her image away and focused on the angel standing directly in front of me.

"I came here to talk to you, Connor."

"Me?" He pointed at himself. "That's sweet, Sam. I know we haven't had much time to get to know each other very well."

"No, we haven't. You were the last to arrive, not counting Cassandra."

His expression shadowed at her name. "Yeah, that's right."

"Connor, what did you mean last night about that angel being a distraction?"

He didn't speak for a moment. "What?"

"I heard you. You mumbled it to yourself. You said that she was a distraction and that you didn't know what his game was or where he's hiding. Who's *he*? Who were you talking about?"

Connor's jaw tightened. "I think you must have been hearing things."

"Nope. I'm completely positive about what I heard."

He shot a glance at Jordan, then back at me. "Okay, ladies, lovely chatting with the two of you, but I really need to get back out there and do my job."

When he turned toward the door I ran toward him and grabbed his arm. "Connor, please. You need to talk to me. You know something and you need to tell me what it is."

He turned to face me. "What's your deal, anyway? Why are you even a part of this? How are you not a gray anymore—just like that? Bishop won't tell us anything he knows, but there's something weird about you."

"Tell me about it," Jordan murmured.

"You know way too much about everything," Connor continued, his gaze narrowing. "And how do you see the searchlights? How did you get a message to Bishop about where you were locked up? How do you read our minds?"

"Want me to do it right now?" I asked. "Because I will if you don't start talking."

"You can try. I'm way older than I look so I'm pretty good at blocking that sort of thing, especially if I know to expect it."

He was right. Even staring him right in his eyes I couldn't break through the wall he had up. There had to be another way. I didn't have time for this.

I hissed out a breath of frustration. "If I tell you why I can do stuff, then you have to tell me something about what you know. Can we make that deal?"

Connor cocked his head, considering. "Maybe. If what you've got to say is good enough."

I said it before I second-guessed myself. "I'm a nexus."

His eyes widened. "Excuse me?"

"Sounds like a car," Jordan mused aloud. "An expensive one. Oh, wait. That's Lexus."

I tried to ignore her commentary. "You guessed what I was the moment you got here, but then you doubted yourself."

"Holy crap, you're a nexus. I knew it!" He frowned and shook his head. "Why didn't you tell us?"

"Because Bishop told me not to. He said it was too dangerous."

"Well, yeah. Guaranteed. But really, that mostly depends on who your birth parents were."

I shot him a look of surprise. "What do you mean?"

"Do you know who they were?"

"Sort of. A little." Bishop thought this was the be-all, end-all of secrets, but I didn't regret saying anything. I was really sick of secrets. Secrets had gotten Cassandra killed by her own hand. Secrets had kept Bishop's dark past hidden for far too long. Secrets were what I now wanted to get out of Connor to keep everyone alive.

Secrets only made everything more confusing and helped no one.

"Demon dad or demon mom?" he asked.

"My birth father was a demon named Nathan, who jumped into the Hollow seventeen years ago."

Connor gaped at me. "Holy crap."

"You already said that."

"Nathan. He wouldn't happen to be any relation to the demon named Natalie, would he?"

This time I gaped at him. "You knew about my aunt Natalie? Why didn't you say anything?"

He cringed. "I'll take that as a yes."

"What do you know about them? About *him?*" I grabbed his arm tighter and then looked down at where I held on to him. My unidentified hunger suddenly seemed to wake up and zone in…

On Connor.

My fingers dug deeper into his flesh and Connor started to tremble.

"I can feel that. What are you doing, Sam?" he asked, his voice raspy. "What are you doing to me? Stop it!"

It was his energy. It sparked against my skin like a live wire. I could actually see it. His supernatural energy was the same glowing, celestial blue that an angel's eyes turned. And with a touch, I suddenly realized I could absorb it into myself to feed my brand-new hunger.

And it tasted really, really good.

chapter 32

"Let go of him!" Jordan tried wrenching me away from the angel, but failed. "God, you're like a total monster, aren't you? Forget a hobbit, you're a...like a...oh, I don't know. Some monster thing. You're the movie geek, not me!"

Finally, I let her pull me away and I gasped for breath. Connor fell to his knees, bracing himself against the floor. He looked up at me wearily and grimly.

"I take it you got that little talent from your birth father. Angels don't usually have anomalies like that to pass along."

I reeled from what I'd done, staggering backward.

"I'm sorry." I swallowed hard, clasping my hands together to stop them from trembling. "Did I hurt you?"

"I'll recover. You didn't drain me too much."

I rubbed my fists hard into my eyes as my control returned. "My father was a demon who had an anomaly when he was converted from human. Natalie's was that she hungered for souls, that's what made her the Source of the grays when she came back here and started kissing people and infecting them with her problem. My father, though...Natalie told me that he could absorb life energy."

"Sounds like a fun guy," Jordan said shakily.

My stomach churned. "This can't be happening. I—I already had one hunger to deal with. Now the moment I get rid of that I've suddenly developed this little addiction to supernatural energy?"

"How do you know it's *supernatural* energy?" Jordan asked.

I looked at her. "I didn't feel this way with Colin today at school. Or with you. Only with Connor so far. He's supernatural. You just have some psychic stuff going on, but you're still human."

"Sounds like a good bet it's supernatural only, then," Connor said. "Hooray?"

Jordan helped Connor to his feet, scowling at the both of us. "Okay, angel-guy. Monster-girl told you her little wacko confession from hell. Your turn. What do you know that can help us? What have you been hiding?"

She'd kept up nicely with tonight's program. I couldn't help but be impressed that she hadn't run away from here screaming after everything she'd learned.

"Fine, I'll share." Connor scrubbed a hand over the top of his scalp, then eyed both of us cautiously. "I knew when I came here that something was messed up with the Hollow. Like, seriously messed up. That's the main reason they sent me as an unexpected addition to the team. Heaven knew the Hollow had a leak into Trinity by then, and that was the link to the gray problem. They also knew it was being caused purposefully by someone with an agenda. The leaky part of the Hollow is trapped here, just like the grays are—like *we* are. The barrier keeps it from opening up anywhere else."

I took this in. "So what was your mission?"

"To check it out. To observe. To see if I could figure out if Heaven was right about who's in control of something that isn't supposed to have a controller. The Hollow isn't supposed to be a place you visit and then jump back out. It's a one-way ticket."

Connor also knew that it was a *somebody* controlling the Hollow. It helped confirm what I already knew. "It's supposed to be Heaven and Hell's garbage disposal."

"Essentially. But it's not that anymore."

"Since when?"

"Since about seventeen years ago."

My breath caught. "Seventeen years…"

That was when Natalie and my father—and my mother—were sent into it.

"Nobody knows you exist, Sam." Connor paced back and forth, looking at me as if I was a ghost standing right here in front of him. "Nobody knows a child came out of that relationship, only a whole heap of trouble. But you know what? It explains a whole hell of a lot to me."

"They killed my mother because she loved him." My words were quiet, but they were fueled by the outrage I'd felt about this since first hearing the story. "They killed her with a dagger like Bishop's and tossed her into the Hollow like garbage. My father followed because he loved her and couldn't live without her—just like Roth nearly followed Cassandra if you all hadn't stopped him."

His brows rose. "That's some fairy tale."

"Heaven was responsible for murdering my mother. All because she loved somebody she wasn't supposed to." Tears streaked down my cheeks. "How's that for fair? How's that for keeping the balance?"

"Who told you this?" he asked softly.

"What difference does it make?"

"A big one, actually. Because whoever told you this didn't have their facts straight—or they were straight-up lying to you." There wasn't an ounce of humor on Connor's face as he regarded me. "I was there, Sam. That night when everything went down seventeen years ago. I was part of that team, too."

I couldn't breathe. "*You* were?"

He nodded. "Damn—now, looking at you, I should have known from the moment I saw you. You look a lot like your mom, but you got your coloring from your dad. He had dark hair, brown eyes. Good-looking guy. Crazy as a loon, but good-looking."

"Crazy?"

"He was exiled from Hell. That was his punishment for falling for an angel—no pun intended. You think we kill those who break a rule like that without thinking twice? Way harsh. Exiling takes care of any universal balance issues, especially when there is a list of previous offenses to go along with it. Nathan's tendency for draining other supernaturals of their life energy, that handy little talent you seem to have inherited—although I was told he could do it with humans, too— wasn't welcomed with open arms. He did some damage before they finally got the hint and gave him the boot. Anna, your mother, she would have been given another chance in Heaven if she broke it off with him. But she didn't. She went to him immediately when she learned of his exile. I guess they really were in love, I'll give you that much. But he was no good for her. He drained her energy a little at a time to keep a hold on his sanity now that he was souled. My team was dispatched to take care of Natalie when she made her last visit here. It became a two-for-one deal when your father got involved. And, Anna..." Connor's eyes were haunted. "She was weakened by how much he'd been feeding on her and she...she got in the way. It was never supposed to be her, Sam. It wasn't. But she got in the way of my blade..."

I stared at him, stunned. "*You're* the one who killed her."

Connor blinked hard. "It was the worst moment of my entire existence when I realized what happened."

I could barely form words, my throat was so thick. "This is too much."

"I'm sorry, Sam." His expression darkened. "It should never have been Anna who was destroyed. But it all happened so fast. The Hollow took her. And Nathan nearly killed all of us before he jumped in after her. Thought that was the end of it. Wrong."

Connor...it was *Connor* who'd killed my birth mother. Natalie had told me a different story—told me Nathan and Anna were part of the team to track down Natalie who'd escaped from Hell with her little hunger problem. It was how they'd originally met.

And I'd believed every word.

I shoved Connor against the wall. "Are you lying to me?"

He looked at me bleakly. "If I was going to lie, I wouldn't admit being the one who killed your mother, would I?"

"Samantha," Jordan said uneasily. "Don't hurt him."

I laughed at that, a hollow sound that hurt my throat. "Hurt him? He's an ageless, immortal angel. You really think I could hurt him?"

"Uh, yeah. I really do. Remember, it's all fun and games until somebody loses an eye. Or a wing. Or...whatever angels have worth losing."

"Great," I murmured. "Jordan Fitzpatrick, resident guardian angel to angels."

"I'm sorry, Sam," Connor said again. "But none of this changes anything. The Hollow and the one controlling it need to be dealt with. And it needs to be soon."

"Sounds like we're going to have to have a long talk, Connor." Another voice cut through my concentration. I swiveled to see Bishop standing at the end of the hall, just past the open door. "You've been keeping information from the rest of us?"

"How much did you hear?" Connor asked grimly.

"More than enough."

I stepped back from Connor and crossed my arms as the other angel drew closer.

Adam Drake. Guilty of the murder of twenty-five victims including his older brother, James. Sentenced to death by hanging for his crimes.

Connor hissed out a breath. "I was told not to say anything. Not until I knew more."

"And what do you know now?" Bishop's voice was low and dangerous.

"It's my father," I said quietly as the pieces clicked together. "I'm right, aren't I, Connor? It's him. He's the one in control of the Hollow. He's the one who let Natalie out, who let Marissa out. He's trying to distract—who? You guys? The city? Everybody? What's his big plan? What's he trying to do?"

Connor nodded. "Heaven believes that Nathan used his ability to absorb energy to essentially draw the power of the Hollow into himself fueled by his rage and grief over what happened with Anna."

"What else does Heaven believe that they didn't bother to tell me?" Bishop asked.

"This was all decided after you left, so don't take it personally." Connor grimaced. "They believe he's still trapped inside, that absorbing the power of the Hollow changed him in ways that prevent him from escaping."

"Well, that's a good thing, right?" Jordan said. "If there's a badass, hate-filled demon who can suck up energy and kill people with a touch, I think it's probably good that he can't get out."

"If he's not in the Hollow itself, he's well hidden. Watching, waiting." Connor shook his head. "But for what? I haven't figured that out yet."

"Natalie and Marissa were tests," I said, feeling cold.

"I'm sure of it." Connor nodded. "And we took them both down. Nathan must know this and he'll...adjust his plans—whatever they are. There's only one problem I can think of now."

"Only one?" Jordan regarded him like he'd just grown another head. "Wow, you must be looking at a whole other craptastic situation than the one *I'm* looking at."

Connor eyed her. "Who invited you here again?"

"That would be me." I tried not to be even slightly amused by Jordan's bluntness. Everybody was the victim of it, not just me. "So what's the problem you can see?"

Connor looked directly at me. "You are."

I gaped at him. "Me?"

"If we're right about the ultimate threat being Nathan, then he must know you're here. It's too big of a coincidence otherwise. Why would he release Natalie into your city in particular?"

Damn. He had a point. A really pointy one.

I felt Bishop's searing gaze on the side of my face like fire and finally risked a look directly at him.

"What?"

"You told Connor your secret?"

"Yeah, I told him."

He groaned. "Fantastic. We definitely need to talk."

I narrowed my eyes. "Trust me, Bishop. We're talking, and not only about me being a blabbermouth about my paranormal parentage. I need time to wrap my head around my birth father being the potential big bad of the entire universe. Actually, come to think of it. Let's talk *now*."

Bishop's brows rose as he regarded me cautiously. "All right."

"Stay here," I told Jordan.

Her brows were raised, as well. "Wow, did you just change into your bitch pants? Relax, monster-girl. I won't budge an inch."

I sent a dirty look at her then turned to walk down the hall past Bishop and toward the door. I shoved it open and went outside, inhaling the cold air deep into my lungs and trying to do as Jordan suggested and relax.

Yeah, right. That was currently impossible.

The door creaked shut behind Bishop. "Want to fill me in on what's going on? What are you doing here?"

I let out a long, shaky breath. "In a nutshell? I remembered something Connor said that made me think he knew more than he was letting on. I was right. And I had another vision—another apocalyptic-style one like the one I had the night I met you. The city destroyed, sucked into the Hollow. Nothing left. But there was a voice in my head this time telling me that I was a part of it. That whoever is behind all of this needs my help. It's my father. It's him. He's controlling the Hollow and he's still driven by grief and hate after losing my mother. He wants revenge."

"You might be right. But you still shouldn't have said anything to Connor about what you are." Bishop's face was etched in concern and he came closer to me, taking me by my arms to turn me to face him. "It's too dangerous. If Heaven finds out about your secret...you won't be safe."

"Screw secrets," I blurted out. "Seriously, just screw them. I'm sick of it. Secrets have messed everything up. I have my father's hunger now. I don't crave souls anymore like a gray, but I crave supernatural energy just like my father did. That's how he was able to allegedly suck up the Hollow and mess everything up. And he sent my aunt out to be some sort of a foot soldier for him, to tell me lies and try to get me to join their side. Lies and secrets. They only make everything worse. Know what I mean, Adam?"

"I know it's been difficult for you, but you have to listen to me. You have to…" His voice trailed off and his blue eyes widened. "What did you just call me?"

The night went quiet all around us so all I could hear was the sound of my heart pounding hard against my rib cage. "Adam."

He let go of me and took a step backward. "That's not my name."

"Yes, it is." I clasped my hands together to keep them from trembling. "Adam Drake. It's your name, so don't even try lying to me. Like I said, I'm sick of lies and secrets. You could have told me the truth, but you didn't. I had to hear it from somebody else."

He shook his head, his expression bleak and pale. "No."

"Adam Drake, eighteen years old in 1878. You killed all those people. It wasn't only Kraven you murdered. You killed them and you were put to death for it. And yet you still became an angel. Such a mystery, huh? One I'm trying like hell to figure out before it drives me completely insane."

His eyes glowed blue now, the rest of his face a mask of misery. "How did you—"

"There wasn't much information about your victims online, but there's that number that keeps flashing in my mind. Twenty-five victims, starting with your brother. Is that why Heaven thought you'd make a stellar angel of death—because you sent him to Hell? How many have you killed since then?"

He kept walking back as I moved closer until he hit the wall of the church. He stared at me as if every word that spilled from my mouth stunned him. "Countless, Samantha. I've killed countless people in Heaven's name. All people who've deserved my blade for what they've done—for the threat they presented to the balance."

"What about the ones when you were alive? Answer me, Bishop." I had to use that name since it was how I knew him. His real name might be Adam, but he would always be Bishop to me. "Did they deserve it, too? Do you remember killing them?"

"Yes." His jaw tightened so much it looked painful, and anguish slid through his eyes. "I remember every single one. But I don't remember *why* I did it. That's the worst part. I remember killing them, killing James, but I don't remember what made me do it. Maybe I snapped. Maybe I've always been crazy."

I turned to look at him again, my fists clenched at my sides. I'd wanted some tidy answers, but all I got were more messy questions.

The crunch of gravel alerted me to someone's approach.

"Well, well, well," Kraven drawled. "Look who it is. My little brother and his one and only true love. Sorry to interrupt any outdoor sexcapades. Happily, you still have your clothes on. It is a little chilly tonight."

Bishop's glowing gaze moved to the demon. "You told her, didn't you?"

"Told her? Told her what?" A smile tugged at the corner of his mouth. "Oh, *that*. Oops. Shouldn't I have said anything?"

"You son of a bitch."

"You got that much right."

"Why?" Bishop's voice was soft, but his gaze hardened. "Why would you tell her? What good does it do anyone?"

"Good?" Kraven snorted. "Sorry, I think you're forgetting I'm a demon. We don't really specialize in good. Mayhem, chaos, misery—that's more my ticket. Get all those malicious feelings out. Balance scales to the dark side a smidgeon. Delicious."

"You really hate me that much?"

Kraven's eyes glowed red. "Oh, little brother. I can't even express in words how much I hate you. How much I want to see you suffer for what you did to me. So if I can cause any additional pain in that deteriorating brain of yours, I consider it a personal victory. Does she hate you now because of this? Sweetness might be a nexus, but right now she seems to trend toward the lighter side of the scale. She can't deal with the true nastiness that comes with falling for something like you." He laughed. "So now what happens, little brother? Do you kill her, too? Do you fulfill your Heavenly mission, no matter who your victim has to be? Whatever they say, right? Come on, where's that shiny dagger of yours? Let's get this party started!"

"I'm not killing her," Bishop said evenly, every word as sharp as a blade. "Even if Heaven made it a direct order—I wouldn't do it. I don't care if they destroy this city, if they destroy this entire damn world. I would never hurt her."

Kraven made a face. "I think I just threw up a little in my mouth."

I stared at Bishop. Even though there was that edge of madness in his words tonight, he sounded so damn sincere.

For a moment, I'd doubted. After everything that had happened between us, I'd still doubted him.

I was such an idiot.

From the first moment I saw him, there was something there. And yeah, maybe it started off as an instant attraction to his soul, but it was *something*. And it had only grown since that night when my life had changed irrevocably. Now it wasn't due to a soul or an instinct or a moment of irresistible craving…for me it was *real*.

I could never love somebody who hurt people for fun. Who killed because it was a rush, a hobby, something they felt no remorse for. I wasn't interested in falling for a sociopath now or ever, no matter who he was.

I'd never really totally trusted my heart, even when it was yelling so loudly it was impossible to ignore. And I didn't really favor doing spontaneous things—things that could get me in trouble at school or put into the backseat of a police car.

Sometimes, though, I had no other choice.

Sometimes, there was only one answer and it appeared with crystal clarity and stubbornly stuck around even when challenged again and again.

I couldn't ignore that.

"Let me see." I said it so quietly I wasn't sure anyone had heard me.

Bishop watched me steadily, his gaze not leaving mine for a moment. "Samantha…"

"Let me see your memories. Drop your walls completely and let me see what happened back then. This has tormented you for over a hundred years. I know it has. But I think I can help you learn what really happened."

"What really happened?" Kraven scoffed. "He made a deal with Heaven and got a big shiny knife and a pair of fluffy wings for his troubles. I remember how that knife felt when he sank it into my back."

It wasn't until I looked at the demon that I felt a hot tear splash to my cheek. His brows drew together as if whatever expression was on my face was the exact opposite of what he'd expected.

"Don't look at me like that, sweetness. I don't want your pity."

He called it pity. I called it empathy. "You've suffered all this time, too, but for a different reason. You believe the brother you loved more than anybody else betrayed you for some sort of prize. You would have done anything for him, I know you would have. Even now, you can't help yourself when it comes to Bishop—"

"Adam," Kraven bit out the name. "And he can't even admit to his own damn name. Pathetic."

"—you still want to help him when he gets in trouble. You still want to save him when he's in danger. You can tell yourself you hate him and that you only took this assignment to get the chance to make him suffer, but you're lying to yourself. Theme of the night—no more lies. No more secrets. You think you're so damn tough, Kraven…"

"I am," he gritted out.

"You are," I agreed. "But not when it comes to Bishop. You still love him, you can't help it. That sort of love is unconditional, even if he hurts you. Even if he…kills you." I turned from Kraven's now stricken expression to look at Bishop. "Will you let me see your memories? You can't fight me on this if I try. I have no damn idea what I'm doing or even if it'll work. It's always been accidental before."

Bishop was silent for so long I was certain he was ready to walk away and try to forget about this.

But finally, he nodded. "We can try."

"This is ridiculous," Kraven said, but there was an edge to his voice now. Something raw and pained that went miles deeper than the surface. This pain he felt toward his brother went right to the center of his entire being. "You two have your sexy little mind-meld experiment. I have better things to do."

When I reached out and grabbed his wrist he turned a very dark look on me that once would have scared me to my very core. To be completely honest, it still did.

"No." I tightened my grip on him. "You're not going any-where."

He raised an eyebrow. "I'm not?"

I shook my head. "It's time for the truth. Are you ready to see it?"

chapter 33

Kraven glanced down at my hand on his wrist. "That feels kind of tingly. I like it. What are you doing now, sweetness?"

My new hunger was currently at a very controllably low level, which was good. I couldn't let my new problem interrupt this. "Ignore it."

"I'll try my best."

I took hold of Bishop's hand. He eyed me uneasily. "So you're going to try to be a true connection between Heaven and Hell tonight, are you?"

"It might even work."

"You literally have thirty seconds before I'm out of here," Kraven said, his jaw tight. "Tick tock."

No pressure there.

I looked at Bishop. "Try thinking about back then, when everything went wrong. When your memories first got faulty."

His expression tensed. "I'll try."

I nodded, holding his gaze—holding it harder than I ever had before since I knew this was so important.

If it worked—and that was a big *if*—this could go either way. It might only confirm that Bishop snapped and went on a murdering rampage. Or that he'd made some deal that required the life of his brother offered up to Hell on a silver platter.

What I was trying to do might possibly make everything worse.

Doubt worked its way under my skin in record time.

Maybe I shouldn't do this. Maybe I should put it off till another night when there was less on my mind and I had more answers about Nathan…

Maybe—

Snap!

James was right. My sight's back to normal. Hell, it's better than normal. Walking around without thick glasses and the constant threat of going blind is an amazing feeling.

Magic. I never would have thought it'd work.

The man who helped me, who James had found through one of Kara's contacts in the city, cost a small fortune—James has yet to tell me how much—but it worked.

Time to find my brother and thank him for saving my eyes.

I get back to Kara's place thinking I might find him here. James and I have our own house, an abandoned one on the east side we've taken unofficial ownership of. We saw our mother enough before and after the jobs she sent us out on. One day we'd find jobs that didn't require us to be indebted to her any longer. Jobs that didn't require weekly visits to the cemetery.

"Where's James?" I ask the moment I see her.

She gives me a stiff smile and pats back her hair, which is a golden shade I know she still uses like money to earn the attentive gazes of many men. "Haven't seen him today."

"Let him know I'm looking for him." I turn away.

"Adam, darling. Wait. I know you're angry with me."

I tense up. "Forget it."

"I can't forget it."

"I don't want to interrupt your meeting. You're having one now, right?"

She glances back toward the door to the basement, the one part of this house I've never been invited to see. For years, it's only been a mysterious locked door leading to the place she holds her secret meetings.

Her secret magic meetings. The same ones I've always laughed at behind her back.

Now that my eyes are fixed, I'm not laughing quite as loud.

"You should be careful," I warn her. "I don't know what you all get up to down there…or why you need the bodies you don't send on to the medical school…"

"Darling, please forget all of that." She gives me a tense smile that fans fine lines out around her eyes. "It's my little thing. Nothing to worry yourself about."

"I never said I was worried."

She presses her hands to my cheeks and looks deep into my eyes. "So much like your father, always trying to do the right thing, to convert me from my wild ways."

The subject of my father's always been a sore point. Mostly because she's told me next to nothing about him other than the fact he'd left her. I wasn't even sure if he knew I existed.

"Not like James's father," she says, her expression darkening.

She hates Thomas Kraven and has for nineteen years since he got her pregnant and discarded her. He already had a wife and two mistresses, so he didn't want any more obligations. When she threatened to go public with James and tell everyone that he was Thomas's child, he'd made it clear that both she and James would die if word got out about his bastard. He would never acknowledge James as his son, and Kara would never get any money from him.

He was a cold and heartless man—and very dangerous. Kara never doubted he'd follow through with his threats.

My mother has changed since those days. Now she took money for other people's bodies…but not her own. At least, not to my knowledge.

"You need to let go of the hate you have for him." This isn't the first time I've told her this.

"I can't."

"You're not even trying. It's consumed you all these years."

Something in her eyes sparks. "Perhaps it's finally time for those who've wronged me to get what they deserve."

A shiver goes down my spine when she talks like this because I know she means every word.

"I love you, Adam." She pulls me into a hug that I try to return. "You're the only one who cares if I live or die."

"James does."

"James is just like his father. Arrogant, selfish, a user from the day he was born."

Always exaggerating, my mother. "From the day he was born? An arrogant, selfish infant?"

"You know what I mean." She pulls away, her eyes damp with tears. "You've always been my favorite."

"Don't say that." I hate it when she dismisses James as if he's meaningless to her.

"But it's true. Your father was my one true love."

"A man who abandoned you and never looked back?"

"He had his reasons. One day you might learn what they were."

"Yeah, right." I had to get out of here. "If you see James, tell him I'm looking for him."

"Yes, my darling."

She hasn't even noticed I'm not wearing my specs. Hasn't noticed that I can see without bumping into things for the first time in ages.

Her favorite. Sure, I am.

As I reach the front door, I freeze when I hear a sound.

Raised voices coming from downstairs. One I recognize immediately as James's.

But Kara said he wasn't here.

Instead of leaving, I turn and slowly and quietly move toward the *door leading to the basement. Kara's already gone downstairs, but she left the door slightly ajar behind her.*

I push the door open farther and take a step down. The stairwell leads to a short hallway and a room beyond. It's in there that Kara must have her meetings. It's there that I'm drawn to as if I have no choice but to see for myself what's going on.

"Get away from me!" James's voice is raised, angry.

"Stop acting like a fool," our mother replies. "You agreed to this."

"Agreed? To join your little soirée? Yeah, I agreed to check it out. Wanted to finally see what you all get up to every week. But if your friend touches me again with that, I swear I'm going to cut off his hand."

"James," Kara soothes, her words strong and steady. "To be welcomed as a new member of the group we must first draw these symbols on you."

"Maybe I don't want to join anymore."

"Strange. You were so eager last week when I promised to give you the name of the man that could help your brother."

"That was then."

I move closer and peer around the edge of the doorway to see them inside. James's back is to the door and he stands shirtless before Kara and five men dressed in black robes. The room is dark, lit only by candles and torches set into the stone walls. There's a pit filled with smoldering ash in the center of the room. Chains and manacles are attached to the walls.

It looks chillingly like a dungeon.

"We helped you." Kara gives him one of her special smiles, the one that's made many men over the years lose their coins into her purse. "And now you will help us."

"Not sure about that, Mother."

She grimaces. "I've asked you not to call me that."

"Sorry, keep forgetting. Don't want these nice men to know you're ancient enough to have a son my age, do you?"

She nods at another man, her expression impassive. "He's going to be a problem."

"What should I do?"

"Whatever you feel you must to gain control over this situation."

He draws out a long metal bar from under his robes. James doesn't even see it coming as he's struck in the back of the head. He falls to the ground unconscious and bleeding.

I don't hesitate before racing into the room.

"What are you doing?" I demand.

Kara looks at me with shock, which shifts swiftly to disappointment. "Adam, you shouldn't be here."

"Why did you knock him out? You told me he wasn't even here and now you do this to him?"

"He agreed to be a part of this."

"Sounded like he changed his mind."

"It was stupid to render the boy unconscious," another man in robes says through clenched teeth. "The vessel needs to be conscious. It has already begun. There's no stopping it now."

The ashes in the pit begin to swirl as if touched by an unseen wind and the room grows colder until I can see my breath freeze before me with each exhale. I crouch over James, a fierce need to protect him from these strangers—even Kara, whom I've never totally trusted but never considered a true threat.

"Oh, Adam," she says, shaking her head. "You don't know what you've interrupted here."

"Some sick ritual to help you get revenge over Thomas Kraven?"

"Him and many others."

"Is that all that matters to you? Revenge, power, money?"

She looks at me as if confused. "Yes, of course. It's what I want, what I've been working for all these years. Why I had two children—one to sacrifice to the darkness when the time came. It was never supposed to be you, my darling. James's soul is already spoken for."

Three years ago she admitted to selling James's soul to give her access to black magic. I'd assumed she was drunk and hadn't taken a word she said seriously. But James had gone very quiet.

He believed. He's always been the one to believe in Heaven and Hell. Every time we dug up a body for Kara, he'd pray to be absolved of his sins afterward. He didn't think I heard him, but I did.

The idea that his mother had sold his soul for her own gain had hit him hard even when I tried convincing him it was all lies. He'd barely spoken to her since, even when I tried to convince him she'd been lying.

"Do it," Kara now says quietly.

Two of the men grab me, their grips so tight I can't break free. Another man cuts open my shirt with a dagger, then dips his finger into a bowl of thick red liquid and begins to trace symbols on my chest. It's blood. He's drawing on me with blood.

My stomach clenches with fear and disgust.

"What are these symbols? What are you doing to me?"

Kara nods. "It's right that it's you. This is a true sacrifice. They will see that and they will reward me."

"Kara!"

"You should have minded your own business. Your brother didn't need your help. You think you've saved him?" She pats my cheek hard enough to hurt. "There's no saving him. His soul belongs to Hell."

"You're such a bitch."

"Only because life presented me with no other options, my darling." She looks over her shoulder at the swirling ashes. "It's here."

The two words turn my blood to ice.

The ashes begin to rise up from the pit. The air is so cold it's like it's suddenly the dead of winter despite it being midsummer.

They wanted to do this to James. Whatever this is.

I can't move. All I can do is stare at the ashes as they draw closer to me, forming a line like a rope that slithers around my wrists, my waist, my throat. It's choking me. It's killing me...

But as quickly as it starts, it's all over.

I fall to my knees, reaching out to grab James's arm, hoping to shake him awake so we can get out of here. I've survived whatever the hell that was and I'll be damned if I'll let anyone hurt my brother. He's always been there for me and I'd give my own life to save his.

To save him from our own mother, who doesn't care if we live or die.

"Good," Kara says, smiling again. "It's done."

"What's done?" I grit out.

"You'll kill them for me, my darling. Every last one who's ever done me harm or stood in my way."

"I'll kill nobody for you. I dig up your dead bodies, but I don't make them dead."

Her expression hardens. "You'll do exactly as I say now, child. Stand up."

I stand up as if there are strings attached to my shoulders.

Her eyes are so cold they freeze me in place. "You've made me very angry, Adam. You made me sacrifice my favorite son. You've made me sacrifice you."

"Sacrifice?" I frown, confused. Frightened. "But I'm still here. I'm still breathing."

"I wanted to protect you because I loved your father. You took that from me. You gave me no other choice. I take revenge toward those who've done me wrong. You've now done me wrong, Adam, my sweet. So now you will kill my enemies one by one without hesitation, without question. And tomorrow, when I've ensured he's forgotten all about his little visit down here, you will kill James. You will kill him as your punishment so you have no one left alive who cares for you. No one who wants to help you. Do you understand me?"

I stare at her with horror. "Mother, no…"

"Say it, Adam. Say it!"

Just as the ashes wrapped around my throat, now something invisible tightens in their place, leaving me cold and empty and unable to fight. My mind fogs—the past unclear, the present hazy, the future entirely at her command. "Tomorrow I will kill James. For you, Kara."

She smiles again. "That's my good boy."

Michelle Rowen

I will do whatever she tells me to. I have no choice.
No choice.
She's damned me every bit as much as she's damned my brother.

chapter 34

Snap!

Both Bishop and Kraven let go of me at the same time and staggered backward. It had all been so real. As if *I* was Bishop, experiencing every painful emotion, every horrible thought. I felt his fear, his disgust and his inability to resist whatever dark magic his mother and her friends had performed on him.

Symbols drawn in blood. The darkness and evil in the ashes rising up and taking him over, clouding his memories, but leaving him conscious enough of what he was doing. Just not *why* he did it.

"It was supposed to be me," Kraven whispered. "But that selfish, murderous bitch didn't care in the end, as long as it got done. She made me forget being down there with them, but now I've seen it. I've seen it all."

Bishop's expression was stone, but there was something in his eyes that worried me. What he'd been forced to remember, forced to *see,* had unhinged him. I reached for him, hoping to lend him some sanity, but there was no spark of energy this time when I touched his skin. He looked down at where my fingers curled around his wrist, his expression grim.

"Wasn't sure when that would stop working. Guess it's to-night."

"Bishop, no." Guilt lanced through me. "I shouldn't have done it. I shouldn't have done the memory meld. It must have messed this up."

"I think it's just a coincidence and was bound to happen sooner or later. But my mind..." He pressed his hands to either side of his head and swore under his breath. "It's getting worse by the minute."

Kraven had gone silent, watching us from the shadows as if we were complete strangers. "How long do you have before you lose it completely?"

"Don't know. Not long."

The demon's expression was guarded, untrusting. "I don't know what to think right now. How do I know if any of that was real? Maybe you're lying to me, trying to manipulate me."

I shot him a look. "I guess that's something you're going to have to work out for yourself. But if you ask me, it was real. Totally real. And if there's somebody you should hate, it's your mother."

"Believe me, I'm way ahead of you on that one."

"What happened wasn't Bishop's fault. And it wasn't your fault, either. You thought he killed you of his own free will to get some sort of Heavenly reward. Well, guess what, James? You were wrong. And for a hundred years you've hated the one person who would have done anything for you."

He just stared at me bleakly before turning away and going into the church without another word.

"So he chooses avoidance when faced with the truth," I muttered. "Not a huge surprise."

"I need to talk to Connor," Bishop said, his voice hoarse. "I can't get sidetracked by any of this. Not now. If what he said about your father is true, then we need a plan in place to deal with it."

He was right. The many problems between the brothers weren't going to be fixed in a few minutes. Even with the truth about Bishop still playing like a movie in my head, I knew I had to stay focused.

"This isn't over yet, you know," I told him. "None of it, so don't lose hope. You can still be fixed."

"There's no fallen angel who's ever been welcomed back to Heaven."

"You're no normal fallen angel, Bishop." I actually smiled at that as I pulled him closer to me. What I'd seen had been horrible, but it had set my mind at ease about him being evil. "Seriously, you're the most *ab*normal guy I've ever met in my life."

His lips twitched. "Thanks. I think."

Bishop went back into the church, but I stood out there for a few more minutes trying to breathe. Trying to stay calm. Trying not to get overwhelmed.

Yeah. Good luck with that.

It had been exhausting, but if there was one thing I'd done right tonight, it was to show Kraven and Bishop the truth. What they'd do with it after so many years of bad blood between them, I honestly didn't know.

As I turned toward the door to go back inside and join the others, something caught my eye. Somebody was walking along the sidewalk on the other side of the road without sparing a glance toward the church.

It was Roth.

Despite our many issues, my heart ached for him. It was only last night that Cassandra had been lost to the Hollow— torn right out of his arms.

Is this what he'd been doing ever since? Walking the city all alone?

I needed to talk to him, to tell him to come back to St. Andrew's to be with people who cared about him, who might be able to help him with his grief.

Before he turned the corner up ahead, I started after him. I was about to call out his name when a hand clamped down on my shoulder.

A scream caught in my throat and I spun around to face… Jordan.

"Hey," she said, her brows drawn together. "Where do you think you're going?"

"Uh…I need to—"

"You're just going to leave me here with the Three Stooges? By the way, for three hot guys, they are seriously weird, and not just because they're all supernatural. If you're leaving, so am I."

Roth was getting farther away and I couldn't let him out of my sight. I grabbed Jordan's arm and started walking faster. Her long legs helped her more than keep up.

"Where are we going?" she asked.

"I need to talk to Roth."

The demon was fifty yards ahead of us and moving fast. "Doesn't look like he wants to talk to you."

"I need to help him."

"From what I've heard tonight, you need to be a little more concerned with helping yourself." She glanced to the left to see the outline of downtown, including skyscrapers and office buildings. The glow from the sign on the side of the massive St. Edward's hospital lit up the night.

"Thank you for your opinion."

Her gaze tracked behind us and there was something about her expression. Something wounded and lost.

"What's wrong?" I asked.

"He's close."

"Who's close?" Then I grimaced. "Are you talking about Stephen?"

She inhaled sharply. "Who else? He's around, Samantha. I can feel it."

I hesitated, knowing this was a dangerous subject to get into with Jordan. "It was rough for a couple days there, but I honestly don't think he's going to try to hurt you again, if that's what you're afraid of."

"I should hate him."

"You have every right to feel that way."

Her arms were crossed tightly over her chest and I couldn't help but notice her eyes were now glistening. "I'm not like those girls who are into guys who treat them like crap. I see it all the time, some of my friends are so pathetic when it comes to loser guys who obviously don't really love them. They cheat on them, hurt them, treat them like garbage, borrow money from them and never pay them back…and yet as soon as the guy texts, they're all excited again. Pathetic."

"I have to agree."

"I'm *not* like that."

"Trust me, Jordan. I don't believe you're like that, either."

A tear slipped down her cheek and she angrily wiped it away. "Then why can't I hate him?"

My heart twisted. "I guess because real love's not that easy to destroy."

"That's really stupid."

"Yeah, it is." I took a deep breath and let it out slowly. "But you need to prepare yourself. Things aren't going to get better for him. His soul is gone. He's a gray—possibly the last one in the city. If the guys find him, it's their mission to kill him. He's a threat and he can't be helped."

"There has to be a way," she whispered.

"I wish there was."

She looked directly at me as we continued to walk. "Do you really mean that?"

I nodded. "I really do."

And then I slammed right into Roth's chest.

"Following me?" he asked when I realized what had happened.

He'd stopped walking, turned around to watch our approach, and I hadn't noticed a damn thing since I'd been discussing Jordan's love life, which was, quite possibly, even more complicated than my own.

I searched his face, my heart pounding hard. "Roth, I'm glad you stopped. You need to come back to the church. The guys are worried about you."

"What about you, Samantha?" His face twisted into an unpleasant smile. "Are you worried, too?"

His tone could easily be described as the opposite of friendly.

"Actually, yes. I am. Look, I know what happened last night was horrible. It was hard for all of us. But you need to—"

"Shh." He pressed his index finger to his lips. "Do you hear that?"

I stopped and listened. "Hear what?"

"Me not caring about your opinion. But thank you for attempting to give it to me anyway. Do you think you can fix everything with a few words? You're a teenager, barely out of diapers. You could never understand how I feel. And I don't really want you to try. Okay?" His cruel grin stretched. "But I am really glad you followed me, even if you brought a friend. Won't matter in the end, I suppose."

"And I thought the *other* demon was a jerk." Jordan eyed Roth with distaste. "Color me wrong."

I frowned. "You're glad I followed you? What are you talking about?"

"He said you'd follow me." Roth shrugged. "And here we are. Right where I said I'd bring you." He turned around in a slow circle. "Okay, she's here. I did what you asked. Let's get on with it."

I suddenly realized where we were. It was a grocery store—or at least, it used to be. It had closed down, the sign broken, the parking lot a large expanse of concrete and dark emptiness.

I'd seen this place before—it was in my vision.

My throat tightened. "What's going on? Who wanted you to bring me here?"

A lone streetlamp still worked and cast a long shadow as the figure approached from the darkness. Other lamps along the street were broken or flickering.

"Beautiful star," Seth said, a smile wide on his face. "You're here. I'm glad."

Part of me relaxed at seeing it was only him. The other part didn't relax at all. Just the opposite. Especially after him having a starring role in my after-death experience. "Seth... what are you doing here? You know Roth?"

He raised an eyebrow and glanced at the demon. "It's a very recent development, but yes."

I scanned the length of the fallen angel. His clothes were dusty and torn, just like usual. His beard seemed even thicker than the last time I'd seen him, the night we'd been at Ambrosia. The strange marks on his arms I'd noticed before had grown even darker and larger. They also trailed up his throat now.

"Um, who is this dude?" Jordan asked, scrunching her nose.

"This—this is Seth," I said. "He's a fallen angel who's been in Trinity a long time. Seth, this is Jordan."

"Charmed," Jordan said as insincerely as possible. She eyed

Seth as if he was something she'd found stuck to the bottom of her shoe. "Can we wrap this up? I really want to get back to my car and go home. I suddenly feel the need to have a long shower."

"Seth, what's going on?" I asked. "You never stick around very long to answer my questions, but I have a lot of them. Why did you want Roth to bring me to you? What do you need to tell me? Have you seen something that might help us?"

"Help," he murmured. "Yes, that's what this is about. I'm glad to see you're better now. All fixed. All improved. Much more useful to me this way."

A churning had started inside me. There was something going on here. Something worse than it seemed. Why couldn't I figure out what it was?

Probably because of the one thing I'd always valued most about myself—my ability to be a realist. Even now that I knew that there were strange and magical things in this world happening all the time all around us, I refused to totally accept it. I needed proof. Needed evidence to support the data.

I thought I'd be a writer one day. Maybe a nonfiction one where facts counted more than fantasy. But that's where my head had been for seventeen years. And right now, it wasn't doing me any favors.

I had to think beyond what my eyes told me.

Right now, it had to be my gut I listened closest to.

"I dreamed about you," I said, my mouth dry. "When I was dead for twenty minutes. My unconscious mind conjured you up in particular—all clean and well-dressed and totally sane. Why you?"

"I have no idea what you're talking about," Seth replied.

"That makes two of us, hobo guy." Jordan tapped her foot. "Samantha, come on. Let's go."

"You're not going anywhere," Roth told her.

She gave him a withering look. "You really are a jerk, aren't you?"

"You have no idea."

"What's your deal, anyway? Are you working for this weirdo?"

"You could say that."

I frowned at Roth. "What does that mean? If you know Seth, why wouldn't you bring him back to meet the rest of the team? He could help Bishop—they're both fallen angels with souls to deal with."

"It's strange, really," Seth mused, stroking his beard absently. "Almost funny."

I tensed. I'd decided to listen to my gut and right now it was telling me something very important. Seth didn't sound all that crazy tonight. And Seth *always* sounded crazy—except in my dream.

I looked directly at him. "What's strange?"

"Why did you assume I was an angel?"

I tried to say something immediately in reply, but faltered. "Well, you told me you were."

"No. I never said anything like that at all." He cocked his head, studying me. "You made assumptions based on your dealings with the other angel, the one who occupied your thoughts so much that you barely even noticed me."

"I sensed your soul." I frowned, trying to remember what had been said during the first couple of meetings with Seth outside of Crave.

"They're tricky things, souls. Meant to be a punishment far worse than being destroyed. Humans were meant to have souls. I had a soul when I was human, before I went through the transition and never had a problem with it because it was natural." He touched his chest. "This one, though, that they seared into me, has always been a challenge. But it's also been very motivating."

Seth had been on the streets long enough that there was no helping him with a touch, as I'd been able to do with Bishop up until tonight. His mind had been permanently messed up, his punishment for falling from…Heaven.

Or so I thought.

"Show me your imprint," I said as firmly as I could. Some things I had to see to understand. To believe. Even when my gut was shouting at me that I already had more than enough proof to know what he really was.

He raised a dark eyebrow as if amused by my request, then turned a little, pulling up the edge of his dirty shirt to show the thick, dark lines of his bat's-wing-like imprint—the imprint of a demon. My stomach lurched.

"See, beautiful star? I was never an angel. I would take it as a compliment that you assumed me to be one if I was fond of that particular breed of creature. But there's only been one angel I could ever tolerate. Only one who could tolerate me in return."

All I could do was stare at him.

Jordan fished into her purse to pull out her phone. Roth snatched it out of her grip and smashed it on the ground.

She shoved him hard, but it didn't make him budge an inch. "You creep! That was brand-new!"

"I don't care."

"You owe me for a new phone."

"Bill me. And shut the hell up."

"Samantha!"

But I wasn't paying attention to her, not to Roth, either. My attention was fully fixed on the demon in front of me, the one I'd assumed from nearly the first moment I'd met him was an angel…just like Bishop. One lost and abandoned by Heaven with no chance to return. No one to help him. No one to care.

He was an exiled demon.

"You're a smart girl," Seth said to me. "You already know the truth, don't you?"

No, please. It can't be.

I couldn't have been this blind.

Then Seth moaned as if in pain, bracing his hands on his thighs, his back hunching over. With alarm, I looked down to see the strange, branching black lines move farther down to his hands and onto his fingers.

"What's happening to you?" I asked, breathless.

"It's a little sooner than I'd anticipated." He laughed, a low, pained sound deep in his throat. "Oh, who am I kidding? This is a *lot* sooner than I'd anticipated, but sometimes, beautiful star, you must make adjustments when necessary. Quick like a bunny. Race to the end so everything can be tied up in a nice, shiny bow. Now, tonight. It will all happen tonight whether I like it or not."

There was that mad tone of his I recognized more. "Who are you? Who are you, *really*?"

His gaze moved toward the cityscape to the left. He nodded at the huge outline of the hospital. "When I was first exiled, I woke up in the shadow of St. Edward's. I took it as a sign that this was where my new life would begin. I wasn't like the others, I didn't accept that this was an end and that I had to make peace with losing my mind and losing my power for all eternity. There are always other choices, you just have to know where to look and be willing to do just about anything to achieve your goals. That hospital was my new birthplace. And inspired by that hospital, I was reborn as something much different than I was before."

I followed his gaze to the tall building with its glowing sign like a beacon in the distance.

St. Edward's Trinity Hospital.

Each capital letter was large and blue, while the rest of the letters were smaller and white and the now-obvious acronym burned into my eyes.

S.E.T.H.

"My original name was Nathan," he said softly. "I'm your father, Samantha."

chapter 35

It wasn't shock that hit me like a sucker punch to the gut over this revelation, but more of a sick, sinking sensation that left me cold and shaky. Part of me had already suspected the truth, but my rational mind hadn't wanted to give it any conscious thought.

Seth wasn't a fallen angel who'd been in Trinity for years and years while losing his mind to the point that he was stuck on the streets with no home to call his own.

He was Nathan, an exiled demon who allegedly controlled the Hollow and had vengeance as his number-one priority.

My father.

I was having a serious Luke Skywalker moment.

"He's your father?" Jordan's words dripped with disbelief. "Seriously?"

All I could do was stare at him—and I tried to use what little clearheadedness I had left to read his mind when he met my gaze directly.

I could read the minds of angels and demons; I'd done it before.

I could find the real truth beyond his twisting words before it was too late. Although, I honestly didn't know how much more truth I could handle and still remain vertical.

His brown eyes, not quite the same shade as mine—but now that I was looking, pretty darn close—weren't giving away any secrets. His walls were up and they were as thick as the concrete we currently stood on. It would take a long time to break through.

"So, I brought her to you like you asked me to," Roth said tightly. "Time for your side of the bargain."

"You bargained with him?" I asked, my voice quiet.

"I sure did." Roth didn't sound the least bit ashamed.

"For what?"

There was a pause before he answered. "For Cassandra."

I couldn't help but tear my gaze off the man standing before me to look at the other demon. He tried to hide it but I saw it, that bottomless grief in his dark eyes.

My throat was thick. "Cassandra's dead."

He shook his head. "No, she's not. She was hurt, but she wasn't dead yet."

"The Hollow wouldn't have taken her if she wasn't a split second from death."

"But now I know who controls it and can give her back."

Right. That would be Nathan. "If he promised you that, he was lying. Cassandra's gone. I wish it was different, too, Roth, but it's the truth."

Jordan had gone very quiet, standing off to my left. I wasn't sure if she'd started trembling due to the temperature or from the subject matter. Likely both.

"Roth, you have served me well tonight," Nathan said. It was time I stopped thinking of him as Seth, a name I associated with an angel I'd wanted to help. "You will be well rewarded when the time comes."

"I don't want any damn reward. All I want is Cassandra

returned here like you promised." His brows drew together. "Is Samantha right? Were you lying to me? Is she…dead? Forever?"

Nathan took in a deep breath and let it out slowly. He didn't reply to Roth; instead, he directed his attention toward me again. "It's difficult, being a demon who was once human. There are certain requirements for the job, very few all that pleasant. You know, I'm sure, all about the balance that must be maintained, don't you, Samantha?"

"It's all about balance," I replied.

"So bloody important, this balance. What do they think will happen if something disturbs it? Will the whole universe implode?" Nathan's lips curled under his beard into a very unpleasant smile. "No. Not the whole universe. Only Heaven and Hell. They believe they are timeless and immortal, but they're dependent on souls. My sister messed that up—or at least, they saw her as a threat. My kid sister, a threat to Heaven and Hell. They think the same about nexi, Samantha, never doubt it. For two vastly different places, they have many similar goals. Keep the balance, follow the rules, toss out those who don't toe the line. Destroy those who are a threat or make them too crazy to try to seek revenge."

"And that's what you're doing. Seeking revenge."

"They did this to me." His jaw clenched and again he grimaced as if a tremor of unbearable pain rippled through him. The branching lines extended farther like vines traveling over his hands and up his neck to trace his jawline. "And they will feel my wrath like nothing they've ever known before."

I swear, I felt a rumbling beneath my feet like a small earthquake.

Jordan's gaze darted around as she tried to steady herself on what should have been solid ground. "What was that?"

The image of the city being sucked into the dark vortex

made a chill race down my spine. This was the place. This parking lot. This is where the vortex appeared and took everything with it, leaving nothing behind.

Just how powerful was this demon?

"If that's so, why haven't you done it already?" I asked, swallowing my fear. "It's been seventeen years since Anna was killed. Why have you waited this long for revenge?"

His expression tightened at the mention of her name. "You know about Anna."

"Natalie told me a lot."

"Of course she did." His jaw clenched. "Natalie loved to talk. Seventeen years of endless talk. I was glad to finally be rid of her."

Roth glared at the demon. "You made me a deal. Are you reneging on it?"

Nathan hissed out a breath. "Being burdened with a soul is not an easy thing. Sometimes the madness grips me when I stay here too long. It can't be helped. If I don't return to the Hollow right away, I have found other ways to cope."

He reached out and gripped Roth's throat.

The demon gasped. "What are you doing?"

Nathan's eyes glowed red. "Coping."

Roth dropped to his knees as if the strength had left him in a rush. And I could feel it like a tingling sensation on the surface of my skin—his energy. Nathan was stealing his life energy.

I grabbed Nathan's arm. "Don't kill him!"

"If I was trying to kill him, it wouldn't take this long." He released the demon who collapsed all the way to the pavement. "Trust me, beautiful star. I have full control over this power. And I have no doubt, you do, too."

Roth's chest heaved as Nathan loomed over him.

"The angel is lost to you. Forget her and move on. Trust me, boy, obsession of this kind will only destroy you."

A moment later, Roth's eyes closed and he slumped to his side, unconscious.

A cry of fear escaped Jordan's throat and she stumbled back a few more steps.

Nathan's gaze tracked to her. "You...you're the one who has always given Samantha difficulties. Called her names, treated her poorly. Do you want to kill her, Samantha? I can show you how. It will be quick and painless. Or just the opposite—your choice."

"What?" Jordan yelped. "No, no, not a good idea. I mean, I've said some stuff, but so has she. And it's different now. We have, like, an understanding. We've been through a lot together. That means something, right, Samantha?"

Nathan laughed at this, a dry sound still edged in madness, despite his recent meal.

"I don't want to kill Jordan," I said evenly. "Just because I've had some problems with her in the past, doesn't mean I want her to die."

"Very well. Then she'll be spared."

But if my vision was right—and if it was something that would happen tonight—*no one* would be spared.

"What do you want from me?" I asked. "Enough of the small talk, tell me the truth. You wanted Roth to bring me here to talk to you. Whatever's happening to you right now seems—" I swept a gaze over his scary, branching lines "—severe. So tell me why I'm here. Why now? And why me?"

He was silent for a moment, his hands fisted at his sides. "I need your help."

"My help?" I shook my head, sickened by what he could be suggesting. "To do what? To help you destroy Heaven and Hell? This world? All out of your need to avenge Anna's death? Is it really as hard for you now as it was then to accept that she's gone?"

A tremor went through him, and again I felt its echo beneath my feet.

Nathan didn't turn away, didn't convulse with whatever pain he was experiencing. He just watched me as if curious. The insanity that had been growing in his eyes a minute ago had dissipated, thanks to his light snack on Roth's energy. I spared a quick glance at the demon who was still unconscious nearby. Jordan stood next to his still form, wringing her hands.

I wanted her to run. But I had a funny feeling she wouldn't get very far.

"Can I tell you something important about yourself, Samantha?" Nathan asked. "Something that is vital for you to know, to believe and to accept?"

"I already know a bunch, no thanks to you." I inhaled slowly, trying to stay calm. Or as calm as I possibly could. "I'm a nexus. Demon father, angel mother. I can see things others can't—things that have to do with the supernatural. I can read the minds of the team members if they don't try to fight me too hard. I could see the searchlights that helped find the lost demons and angels sent to this city on this mission."

I can zap you really hard if you come close to me and I might be able to knock you out, too.

And I have a special dagger strapped to my thigh that an angel gave me to help protect myself when needed.

I didn't share these facts, of course. I had to keep a couple surprises at the ready. I had a very strong feeling I would need them before the night was over.

"What else?" he asked.

"Now that I'm free from having the symptoms of a gray, I can absorb energy. From one hunger to another. I guess I have you to thank for that, too, right?"

This made him smile, but it wasn't an expression filled with joy. "Right. And that is key to what I need tonight from you, beautiful star."

"Why do you call me that? You've called me that since the beginning."

Nathan looked up at the velvet-black sky dotted with bright stars. "Stars once were navigation points. Still are for those who know how read such things. For me, finding you was like finding my way again. I had worried that all was lost. And yet, there you were. Like magic."

"Actually, I've been here in Trinity since I was born. Anna dropped me off at a local adoption agency. Never left this city for seventeen years, so don't try to act all surprised I'm here." I snorted. "And don't try to convince me that you're my dear old dad who finally wants to connect. Maybe see a movie on the weekends? You want to convince me you care about my future and that when you look at me you see Anna and how much you loved her?"

I expected my words to affect him, maybe reach down under those dirty clothes and grab hold of whatever heart he still had left. Instead, he regarded me with a wry smile.

"Psychology. And I thought you were only a high school student."

I swallowed hard. "I need answers, Nathan. You said you wanted to tell me something important about myself, right? What is it that I don't already know?"

His gaze turned thoughtful as he swept his brown eyes over the length of me until they returned to my face. "That you shouldn't exist."

My breath caught. That was actually the last thing I expected him to say. "What?"

"Throughout history, nexi have always been destroyed by Heaven and Hell on the rare occasion they are created either through a forbidden romance or through…darker means." He didn't go into detail about what "darker means" meant, which was a relief. "You are something that is so unnatural and wrong that the fact you've managed to live this long is a genuine surprise to me."

Every word worked its way under my skin, each as painful as a sharp sliver.

Unnatural. Wrong. Shouldn't exist.

I half expected Jordan to add a well-placed quip agreeing with him, that I'm a freak of nature. She remained silent.

"When I look at you, I don't see Anna. Frankly, I don't want to see Anna. She's gone. A long time ago. It's given me plenty of opportunity to reflect over what I was willing to give up for her. It was our relationship that exiled me. The pain I've felt since then is entirely her fault."

If there was one thing I believed since I learned the truth about my origins, it was that Nathan and Anna had been deeply in love. To me, their love was epic and immortal, surviving even after tragedy and death.

Who knew I was such a romantic?

It was an unexpected blow to my spirit to know it wasn't like that at all.

"You blame her?" I asked quietly.

"I did for a time. I've since come to realize that there is only Heaven and Hell to blame—for everything. I will destroy them, Samantha. But first I will take their little world filled with souls. The Hollow will rise up and swallow all of this so I will control those souls. I will control all the mortals that walk this world…instead, they will walk mine. And I will be able to watch as Heaven and Hell begin to fight in earnest against each other for survival."

"Why would you do that if you don't care about Anna

anymore, enough to get vengeance for her death? What's the point?"

Again, he stroked his beard thoughtfully. "There are those who create and those who destroy. Chaos doesn't need a reason to exist."

I saw it then all too clearly. His insanity went far deeper than the surface and couldn't be fixed by absorbing Roth's—or anyone's—life energy. And it wasn't only because of his soul. The Hollow's supernatural junkyard of dark energy had changed him over the years, bleeding his sanity—his love for Anna—away drop by drop until there was nothing left to salvage.

I cast another glance at Jordan and our eyes met. I saw the same realization on her face that I felt inside myself.

We were in very deep trouble.

But I already knew that.

I returned my attention to my birth father. "If I'm so unworthy of breathing, what do you need me for?"

His dark brows drew together. "I never said you were unworthy to me. Just to *them* you are. They would kill you in a heartbeat and they would use you for their own gain—as they already have."

"And you don't want to use me?"

This earned the shadow of a grin. "Touché. The truth is, I need what you and I share. That hunger that has awoken inside you. It's powerful, that hunger. Some might call it an anomaly, but it's an asset. It's not like what you felt before with the need to devour souls. This serves you…and it can serve me."

My stomach convulsed at what he was suggesting. "I'm not helping you destroy the world."

"Of course not. I know you wouldn't agree to such a thing. Not now, anyway." He grimaced again and the lines moved all the way down his hands to his fingertips. He looked at them grimly. "Seventeen years of absorbing the energy of the Hollow—the energy of each discarded demon or angel who found his or her way into its belly. I took as much of it as I could get. It wasn't until it was too late that I realized it was too much."

"What do you mean, too much?"

"The energy is overwhelming me. I need to release it so I can gather my strength again. Otherwise, it will break me into pieces." A glimmer of knowledge came over his expression and, if I wasn't mistaken, an edge of fear.

"Sorry, *Dad*." I said it as harshly as I could, despite quaking inside. "But you being destroyed before you put your nasty plan into action? Doesn't sound like a tragedy to me."

He laughed at this, a sharp crack of a sound. "No, I'm sure you'd think that, given all evidence to the contrary. But you're wrong. Those pieces of me will each become a Hollow of its own. Countless hungry mouths seeking energy with no conscious being controlling it. I might relish chaos and the destruction of my enemies, but not at the risk of my own existence. I want to be the one to destroy Heaven and Hell. Me alone."

Could it be that the power inside Nathan was ready to shatter tonight and that one of those pieces was what destroyed Trinity as it did in my vision?

No one to control it. No one to stop, because there was no one *to* stop.

My throat tightened, as if gripped by an invisible hand as I stared with fear at the man I'd always thought harmless from the moment I met him. Harmless and in need of help. I'd been only half right. "You want me to take some of that power away with a touch because I'm the only one who can. Take it into myself—that poison you're dealing with right now that's causing you so much pain."

"From what I've seen of you, beautiful star, you have a need to help others. Even though they would turn their backs on you, abuse you, use you and underappreciate you. You want to help them. You want to save them." His jaw, covered in those strange black lines, tightened. "This is the only way you can."

Jordan continued to look on in shock, following this conversation as if fascinated and horrified by everything said.

That made two of us.

What Nathan was asking settled over me like a rancid, moldy blanket. "You're asking me to sacrifice myself tonight to save this city."

He shook his head. "No, not sacrifice your life—that would require taking all of my power. I'm the only one capable of using that power to destroy. You're too young, too fragile to handle that. It would kill you."

"Sam, no…" Jordan whispered.

"You don't belong here, beautiful star," Nathan continued. "Not here. You're not one of them and you never have been. Taking part of my energy to relieve the pressure on me temporarily will not kill you, but it will change you into what you were always meant to be. You will become a permanent part of the Hollow, just as I am. And if you refuse, everything in the world will suffer and there's not even anything I can do to stop it. It's as simple as that."

"Simple." I swallowed. "You think any of this is simple?"

"It is to me. I see the truth. Even your adoptive family rejects you. Nobody cares about you at school. Even the girl who stands here shivering before us both hates you and has caused you only pain."

"He's wrong, you know," Jordan spoke up, her voice strained but steady. "I don't hate you. I actually like you. I think you're all kinds of strange and make stupid decisions nearly every day, but I like you. Normally I wouldn't admit this out loud, but I feel like the situation sort of calls for it."

I turned to her with surprise, my eyes stinging. But before I could say anything, the demon surged forward until he was right in front of her.

"If I wanted your opinion, I'd ask." Nathan backhanded her and she went flying through the air and slammed down against the pavement fifteen feet away.

It had happened so fast, all I could do was look at him in shock and fury.

Out of the darkness, another figure now approached. Fast. It was Stephen, a furious expression on his face.

"I'm going to kill you for that," he snarled.

Nathan sighed. "More teenage romantic drama. Never ends well, boy. Consider this a lesson for you."

As Stephen's fist was about to make contact with Nathan's jaw, the demon grabbed it, twisting. I heard Stephen's wrist break and he gasped in pain.

Nathan held on tight and Stephen made a wheezing sound, as if he couldn't get any air into his lungs. The demon was feeding on more life energy, draining Stephen of his life right before my eyes.

"Stop it," I yelled. "Stop it now! If you want me to help you, don't do this!"

Nathan let go of Stephen and the gray crumpled to the ground, unconscious.

I stood there facing my demonic birth father with three unconscious bodies surrounding us as if this was a battlefield.

"You'll help me?" he asked.

I'd quickly found myself cornered with no chance to run, no opportunity for escape. Natalie may have lied shamelessly to me in order to attempt to get me to do what she wanted. But with Nathan—I had no doubt he'd been telling the truth.

wicked kiss

Unless I took away some of the energy that was currently trying to shatter him into countless pieces and which would then destroy everything in their paths, everyone and everything was doomed.

This definitely wasn't a multiple-choice quiz with the possibility of full marks.

"I'll help you," I said finally, my chest tight. "But I need you to do something for me first."

"What?"

"Bring Carly back."

"Your little blonde friend."

"She was taken still alive. And I know you can release people like that. You did it for Natalie. Do it for Carly, too."

He cocked his head. "Always trying to help others. You must get that from your mother's genes."

Nathan's eyes began to glow red and a moment later, the Hollow opened up behind him. Just like that. One moment there was nothing there, the next, a swirling black vortex, eight feet in diameter, hung in the air. The sound was as thunderous and ear-splitting as always.

The vortex disappeared a moment later, but there was someone left standing in its place with her back to us. Someone very familiar.

It was Carly.

417

chapter 36

She scanned the area and slowly swiveled around to face me, her face even paler than her light blond hair. "Sam?"

"Carly! You're here!" I jerkily moved toward her, grabbing her shoulders so I could inspect her for injury. She looked fine—unhurt, undamaged, healthy—and she wore the same clothes as the last time I'd seen her: a cute dress that hugged her curves she'd worn the night I'd confronted Natalie at Crave.

She blinked hard. "What the hell just happened? I shoved that knife in Natalie and—that black thing grabbed me and... and suddenly I'm here." She glanced around. "In the middle of freaking nowhere. With that weird homeless guy and... oh, my God. Is that Jordan Fitzpatrick? Can I suck out her soul? Please?"

She didn't remember anything about the Hollow. But she was still a gray.

I'd wanted to save her from the Hollow. Mission accomplished. But now, before I could allow myself a measure of relief that she'd be okay, I had the chance to save her from being a gray.

Stephen was waking up and I left my best friend to run

back toward him, frantic. "I need Carly's soul. I need it now, Stephen. She can still be saved."

He'd crawled over toward Jordan to check on her, but she was still unconscious. He cradled her head in his lap.

"Stephen!" I yelled, punching him hard in his shoulder. "I need it *now.*"

He just shook his head. "It's gone."

That imaginary hand that had been around my throat now clutched my heart. "It can't be gone. You saved mine, you said you saved hers, too."

His expression was grim. "Natalie wanted me to, but it's different. It was different from yours. Yours was stronger, it survived the transfer. Carly's was… It fell apart when I was trying to encase it. I lied so she wouldn't be mad. Carly's soul is gone, just like mine is, Samantha. I'm sorry."

I went cold inside, so cold that I couldn't even get angry. I couldn't yell or scream at him. The promise that I could make Carly the way she used to be was gone.

Now that she was back, soon she'd go through stasis. And knowing how the other grays had fared, she likely wouldn't survive it.

"Sam, what the hell is going on?" Carly's words now twisted with panic.

The tremor that shook the ground brought my attention back to Nathan. His face was covered in black lines now and he convulsed, bending over as if he couldn't stand the pain a moment longer. "No time," he gasped. "You must do it now or everything ends."

A demon who had caused so much pain now experienced it himself.

I should be happy about that. I wasn't.

My vision was about become a reality if I didn't do something to stop it.

And Nathan was very right about one thing. There was no time. No time to try to contact Bishop through that thread that joined us. For all I knew, it wouldn't work anymore, now that I wasn't a gray. Maybe the part of his soul I had inside me was gone now, too, just like the power to help him fight his madness.

Jordan inhaled sharply as she finally woke up, her gaze darting around the scene before her she probably hoped had been a nightmare. "The demon...the creep. Where'd he go?"

I shot a look over to where Roth had been. She was right; he'd disappeared. The moment he'd had the chance, he'd taken off and left us all behind to deal with this mess. He didn't get his end of the bargain, so he'd settle for self-preservation.

I wasn't all that surprised. Disappointed, but not surprised.

"I think my ankle's broken," Jordan groaned, sliding her hand down her leg. Then she glanced at the person sitting on the ground holding her. "Oh, hell. Stephen...it's you."

"Yeah. It's me."

She sat up and quickly scooted away from him, grimacing from the pain in her ankle. "Why— Where did you come from? What are you doing?"

He looked at her bleakly, shrugging. "I have this weird impulse to protect you."

That earned him a dark look of disdain. "When you're not knocking me unconscious and holding me prisoner while asking someone else to devour my soul? Based on recent experience, the only person I need protection from is you. Well, and the homeless demon dude who's about to go all apocalyptic."

"Good point. And yet, here I am anyway, when I should be anywhere else."

"Sam," Carly said, drawing close enough to touch my arm. "Can you please explain to me what's going on?"

I looked into the face of my best friend since we were little kids, playing in sandboxes and swimming pools. Running through sprinklers. Catching frogs and kissing them, hoping they might turn into princes.

It was a phase when we were ten. It passed.

I thought I'd be able to save her.

At the moment, it seemed as if there was only one person I might be able to save. And it was the last person who deserved it.

The tremors were growing more intense. The entire city shook as if the earth was about ready to split open and swallow it whole.

I took a deep breath in. "You know how I've always been a realist, despite loving monster movies? How I've always looked at facts and figures and tried to understand things in black-and-white terms?"

"Yeah. So annoying." Carly laughed shakily. "Why?"

I hugged her hard. "If I was a dreamer, I'd believe there was another solution. But there's not. Not this time."

"Wait, Sam, what are you talking about?"

I let go of her and walked straight over to Nathan. The lines on his skin were alive, writhing, and in between, there was a glow emanating from them, as if the energy inside him was ready to burst free and shatter him into a million sharp and hungry pieces.

I reached my hand out to him. It trembled.

He grabbed it so tightly, I winced.

"Do it," he gritted out. "Save me, Samantha."

"I'm not doing this for you."

This ability was still new to me and it had happened with Connor by accident. Still, that hunger woke up again now the moment I touched Nathan. Supernatural energy surged beneath my touch, bigger and brighter than anything I'd ever felt.

Dark energy. It had no purity to it, no true light. It was messy, cluttered, angry and filled with muck. And yet, I hungered for it anyway.

Nathan had said he was in control of this ability—and so was I.

I guessed we'd soon find out if that was true.

A greediness rose up inside of me and I began to absorb that energy into myself. So natural, it was as if I'd done this all my life—same as drinking a milkshake. And it was much different from being a gray. This ability—this anomaly—felt right.

After a minute, Nathan's shoulders relaxed. "That's right, beautiful star. You're doing so well."

I gripped his other hand and we stood there, face-to-face, as I absorbed his supernatural energy—the energy of the Hollow he'd taken so he could control it; that had begun to control him, to destroy him.

I took enough of it to save him and keep him from destroying the world.

But then I kept taking some more.

My stomach roiled from the darkness of it, like mounds of junk food, full of fat and sodium, with no nutritional value. This was the Hollow. Bad things had been cast inside. This was the essence of that.

No wonder it had changed Nathan so much. After all, you are what you eat.

I could still think, still reason. This wasn't controlling me, I was controlling it.

Good.

"You said before that there are those destined to create," I said, "and those destined to destroy."

He managed a smile. "I did say that. Which are you?"

I locked gazes with him. "Let's just say, I think I take after my father."

I tightened my grip on him and his grin faltered at the edges. "You've taken enough now. Let go of me."

I didn't let go. I continued to absorb his energy. And the more I took, the more I wanted.

He hissed, trying to pull away, but failing. "Let go of me. I told you already, you can't take too much or it will kill you."

"Yeah, you did say that, didn't you? But this is the only way you'll be stopped. The power of the Hollow—the part that you were able to control—is going to die with me."

"Samantha, no! Don't do this!" Jordan yelled this while the other two looked on with shock.

"Get out of here!" I yelled over my shoulder at them as I felt the moment when I'd taken everything I could from Nathan. "I honestly don't know how this is going to end. Get somewhere safe where you can—"

Then something hit me, grabbing hold of me and pulling me to the side and away from the demon. I landed on the ground and Bishop was there, staring down at me.

"Samantha, what did he do to you? Are you all right?"

Funny, I felt fine. I felt really good, all satiated and satisfied. But that feeling began to fade as soon as it arrived.

"How did you know to come here?" I said, not answering his question.

"Roth came for us, told us what was going on."

I tried to laugh, but it sounded more like a sob. "I thought he'd taken off, abandoned us. Of course not. He really cared for Cassandra… He has a heart buried deep down somewhere. Even though he's a demon, he isn't a monster. He's not like my father."

Bishop pulled me up into a sitting position. His expression was etched in worry. "You don't sound right."

"She took it all." Nathan growled as he rose up off the

ground. The lines were gone from his skin, but his eyes blazed red with fury. "Give it back, you little bitch."

I narrowed my eyes at him, shaking my head. "Sorry, can't. I'm busy digesting that nasty-ass meal. Shouldn't take much more than a minute or two."

"You're going to die if you don't do as I say right now."

"Sorry, *Daddy*. But you can bite me."

Bishop turned a look of horror on me. "What did you do, Samantha?"

Kraven came into my peripheral vision as he moved swiftly to hold Nathan in place.

"What now?" he asked, his expression grim.

Nathan turned a furious glare on the demon and I knew he was about to drain his energy. I tried to open my mouth, to warn him, but then both Roth and Connor were there to shove Nathan back.

"This isn't what I wanted." There was madness on the demon's face, true madness that chilled me even now that it was too late.

Too late to help him, to help myself.

"Give it back!" He surged toward me and shoved Bishop out of the way to grasp me by my throat, raising me up off the ground. His fingers dug in so tight I couldn't breathe. He was going to crush my larynx.

Now that I wasn't draining him anymore, he had every last bit of his demonic strength back.

And zero sanity in those blazing red eyes.

You could take the demon out of Hell, but you couldn't take Hell out of the demon.

It took all four guys to pull him off me. A moment later, the bright glow from Bishop's dagger caught my eye as I sputtered and wheezed in a heap on the ground.

As Nathan lunged forward to attack anyone who stood

in the way from getting to me, Bishop sank the Hallowed Blade deep into the demon's chest and immediately pulled it back out.

He hadn't hesitated.

This was his specialty, after all—he was an angel of death.

Nathan staggered backward a step, finally stilling as if all the fight had left him in the space of a single breath. The hellfire left his eyes so they returned to their normal shade of brown.

"Too late to save her," he whispered. "Gone forever. No second chances. Should have been me…never her. I didn't deserve her. I never did."

I knew he was talking about Anna.

The Hollow opened its roaring mouth behind him.

His gaze found me in the shadows. "You didn't have to die tonight, beautiful star."

I shook my head. "Neither did you."

And then he was gone. And when the Hollow closed up this time, I felt the power I'd stolen from Nathan bristling under my skin. I sensed that it had closed forever this time.

Connor swept his gaze over the rest of us. "That was close."

"Too damn close," Roth agreed.

"Says the guy who nearly helped that dude destroy the universe." Kraven didn't give the other demon a friendly look. "Not exactly forgiving you for that yet. Or probably ever."

Roth returned the glare with one of his own. "If I didn't come get you losers, you never would have realized anything was happening. It was a mistake, I see that now. But it's over and everything's all right."

"You're right." Kraven scanned the area, his gaze landing on Carly and Stephen. "Looky here. It's the last two grays in the city all lined up, no waiting. Who ordered delivery?"

"No…" I grabbed Bishop's arm. "Please. You can't let him hurt them."

"What's wrong with you?" Kraven asked. "Hard night, sweetness? Too much for you to handle? Considering what just went down, I'm thinking we're all lucky to still be breathing."

Bishop hadn't taken his attention from me for a second. "Was he telling the truth? Are you dying?"

The pain gripped me a moment later and I cried out. I looked down at my arms to see the black lines branching now down my skin. "It's okay. It won't hurt anyone else. I have it contained. When I'm gone, it'll be gone, too. The Hollow's closed for business."

"Samantha!" Carly cried out. Connor had taken her firmly by her arm, holding her in place. Roth did the same with Stephen, wrenching him away from Jordan.

Only two grays left alive in the city. Right here, right now. And there wasn't anything I could do to stop this.

It wasn't supposed to end like this. Carly was supposed to get her soul back. And Stephen...Stephen was supposed to be one hundred percent evil so I didn't care if he lived or died.

But I cared.

"Talk to me, Samantha." Bishop dropped his dagger and kneeled in front of me, holding my face between his hands.

"I can feel it," I managed. "The energy from the Hollow, it's so dark. Even worse than I thought it would be, but I guess it makes sense." I cried out as another wave of pain descended. I could feel the branching lines move up onto my face now like icy, cold fingers scraping over my skin.

Close—very close now. I'd chosen this and it was the right thing to do.

Still, I was so scared. My bravery only went so far.

"Damn it," he growled. "Why did you do this? Why did you want to sacrifice yourself like this?"

I knew the answer to this one. It was a test I definitely wouldn't fail.

It was something that occurred to me when Nathan was busy telling me how unnatural I was. How unwanted. How unloved.

That was exactly how I'd felt for ages, ever since my parents separated. My father barely emailed anymore, too busy over in England with his new girlfriend to spare more than a thought toward me. I hated him for that, feeling abandoned, just like I felt abandoned by my mother working so hard at her job that she was barely around. They made me feel like they'd never wanted me.

But I now knew they adopted me because they couldn't have their own biological child. That meant they wanted me— me, in particular.

And my father didn't stay in touch lately because the last time I spoke with him I told him I never wanted to see him again.

Funny how we forget that every story has two sides, even when one of those sides is our own.

My mother had never abandoned me, she'd just been trying to keep busy while nursing a broken heart. My father hadn't abandoned me, either. He was giving me space until I got over my deep-seated feelings of betrayal about the choices he'd made to try to find his own happiness.

But they still loved me. They still wanted me. And they had from the very beginning.

I'd never realized how lucky I was.

Until now.

"Why, Samantha?" Bishop asked again. "Why sacrifice yourself?"

For family, for friendship, even for people I couldn't stand the sight of. For movies about zombies, especially the really bad ones. For sunrises and sunsets. For the possibility of acing a test and going to my first-choice college and maybe becoming a writer or something equally awesome. For my mother's ability to order Chinese food like a champ. For sandboxes, and swimming pools, and kissing frogs hoping they might turn into princes.

For real love—the kind that lasted forever.

"Because," I whispered, "some things are worth dying for."

He held on to me tightly as my life ebbed away. "I couldn't agree more."

Then he drew closer and pressed his lips against mine.

A last kiss. I thought that was a nice touch. To kiss the boy I loved before I died.

But I quickly realized it wasn't that kind of a kiss.

I gripped the material of his shirt and forced my mouth away from his. "What are you doing?"

"I told you I still had the ability to heal—a little left. I'm using it to heal you." Then he crushed his mouth against mine again.

I tried to stop him, to tear myself away, but he held me too tightly.

He couldn't do this. To heal me while in his condition, burdened with a soul which dampened all of his celestial abilities—it would take every last bit of life energy he had left.

It would kill him.

And he knew it.

Tears slipped down my cheeks as he kept me locked in this bruisingly hard kiss, and I felt that healing energy move through me, burning away the parts that had been damaged from taking Nathan's power away.

Then Bishop finally drew back, still holding my face between his hands, which continued to channel the healing into me. His eyes glowed bright blue before the light doused from them completely and he slumped forward against me.

He'd healed me. The dark and deadly energy I'd taken from

Nathan was gone as if it had never been here. The pain was only a bad memory. Physically, I felt better than I had in ages.

And Bishop was dying in my arms.

Kraven loomed over us, his expression filled with every emotion I could name—fury, confusion, hate, anguish. All of it directed not at me, but at Bishop.

"This can't happen," he growled. "Not now. I won't let it."

"What can you do?" I choked out.

"The barrier's what's trapping him here. And there's only two things left keeping that barrier in place." He turned from us and I saw that he now had the dagger in his grip.

Carly and Stephen. He was going to kill them to complete the mission.

"Sam," Bishop whispered. "Take this. Be normal again, I know it's what you want."

He yanked the chain from around his neck and handed me back the locket I'd given him only last night.

Then his eyes closed and he went still in my arms.

I stared at him, unblinking, squeezing the locket so tightly that it would hurt if I could feel anything other than cold shock.

Be normal again.

"You think it's that easy?" My words trembled as I eased him down to the ground and stroked the dark hair back from his forehead. "Well, it's not. I need you, Bishop. Please, don't leave me. Not yet."

It was supposed to be the dagger that killed a demon or an angel, not this. Not because he saved my life. It wasn't fair.

"Both of you are dead," Kraven snarled, moving toward Carly and Stephen.

"No!" I leaped up from the ground and ran over to block them.

"Get out of my way."

"Not a chance."

His eyes blazed bright red. "You don't think I'll use this on you, too?"

I had no doubt he would if he had to. None at all. "I *knew* you still cared about your brother. This is proof."

"And now he's dead. Still not too late—the Hollow didn't take his body. Still a chance to make this right, but the barrier needs to go. This mission needs to end."

"I agree." I turned to face Carly and Stephen.

"Sam, do something! Help me!" Tears streamed down Carly's cheeks.

"Kill me," Stephen said, his expression stone.

"No!" Jordan shrieked. "Don't—please don't!"

He didn't look at her, instead his gaze moved to me. "I deserve to die after what I've done to Jordan, to you. To...other people—so many other people. I can't take any of it back."

"You're right," I said. "You can't take it back. But death's not an option. Not tonight. And not for anybody else."

Please let this work.

I slid my fingernail into the locket and opened it up. There was something inside, something that shimmered like a translucent ribbon. I pulled it out to see that it was so long and so wide to be able to fit into something so small. I held it in my hand, mesmerized by its beauty and warmth.

My soul.

Be normal again, I know it's what you want.

"Not anymore, Bishop," I said aloud. "Not without you."

Not wasting another second, I tore the soul into two pieces and shoved them each into Carly's and Stephen's mouths. They gasped and choked as if I was making them swallow something large and unpleasant.

Please work. Please.

Both gasped, inhaling sharply. The halved soul disappeared into the two grays.

Then there was another tremor—although this one felt more like a lightning strike.

"Don't know how," Kraven muttered. "But you did it, sweetness. Congrats."

Connor and Roth looked at each other with shock as they both let go of Carly and Stephen at the exact same time. I spun around to see Bishop lying so still on the ground. Not moving. Not breathing.

Then the sky flashed with bright, white light and another thunderclap shook the world beneath my feet. The flash of light momentarily blinded me and I shielded my eyes from its glare. The skies darkened again an instant later and I looked around, stunned.

Bishop was gone, a scorch mark where he'd been lying the only evidence he'd ever been here.

Same for Kraven, Connor and Roth.

They were gone.

It had worked. The last of the grays were gone and the barrier had disappeared immediately. The team had been pulled back to Heaven and Hell.

A sob rose in my throat.

Someone grabbed me, pulling me to them and hugging me hard. It was Jordan.

"I thought— Oh, God. You're alive. You're, like, seriously the most bizarre person I've ever met in my life, but you're alive. And I'm alive. And...Stephen..."

Stephen and Carly had fallen to the ground, both unconscious.

I rushed toward my friend as she started to come to. Jordan limped over to where Stephen lay and gripped his shoulders as he blinked up at her.

"What...?" he began. "Where am I?"

Carly pushed up from the ground. "Uh, what happened? Why was I lying on my back in a parking lot?"

"What do you remember?" I asked tentatively.

"Crave. We went there to confront Stephen about being a total dick to you. You met up with that hot guy named Bishop and totally blew me off. Nice, by the way. And now I'm here." She glanced to her left and made a face. "Hey, the total dick's here, too. Oh, and Jordan Fitzpatrick. Awesome."

Jordan and I exchanged a glance.

"What about you?" Jordan asked Stephen. "What do you remember?"

He rubbed his forehead. "I also remember being at Crave. I'd come back to visit you. University sucked and...I don't know. Nothing's working out the way I wanted it to, except, well, I needed to see you." He frowned deeply. "That's it. That's all I remember...and now I'm here."

They didn't remember being grays and they didn't remember losing their souls.

They had no idea I'd given my soul to save their lives.

And Bishop had sacrificed his existence to save mine.

"You fixed them. You did it." Jordan's voice was hoarse. She reached out and pulled me into another tight hug. "And for the record, I remember. I remember everything, okay? You're not alone."

I was glad to hear it. But all I could do right now was nod as the tears streamed down my cheeks.

chapter 37

I guess you could say life went back to normal after that night.

Normal, however, was a relative term now.

Carly and Stephen didn't remember anything about being grays. It was for the best, especially for Stephen. He'd unquestionably done some bad things. To have to live with that now that he understood what he'd done wrong when his morals had been unnaturally off balance, well...I wouldn't wish that on my worst enemy. Which Stephen actually was for a short time.

Carly, admittedly, had to deal with everyone who thought she'd run away from home with some random guy and had now come crawling back. She was understandably confused, but couldn't account for the missing time. Therefore, she decided that that's exactly what must have happened. She'd had a romantic adventure and then—she figured—hit her head and got temporary amnesia.

If she believed such a fantastical explanation, I wasn't going to try to convince her otherwise. Bottom line, I was just happy beyond words to have my best friend back.

And speaking of friends, I now counted Jordan Fitzpatrick, my former nemesis and tormenter, among them, as crazy as that sounded. But I guess it didn't sound all that crazy. What we'd experienced together…well, it changed us forever. Both of us.

Jordan knew things about me that nobody else knew. And if she tried to tell anybody, they'd think she was nuts. For the foundation of a new friendship, that was about as solid as it got. She could still be a total bitch from hell, though. Now I preferred to think of it as part of her charm.

She was still seeing Stephen. Even if he didn't remember the bad stuff that had happened, she remembered the good stuff—that even when he'd been turned into a super-gray, he still loved her. They were kind of meant for each other if you asked me.

My mother returned from Hawaii with a fantastic tan and a digital camera full of pictures. She was as relaxed and happy as I ever remembered her being. And, total bonus, she'd met a man while away, one who lived in a city only a couple hours' drive from Trinity.

She didn't understand why I was being extra nice to her, more talkative, more interested in what she was doing. I just told her I'd missed her. And I said the same thing in an email to my father in England. I missed him, and I hoped he'd visit me again soon.

He replied only a half hour later telling me that he'd be here for Christmas and was so happy to hear from me it had brought tears to his eyes. And that he loved me very much.

The email made me cry, too. Happy tears. All this time, I thought he was the one ignoring me, but it was actually the other way around.

I went to school every day. No sick days permitted for someone who died one night and came literally a breath away from death the next.

Colin had happily transferred his current crush to someone else, someone who was able to completely return it. Someone who didn't give him mixed signals due to hungers, which were now an unpleasant memory.

It was his ability to deal with only a partial soul that had made me realize Carly and Stephen could survive with the same. It was a hypothesis. Luckily, one that had worked.

So, yeah, I was still a nexus. Still one that would forever hunger for supernatural energy, but all in all, I was doing pretty darn good, thank you very much.

Even though I thought about him every day. Every night. Every moment in between.

He'd given everything he had left to save my life and I'd failed to return the favor.

"I'd like to introduce a new student," Mr. Saunders announced at the beginning of English class on Friday. I scribbled in my binder randomly, a sketch of wings in black ink that covered the entire page of a previously graded test. "If you could all help him catch up this late in the semester, that would be much appreciated. Please introduce yourself, young man."

"My name's Adam. Adam Bishop."

My pen froze and my gaze shot up from the page.

Bishop stood at the front of the classroom.

"Where do you hail from, Adam?" Mr. Saunders asked.

"All over the place. But I'll be staying in Trinity for a while."

"Well, welcome. Please take a seat."

He took an empty seat near the door at the front of class without looking at me.

Bishop was here.

Here in my English class.

What was going on?

Seven days had passed. Seven horrible days since the whole team had disappeared, leaving no trace except for the scorch marks that I'd visited three more times since. I'd hoped they might come back—all of them, any of them.

Now Bishop had just strolled into class like he was any other transfer student starting school in a new city.

It was impossible to pay attention to a single thing Mr. Saunders said as I counted down the minutes until the end of class. When the bell rang, Bishop stood up and was one of the first out of the room. I threaded my way through the crowd, keeping him locked in my sights. I trailed after him through the halls, past my locker and out the exit, practically tripping down the stairs in my effort to keep up with his long legs.

"Bishop!" I shouted after him when he reached the pathway leading toward the parking lot.

He stopped and turned to glance back at me.

I'd had time to figure this out. An hour to work over every possibility in my head.

He was dead, lost to me. He'd given his last bit of energy to heal me.

If he'd somehow been resurrected by Heaven, I would bet that, just like Carly and Stephen, he now had no clue who I was. He had amnesia!

However, he was alive.

I could work with amnesia.

"I know this is going to sound crazy…" My words tripped over each other in their race to leave my mouth. "But you already know me. I'm Samantha. You were here before and some bad things happened. I—I thought you were dead! You were dead, but I guess you're not anymore. You're here. And you must be here for a reason. Bishop, this is wonderful. You have to remember me, we went through so much together. You have to!"

Bishop cocked his head to the side, a smile curling the corner of his mouth. "Oh, don't worry, Samantha. I remember everything."

I gaped at him. "You do?"

"And for the record, I wasn't totally dead. Just mostly dead." He swept his gaze over the area lined with trees that had lost almost all their leaves this late in the fall. "I'm glad you followed me. I needed to speak with you alone."

I stared at him. "How can you act so 'whatever' about this? You nearly died! You were pulled back to Heaven and…it's no big deal?"

"You're angry."

"Furious. Seven days, Bishop! I've been grieving you for seven days. I thought I'd lost you and…and you just randomly start going to my school? Why are you back?"

"I would have contacted you before, but I couldn't." He raised an eyebrow. "Sounds like you missed me."

I crossed my arms, glaring at him even though my previously shattered heart was now pounding with sheer joy. "Less and less each moment that passes and you don't tell me what happened."

This made him laugh, and for the first time, there wasn't an edge of insanity to it that I could hear.

"You're fixed?" I asked, breathless. "The soul you had…"

He nodded. "Gone. They tried to fix me and they did a good job. However, it couldn't all be reversed. I guess I'll always be a little unhinged." He crossed his arms and regarded me carefully. "You're still a nexus. You gave your soul away to save Carly and Stephen."

I tensed. "I had no choice. If I didn't, they'd be dead."

His expression turned serious again. "Heaven and Hell aren't big fans of nexi."

"So I've heard." I took a deep breath. "So, what now? Are

you back as a new student of McCarthy High, or an angel of death to take care of a little problem named Samantha Day?"

"Both. Heaven knows what you did, Samantha. What you were willing to do to save the world from your father, to save your friends. It's earned you some respect. But you're still a nexus, which means you need to be watched."

"Watched," I said tentatively. "Not killed."

"No, not killed. So that's why I'm here. I requested this new mission personally. Consider me your brand-new guardian angel." He gave me a wicked grin. "If that's okay with you?"

This was the last thing I expected. I had no words to reply— not right away. It was all too incredible.

Again, he sobered. "I mean, if you want them to assign someone else…I know Connor could handle it and…"

"No," I said quickly, not able to repress my smile a moment longer. "I'm more than okay with this arrangement."

His grin returned. "Well, good. And by the way, the future's not set. As a nexus, you have the powers of both Heaven and Hell inside you and with your special status in the eyes of Heaven, you have the opportunity to be transitioned to fully angel if you choose to be."

"Angel?" I said, startled. "Me? Are you serious?"

"Very serious." He drew closer, until we were almost touching. "I think you'd make an amazing angel, Samantha."

"Nah," another familiar voice said nearby. "She'd make a way cooler demon."

My gaze shot to the left to see Kraven approach.

The demon grinned at me. "For the record, I remember everything just fine and dandy, too, and I have my entire mental faculties intact, unlike ninety-eight percent over here."

Bishop's jaw tightened. "I thought you were going to let me talk to her on my own first."

"I lied. Deal with it." Kraven walked a slow circle around

me, his gaze sweeping the length of my body. "So, sweetness, I'm back. Don't throw yourself into my arms and embarrass yourself. We got plenty of time for that."

I knew he was joking, but at this very moment, I kind of felt like giving the demon a huge hug since I was genuinely delighted to see him. Instead, I restrained myself and tried to act blasé. "You're here, too? Why?"

"Balance. Duh." He shrugged. "Heaven sent someone to keep an eye on the potentially dangerous little nexus. Hell had to ante up, as well. And I'm the one they sent. Shocker, right?"

"Total shocker." Of course. The balance, couldn't forget about that. Heaven and Hell working together yet again, and I was the reason for it this time. I was both amused and a little disconcerted that they thought I might be that much of a threat someday. For now, anyway, I felt as close to normal as I ever could, even with the supernatural energy emanating off both boys now nudging my inherited hunger back to life.

"Roth gives his regards," Kraven said. "Back to his regular routine. Hopefully he'll forget all about that angel."

"You think that's possible?"

"Not a chance. Anyway, don't be too disappointed, but I gotta skedaddle. Things to do, places to go, gorgeous women to meet. I'm sure my little brother will keep a close eye on you and he won't mind me slacking a bit. Right, kid?"

"Don't call me kid," Bishop said.

"Remember my offer on the demon thing, sweetness," Kraven said. "Infernal transitions don't always go smoothly, but there's never a dull day. But for now I'll leave you two alone. Enjoy it while it lasts."

Without another word, he strolled away down the path. I watched him leave, shaking my head with disbelief.

"So you two are…reconciled?" I ventured.

"Let's just say, it's an interesting work in progress. I guess we're going to have lots of time to spend with each other to see what happens." He curled his hand around mine. Touching him was pure bliss, something I never thought I'd experience again.

Then he let out a low snort of laughter.

"What's so funny?" I asked.

"Nothing, it's just—it seems that the inconvenient addiction of mine, the moth to the flame…hasn't gone anywhere, after all. I guess it was more than that all along."

I couldn't help but smile at that. "I knew it."

"You did?"

"Well, I knew it for *me*." I shook my head, looking up at him, still stunned this was real. "So we're just two unsouled supernatural beings now who go to high school together and are kind of crazy about each other, huh?"

His blue-eyed gaze met mine and held. "Pretty much, with varying degrees of crazy. Does that work for you?"

I pulled his face down to mine and kissed him. "It works just fine."

Bishop was back. He was my guardian angel. And just like rebuilding his relationship with his brother, we now had plenty of time to see what might happen next.

I honestly couldn't wait.

★ ★ ★ ★ ★

aknowledgments

Thank you to you, dear reader—yes, you! You're smart, savvy and gorgeous—never doubt it. Follow your angels and try your best to ignore the demons. Even the really cute, snarky ones.

Thank you to my family and friends—without your love, support and encouragement, I'm not sure what I'd do. Like, seriously.

Thank you to T. S. Ferguson and Natashya Wilson for letting me share this duo of Nightwatchers books with the world, and for giving me the time and the opportunity to extenda-mix the ending of this one to make it just a little more wicked than it was to begin with.

Thank you to my story fairy. Never stop launching shiny new ideas in my direction. It's big fun to chase after them and see where they land…. Look, there goes another one now….

Be sure to read the first book
in the Nightwatchers series, *Dark Kiss*.

Samantha Day knows the
kiss she shared with a hot
guy at the club changed
her somehow. But when
angels and demons come
after her—together—she
knows something beyond
evil is happening. Can a
kiss steal your soul? If so,
what has she become? And
can she control her need to
share the kiss with Bishop,
an angel who might just be
her fatal weakness?

Available wherever books are sold!

"More, please! Gorgeous angels, suspense and
romance...this book has everything I love.
I was pulled in from the very first sentence."

—Richelle Mead, #1 bestselling author
of the Vampire Academy series

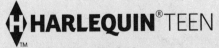